FIXES

FIXES

EUGENE KENNEDY

DOUBLEDAY

NEW YORK · LONDON · TORONTO · SYDNEY · AUCKLAND

Published by Doubleday, a division of Bantam Doubleday Dell Publishing Group, Inc., 666 Fifth Avenue, New York, New York 10103

DOUBLEDAY and the portrayal of an anchor with a dolphin are trademarks of Doubleday, a division of Bantam Doubleday Dell Publishing Group, Inc.

Library of Congress Cataloging-in-Publication Data

Kennedy, Eugene C.
Fixes / by Eugene Kennedy.—1st ed.
p.   cm.
I. Title
PS3561.E4258F5   1989   88-29952
813'.54—dc19

For Saul

Too long a sacrifice
Can make a stone of the heart . . .

— W. B. YEATS

Before

The pope was dead, to begin with. The French one, only sixty. On the floor of his private chapel, staring like a man surprised he made the train, you'll never catch me now. Well, he wasn't dead, not quite yet, when it all started, and he wasn't the only one dead when it finished. I'm getting ahead of myself.

My name is Tracy, James, forty-five years old, the new-style Notre Dame grad, married but separated. Four children back in Chicago, three boys and a red-haired girl of eighteen, the youngest, the very mirror of her mother without the anger, nobody is as angry as Maureen, nobody I know. That, however, is another story. I'm a sinning Catholic, that's the only kind there is, really. But I was raised when the church, like the movies, was what it was supposed to be, and the priests were tough and more concerned about saving your fevered adolescent soul than running illegal wetbacks through the sanctuary.

The family I came from—Mom the traditional homemaker, Dad the police captain, along with the child of early grace, the little brother I'll get to presently—called me Jimbo, sometimes J.B., a lot of people still do. Some of them think I look like another Tracy—Spencer. In his prime, in *Woman of the Year,* maybe, when he was a sportswriter escorting Kate Hepburn to baseball games. I was a sports columnist once myself, used to be chief *Time* correspondent in Rome, too. Which is where we started.

It was the night my kid brother Mike—Monsignor Michael Tracy, that is —arrived for one of his regular visits at the Vatican. Mike was a VIP, a *very important priest,* back in Chicago, a member of the golden-boy network of clergy, the bright ones with even white teeth as destined as the jeweler's finest chalices for prominent display in the church. Mike was a shoo-in to become a bishop and old Father Fitzsimmons, our pastor, would raise a glass —a nice easy motion Fitzie had from all the practice—and wryly ask, "And won't a red hat sit grandly one day on Michael's fine head of black hair?" Mike accepted his future grandeur as a matter of course, in the way of handsome men who have never known anything but success and preferment.

Michael always got first place in everything, including his doctoral studies in theology and in his assignments. Everybody seemed as eager to please him as Mom had been. Maybe you don't know how an Irish Catholic mother treats a priest son, her pride and joy, the immaculate conception himself, she'd never lose him to another woman, she'd have him until, silver-haired himself, he'd lower her coffin on groaning straps down into the grave, hers to the end without a rival. Such women, even those without priest sons, bound the Catholic Church together in America in its great days, no telling what will happen when the last one of them is gone. You can still see them, chatting in little knots in parking lots outside churches after the 8 A.M. morning Mass, the "eight," as they say, huddled together in a last stand of a great cultural period.

Mike was a writer, too, words slap like wavelets in the Irish genes, along with the booze and the pessimism and the grand dreaminess. He wrote theology books, mostly, but a lot of popular stuff on the side, and he was a favorite speaker, especially at conferences of nuns, saving the saved, I'd tell him, the matinee idol priest stuck in their fancies like a holy card in their prayer books. But Mike, being so accustomed to attention that he didn't notice it, was infected with holy naiveté and acted as if he didn't know what the hell I was talking about. That made him a shade too sure of his own opinions. For example, Mike was convinced that most of the troubles in my marriage were my fault, simple as that. He didn't mean to hurt you, priests never do, it's a function of their infallibility complex, an occupational hazard of the clergy.

Mike was a regular visitor to Rome on one kind of ecclesiastical business or other, usually something delicate, like how do we handle some bishop who's gone around the bend, sure he's St. Francis and handing out diocesan funds like Monopoly money to street people. Or the big-shot monsignor who's flashing in his Burberry on a bridge over the expressway, entertaining Lake Shore Drive matrons on their way home from the malls. Mike would get the emergency call, and net the Right Reverend as gently as a butterfly. Catch them, don't squash them, that was his motto, then get the poor bastards to the doctors and square the details all around, Monsignor is away on retreat, yes, you're right, a very holy man.

It was Mike's face that was his fortune, however, with those blue eyes with no mud stirred up from the bottoms, that innocent look, smooth as the finest Limoges, of those who haven't been ill-used or spoiled by life, yet. It's that Mick kisser of yours, I used to say to him, people can't resist it, they trust you, that's why you get away with all this shit.

So I wasn't surprised to hear that Mike was in town, although I liked a little advance notice before he showed up at my apartment on Monte Mario, not wanting to overdo my public sinner act with him, or cause his dark eyebrows to arch at the sight of lace things trailing out from beneath the bed, or silk stockings hanging in the bathroom, something shocking in the medicine cabinet. Confess your sins, the old man used to say, don't advertise them. The coast was clear when Mike arrived one evening about eight.

"What is it now, Michael-o, some diocesan official caught trying to screw a tree?"

"Nothing so colorful, Jimbo. Or, I hope, with such potential side effects." He looked weary as he loosened his Roman collar. "Actually, I'm here on business . . ." He hesitated, smiled, shifted to a hokey preacher's tones. "Don't you know I must be about my Father's business?"

"*Very* funny." I opened a bottle of Frascati at my makeshift bar. "What kind of business?"

"Oh, bureaucratic business. What else is there in Rome?"

"Indulgences, canonizations, your usual miraculous fixes." I filled two glasses, sloppily. Mike seemed to be looking beyond my shoulder. "Like that book you're writing on the saints. Is it true they canonized Maria Goretti because she's the only recorded case of an Italian girl saying no?"

Mike didn't seem to hear me, then he inhaled, got me back in focus. I wiped the side of his glass, handed him the wine. "Actually, Jimbo, I'm here on personal business."

"*Personal* business?" We dipped our glasses at each other but Mike lowered his immediately, his automatic half smile collapsing. "I didn't think you future bishops were allowed personal business."

"I'm here to be questioned. *Interrogated,* as they put it . . ."

"As *who* put it?" I felt uneasiness kicking in. "Who the hell is *they?*"

"I've got an appointment at the Congregation for the Doctrine of the Faith tomorrow."

"A.K.A. the Holy Office, not so long ago the Inquisition?"

Mike nodded neutrally.

"What in God's name for? You're one of their agents, or double agents, aren't you?"

Mike blinkered a Lafayette Escadrille, death awaits the brave smile, raised his glass, "Well, they think that they can never be too careful . . ."

"Is it something you wrote? One of those sweet tracts for nuns, start the periods going among the retired set in some motherhouse, something like that?" Mike didn't answer, just sat there pensively, quietly sure of himself again. "What the hell could they object to in what you write? Or say? These are the guys you've been running interference for, the guys you've been making look good for years . . ." The bar wobbled slightly as I leaned against it. Mike sipped his wine. I raised my glass again, held it in midair. "Mom know this?"

"Just that I'm in Rome."

"This isn't a big deal, is it? I mean, what can they give you, two to ten? With good behavior . . ."

Mike lowered his glass to the arm of his chair, stared up at me, that wholesome Irish face turned full at me like a satellite dish. "Jimbo, I'm going to leave the priesthood."

The wind went out of me, as if I'd taken a surprise punch. I rocked back and forth a moment, stunned, watching my brother come in and out of focus. "Oh Christ!" I blurted out. "Oh, Mike, what the hell . . ."

"That's really why I'm being questioned at the Holy Office."

I studied Mike, who seemed calm but not as innocent, not as much a little brother as he had been a minute before. "You've got to be kidding me, Mike, I mean . . ."

"This hasn't been an easy decision, Jimbo."

"Decision, *decision,* what the hell has been going on anyway? You don't know what you're doing, you're overtired, you're just jumping at something . . ."

"There's nothing impulsive about this, Jimbo. I'm thirty-eight years old. You don't have to walk me to school anymore."

I felt hot all over, his tone of certitude got to me, as if I couldn't possibly know what I was talking about, that my opinion didn't count. What the hell was he doing, and for what? Or, more likely, for whom? "Don't tell me you're in love."

His eyes flashed. "That's what the old man called a dirty Irish trick, Jimbo, asking me a question, then telling me how not to answer it. Or is it your *Time* style? I came here hoping that you, of all people, would understand."

"Understand?" I paced back and forth, my shadow falling across his upturned altar boy's face. I stopped. "This is all pretty quick, you know. Have you thought about the way this will affect others? This *does* affect other people, you know. All those people, like the good nuns who read your books, your friends . . ." I put my wine glass on the bar. "Your family . . ."

"Whatever I do, Jimbo," he said evenly, "somebody is going to be hurt. I've talked this over, I've prayed about it . . ."

"Oh Christ, Mike, don't give me that pious crap."

"Call it what you want. I'm not doing this on some whim, the devil hasn't appeared to me in female form."

I stared at him for a long moment, the room creaked in the suddenly heavy silence. Something that stabilized my life more than I knew was coming loose, a cornerstone was cracking, disgorging its tin box of memory. "Bullshit!" I snapped angrily. "For one thing, you don't have the slightest idea what marriage is all about. What you know is all from books, or looking into the eyes of brides at their best, full of moon juice on the altar steps, just after they've hooked some sucker." I reached for my glass, gulped most of its contents. "You're naive, Mike. Hell, you're more than naive. Or *less* than naive, maybe that's it. Don't you know what marriage really means? You spend your life consorting with the enemy, that's what it means." I was shaking, surprised how much stored-up irritation I had with the star pupil who always brought the medals home and got all the atten-

7

tion. The favored child, fuck him. "Have you thought what this'll do to Mom?"

"I can't stay a priest to please Mom. Too many guys do that . . ." He gave me his all-American Mick look, the puppy's eyes in my gunsight. "Maybe you underestimate her."

It was not a pleasant moment. Betrayed, that's what I felt, goddamned seething betrayed. Little Michael was supposed to remain in place, that's what we all had given up so much for, so he could be special, the priest brother, the darling of the family, almost a fetish in the Catholic culture, one that kept things timeless if not eternal, that's why there was nothing ever too good for Father . . .

"I'm not planning to stay here." Mike stood up. "I'm sorry to spring this on you so suddenly." He looked earnestly at me. "I'm really sorry, Jimbo, I don't want to hurt anybody, and I know this is disappointing but . . ."

"*Disappointing?* Is that the best word you can find, as if you were just announcing the cancellation of the Bingo after the novena services? *Disappointing!* I'm just glad the old man isn't alive to hear you talk this way." The room ached around us. I wasn't finished, I was drawing on deep deposits of sarcasm, the finest of Irish poisons, it had killed more Micks than the Famine. "What is it, you find there was postage due on the letter from Fatima?" I walked to the windows, turned. Irish brothers have a great capacity for kicking hell out of each other, then embracing, we weren't going to get to the second part tonight. "Don't tell me your troubles with faith, maybe you learned your guardian angel is gay, been giving you those funny dreams. I'd rather hear something simple. You learned about fucking, right? Tell me it's the fucking, talk to me about something I understand. Big deal. Fucking is fucking. Here's the wisdom of a lifetime: rent, don't buy."

We stared at each other wordlessly. I was mad at myself for being so mad at him. "Mike, you don't know what a mean bastard the real world is, you *think* you know, you don't know shit, not really." I paused, took a deep breath. "I don't mean to hurt your feelings, but have you thought that maybe you owe other people something, people who made sacrifices for you?"

He started to say something, stopped, shook his head.

"You know when you're a real pain in the ass, Monsignor? When you act so superior, nobody can tell you anything, *you* know everything."

Mike gazed steadily at me, patiently letting me spew out my feelings all over him.

"And don't give me your long-suffering act, like I'm the villain here. You need *somebody* to tell you the truth. There's obligations in everybody's life they can't get out of. That's what life is, doing your time, you don't have any choice. Life *is* the sentence." I sighed. "Goddammit, at least *I* know I've really been married to Maureen. I'm not kidding myself that I didn't know what I was doing, that there never was a marriage, that great contemporary bullshit, that our kids are illegitimate, that I can get it annulled, here's the fee, where's the nearest exit? Christ, Michael, you've spent your life in the unhappiness business. You ought to know better."

Mike placed his wine glass carefully on my improvised bar, adjusted his collar. The atmosphere was dry and tight.

"It's not that nun friend of yours, is it?"

He walked slowly to the door. "You're a real thick Mick, Jimbo, did you know that?" He closed the door quietly behind him. I threw my glass at it. So sure of yourself. You think you know everything, and you're so goddam dumb . . .

But I really am getting ahead of myself.

GENESIS

ONE

Mother Hilda didn't eat anything, the Communion wafer and a little water, that was it. West Germany hadn't seen anybody like her since Theresa Neumann did the same thing back in the thirties and forties. And there had been rumors that Theresa kept a basket of food under her bed, a couple of slices of kuchen, maybe a little schnapps for the cold winter nights. These days, aside from scattered weeping statues usually located directly beneath leaking water pipes, Monsignor Michael Tracy thought that Catholic enthusiasm for holiness and for the miraculous, including his own, had flown out the window opened by the Second Vatican Council.

A couple of examples. Padre Pio, the Italian priest who wore Dickensian clerk's gloves over his bleeding hands while saying Mass, was dead and almost completely forgotten. Go to confession, Padre Pio will read your soul, the story was that he read Graham Greene's once, scared hell out of him, a real living saint, *il padre,* crowds knocking his door down. Now you could only get Padre Pio on videocassette, *Fifty Years of Thorns and Roses,* $55 American from some outfit in Canada, please specify VHS or Beta.

Otherwise there wasn't much interest in live saints, stigmata, or confession for that matter, anymore. High-toned Protestants were more nostalgic about them than most Catholics.

Nobody had thrown their crutches away at Lourdes lately, the crowds had kept up but the cures had gone way down since Vatican II. Something had definitely happened, Monsignor Tracy felt, and he was exhibit A. After all, wasn't one of his reasons for being in Rome a date to be questioned about his plans to leave the priesthood and marry? He was firmly decided about marriage, but his head was as filled as that of any new discoverer of love with the special helium of infatuation. Beyond the arid valley of duty in which he had lived acceptantly he had entered the fresh uplands of love. It was all new to him, falling in love had been well named, you lost your balance, you couldn't do anything about it. So Michael was like Adam, just awakened, rubbing his sore side, beholding Eve for the first time. Ann. *Ann.* He loved the sound of her name, it had crowded the obsessive little prayers of a lifetime out of his head. Ann. Ann Coleman.

Michael was afloat more than afoot as, waiting for his Holy Office appointment, he bobbed around the Eternal City gathering information for a book on sanctity in the modern world. He was going to do a preliminary article on the subject for the *New York Times Magazine.* Ann's blond-haired good looks filled his imagination, making double exposures of every Roman scene. Ann was a former nun who was now a cardiologist in Chicago, imagine, a priest falling in love with a nun, that's the kind of thing they used to warn about in the seminary, *that* was what Martin Luther had done! Michael surveyed the massive water- and age-stained facade of St. Peter's Basilica, the statued apostles looking down suspiciously at him, we know what you're up to. Oh, Annie, he groaned inwardly, I wish this were over with and that we were together for good. He looked away from the disapproving statues, felt an unfamiliar anxiety. Jimbo hadn't been much help. Dear old Jimbo, he thinks I don't know what I'm doing. Do I? Ann's face reappeared brightly, he felt that he might explode with love and longing, why didn't I know about this a long time ago?

Michael thought of Mother Hilda as he sat in the all-beige waiting room of the Congregation for the Causes of Saints in a blank-faced building that pleaded nolo contendere in the midst of Roman splendor. Mother Hilda was popularly considered to be a living saint. She was acclaimed, for example, by thousands of priests who had sought her out for one of her famous brief visionary counseling interviews, in which she drew on impressionistic images to read their troubled hearts and to give pointed advice. Monsignor Tracy sighed, what pictures will flash into her head when she meets me? An officious-looking cleric wiggled across the room like a fish in an aquarium tank, there is a slight delay, the prefect will be with you shortly. Mike watched for a trail of bubbles as he floated away.

Monsignor Tracy closed his eyes. Mother Hilda, the seeress of Munich, mother confessor to priests and helper of that city's lost souls, street people, what have you, she even ran a house for broken-down prostitutes on the edge of the red-light district, took them in, sometimes their customers too, the pimps were pissed off at her, she was bad for business. She was in Rome, too, and, the day before, Michael had watched her at the main altar of St. Peter's Basilica, kneeling thin as a furled black flag between the massive pretzel-twist pillars supporting the baldachin. Nun followers in gray capes had knelt in a semicircle just behind her. Their intense concentration had spread a wake of silence behind them, causing the normally noisy pilgrims to halt, sign themselves, hesitate to proceed, it was like a spell, the questing monsignor had thought, maybe prayer generates a never-measured magnetic field, maybe holiness is made up of subatomic particles. Or maybe it's simpler, maybe Mother Hilda *does* have it right . . .

The clerical grapevine, Rome's famous *murmurantes,* said Hilda was at the Vatican not only to give advice to curial officials, but also to pass on a message directly from Jesus to the pope, Federal Express, get the world ready for Apocalypse. It sounded more like a television evangelist's threat than a saint's encouragement for a troubled world. Did holiness scour the soul with fear or fill the heart with love? What kind of a move am *I* making? The goldfish cleric touched his shoulder lightly, Michael opened his eyes, the prefect will see you now.

TWO

"Monsignor Tracy, it is good to see you again." Monsignor Federico Lanza offered a warm but dry greeting. They had met on some of the Chicagoan's previous trips to Rome and respected each other as a couple of ecclesiastical professionals. Lanza was engagingly direct yet mysterious, Rudolph Valentino survived into middle age, cured in irony; he looked as if he had once danced a lot, watched riots from a café table, been a second at duels, swallowed a thousand secrets without indigestion. Michael batted away the multiplication of images, watched Lanza deftly flick back the red-lined wings of his cassock cape, light a cigarette, and lean back as if presiding over a timeless zone, which, indeed, he was. "How have you been?"

Such questions, like the hooded stares from the statues of saints, tugged at the loose flap of Michael's anxiety. Rome was a gossip factory, Lanza might very well know about his Holy Office appointment, judge him much as Jimbo had, another clerical Tristan. Tracy skipped small talk, quickly explained his interest in sanctity, his proposed book and magazine article, felt Lanza's gaze pore over him as lightly and surely as spring sunshine. "What exactly is the working definition of holiness you use here in deciding in today's world if someone is a saint or not?"

"Ah!" Lanza smiled appreciatively. "The American question! You want to know things exactly. The moment of birth, the moment of death. I tell you, Monsignor, what St. John of the Cross inscribed on the mount of perfection. 'There is no way here.'" He paused, as if enjoying his own observations. "Sanctity is like natural light in a neon world, real but obscured by the artificial brightness all around it. *Everybody* knows what it is." He placed his cigarette on a cut-glass ashtray, held his hands above his desk blotter, index fingers to thumbs, as if saying Mass. "And *nobody* can tell you what it is. It is a subtle subject." He picked up his cigarette. "Still, the world needs models of goodness more than it ever has, yes? So we continue to look for them. And, since Vatican Two, when we got rid of the lawyers that used to infest this office, we have placed the emphasis on character, on how people meet the obligations of their ordinary lives, on what we call 'heroic virtue.'" Lanza interrupted himself, changed his tone. "Incidentally, we now employ the historical critical method to the examination of the lives of individuals whose causes are introduced. It is very scholarly. People seem surprised to learn that there is nobody here with the title *advocatus diaboli,* the devil's advocate. I am sorry if this takes some of the drama out of our work."

Lanza paused, as if expecting a question. Michael remained silent. "Evil," Lanza continued, "does not hide itself. Goodness does all the time. It is found in simple things: spouses who are faithful and who love their children, priests who say their prayers . . ."

Simple goodness. Ann smiled inside his head and Michael's attention floated away from the urbane Lanza. He sensed that he was drifting with his fantasy into a becalmed silence, looked up into Lanza's eyes. "What, Monsignor, about supernatural signs?"

"You mean miracles," Lanza said serenely, taking Michael's measure again with his cellophane-wrapped-caramel eyes. "We have an undeserved reputation for measuring holiness solely by thaumaturgy. Miracles, I must tell you, are a problem. We are not running a wonder factory here. And wonders . . ." He picked up a thick folder, hefted it. "Wonders are easy to find, and very difficult to verify. And, I might also add, very expensive to investigate. A truly good life, even without miracles, is where we start."

"Miracles are no longer regarded as evidence of sanctity?"

"I wouldn't put it quite that way. But it is true that you can have marvelous phenomena of all kinds without goodness being involved at all. Just to establish goodness clearly is, shall we say, a laudable beginning."

"But how do you decide about that?"

"Well, sometimes it is easy. As with Pope John XXIII. The whole world, non-Catholics included, recognized that he was a good man, a holy man."

"But he hasn't been canonized."

"That, my dear Monsignor, is where church politics enter. Pope John's cause was coupled at its introduction with that of his predecessor, Pope Pius XII." Lanza frowned. "One cannot advance without the other and the latter, I hardly need tell you, is a cause not without difficulties . . ." His face brightened again. "It is not so hard to identify good persons. It is hard to canonize them."

"Why should it be, if, as you say, the world is so in need of good example?"

"Time! Joan of Arc was burned at the stake in 1431 but she was not canonized until 1920. They have been investigating Christopher Columbus for centuries and he is no closer to canonization than he was to America when he stood pleading for funds in the court of Queen Isabella. There is no hurry here. And no way to speed things up. All the machinery here is designed to function on Eternal Standard . . ." Lanza laughed. "You must learn to live with it just as dear Pope Jean has. When he first came from Paris, he wanted to abolish the custom of the Italian siesta. He didn't succeed, of course, and our French Holy Father no longer even fights it." He smiled complacently. "The Catholic Church is fortunate to be here. Time is the Roman gift."

"Let me ask you about some people the world considers good right now . . ."

Lanza raised his right hand in a friendly, fending-off gesture, hunched forward. "We would *love* to identify more candidates for sanctity from the present century. We are oversupplied with friars and nuns from the Middle Ages, with martyrs from the early Roman times. We are in great need, for example, of models of married couples, of men and women who lived faithfully and lovingly. Yes, of course, we would like them. Perhaps couples like Jacques and Raissa Maritain, the philosophers. But many people want the miracles you spoke of, and to get the Maritains into the pipeline, as Americans like to put it, is impossible . . ."

"What about Mother Hilda?"

The lines in Lanza's face tightened, he pursed his lips, leaned back suddenly silent, charm withdrawn like a counter from a gaming table.

"The seeress of Munich," Michael intoned, more enthusiastically than he expected, pushing against the invisible siding of Lanza's genial resistance, "has helped thousands of people. I understand there are many cures attributed to her. She has been a counselor to priests all over the world, including some who work here in Rome. What about her?"

Lanza smiled paternally. "Well, Monsignor, let me say this. There is one insurmountable problem with Mother Hilda. She is alive." He waved his hand, dismissing a line of witnesses, quickly formed, ready to testify. "We are, if I may put it bluntly, concerned only with the dead here. We can settle controversies about the dead. We have, in fact, become very good at it. We are not concerned about doing that for the living." He glanced down at the hooked ash of his cigarette. "It might be well for the success of your research if you didn't do so either . . ."

THREE

Pope Jean watched Mother Hilda leave St. Peter's from his apartment window, his right hand cradling the side of his sensitive scholar's face. Is she from God or not? A question popes asked hundreds of years ago when fasting and miracle-working could have been Olympic specialties in Italy, with gaunt holy women popping up in every little town with visions and advice on how to run the church. Pope Jean had received Mother Hilda yesterday. She had spoken simply, directly, looking right at him. "If my visions are from God, then you must heed them. If they are from the devil, it is only because God permits it, and if I am asked to receive them in my body, you are asked to interpret them in your soul."

Mother Hilda had told him of the images that came spontaneously to her, spectral scenes of Roman streets, black-cloaked horsemen, faces hidden, thundering over stones rubbed smooth long before Jesus had been born. The pope frowned, felt her unfaded presence, the steady tone of her voice as she had warned him, "Be on guard, be on guard . . ." He glanced at the antique clock on his desk. Even the pope could not keep Franz Cardinal

Kiejson, prefect of the Congregation for the Doctrine of the Faith, once the Holy Office, waiting too long. Meetings! I lived through a purgatory of meetings when I was archbishop of Paris . . .

A solemn-looking monsignor, clutching a folder, waited in the hall. All business, *he* would never have a vision, unless perhaps ordered to do so. The pope hesitated, patted the side pocket of his cassock. My pills. The monsignor's cold clear eyes telegraphed expectation, duty, all the burdens of the papacy. I'll get the medicine later. The pope nodded, followed the cleric down the corridor into a large gilt and gray conference room. After the ritual greetings the pope took his chair, studied Cardinal Kiejson as the tall, silver-haired Dutch prelate sat down opposite him. The sixty-two-year-old Kiejson was lean and, except for a wartime scar on his right cheek, imperially handsome, a victorious knight in a time-darkened painting. He would never have visions either. The Dutch cardinal flickered a smile as he flattened the pages bulging out of an open binder in front of him. "Holiness," he said in tones of hard-won assurance, "it is time to choose a course of action regarding the church in the United States."

The pope seemed preoccupied, stood up, walked slowly to the window. "Have you ever wondered, *Eminenza,* about the inner nature of belief?"

Kiejson forced a smile over his uneasiness. Ah, the French philosopher pope, ever predictable. Bring up a practical matter and he immediately counters with an abstraction. "I am concerned about it all the time."

"In Paris," the pope responded, returning, head lowered, to his chair, "the museums are crowded and the churches are empty. The museums have become the churches, I am afraid, and the churches are now the museums. The churches are quiet, as only places long empty, their moment past, can be. The reverence, the listening, the waiting for revelation about life: these are all in the museums now." He looked up at the Dutch cardinal. "The churches or the museums. In which do we find true belief?"

"We were speaking of the United States, Holy Father."

The pope leaned forward, tented his fingers. "Yes. I read your summary. Do you really believe, *Eminenza,* that schism is near?"

"Something more insidious. The American mindset is unique. Even Charles Dickens described it when he visited there over a century ago. Authority exists not to be obeyed but to be tested constantly. And whoever claims authority is pulled down immediately. We are questioning theologians and writers from the United States right now. Americans are generous and likable, but they bring their positivism, their doubt, their excessive self-confidence into the church. Nothing is ever settled in America." Kiejson gestured, the thickly packed pages beneath his raised hand hunched, began to close. The pope gazed thoughtfully over his fingertips at him.

Kiejson pushed the protesting pages flat. "I have, on the basis of these reports and my conversations with the American ambassador, Mr. Wingate, concluded that, if papal teaching authority, the *Magisterium,* is to survive there, then strong disciplinary action must be taken soon. And not only for purity of theology. The American bishops, acting as a group, have involved themselves in such questions as nuclear arms and foreign policy. But for them, and some others, the United States would have smashed the Communist infiltration in Latin America by now. American bishops seem persuaded by every left-wing cause. They simply do not understand the Communist threat as we in Europe do."

The pope shook his head slowly, lowered his hands to the tabletop. "What kind of 'disciplinary action' do you suggest?"

"We must, for example, move against Archbishop Canfield. He has been the subject of hundreds of complaints. Not only has he interfered with his government's foreign policy by publicly picketing the defense plants in his archdiocese, but he is uncertain doctrinally as well."

The pope felt a twinge of discomfort in his left arm, lowered his eyes, gripped the table edge, spoke deliberately. "I had expected you to speak first of Cardinal Casey . . ."

FOUR

Thomas Cardinal Casey, the sixty-eight-year-old archbishop of Chicago, had lost the plump, vigilant owl's face of his youth. Feathers had been badly ruffled in battles over the years, he was as hard and worn-looking as a statue's pilgrim-kissed foot, but he had few complaints, except for a stomach ulcer and a mostly under control anxiety about his role in certain Vatican bank dealings. He held a glass of medicine in his left hand, a telephone in his right. "Missy, I can't hear you very well."

"It's only six o'clock in the morning here in Chicago."

"I know, but I wanted to speak with you before I saw the Holy Father."

"You just set him straight, Tom. I don't think these Italians tell him everything, they don't believe in it . . ."

"Well . . ."

"Are you taking your medicine, the way the doctor said you should?"

Casey gazed unhappily at the glass in his left hand, lowered it to a side table. "I've got it right here."

"That's not the same as taking it. Now you just tell the pope that a lot of these people working for him should be grateful to you, all the money you've collected for them. Butchers' and bakers' sons, the lot of them, living high and comfortable, you paying the bills."

"They're small people, Missy, office boys, that's all. They're not the ones to worry about."

"Momma used to say you could ignore the fly only for so long, then you showed it what the swatter was for."

"Listen, Missy, I talked to Franz last night."

"That Dutch cardinal you've been so good to all these years, paying his way when he comes to America and everything?"

"Yes, he, well, he's been handling everything and he felt that everything was taken care of . . ."

"Well, isn't it?"

"It's a question of how much pressure they may put on the pope."

"They? Who are *they?*"

"Well, there's been a lot of misunderstanding about the Vatican bank. I've talked to Max Hampton and he doesn't seem to think there's anything to worry about."

"Max Hampton, that Orangeman lawyer of yours? Momma would have told you a thing or two about that. Throw a sock full of diarrhea at the Orangemen's front door, that's what she said to do on Halloween, that's what I think of your man Hampton. Now listen, Tom, you tell the pope he ought to worry more about these pinko bishops like Canfield, out trying to weaken the country's defenses, always criticizing the president . . ."

FIVE

Angelo Cardinal Solieri heard the phone ringing in his secretary's office. Where is Father Paul anyway? He pushed the old manuscript away gently, lowered a magnifying glass carefully onto the table next to it. He smiled as he rose from his chair, I am like everything else here in the archives, a relic with a cracked binding and loose pages. Solieri entered his assistant's book-piled office, nudged some papers aside, picked up the receiver. "Yes, yes, this is the Vatican archives. Speaking. The Holy Father wishes me to hear his confession? Yes, I know, it is the regular day. Yes, in his private chapel." He fished inside his plain black cassock for an old pocket watch, looped on a shoestring to his belt. "One-thirty? *Bene. Pronto.*" He replaced the receiver, mounded the papers over it again, and returned to his office.

SIX

Monsignor Tracy sat in the dim parlor of Mother Hilda's small headquarters on Via Remalda. The surfaces of the two chairs, one plain table, and cabinet were eggshell-smooth and, save for the gorily painted crucifix hanging on the whitewashed wall, were the only objects in the room. The chair groaned in the eerie silence as he bent to look at his watch. Two P.M. A door opened. Mother Hilda, face shadowed above the mantle formed by her arms slightly raised and crossed beneath her habit, floated through. "Sit, please," she said softly as the priest started to rise. She settled vaporously onto the chair on the other side of the plain table. "You wish to see me, yes?"

"Yes, Mother . . ." Michael Tracy sounded foolish to himself, broke off, studied her bone-china face, her silver-bright eyes. She had to be in her fifties, she could have been any age.

"It is you who asked to see me." Her tone was benign, controlled, compelling.

"I am writing an article—and a book—on sanctity, on holiness in general and particular, in the Catholic tradition."

She studied him for a long moment, spoke quietly. "But you yourself are in conflict with the church."

Michael cleared his throat, glanced down at his gleaming black shoes. "Maybe we could begin with your own work. You have been a counselor on the spiritual life for priests all over the world. You saw the pope in a private audience the other day. What did you tell him?"

She cocked her head slightly, studied him as if she saw better with one eye. "My message is found in the love of Jesus, nothing more." She kept her lopsided, intense gaze fixed on Michael. He shifted in his complaining chair. The room seemed detached, as if forming itself at her direction, then breaking free, as a child's balloon would, from its earthly mooring.

"What did you tell the Holy Father?" The room steadied itself.

"I do not feel that I know you yet, Father." Her eyes played fluidly across Tracy, making him think of childhood views of the northern lights. "Some souls," she said very calmly, "are receptive, some are not. The devil tempts me in many ways."

Mike lowered his eyes, rubbed his chin, tried a smile, the old clerical charm. "Well, I'm here for the *New York Times Magazine*. Even the devil wouldn't work there . . ."

Her eyes remained skeptical, hesitant, vigilant. "I am trying to get an impression of you. I sense certain things that I do not yet understand." She lowered her arms inside her habit, the stiff collar beneath her chin dropped, revealing the tallow-smooth skin of her neck, a fleeting shimmer of the flesh long under control.

"Mother Hilda, you just said that you were trying to get an impression of me. It is said that your spiritual advice is built on spontaneous images that come to you when you are with others."

"Yes, God gives me these pictures. Yes, that is so. If, on meeting a priest for the first time, I receive an impression of a barren field, I know that I am looking at a soul that is parched because of a lack of prayer. It is simple. God is very simple, you know."

"What about fasting? It is also said that you eat very little, perhaps only the Communion wafer and water. Is this . . . ?"

She shook her head, said softly, "I cannot speak about this."

"American Catholics are interested in knowing whether your fasting is an ideal you encourage for everyone, or if it's for some private, perhaps penitential, purpose."

Mother Hilda leaned slightly forward, smiled as she spoke. "Perhaps you Americans are curious because you eat so well and remain so hungry."

"You mean spiritually?"

She raised her right hand, bound across the palm with gauze. *"You,"* the nun said intensely, warmly, ducking her hand back inside her habit. "There is a conflict in you, yes, you are in doubt about yourself." She closed her eyes. "I see an altar prepared for Mass. But the priest refuses to come . . ." The nun opened her eyes, looked in a kindly way at Michael, spoke in a low, tender, sorrowful voice. "You, it is *you* who are turning away from the altar. I see, yes, I see . . ."

Bells began booming sadly in the distance, a mournful cannonade of tolling, catching her on the blind side of her concentration. She gasped, abandoned reading Tracy, raised her bandaged hand again as if warding off something. She shuddered slightly, opened her eyes, looked blankly beyond the priest. "Yes," she whispered, dragging the word out, *"yes* . . . I heard the bells . . ."

Mother Hilda rose from her chair, Monsignor Tracy did the same as she let out a low groan, groped across the table toward him. He thought he heard nuns scurrying nearby, the door opening . . .

Mother Hilda became motionless, her arm extended, her eyes glowing, staring into another world. "I saw Death riding into the streets of Rome . . ."

SEVEN

"Eminenza!" Cardinal Solieri said almost musically, nearly colliding with Thomas Cardinal Casey at a joint in the corridors near the papal apartments. As they entered the parlor outside the pope's study, the archivist nodded cheerfully to the man known in Vatican shorthand as *Chicago;* the solid, chunky word summed up the city and its archbishop. "I will not be long." Solieri smiled, hurried through the ornate door to the hallway leading to the private chapel.

Cardinal Casey mused briefly, touched the envelope in his cassock pocket. A check for $100,000, a gift for the Holy Father from the Catholic people of Chicago. Never go calling on your betters, Momma used to say, with one hand as long as the other. He sat down, rearranged his crimson sash, inspected his wristwatch, thought he heard muffled noises. What is old Solieri doing in there anyway? And he should throw away that greenish black cassock, he's a cardinal now.

A flurry of steps, the parlor door burst open. Egidio Cardinal Maestrini, the shrunken eighty-seven-year-old dean of the college of cardinals, hurried through, followed by two young priests. They ignored Casey, surefootedly took the same route Solieri had. Their clacking heels blended with voices farther down the corridor. Casey rose, followed them uneasily to the papal chapel.

Pope Jean lay on the floor, that unmistakable glassy good-bye look in his eyes. His white skullcap had flopped back like a halo on the carpet beneath his head, and his right arm was stretched out toward a tumbled prie-dieu. Fingernail marks furrowed its red velvet trim where he had clawed at it as he went down. His left arm was wedged beneath his body, his hand jammed into the side pocket of the flared cassock skirt. He had let go of the power and the glory and everything else, soiling his white pants at that flashpoint of dying.

Franz Cardinal Kiejson knelt numbly at his side in the charged silence. Solieri made a small sign of the cross in chrism on the pontiff's forehead. *"Per istam sanctam unctionem et suam piisimam misericordiam . . ."* Maestrini and his aides lowered themselves in a rustle of silk next to Kiejson. Casey remained standing, in shock, outside the emergency, not comprehending immediately what had happened to the man in whose hands, until a moment ago, his own fate had uncertainly rested. The Chicago cardinal had looked forward to the meeting so long and so anxiously, had prepared, according to his lights, so well, that he could not easily grasp that it would never take place. The *pope* is dead, the pope is *dead . . .*

". . . indulgeat tibi Dominus quidquid deliquisti. In nomine Patris et Filii et Spiritus Sancti." Amen rumbled out of the stunned onlookers. They rose slowly, caged in self-preoccupation, each one's private papal agenda had been torn away like a ragged calendar page. "The Holy Father," Kiejson said in a blank, automatic, justifier's voice, "had asked me for a draft of some papers . . ." His explaining talent failed him, a tear coursed down his right cheek, ran sideways on the welt of his scar, dropped into the silent void.

"Yes, yes," Maestrini's ancient voice crackled urgently. "What, what exactly happened?"

"Pope Jean was not in his study," Kiejson continued numbly. "I waited, as usual, then became concerned. I entered the chapel and . . ." Solieri watched Kiejson closely as the head of the Holy Office lowered his head, paused, dabbed his ringed hand at his cheek. "It was a terrible shock. The Holy Father had seemed fine just an hour before." He looked searchingly at the archivist for a brief moment, spoke as if seeking confirmation. "Then

Cardinal Solieri arrived . . ." He gestured from one to the other. "Then I called you . . ."

Noise, suppressed yet definite at the chapel door. The black-bearded Count Rafallo, the pope's physician, made an operatic entrance, taking charge, pressing questions on everyone, shooing the onlookers back from the pope's body. He removed a stethoscope from his medical bag, unbuttoned the white cassock above the unmoving chest, mumbled, half turned from his examination. *"Why* didn't you call me immediately?"

"Does it matter?" Cardinal Maestrini asked in a relic-dry voice. He scanned the group slowly, establishing his authority. "I doubt that you, or anyone, could have done anything at all. Let us be clear about that." He traced a cross in the air. "May God have mercy on his soul." He surveyed the group again, lowered his tone. "As dean of the college of cardinals, and unworthy as I may be, I now assume direction, *sede vacante,* of our Holy Church." Maestrini looked past the prelates, above the head of the fussing Rafallo, to the younger priests. "I want the pope's body brought to his bedroom. There are many things to be done."

"But . . ."

The old cardinal glared at Rafallo, whispered instructions to his priest aides. Within a few minutes Swiss Guards had moved the pope's body and the small band of mismatched witnesses had gathered around the bed where it now lay, a sheet covering the Holy Father's final dishevelment. Nuns of the papal household arrived, lit candles throughout the room as a monsignor arrived and handed a small silver mallet on a tray to Cardinal Maestrini. Tense silence. Maestrini raised the hammer above the pope's forehead, tapped it gently. "François Alouf, are you dead?"

Casey took a deep breath, felt the envelope buckle in his pocket as he shifted from one knee to the other. The Chicagoan sighed quietly, Momma was right, God has his ways. He looked across the white mound on the bed into Solieri's observant brown eyes, panned uncomfortably across Maestrini to Kiejson, whose pink scar throbbed in his ashen face.

"François Alouf, are you dead?" The wizened, gnomelike cardinal tapped the pope's forehead again, then once more, asking almost unintelligibly, "François Alouf, are you dead?"

Maestrini turned, accepted the dead pope's ring of the fisherman, the symbol of his authority, placed it in the small tray on the night table, smashed it, the hammerhead flashing in the candlelight. He gazed at the dead pope's face for a long moment. The bells of St. Peter's began to toll.

EIGHT

The Vatican press conference was bedlam when Monsignor Tracy arrived, still trying to sort out the entangled threads and strands of his feelings. Georges Bonat, the papal spokesman, gestured and shrugged like an embarrassed hotel clerk as he struggled to impose some order on the shouting correspondents. Bruno Schmidt of *Der Spiegel* huffily demanded the Holy Father's medical records, they cannot be hidden, *nein, nein,* not at such a time. Michael Tracy sighed, he was sorry about the pope's death, for Jean I had been a humane and intellectual Holy Father, who savored truth and understood that faith involved questions as well as answers. I wonder what he thought about holiness. Mother Hilda supplanted him in Michael's fancy, she had taken up squatter's rights there and he could not seem to get her out. He shook his head, thought of Ann, I miss you, Annie, this isn't real life for me anymore, it's exciting but it isn't real life . . .

"You saw the pope every day, what did you, Bonat, know of his health?" Ted Fielding of the London *Times* had the floor. "Doesn't it seem strange that the pope should die *alone,* that, of all people in the world, *he* should die without a priest?" Bonat opened his hands in surprise. "The pope prayed alone often. What could be more fitting? It is not odd, no, it is not strange . . ."

Michael's thoughts drifted back to Chicago. What time is it there and what is Annie doing?

Mother Hilda lighted in his imagination again, Mother Hilda who had stiffened, gone almost rigid, when the little nun came in and told her that the pope was dead. Michael didn't know what to make of his visit with her; he wasn't sure whether in meeting her he had experienced a near-miss with an astral flight or a close encounter of a kind the positivistic world ruled out of currently acceptable categories, a descent into a kingdom of fire and ice whose blinding light was that of real holiness. Somehow, it should be easier to tell if something or somebody is holy or wacko.

Michael trembled slightly, tried to straighten Ann's calm image in his mind. Hilda was like an old rectory housekeeper, you could tell she had been in a room because all the pictures were crooked. There, Annie, that's better. Annie, I love you. Mother Hilda edged in again next to Ann. The explosion of Roman bells had unsettled the seeress of Munich as if they were fulfilling some prophecy, telling her something she already knew, something she dreaded . . .

The questions droned on around him as Michael concentrated on Ann. But Mother Hilda doesn't want me to think of Annie, she's sending signals from halfway across Rome out of her semi-trance, she's reminding me of the duties of the priesthood. To her, I'm just another falling angel, tumbling down like Lucifer, another foolish man abandoning the altar for a beautiful woman. Jimbo would like Mother Hilda alright. But Annie isn't a temptress, she isn't anything of the kind, and haven't we searched our souls raw about love and its disruption of our lives?

Michael remembered a dying priest he had visited on his deathbed years ago. Father Torpey was in his eighties and his lined face was framed with wispy white hair. Michael had sat by his bedside in the Old Ironsides rectory bucking and heaving in a November storm. Rain pebbled against the window as the old priest took Michael's hand. "You're a young priest, Father," he had said in a remarkably firm voice, "and I'd like to go to confession." Michael had nodded, removed his pocket stole, draped it over his shoulders. "Bless me, Father," the old priest had begun, then paused, wondering, Michael supposed, whether he could tell the younger priest what was on his mind. "I have been a priest sixty years, Father, and I am sorry for all my sins, especially when I was too harsh with people." He had begun to cough, then cleared his throat. "I was too hard at times, thinking I knew what was right." The cough had interrupted him again. "And I have that as a great regret. And one other. I refused the only real love that ever came into my life." Tears had welled in his vein-webbed eyes. "I don't think you can afford to say no to love. It only comes once, a great love, if a man is lucky . . ." He had broken off, storms crackling in his lungs, and Michael had reassured him briefly. "God knows you've been a faithful priest." And he had absolved him, the old man's watery eyes fixed on him questioningly, are you too young to understand?

Yes, Michael thought, I really was too young, the oils of ordination still fresh on my hands, as the saying went. Father Torpey was a holy old man. I wonder what had happened in his life and at the price of what heartbreak. Meeting Mother Hilda was like meeting the keeper of all the things about human emotion I can't believe anymore. No wonder Monsignor Lanza wants to deal only with the dead.

Mike felt suddenly estranged from the world of the mystical, as if, as a result of deciding to marry, a scarlet A had sprouted on his black coat sleeve; he had become an outsider in the holiness organization and ascetic higher-ups had changed the locks on his office. Mother Hilda's combination of intensity and gentleness had somehow diminished him, had banded him the way naturalists tagged birds to monitor them, he wished he hadn't started this research on saints. Saints! As in that old movie about St. Bernadette, if you have faith no explanation is necessary, if you don't no explanation is possible. Spiritual insights from Beverly Hills moguls! Michael struggled to attune his receptors to the prison-yard mood of the press conference, with its overtones of dangerous possibilities, of something big being up.

Bonat waved away a question about alleged Kremlin involvement in threats on the pope's life, hurriedly introduced Count Rafallo. The burly physician fluffed his beard, adjusted his aviator glasses, spoke gravely but with confident relish of the pope's death, gesturing occasionally as if he were Fellini composing a scene. Pope Jean had been in good health for a man of sixty, some very minor ailments, yes, but nothing unusual for a man of his years and stressful responsibilities; there would be a fuller report when it was appropriate. Michael smiled. Rafallo sounded like Mayor Daley at his evasive best, Chicago's late mayor was always promising reports "at the proper time."

Appropriate? The editor of the Catholic paper in Milan was not sympathetic to Rafallo's strategy. When could be more appropriate than *now?* The papal physician calmly ignored him. A real professional, this Rafallo. Had Pope Jean been under treatment for anything? Had he been taking any medication? Rafallo shook his head, removed his glasses. Will there be an autopsy? The doctor stared down at the audience, everything will come, he repeated, at an appropriate time, then he turned, stepped down from the platform, and headed for a door a few feet away.

A shower of questions fell on Rafallo's back as Bonat raised his arms for quiet. No, nothing on the funeral arrangements yet, there will be no other announcements at this time. Any idea who the next pope might be? When will the consistory be held? Can you give us a list of cardinals? Bonat shook his head, held his hands palms outward, that is all, monsieurs. Reporters rushed forward, surrounded, penned the Frenchman in. Monsignor Tracy watched them for a moment. I'm suffering from mystery overload today, first the mystical nun, now the dead pope, more mysteries than the rosary. He headed for the rear exit. His brother Jimbo hurried after him.

NINE

Jimbo overtook his priest brother, put his arm around his shoulder, how you doing, Michael-o, what do you think of Charlie Chan at the Vatican? The journalist brother insisted that they have a drink, not every day the pope dies, it'll be good for you, bluff camaraderie, arm around the priest's shoulder, there's just the two of us, you know, no mention of their clash the night before, very Irish. Jimbo talked expansively as they headed toward the Via della Conciliazione, know just the place, nice and quiet, Mike didn't have a chance to talk, he was thinking about Ann anyway.

The brothers sized each other up awkwardly as the waiter languidly wiped the table top.

"About last night . . ."

"Your position was quite clear. Faith and family. You'd be a big hit at a Knights of Columbus Communion breakfast."

"Very funny. The wisecrack is a Tracy family weakness. You know, there might be something worth listening to in what I say."

"What am I supposed to tell you, Jimbo, you're not heavy, you're just my brother?"

The waiter interrupted, they disengaged, ordered Frascati. They confronted each other like a science experiment, two Erector-set poles with electricity crackling between them.

"What happened at the Holy Office? How'd it go this morning?"

"They put off my appointment. I went to see Mother Hilda instead."

Jimbo Tracy lit a cigarette, coughed as he inhaled. "Doing a piece on her?"

"To fill in time before I'm burned at the stake." The brothers looked away from each other.

"Did you know, Mike, that your cardinal archbishop was at the papal deathbed?"

"Casey? I didn't even know he was in Rome."

"Oh yes, the sight of the old fraud probably caused the pope to take a stroke, as the old-timers used to say. Of course, the pope's dying was better for Casey than having to move to Brazil, or some other place there's no extradition treaty."

"Jimbo . . ."

"Count on Casey to be right there to see good Pope Jean back into the Underground. The Holy Father was in it, as I recall, during the war. Him and every other Frenchman I ever met. Did you ever meet a Frenchman who didn't blow up rail lines in the dark of night all through World War Two?"

The priest looked at his brother, what's really on your mind is that you want the family's four-leaf-clover padre to stay above ground, in his collar. There were no hints of that, however, in Jimbo's rapid-fire review of the day's rumors, Moscow contracts, Chinese agents, hidden diseases, it's like a fucking treasure hunt, what do *you* hear, Mike?

"Very little, Jimbo. I've been pursuing other interests, the seeress of Munich, last seen circling Da Vinci airport . . ."

"Do I detect a note of skepticism in Monsignor's tones? What did she do, get under your skin?"

"You and she do talk the same language."

"Faith, it's called, Mike, faith of our fathers."

"We've covered that subject, Jimbo. Is there something else you want to talk about?"

"Mike, there *is* something peculiar about the pope's death. What do you hear about it, seriously?"

"Seriously, nothing. You heard the news conference, same as I did. You don't want to talk about that, admit it. Underneath all this male bonding, you want to review my standing in the priesthood."

"Farthest thing from my mind. Bigger things are happening than that the Tracy boys have had a little difference of opinion. Besides, I've thought about it. You do what you want, you always have anyway."

Mike frowned, pushed his chair back as the waiter placed water-flecked wine glasses in front of them, filled them from a carafe.

"What did the pope *really* die of? If it's as simple as they say, Michael, why does this have all the signs of a cover-up? And who would benefit from the pope's dying suddenly?"

"Round up the usual suspects."

"Come on, Mike. This *is* what I really want to talk about. There is something goddam odd going on. Like old Aunt Agnes used to say, she could tell cockeyes, false hair, and false teeth, she had an eye for phoniness, Agnes. After reporting on the Vatican for a long time, you get used to their timing, you feel it when it's off, it's like the Ferris wheel stopping suddenly, everybody lurches. I inherited Agnes's instincts. I'm picking up something funny." He tapped his chest. "In here, the instincts never fail."

"I've seen one reader of hearts already today."

"Look, Mike, the Vatican has had two thousand years of practice with dead popes, it's one of the things they're good at." He fiddled with the damp napkin beneath his wine glass. "But they're rattled today. That press conference was a mess. Way out of control. Inspector Clouseau and Doctor Caligari on the same bill." He leaned forward, spoke intensely. "They're on the *defensive*. They're hiding something. You can tell it a mile off."

Monsignor Tracy smiled ruefully at his brother. "Jimbo, you've been like this all your life. You make a big scene, then you escape by charm and sleight of hand; the audience loves it."

"It's providential," Jimbo continued, "that you're here in Rome, Mike. *Think* of what we can do with this story. What *did* the pope die of? Who was the last person to see the pope? What are the implications for the church right now? The pope was at the very center of world politics as well as world religion. Not everybody wants peace the way he did, not everybody wants the big religions to get together either. There'll be a hundred reporters on this, probably more, but we're the team to beat, you and me, me with *Time*'s contacts, you with your inside Vatican sources. The Tracy brothers,

Mister Inside and Mister Outside. Monsignor Inside, if you prefer. Jesus, the old man would love it, wouldn't he?"

The old man having been a Chicago police inspector, Captain Dennis Tracy. Sweet old Denny, dead at forty-nine from a broken heart he had sustained in the very steep fall he had to take, the innocent sacrificed for a Chicago City Council scandal.

"It'd be kind of a sweet revenge, something to do for the old man, Mike. After all, he went down because of a cover-up. Let's uncover one in his memory."

"Let's leave our family honor out of this."

Jimbo sipped his wine, lowered and cradled the glass in his hands, spoke in a low, intense voice. "How do you think Mom and Dad really got along with each other?"

Monsignor Tracy felt the heat of discomfort spreading through him, ignored the question.

"You ought to think about it, Mike, you with your romantic ideas of marriage. You think they didn't have a hard time? You think everything was easy? Why do you suppose there was seven years between us? Think the pope staring at them out of that framed blessing on the bedroom wall was the problem?"

"That's enough, Jimbo."

"I'm serious. You think this over, you with your touchy feelings about Denny's memory, and your ideas that love is so wonderful."

Mike inhaled, placed his hands flat on the table. "I know everybody has to struggle."

"Sure, sure," Jimbo said, mockingly, "and you ought to know that the big thing in our folks' marriage was *duty*. Even after the pilot light was out, they stuck together. That's what I'm asking you to think about. There's been enough hurt in our family already. Duty, loyalty, things they don't talk about anymore. They keep the world going. How about doing your duty by the family?"

"You should talk . . ."

"I'm not kidding myself about what I feel, I'm not living on romantic illusions."

Monsignor Tracy exhaled slowly, pushed his chair back, stood up. "This wasn't such a good idea, big brother, this drink together. I, I'll . . ."

"You'll what?"

Suddenly the world shook, an enormous roar filled the air, the windows exploded. The Tracy brothers hit the floor under a blizzard of broken glass and debris. Not half a mile away chunks of mortar and stone rocketed and cascaded through the air, riding the invisible umbrella of the blast that had just shattered a section of the wall of the Castel Sant'Angelo.

TEN

"You know what, Mike?" Jimbo Tracy patted a washcloth cautiously around the adhesive bandage that the *Time* nurse had just applied to his forehead, shouted to overcome the dull ringing in his head. "When I hit the floor and all the crockery was flying, I couldn't remember the Act of Contrition."

Monsignor Tracy winced as the nurse fitted a bandage snugly around his right hand, half turned his head in a clouded show of attention.

"Now I lay me down to sleep, that's what came to me. What would the old man think about that?"

"It's about what Denny would have expected."

The *Time* bureau office seemed subdued and orderly after the thunderous street of screaming people, trumpeting ambulances, sirens, spraying water, the crunch and tinkle of wary movement through broken things. The Tracy brothers had stumbled out of the rubble of the café, dust-covered Lazaruses in murky battlefield light. A bulging sail of white smoke had hung above the coffee-colored Castel Sant'Angelo.

"You should both take it easy," the hard-eyed nurse said as she left. The brothers inspected each other warily, the blast had left their ears humming and momentarily swept the tension between them out of the air.

"Fins?" Jimbo used the truce-invoking word from the rough and tumble of their growing up together. Mike nodded as Jimbo continued. "I was older and heavier than you but you were a tough kid at that, like a bug you couldn't squash. 'Fins,' you'd say, 'isn't the same as surrender.' "

"It still isn't."

Jimbo sighed, fingered the margins of the bandage above his eyes.

"Well, Mike, during this break in the action, let's talk about the story breaking all around us." Jimbo's phone rang and the journalist sat down carefully to answer it. He scratched notes on a pad as his priest brother tested the mechanics of his aching right arm. Mike had tried to comfort the injured, absolving a dozen of them in the littered roadway. He had noticed his own bleeding hand as he helped lift a victim into an ambulance just before the police ordered everyone—*sì, sì,* you too—off the street.

Jimbo shielded the receiver with a knuckle-skinned hand. "They've found another bomb. In the Termini." His nerves were firing again, the forget-the-wife-and-kids look lighted his eyes. "They got a warning, from some group claiming responsibility, and the police found it okay." He breathed deeply, blinked at his own scribbles, stood up. "I told you we were in the middle of a big story. You want in with me on this, don't you?"

"I'm working for another magazine."

"Fins, Michael-o, remember? And don't you think, as the nuns used to say, God has preserved our lives for some great work? As to *Time* and the *Times,* we can work something out." The phone rang again. Monsignor Tracy inspected his clergyman's suit, its fabric torn and clotted with dust; it resembled floured meat ready for searing. The journalist brother hung up.

"The New Century Movement, that's what they're calling themselves . . ."

"Jimbo, before you get too involved, maybe you ought to call our mother, tell her that we're okay."

"Ah, Monsignor Michael, so considerate, and wouldn't every mother be proud to have a son like that in the priesthood."

"And you might call Maureen, too. Your kids'll be worried."

"You're full of family advice for a guy who says fuck off when somebody gives any to him."

Michael's hand smarted as he made a pass at brushing his suit jacket. He sighed, stepped toward the door.

"Sure there isn't somebody you want to call, Monsignor?" Jimbo picked up the phone. "Since you're so concerned about loved ones." It rang in his hand. "Yeah . . ." The priest paused, his bandaged hand lightly touching the doorknob.

"They're promising new bombings." Jimbo sighed as he lowered the phone back onto his desk. "Some with warnings, some without."

"Who is *they?*"

"The New Century Movement, who the hell do you think, the College of Cardinals?" He let a rush of air out of his puckered lips. "This is all connected, Mike, you can bet that red-edged black dickey of yours on that. First the pope dies, then the Castel Sant'Angelo gets its rocks off all over the tourists, and there'd be commuters splattered all over the railroad station if the police hadn't located the second bomb. Imagine! The Italian police *found* it. Write that down, that's as good a miracle as Maria Goretti for you."

"Easy, Jimbo. There's nothing to connect these incidents to the death of the pope. Whatever he died of, he wasn't blown up."

"How do you know? You seen him yet? Why did Frog One and the Dago count dodge all the questions about medical records, about an autopsy? Maybe he's spread out like a jigsaw puzzle and they can't fit him together."

"Come on, Jimbo, your Celtic imagination outstrips even your notable gift for sarcasm."

"Well, what do you make of their motto? *We are death riding into Rome.* There's your connection. What else could it mean?"

"Death riding into Rome?" Mother Hilda descended from the flies of Michael's imagination. "You're *sure* of that?"

"That's what that call was about. You suddenly look interested. How come?"

"Nothing, Jimbo." Michael managed a tight grin. "It's just a striking name. Apocalyptic, you might say."

"Oh, come now, Don Camillo, don't try to kid me. Save that shit-eating, monsignor-in-charge-of-the-secrets look for suckers. The light bulb just went on over your head."

"It's the contrast. It's too poetic for terrorists. Baader-Meinhof, tough

Germanic consonants, dread in every syllable, that's what they usually like."
Michael felt a pang in his right hand as he glanced down at his watch.

Jimbo studied his brother for a moment. "Okay, okay."

Monsignor Tracy opened the door. *"Ciao,* Jimbo."

"You could call her from here just as easy."

ELEVEN

Thin tendrils of cloud stretched above the city's snail shell winding of streets, its grids of park and monument, its great squares, silent and empty as wartime. The daily opera of Roman life had been cancelled, the orchestra and the audience had hurried home before something else happened. Monsignor Tracy waited in the tense Cavalieri Hilton lobby while a search for a rumored bomb was being completed. Nobody paid any attention to his battered dust-powdered suit as he sat reading a message from the editor of the *New York Times Magazine. Call focusshift Hilda story.* Hilda, Hilda. He shook her image out of his head, thought about Ann, oh Annie, we've known each other three, almost four years now . . .

Monsignor Tracy was coughing when he set out on that emergency expedition. He was so accustomed to them by then, so confident that he was doing the right thing in protecting the good name of the church, *ad majorem Dei gloriam,* that he had never questioned his purpose, never examined in depth why so many clergy had such complex emotional problems. Easing their pain and smoothing things over, Michael's specialty in a nutshell.

That time it was an alcoholic bishop, a bluff good fellow in his late fifties with faded blue eyes above vein-sprung cheeks, melancholy Mick eyes that looked sad even as he rattled off protective jokes like strings of firecrackers. Bishop John Patrick Muldoon of a small diocese that straddled the Mason-Dixon line, Bishop Muldoon, the final whistle blown when, in preaching to the cloistered nuns, he had referred to champagne as "angel piss." Good old Muldoon kept a shooting range in the basement of his residence. "They're saving me for Chicago," he would tell visitors with a wink to explain his off-the-beaten-track assignment. He repeated that to the sniffling and coughing Michael as, in his red-trimmed cassock, he led him downstairs, talking steadily, trying to keep Monsignor Tracy from ever announcing the reason for his visit.

Bishop Muldoon moved the chain of his pectoral cross aside, rested the gun on his shoulder, pointed his ring finger hand toward the target. "But you must know that, Monsignor, coming from Chicago as you do."

Michael watched him as he squeezed the trigger. BLAM! BLAM! Muldoon's shots struck outside the bulls eye. Michael watched him silently, sensing something tragic, something inevitable unfolding before him. He suppressed a cough as the bishop turned. "The problem is, Monsignor, everybody who tries to do things right has these critics, these enemies who misinterpret everything, who make up lies . . ." He shouldered the gun again. BLAM! BLAM! He blew a hole in the basement wall, then broke down in tears.

Michael accompanied him to the private clinic, felt as if he were abandoning the bishop like a child at an orphanage, then, feeling much sicker himself, headed back to Chicago. The whole incident weighed on him, the awful mingled aromas of martinis, gunpowder, and loneliness. Michael was coughing badly and ached everywhere when he arrived home. The priest who sat across from him at dinner that evening said, in the classical tone of rectory life, "I read about a guy had symptoms like yours, Mike. He was dead in a week. Well, I've go to be off . . ." Monsignor Tracy entered the hospital the next day.

When he complained of sudden chest pains that evening, they sent for the chief resident in cardiology. A nun in a white habit strode self-assuredly into his room, all business.

"Pull up your shirt, Father," she said, lowering the chill mouth of the stethoscope to his chest. She listened carefully, looked up. "You're okay, Father." But their eyes met. Behind rimless glasses hers were blue. She had perfectly even features and no makeup. She glanced at his chart, raised her eyes again, spoke as if standing on an equal plane with him, with a dash of mischief in her tone. "I should say, you're okay, *Monsignor.*"

And in that instant against all his expectations, counter to years of retreatmaster warnings about the twin dangers in the priesthood, Punch and Judy, drink and women, if one doesn't get you the other one will, Michael fell in love. It was as if his experience with bedeviled clerics had reached critical mass and that, beneath his consciousness, he was ready for this moment of revelation. It was like stepping through a door, coming in from a storm. "What's your name, Sister?"

"Sister Ann," she had answered easily, making a notation. "Are you stationed here in Chicago?"

So much for clerical fame. Michael felt amiably deflated. "Are you on the staff here?"

"I'm finishing my residency in cardiology," she said, strapping the blood pressure cuff onto his arm.

"Then what are you going to do?"

"Shh!" She pumped the device, watched the mercury column adjust. He watched her, sensing that something had awakened inside him, something healthy, like the first tiny bud poking through the volcanic ash of Mt. St. Helen's. Whatever it was, it was not a temptation, no, this was something else altogether.

"That's up to Mother Superior," she said, packing up the blood pressure gear. The phrase depressed Michael, it was as heavy as a convent. A weight of institutional expectation suddenly reasserted itself, threatening to crush him. "I may work with our retired sisters. But it isn't settled." Then she looked into his eyes again. And Michael knew something had happened to her, too.

Michael's reverie broke as a uniformed man announced that the search was ended, everything was all right, the guests could go to their rooms. Michael was filled with longing as he called Ann. "No, Annie, I'm okay. Really. Just a few new chest pains, in the region of the heart. I've had heart trouble since the first moment I saw you." He sat on the edge of his hotel bed. "Actually, I have a few scratches. We went to Jim's office. *Time* had a nurse take a look at us. All I had to do was take out a lifetime subscription."

"Come on, Mike, I've been worried about you."

"Come on now, Annie, you're the great downplayer of illness, especially among priests. It's over. I'm sorry I couldn't call earlier."

"It's okay, I just finished for the day. I only heard bits and pieces of what was going on. It sounded like all Rome was blowing up. You're sure you're alright?"

"I wouldn't kid a doctor, not this one."

She paused the space of a sigh. "We had such a wonderful time just before you left . . ."

"You'll get sick of me when I'm around the house all the time."

"I miss you terribly . . ."

"Me, too. I feel as if some part of me is missing. My arm or something."

"I know, I know . . ."

"You know, Annie, as the café fell down around us, I thought this is a hell of a way to keep me in the priesthood. Jimbo, of course, reads it as a sign of divine intervention, God's way of keeping us from getting married."

"I'm afraid that I'm not Jim's favorite person."

"That's just his veneer. Warped, and a little wormy, but only an eighth of an inch thick."

"Jimbo sees me as some sort of rival for your affections, the temptress breaking up the Tracy family."

"A great trait of the Irish. Their biggest cash crop is bachelors, you know. They get high on celibacy. Irish priests do a few lines of it every morning before Mass."

"No, Mike, it's the Irish mothers. They protect their boys, they don't want to let go of them."

"Tell me about it. Old Bishop Hafey tried to figure a way to slip 'A Mother's Love's a Blessing' into High Mass. He loved that last line, about not appreciating a mother's love 'till she's buried in the grave.' Grand Irish stuff, celibacy and funerals. Did you know they call the obituary page the 'Irish scratch sheet'?"

"It's really not funny. Irish mothers are tough, they don't give up ground easily. You should have known my grandmother, my father's mother, back in Brooklyn. Every Sunday she expected her married sons to visit her. Her 'boys,' she called them. She took them into the back parlor to talk to them, all five of them, and let their wives know very clearly that they were not welcome."

"And the daughters-in-law poisoned her soda bread one day, is that the one?"

Annie paused, it hurt too much to be funny. "What about our permission? Did you find out anything?"

"Well, the death of the pope has thrown everything off. And my appointment at the Holy Office had been delayed even before that happened. So I'll have to call my friend Monsignor Lanza about how to proceed from here. Everything is put on hold in the bureaucracy when a pope dies. They're afraid someone will clean out the store."

A pause. "That means more waiting . . ."

"I know, I know." He felt as if he were suffocating. "It's been tougher than I thought to get this permission. They've asked for everything but blood."

"It's been over a year and a half now . . ."

Mike was silent, he had run out of wisecracks, they didn't work in these painful moments, anyway.

"Holy Mother Church," Ann said slowly, "doesn't like to let go of her sons either."

EXODUS

ONE

Monsignor Tracy felt like a tourist caught in the midst of somebody else's revolution. The acrid fumes of conspiracy theories wafted down the pitched, cobbled lanes, onto the broad avenues, and hung like yellow fog on the Tiber. The same invisible corrosive had stung the air when flames lighted Nero's face, when the Huns flooded through the city gates, and in 1870 when Pius IX proclaimed his infallibility as lightning flashed through St. Peter's and Garibaldi marched on the papal states: Rome did not get nervous easily. Heavily armed troops swaggered erotically, Mussolini-tough, at every intersection. Michael Tracy turned like a slowly panning camera, surveying the anxious, magical city. What am I doing here, I have no business here anymore, I've got to let go of all this. His right hand throbbed. He unclenched it, inspected the pink-stained bandage.

Jimbo wants me in the three-legged-man's race with him to find out how the pope died. And to keep me in a frame on the family mantelpiece next to the papal blessing and the Lourdes water. I've always *liked* being a priest, I'm not leaving out of protest. Annie's face appeared in his imagination, followed by a surge of longing that could have registered on the Richter scale. We love each other, I believe in that, maybe it's the only thing I do believe in . . . A warm hand squeezed his innards. It was the cardiac meltdown that occurred whenever the day buckled open and light flooded his soul. Michael had invested his store of faith, hope, and love in human experience with Ann, and the world had suddenly revealed its transparency. He had lost interest in abstract vistas on the divine. Love was a great humming magnet pulling on everything within Michael so that when he was separated from Ann he felt wasted, distorted, incomplete. All the furniture had been pushed to one side of his soul and he was intensely aware of the void. Love filled you but first it uncovered your emptiness. Not all of Rome's grandeur or possibilities, not the promise of ecclesiastical power or a crimson hat, could fill that painful cavity in his being.

Michael hailed a cab, gave Monsignor Lanza's Vatican City address. He needed to talk to someone and, in his brief interview with Lanza, he felt something solid and dependable in the worldly wise man in charge of making saints. Lanza was more than a bureaucrat. His dark virility spoke of a complex past, of princesses and dowagers leaning close to him above flickering crystal and silver while cigar-smoking diplomats waited for him in the drawing room, of living gracefully through deep and dangerous times. Surely he would understand a priest in love.

On the other hand, Michael had always been somewhat guileless in trusting near-strangers. It was a healthy but perilous and unguarded urge, akin to his Irish sense of humor which made life's weight of sadness bearable but was sometimes too ready to express itself. Were there really bureaucrats, like ladies of the night, with hearts of gold? Or had Michael's own heart, swelling like a bedouin's tent in a sirocco, enlarged itself falsely for the romantic figure of a desert chieftain he hardly knew? He wondered if his father Denny hadn't forged his final pact with trouble because he trusted people too much. Still, Monsignor Tracy had to talk to somebody or burst. So he called Lanza and the prefect, in a calm, unrevealing voice, had immediately invited him to his apartment.

The taxi slowed as it entered the crowded street that ran along the wall of Vatican City. Monsignor Tracy struggled to push the crowding signs and portents out of his mind: Mother Hilda, reader and advisor, making his conflicts smart as much as his injured hand; the pope's mysterious death suspending all official Vatican business, including his own; a call close

54

enough with flying chunks of the Castel Sant'Angelo to make a man repent. But repent *what?* Of falling in love? Where was the commandment, thou shalt not fall in love? Or, for that matter, thou shalt not trust others? I've been living under duty's bell jar, not enough air in there to commit a really interesting sin. On the other hand, maybe that *was* the hound of heaven barking outside the Hilton last night. Michael felt a knot in his stomach that wit could not loosen, I've thought this through a hundred times . . .

The dome of St. Peter's loomed in the taxi window. They're moving the pope's body into the basilica today, it must be in one piece, the body, that is. The cab driver pounded on his horn as a sleek Mercedes-Benz limousine tried to pass on the right. Monsignor Tracy glanced into the big car. Thomas Cardinal Casey, looking straight ahead in wattled profile, my past is gaining on me everywhere today. The cars inched together, Casey coolly vaulted behind the thick German forged glass that would last a thousand years. My soon-to-be former archbishop. You didn't say much back in Chicago when I told you I wanted to leave, you just shook your head, said I'd change my mind, that I'd get over it, but you were almost nice for a man who, as the clerical gossips said, didn't believe in God. You even promised you'd do everything you could for me. Everybody else, including Jimbo, makes trouble and you don't, it doesn't ring true.

The Mercedes turned into an entrance to Vatican City swarming with carabinieri and Swiss Guards. Mike climbed out of his taxi at a smaller gate about thirty yards beyond. The vestibule guard checked his list, buzzed open the main door of the apartment house. Mike climbed a narrow flight of stairs in the musty ill-lit building. He sniffed the air, they must have burned candles, heretics maybe, until a few years ago. But his ready ironies had begun to create internal dissonance. The Tracy humor only made him more aware of his longing, of the conflict between love and duty that it was trying to cover up. He stumbled on the last step before the landing of the floor on which Lanza lived.

The saint-making monsignor answered the door, looking settled and elegant even though the top buttons of his cassock were undone and his collar was slightly loose. Lanza, Michael thought as his host greeted him, is like Clark Gable, you couldn't make him look bad, he had read once, no matter how you dressed him. Lanza led Michael into dark-paneled masculine quarters hung with original paintings illuminated as softly as a park fountain. A high-intensity light gripped by silver tongs burned above a Louis XIV writing desk in an adjoining study whose walls were girded with well-bound books. Above a leather couch a splendidly vested figure of Christ did not hang as much as step boldly from a wooden cross.

"You admire this Christ?" Lanza asked quietly. Michael nodded, still contemplating it. "I like it very much myself. Much better than the bloody versions. You know, Monsignor, that Augustine spoke of Jesus's 'hurrying toward the cross as a husband to his marriage bed.' An interesting idea." He paused as a professor does looking up from lecture notes. "Many mystics speak of Christ's embracing the cross, of his finding not tragic loss but fulfillment there, of his returning in glory to the Father. So Christ reigns rather than just suffers." Lanza paused again, watching Michael. "It is a very Catholic thought, don't you agree?"

"It's very different from the crucifix at Mother Hilda's."

Lanza shrugged his shoulders, compressing into the movement the entire curial history of cautionary ambivalence.

"Mother Hilda's holiness," Michael continued, "seems to be all denial, all suffering, like her crucifix. You can almost feel that something happened to her a long time ago and that afterward she chose the path of abnegation and has stayed on it unswervingly since."

"You are a poet, Monsignor, at least as much as you are a theologian."

"It's the Irish in me. We're great for intuition."

"Yes. Well what you 'feel' in Mother Hilda may be *metanoia,* a change of heart, a conversion. Not unknown in Catholicism."

"If abnegation is the way," Michael said, gesturing toward the resplendent Jesus, "where does your crucifix come in?"

"I did not say that abnegation was *my* way. I appreciate the unreasonable nature of this approach. Deep spirituality may be intrinsically unreasonable. Christianity says that it is reasonable to lead unreasonable lives. I believe that."

"In your congregation, however, you examine the lives of the saints. You perform spiritual autopsies. Is total abnegation the way with most of them? Or is it only incidental to the way?"

Lanza studied Michael for a moment; the American was more interesting than he had expected him to be. "You ask a perennial question," he said slowly, "about whether holiness consists in giving everything up for God, or finding God in everything."

Michael glanced slowly around the room. How well did it reflect Lanza?

Was it truly warm or was it a comfortable stage set, cool and canvas-thin? The sonar echoes that came back from the prefect were, however, strong and clear. "Let me put this another way," Tracy went on. "Suppose we ask the same question about love. Is it a deception, or is it the closest experience we can have of God?"

"Some psychologists say that love is a form of mania, some say that it is an addiction, others that it is a bad habit. And some suggest that we have invented love in order to rationalize Eros."

"And you, Monsignor Lanza, what do you believe?"

As he pointed to a chair, an inch of tired French cuff emerged from Lanza's black sleeve. He tucked it back in, spoke thoughtfully, deliberately. "What exactly did you come to talk about, Monsignor Tracy? Holiness or love?"

"Both, I suppose . . ." Michael sat down on the couch.

"Would you care for something to drink, coffee perhaps?" Lanza circled around through the study, extinguished the burning coal of light, returned, looked inquiringly at Michael. "In our life here, I share a common chapel with two cardinals who also have apartments on this floor. We have a small, well-stocked kitchenette, too. For those days when the sisters are off . . ." Lanza caught the look of concentration on Michael's face, let his sentence disintegrate, sat down opposite his visitor.

Monsignor Tracy took a deep breath and told the story of his love for Ann in one long, uninterrupted paragraph. "I'm sure about what I want to do in the long run," Michael concluded, "but I don't know what to do next, or how to do it. My family is one thing, getting the permission from the Holy Office is something else. I want to do this the right way. Cardinal Kiejson . . ."

"Who lives down the hall," Lanza interjected as Michael paused, "I know him well. 'If thy eye be single,' the gospel says, 'thy whole body will be full of light.' Cardinal Kiejson, my dear Monsignor, is very single-eyed."

Michael swallowed with difficulty at this quick, dry, unencouraging opinion. "Are you saying that I can't expect much help from him?"

Lanza compressed his lips, frowned, opened his hands in the ambivalent Italian manner. "Everything is always closed here in Rome, Monsignor, and, at the same time, everything may also be open."

"That's not how we Americans operate."

Lanza shrugged. "No, no, I have come to understand that. There is a delegation of Americans in Rome right now badgering me about the cause of someone they want declared a saint practically overnight." He smiled philosophically, indulgently, resistantly. "Remember what I told you about Rome running on Eternal Time, Monsignor."

Michael Tracy studied Lanza. Have I entrusted my heart to the wrong man? "But my application has been in for more than a year and a half. I was told . . ."

Lanza touched the edge of the Roman collar protruding from his cassock collar, eased it back into place. "For you, Monsignor, this is the most important thing in the world. For ancient Rome, with a pope mysteriously dead, with a new one to be elected, and terrorist threats everywhere, your concerns do not seem so pressing." He paused, took Michael's measure again. "You think I am being harsh or unfeeling, yes? That I am the devil's advocate even though I told you he does not exist. Monsignor Tracy, we do not know each other but, in one of those mysterious ways, we have spoken frankly, in trust. I speak on that foundation. I am trying to save you pain. You are in love. You are not the first priest to be in love, nor will you be the last. Romance swells the heart and blurs the vision. I only want you to be realistic, and very few Americans are. We are accustomed to love here in Europe, we live with it as one must with the weather. Sometimes it is good, sometimes bad, but it is natural, always there, and ever capricious." He shifted slightly in his chair. "This may hurt but you must face it. No case is ever closed here, that is true, but nothing, *nothing* will be done officially on your rescript of laicization, *sede vacante. Nothing* happens in the interim between the death of one Holy Father and the choosing of another." Lanza sighed, leaned forward. "You want something to happen now, my friend—I do call you friend—that is not going to happen."

"Nobody can go on waiting forever."

Lanza's unblinking eyes bespoke concern and restraint. Like those of the friendly veterinarian, Michael thought, who wants to put your dog to sleep. Lanza waited a beat, spoke gently. "Let me make a suggestion. Rewrite your petition while you are here in language they will understand. And this time don't mention your friend Ann."

Michael blinked. "You want me to put down Mother Hilda instead?"

"The congregation you've been dealing with does not want to hear about women. *Any* women. Including them, out of American honesty or sincerity, doesn't help procedures."

"But we're talking about love, as in love thy neighbor, the thing the church teaches. They don't want to hear about love?"

Lanza's acceptant expression remained in place, an elegant embodiment of *Romanità,* that composed, contained style Vatican bureaucrats had perfected as they watched kingdoms rise and fall around them, throughout history. Still, Michael sensed Lanza's fundamental benevolence but Michael also understood that Lanza expected to be a cardinal archbishop some day, and that he would go only so far, that he would not imperil that reward for his unswerving, if humane, loyalty to the Holy See.

"The men at that congregation," Lanza said evenly, "can deal with applications from Italian peasant boys whose mothers sent them to the seminary because they didn't want them behind a plow the rest of their lives. Or with priests who had major psychological problems they tried to solve by taking orders. They can accept those things."

"Are you saying that if I alleged motherly coercion or said I was a screwball, I'd get permission to marry?"

"Well . . ." Lanza shrugged, raised a pacifying hand.

"Can't you hear what you're saying, Monsignor? You're suggesting that I will do better with my Roman masters if I lie about the most important thing in my life. I can't do that. It would be sacrilegious. I'd rather find some priest who would be willing to marry Ann and me because it's the right thing to do. Somebody who wouldn't worry about his career or what some Roman official would think about him . . ." Mike broke off. "I'm sorry, I didn't mean . . ."

Lanza cocked his head. "You are upset. I understand." He turned away. "Finding such a priest is one of your choices." He paused. "But I would not want to hear about it, officially, that is."

Michael's temper flared again. *"You* could marry us. You could justify it on pastoral grounds. You *could* do that, Monsignor Lanza, you could do that on your own. It's one of the oldest exemptions in canon law. Anything goes if *omnia parata sunt pro nuptiis,* if everything is ready for the wedding. Maybe it would be your salvation as well as ours."

Lanza let Michael's anger swirl about him, looked thoughtfully at him, responded mildly. "I am a Roman official. You want me to understand you. You must understand me. I would be excommunicated if I married you. You must know that."

Distant sounds. A ticking clock. Michael rose, winced as his hand smarted with pain.

Lanza, eager to do something concrete for Michael, suggested an aspirin. "We have some in the kitchenette." He rose, led Monsignor Tracy down the corridor. He stopped by a door at the far end next to a tarnished metal elevator gate. Dusty cables swayed lightly in the musty shaft behind it. Michael peeked into the darkness. "Did Mr. Otis install this himself? During Vatican One?"

Lanza flashed a smile of uncertain comprehension as he unlocked the door to a cupboard-lined room. A buzzing refrigerator stood next to a 1950s stove and sink. Lanza opened a cabinet above them. A bottle of aspirin stood on the shelf next to an opened cracker box. Michael watched Lanza work the cap off the bottle, shake out two tablets, lay them on the sink as he poured a glass of water. The tension between them dissolved during this busy work. "Most priests I know," Mike said genially, "keep a drugstore above the sink. The last rectory I lived in was nicknamed St. Upjohn's."

Lanza grinned nebulously. "You know, Monsignor," he said as Tracy swallowed the aspirin, "when you called to see me I was sure you were going to ask me about the pope's death. Everybody else has. I even heard today from your brother, the celebrated *Time* correspondent."

Michael rinsed the glass. "Jimbo want you to set a Hav-A-Heart trap for me?"

Lanza hesitated, again puzzled by Michael's reference, closed the cabinet. "He wanted inside information on how Pope Jean died. But, of course, I do not know much. The cardinals have been meeting this morning on the matter. And on the arrangements for the conclave. I understand there's been some trouble with the condition of the body. They don't embalm popes, you know."

"Very quaint." Michael thought of Ann as they walked back toward Lanza's rooms. Annie, why am I here in this crumbling old reliquary where the air hasn't been changed since the Reformation? He was absorbed by a vision of Ann's face, did not at first hear Lanza's question.

"You do know about Mother Hilda I suppose?"

Michael stopped, touched Lanza's arm involuntarily with his bandaged hand, pulled it back. "Know what?"

Lanza paused at his own door. "She supposedly warned the Holy Father earlier this week that he was in great danger, that death was lying in wait for him in the streets of Rome . . ."

Mike started, remembering his own interview with the seeress of Munich. "Did the German holy woman really say that?"

Lanza looked up, surprised at Michael's tone, as he closed the door. "That is what I have heard. One hears many things in Rome. And Mother Hilda is not . . ."

The elevator cage clanged and muffled voices rolled down the hallway. Lanza turned away abruptly, stepped outside, leaving the door open the width of a finger. Michael heard a jumble of voices as Lanza warmly but deferentially offered a greeting. One of the answering voices was very familiar.

"Monsignor Lanza, you must know *eminenza* of Chicago . . ." Michael squinted through the narrow seam to see Cardinal Kiejson presenting Lanza to Cardinal Casey.

"Yes, Monsignor and I have met many times." Casey's nasal tones, that Nixonian imitation geniality, Mike would know it anywhere. He pulled back from the slit of open door. The voices of the prelates overlapped, followed by a volley of laughter. Kiejson, unseen, seemed to stay outside the good humor, as if honoring some vow against excessive spontaneity. The laughter trailed away, the voices became indistinct.

Michael cracked the door open a half inch on a Goyaesque slice of Casey and Kiejson nodding together as Lanza spoke quietly to them. Maybe he's turning me in. Cardinal Casey turned away, bent toward his attentive companions, whispered, then pulled back. What *is* he saying? Then the princes of the church disengaged, walked directly past Michael's vantage point. Kiejson paused, made a parting comment to Lanza. "We must get our friend the *camerlengo* to stop acting as if he were running the Sûreté." They laughed grimly and Lanza came back into the room.

TWO

Several hundred feet of twisting corridors away, Jimbo Tracy dipped a glance at the beribboned uniform he was wearing, remembered what Mayor Daley used to say about putting on a good front when you were uncertain inside: wear your best suit, get a new hat, don't let anybody know how you really feel. Irish trickery, Chicago style, where such sentiments would bring a tear to your eye if someone didn't poke his finger in it first. The uniform was Ownie's idea, Owen Wingate, now ambassador to the Holy See but formerly king of Mazda in Cook County. "A hell of a car," he used to say, "even if the Nips make it." He was a rich Mick who had turned Republican when they started electing black mayors in Chicago. Ownie called it "voodoo politics," which meant that the days of Daley's balanced tickets—nine Irishmen and a Swede—and Ownie's no-bid contracts on fleets of city cars were over for good. Fund-raising for Republicans had earned him the Vatican City appointment and he loved it.

And now, thanks to Ownie, Jimbo was actually inside the Vatican residence complex, close to the papal apartments, sweating but, so far, so good.

That, he thought, would show brother Michael, the monsignor, that Jimbo didn't need his influence to get this story after all. He peered down a deserted hallway, its marble floor patched with light dumped on it from high windows. He started down, toasting his brother mentally, as if getting this far he had put him in his place. Up yours, Michael dear.

"I need an edge, Ownie," he had told the ambassador on the phone, "not much, just something to get ahead of the competition. I'd like to get the atmosphere, the mood, that's all. You remember the way City Hall felt the day Daley died." Ownie agreed to supply Jimbo with the credentials and uniform of a military attaché assigned to the American funeral delegation. "The Italians love uniforms," the ambassador had assured the journalist, "but you're just going for a look around. Nothing more, understand? You fuck around, you'll get fucked." Jimbo thought about that as he made his way down the sun-dappled corridor. The only mood he had picked up so far was the anxiety within himself. He paused at an ornate double door, listened for a moment, inched it open, stepped through.

Jimbo froze as he found himself standing in a tapestried foyer between two husky Swiss Guards. But they ignored him and he forced himself to take one step away from them, then another. A vacuum cleaner whined somewhere nearby. A door opened suddenly on his left and the vacuum noise became louder. Housekeeping nuns moved as gently as Hovercraft over a large gray carpeted floor. Jimbo breathed deeply, entered briskly, intensely aware that he was making a fresh trail of footprints in the deep pile of the rug. The nuns never raised their heads as they closed ranks behind him to smooth out his wake. The old Red Sea ploy, Jimbo said to himself, feeling calmer, sensing that he was near, maybe even in, the papal apartment.

With the invisible padding of silence, Jimbo thought, along with the shanks of streaming sunlight and the keening vacuum, this grand place is just like any other house on the morning after death. He recalled his own father's summertime wake and the greenhouse feel of the flower-choked bungalow and the aromas of food being cooked generously for the crowds of mourners and of the faint trace of liquor from the drinks the men made for themselves in the kitchen. He picked up different smells now, faint but distinct— antiseptic, a hint of carbolic, a whiff of sulfur, astringent medicinal scents, laboratory odors, morgue smells.

He entered another corridor. At its far end, a pair of Swiss Guards lowered and crossed their pikes ominously. Jimbo reminded himself of Mayor

Daley's recipe for Gaelic bravado, kept moving. The odors grew more powerful with each step. The atmosphere weighed down on him—silent, expectant, somber. The Swiss Guards inspected him impassively, checked the plastic-covered credentials he wore on a chain around his neck. In a corridor to the side a burly man in overalls was noiselessly polishing the silver frieze on the side of an ornate catafalque—angels with deployed wings battled devils and serpents along its length. The whole was like a silent movie. The pikes were raised, the Swiss Guard on his right nodded, and Jimbo stepped into a short corridor that ended at another set of double doors. He passed what he took to be the papal chapel, hesitated in front of the doors, turned the curved handles, carefully pushed them open, inched inside, closed and leaned against their inner panels, breathing heavily, almost paralyzed.

The body of the pope, clad in full pontifical vestments, lay on a gurney, silhouetted against the tall windows that framed Rome. The tawny city stretched beyond them like a sleeping lion under the midday sun. The pope's face looked up peacefully from a swaddling of Kleenex, tucked under his chin to protect the edges of the vestments. The room was charged with electricity, with a sense of feverish activity broken off so suddenly that its energy still flooded the air. A green surgeon's gown was tossed on a nearby chair and rubber gloves, twisted half inside out, lay in its folds. On a nearby stand a small damp sponge lolled like a cut blossom next to a tray of cosmetics. On another table lay a place setting of surgical instruments and beyond it a 35 mm camera stood on its side midst a tumble of empty yellow film boxes.

Jimbo inspected the pope's rigid features, their already compromised naturalness further subtracted by a recently applied coating of makeup. Earth tone, the journalist thought irreverently, Williamsburg colors. He stepped back, glanced at a tall, tightly covered stainless steel bucket at the side of the improvised bier. Count Rafallo had been at work preparing the pope's body for transferral to St. Peter's. That much was clear, but what *exactly* had he been doing? Jimbo's eyes passed over the surgeon's tunic and gloves with their stubby, half-reversed fingers still protruding. He picked up the camera. Empty.

The journalist bent, sniffed the strong smell that seeped out of the steel container. Acid, he thought, what the hell *has* been going on here? Voices sounded in the hallway, followed by a rumbling sound. Jimbo hurried through a door into what seemed to be a vacant dressing room. The ghostly outlines of whatever had happened completely disappeared as the double doors opened and Count Rafallo entered, fluffing his spade beard, reconstituting his sense of professional calm. He was followed by Swiss Guards and a troop of young clerics solemnly pushing the gleaming catafalque that would carry the remains of the pope to the basilica of St. Peter's. God damn, Jimbo said to himself, God *damn*. The whole suite shuddered slightly as all Rome's bells began to toll in unison.

THREE

Egidio Cardinal Maestrini, the crimson-capped, white-haired *camerlengo*, entered Kiejson's apartment, hunched as if huddling his strength close to himself, as an old traveler might a meager bundle of possessions. The lines on his forehead were densely packed, one for each deep secret he knew. The bright-eyed wizened prince of the church scanned the Dutch cardinal's quarters thoroughly. "I have always envied the simplicity of your apartment," he said in his dry, dusty voice. "As to my own, it overflows with books and pictures and the many things I have accumulated in my long life."

"Surely, *Eminenza,* we have other matters to consider besides the condition of our living quarters."

"You are businesslike, Cardinal Kiejson, to the point. As detached from things as I am attached to them. Many would see that as admirable." Maestrini turned his head slightly toward Casey as they all sat down. "Don't you agree, *Eminenza?*"

Casey forced a smile. "I agree with you, but I also agree with our host."

"How very like you that is."

"Now, my lord cardinal." Kiejson's voice was thin and metallic as a twanging wire. "The matter at hand . . ." He led his brother cardinals to the alcove sitting room where an extra chair had been put in place for the *camerlengo*.

Maestrini inspected Kiejson as he took his seat. "There is also something to be said for not being completely businesslike. Perhaps it is the difference between the Italians and the Dutch."

"Nonetheless, *Eminenza,* I ask you to consider the situation." Kiejson spoke smoothly, determinedly. "The city is alive with rumors of all kinds. The media are making a great outcry. Terrorists in our midst, the pope dead, a famous monument seriously damaged, and what is the church doing? There has been *no* response, only silence where in the modern world there should be explanation. Leadership *and* explanation."

"About *what* exactly?"

Kiejson and Casey exchanged glances. "Very well," the Dutchman said decisively, "the cardinals must be brought together immediately and briefed on what the Vatican knows about this Communist attack, the state of the church, her finances, problems of priests and nuns, her position vis-à-vis the superpowers and the so-called Third World. In short, *everything.*" He paused, looked directly into the old man's eyes. "And we must deal with the rumors about the Holy Father's death . . ."

Maestrini smiled wryly. "The wisest course, my dear brothers, is self-discipline. We cannot control what the world does but we *can* control what we do. If these stories are *only* rumors, they will vanish as the mist does, without our doing anything about them. To make any statement about the pope's death, or the supposed involvement of the Communists, or this New Century Movement, of which we know little, merely invites questions and further speculation. *That* is the modern world's game. We do well not to play it."

"It is not sensible," Kiejson cut in. "We cannot hide from the times we live in."

"I don't give a fig for the times. The church survives by ignoring the times. When it does not, it is devoured by them."

"We're not getting anywhere in this fashion," Kiejson sighed, "and we *must* begin informing the cardinals, bringing them together for discussions."

"To create rumor mills? I think not. We will have the ordinary general congregations of the cardinals but nothing outside them. We will proceed without any bows to public opinion." He rose carefully from his chair, his glance sweeping across Casey and Kiejson. "You know, when men want to be pope, you can see it in their eyes. I understand perfectly well why you wanted to meet with me. I have attended four conclaves and appreciate how ambition runs in the souls of my brothers. I will do nothing to make it run more swiftly. If either of you is to be chosen, which God forbid, it will happen no matter what I do. Perhaps I trust the Holy Spirit more than you do."

He turned to Casey. "You, my lord cardinal, you have been spared, by some mysterious twist of God's will, what could have been an embarrassing investigation of your advice to the Vatican Bank. And the fate that would have followed. Do either of you know what Pope Jean *really* thought about that matter?" The *camerlengo* raised his bony hands in an exasperated gesture. "I am sorry that I cannot stay longer." He moved toward the door. "My policy stands."

The bells of St. Peter's began to toll, the voices of the cardinals were submerged in the sound that flooded the old building, setting it humming in every joint and seam. The *camerlengo* bowed as if in prayer. The Dutch cardinal shook his head, Casey raised his hands in exasperation. They shrugged and, side by side, followed Maestrini out of the trembling room.

FOUR

A dazed Monsignor Tracy descended the stairs from the prefect's flat. Lanza had offered worldly wisdom along with grim pragmatic insight into the consciences of Roman congregations. *I can't lie about why I want permission to leave the priesthood, and they won't give permission unless I do. Then, their records show that only misfits and momma's boys want out, that no good priest ever just falls in love, and that women, except the Blessed Mother and the saints, mostly as marble statues, don't exist at all. These officials want you to feel ashamed of falling in love. No wonder Cardinal Casey comes to Rome so much, he speaks their language perfectly, Rome and Chicago, capital cities of the fix* . . .

Mike frowned as he watched the crowds moving toward St. Peter's for the reception of the pope's body and the beginning of the lying in state. Ann appeared in Michael's imagination, soothing him. *I love you,* she whispered, *and we'll be together soon. Don't let these small men humiliate you* . . . Ann's image was so vivid that she seemed to be standing next to him and Michael answered her out loud. The security man inside the foyer looked curiously at him as he opened the outside door. The tolling bells were still spreading their jangling kinetic sound across Rome. The Eternal City, Michael thought, was being visited by the angel of deep drill dentistry, unsettling everything and everybody. Oh, Annie, I miss you terribly, I've got to get off this curial milk train at the next stop. He breasted the streaming crowd, headed away from St. Peter's.

Something else was caught on the edge of his mind, demanding attention, listen to me, it seemed to say, you can't deal with anything else until you've paid attention to me. Death lying in wait in the streets of Rome. Mother Hilda gazed at him, smiling enigmatically. Mona Lisa could take lessons from you. Michael worked his way through the surging crowd, hailed a cab, headed for Via Remalda.

Tell her it's important, Michael insisted to the black-eyed mouse of a nun peering at him through the convent door grille, tell her it's Monsignor Tracy, Chicago, the *New York Times Magazine,* the Irish Free State, the Munich Chamber of Commerce. The nun looked confused but the door opened and Michael was ushered into the same white-washed parlor in which Mother Hilda had gone into a trance on the day the pope died. May I have the next trance with you? Michael shook the spoiling rush of humor out of his head, the old man always said that the more depressed the Tracys were the funnier they got. The dying, garishly painted Jesus gazed reproachfully at him from the large crucifix. I know, you're disappointed in me. Everybody else is, too. The numbing Roman bells stopped suddenly. Mother Hilda drifted into the room soundlessly, nodded, sat down, a half-suppressed, hard to read smile on her face, as if she had expected Michael to return bearing the clean oblation of his chastened soul.

Michael cleared his throat. "I have some questions. About the pope and what you told him."

"Yes?"

"You warned him that he was going to die, is that right?"

"I told him what I saw."

"And what was that?"

"I am only the the Lord's instrument. If God sees fit to use me, I must accept that role." She waited a beat, smiled accusingly. "We have no choice about our roles in life."

"I respect your convictions. And your calling. But the pope died *the day after* you told him this. There was also a bombing in the streets that day."

Michael raised his bandaged right hand. "That's pretty accurate prophecy. You had a sense about it, you *knew* something . . ."

The nun ignored him, brought a thin arm from beneath her mantle, pointed at his hand. "You believe that your wound was accidental?"

Michael nodded.

"No, oh, no . . ."

"Let's get back to what you knew—or guessed—about the pope, and why."

"Your wound will not heal."

Mike felt the full force of her intense fraulein's eyes; she could, he thought, do laser surgery with them. "Mother Hilda, the Holy Father is dead. I think you can tell me how he died."

"If you make peace with yourself, your wound will heal." She rose abruptly, like a pop-up page in a childrens' book. "It will heal if you give yourself to God again. Only then."

Mike felt interiorly diminished, as if he had lost whatever advantage he had in the dialogue. She was, Michael thought, recalling Léon Bloy's famous phrase, a real pilgrim of the absolute. Holy, he wasn't so sure of. "Mother Hilda, what *about* the Holy Father? There isn't a lot of time. There's a real mystery connected with the pope's death. I didn't think so at first but I believe it now."

"Mystery, yes." She took a step away, moving sinuously, Monsignor Tracy thought, very sinuously for a holy wraith. "Mystery," she said in a musing faraway voice, "is precisely what the world needs." She stepped back, suddenly businesslike. "My train leaves Rome in an hour, Monsignor. We may not see each other again. You should not concern yourself about the pope. He is with God. You must be concerned about your own soul."

"We're not talking theological mystery, Mother, this is some other kind of mystery."

She sank to her knees. "May I have your blessing for my journey?" She lowered her cowled head. For all its linen-covered modesty, it seemed powerfully sensuous, too. It generated a field of force that would, Michael thought, either cure or repel his bandaged hand as he traced the sign of the cross above it. She looked up, her eyes bright, confident, arresting. "Your hand—that wound—you do understand why God has given you this sign, don't you?"

"Not exactly."

"Perhaps you have stopped trying to hear what the Lord says to you. I see a picture for you, too. A vast empty place, everybody has left . . ." She rose effortlessly, slipped quickly out of the room.

FIVE

Jimbo Tracy scaled his military cap toward a cracked leather chair in the corner of his office. "You don't act as if you believed me, Mike, you don't really think I could have made it inside the Vatican without you . . ."

Monsignor Tracy seemed absorbed in studying his bandaged hand. "Look, Jimbo, I just came by to have this looked at. You said the corporate Joan of Arc would be in today."

The older brother unbuttoned his uniform coat. "She'll be by in a few minutes." He draped the uniform jacket over the back of his chair, touched his forehead gingerly. "The trouble with you, Michael, is that you still haven't recovered from omniscience, the Alzheimer's of the clergy." He snapped on the television set next to his desk, watched a picture form of the pope stretched out beneath St. Peter's dome. "Look at him," Jimbo half growled, "in the shoes of the fisherman, and if my guess is right, he's been cleaned out nice as the catch of the day." He turned toward his brother. "I'm sure that's what was going on. Rafallo had just finished some black art surgery that had to pass for embalming. And he may have removed the only evidence about the cause of the pope's death."

"Your Irish imagination, Jimbo, *if* you were really there."

Jimbo bristled. "I forgot. Nobody can achieve anything in our family except you."

Quiet settled momentarily between them. Michael sighed. "I'm sorry, Jimbo, I'm preoccupied."

Jimbo shrugged his shoulders, flashed a mock grin, the way he did coaxing Mike into a game when they were kids. "You know I'm on to something, don't you? Otherwise you wouldn't be so upset." The journalist leaned over, turned off the television set. "Do you know much about 'the beard,' Rafallo, that is?" Michael shook his head. Jimbo picked up the slack of his own question. "He's the key. Makeup and cover-up, they go together. This situation, as the old man used to say, smells so bad it would drive a dog off a gut wagon."

"Maybe." Michael stared at his throbbing right hand.

"Maybe. *Maybe.* That's getting to be a great word with you. Have them put it on your coat of arms when you're a bishop. If you hang in, that is. *Maybe,* the great American word, it goes along with the question marks that Unitarian Ku Klux Klanners burn on black people's lawns." Jimbo halfgrunted, half-chuckled. "I don't have much faith in love, and you don't have much love for faith. We're like the Spratt family, we've got just enough to get by on between us."

Mike glared at his brother. "There's nothing worse than a cute Irishman, Jimbo. The old man used to say that, too."

"Ah, Monsignor," Jimbo said in elaborate deference, "also known as Your Touchiness. Okay, let's talk about Rafallo. I think if I can be cute enough with him, I'll get a rise out of him, just like with you."

"Did you get one out of Monsignor Lanza?"

"Just making my calls, like a professional. Lanza, as you apparently know, was reasonably helpful."

"He's nothing if not reasonable."

"But I want to play another game with Rafallo. I want to prey on his conscience somehow. Leave the right message for any man and you can rake up something in his conscience. Make him uneasy." Jimbo lit a cigarette, sat on the edge of his desk. "Remember the story about the guy who wired *All is discovered* to ten of the most important men in England? Seven of them left the country that night." He glanced at Michael, who eyed him skeptically. "Happened to me once. I was in Beirut. Got a message that my secretary had called. Then there was a bombing and the communications were knocked out. I couldn't reach her until the next day. But I thought about everything that might have happened to make her call. Maybe one of the kids was sick, maybe Maureen had found out about that Alitalia stewardess, maybe I left something at home the last time I was there, a letter, an American Express slip. Maybe Maureen had told *you* about it. And I thought, Jesus, the last thing I need is little brother flying over to lecture me about the family that prays together stays together . . ." He sighed, puffed his cigarette without breaking the sheath of memory. "Hell, I was ready to plead nolo contendere by the time I finally got in touch with the office. And it was *nothing,* nothing personal, that is. Just that Henry Anatole Grunwald, the editor in chief, was coming to Rome for one of his famous imperial visits. But I really sweated it out. *That* could happen to anybody."

"The fruits of a guilty conscience, Jimbo."

Jimbo studied his brother, quashed his cigarette. "I'll admit it. Will you? What's your friend Mother Hilda got to say about that?"

The nurse knocked on the door, entered without waiting for a response, ordered Jimbo Tracy to sit down, clucked reproachfully as she removed the Band-Aid from his forehead. The journalist kept his brother in half focus under her ministering hands. The nurse applied a fresh dressing and another bandage, then silently moved toward Michael's outstretched hand. He flexed it at her bidding, grimaced as the nurse began to remove the bandage. "I don't know what to make of her." He jerked involuntarily as the bandage came loose.

"She's got you thinking, hasn't she? By God, there's a seed of doubt sprouting in your soul. Nothing like an Irishman's soul for a garden of discontents."

Mike looked up from his hand. "Jimbo, all I said was I don't know what to make of her."

"Monsignor Tracy," the nurse interjected crossly, "you haven't been taking care of your hand *at all.* It's gotten infected. Your wound will not heal. Not this way."

The priest stared at her, then at his hand.

"I've got to clean this and put a fresh dressing on it. Sit right there, don't move. I'm going to take your temperature, too. These infections can get very bad."

Mike· wrinkled his forehead. If you make peace with yourself your wound will heal.

"You've done *something* you shouldn't," the nurse insisted, bending closer. Jimbo walked over, peered down as she spread antibiotic salve on the angry-looking injury.

"He was digging for gold," Jimbo said, "only he got a handful of shit instead." The nurse glared at the journalist.

"I shook hands with a reporter," Mike said flatly, "always danger-ous . . ." His voice trailed off. The baseball-like stitching of Mother Hilda's head cover appeared in the priest's imagination. It could be the seven veils sewn together. Who is she, and what is she doing to me?

III

NUMBERS

ONE

Rome held its breath that afternoon, everything was stiff, at attention—the sky, the streets, the knots of brooding carabinieri, the constricted air. Back at the Hilton, Michael found a batch of messages and a letter from Ann, written before the pope died, before the bomb went off, before he met Mother Hilda.

You just left for Rome. I am sitting here very alone but very much with you. The few days we just had together were so perfect—I have relived the details of the days over and over in my mind—and all I can say is thank God for being so good to us, and I thank Him most of all for you, Michael. My love for you just grows and grows . . .

He folded the letter over as a matronly American tourist tried to sneak a better look at it on the elevator.

"Terrible about the pope, Father."

"Yes."

"You knew him, I suppose . . ."

"No."

"And the *bomb*. Makes a person wonder if you can be safe anywhere these days, don't you think so, Father?"

Michael Tracy forced a smile, Yes, ma'am, I do, and I'll pray for you, and for your sister with the goiter, too. He hurried to his room, finished reading the letter.

Know that I am thinking of you each moment, and praying that you will get the permission for us to marry once and for all. I'll miss seeing you, but God is good for giving us such a happy time and such good memories. I love you so . . .

Mike read the letter again, carried it like a flower in his wounded hand out onto the balcony, gazed at St. Peter's dome, feathered by a stand of jutting cypresses in the foreground. Ann filled his imagination. He thought of their first months of friendship and of how he had volunteered to cover sick calls at the big hospital near Holy Name Cathedral so that by chance, or perhaps not by chance, he might run into Ann. He was absorbed and distracted by his blossoming love for her and, on the one hand, he felt that despite its heartwrenching complexity, it was the first really adult experience he had ever had. The pain was worthwhile for a change, suffering had a different meaning in the context of love. On the other hand, Michael observed himself acting like an adolescent, seeking to meet Ann as if by accident in hospital corridors or at nurses' stations. It had involved him in awkward episodes of reconnoitering and he would blush and seem slightly flustered when candy stripers stopped him cheerfully, can we help you, Father, you've been by here three times already . . .

Except for brief handshakes, Michael had not touched Ann. He had been the restrained and disciplined priest, she the devoted and self-controlled nun doctor. They had talked at length, finding out about each other, and each contact had deepened the dizzying, engulfing, and bewildering attraction they had for each other. I always wanted a sister, he said to her once, and she smiled knowingly and said that she had five brothers and one more was fine. Love seemed to comprise all the seasons at once—a fresh supple spring of life rediscovering itself, a hammered-gold summer of fierce longing, a dead-white winter of desire whispering like water beneath ice, and a bittersweet autumn of important things ending, of good-byes, falling leaves, wood smoke, and hints of death everywhere. Love and death, Michael would sigh in those days, what a combination, ask Romeo and Juliet, they'll tell you.

Still, love delivered the whole year every day, sending Ann and Michael staggering beneath the pressures of its piled-up days, a weight that took their breath away. The irresistible force of their love had met the immovable object of the Catholic Church. Loving each other, they also loved the church to which they had given themselves in what seemed their innocent, long ago, unknowing youth.

Michael had heard stories of priests painfully relinquishing human love, saying that, in the face of the church's demands, they had no choice. And he had known too many clerics whose superficially hearty lives were hollow and lonely, men who played golf a lot and started drinking only after the day ended, good men but unhappy, many of them dead in their fifties. He remembered old Father Torpey in that worn packet ship of a rectory bucking the prairie storm. I don't think you can afford to say no to love, the old priest had whispered, it only comes once, a great love, if a man is lucky. Michael understood Father Torpey now, he felt bad that he hadn't understood him then.

One afternoon when Michael stopped by Ann's office to leave a book, she had come in while he was writing a note at her desk. Mike stood up and as they clumsily maneuvered so that she could pass, they crossed some margin, entered into each other's field in a way they never had before. They caught each other's eyes, hesitated, wordlessly beheld each other, then embraced, uncertainly at first, then intensely, passionately, guiltlessly.

The phone rang in his room.

"Michael, it is you?" Josef Beck, the blond god of German theology, the internationally known Vatican antagonist who always sounded as if he were calling from a ski lodge, frosted goggles propped in his gold metallic curls. "Michael, my old friend, I just learned you were here. It is sad about the Holy Father, yes?"

"Yes."

"I would like to invite you to a meeting. Here at the hotel. We are a small committee, all people you know. We have reports about the pope's death. You are writing for the American papers, yes? The *Times,* yes? You should come. It will be very interesting for you."

"What's this all about, Josef?"

"Poor Pope Jean. A good man, just finding his way. The problem is that the Curia will try to replace him with a hard liner. And those of us who can influence public opinion, well, this is an opportunity to act. We must act now or forever hold our peace. We have very good Vatican contacts through old classmates who work there. We are planning our own intervention in the election."

"Calling the Luftwaffe in for an air strike, are you?"

"Very amusing, Michael, always the light touch. Very good in times of tension."

"I'm glad you're pleased."

Beck chuckled. "This is a very serious meeting. We are developing a political agenda. We have good consultants on this. It is a question of the numbers. We believe we can have an impact on the choice of the next Holy Father."

"I've always been skeptical of clerical politicians, you know that. And political clerics."

"I understand. You will be the dash of bitters we need. The Da Vinci suite. In an hour."

Josef and his brothers, a complicated story in the Bible and here, too. But Josef may be able to tell me something about Mother Hilda. "See you . . ."

TWO

"Your Eminence," Owen Wingate said in a voice from which the scar tissue of Chicago's South Side had never been completely removed, "I am pleased —and I am sure the president is pleased—that you were able to see me this afternoon."

"Sit down, Mr. Ambassador," Kiejson replied, taking his usual chair in his apartment alcove. "It *is* a busy time . . ."

"And such a sad one," Wingate responded, positioning a gold-fitted attaché case on the coffee table. The Dutch cardinal inspected the ambassador's blunt, workingman's hands as they gripped the leather surface of the bag, rich and smooth as butter. The classic American combination, Kiejson thought as Wingate paused, then spoke again. "I have already formally expressed the president's condolences to Cardinal Maestrini." He snapped the case open. "I told him the vice president is coming. Also a delegation including several present and former senators and representatives. The president wanted to come himself. But in view of the terrorist activity . . ."

"Yes, yes . . ."

"However, I wanted to speak to you directly about the . . ."

"Yes?"

"The new pope . . ."

Kiejson nodded.

"We had agreed, you will remember, Your Eminence and I, that is, on the mutual interests of the Vatican and my government. Naturally, it is important that we continue to work closely, the Vatican and the United States, that is. We hope that the new pope will understand our commitment to vigorous anti-communism and to the defense of free market capitalism. It's *the* bulwark of a free world, very Christian. And that's a fact." Wingate cleared his throat. "Pope Jean had, shall we say, confused matters, criticizing both capitalism and communism in the same breath . . ." He paused, searched Kiejson's eyes.

"What is your point?"

"This morning's London *Times* ranks you at the very top of their list of *papabiles.*"

"The new pope will not be chosen by the editorial board of the London *Times.*"

"A tongue of flame won't appear over his head either. He will be *elected.* Ten American cardinals will vote."

Kiejson nodded warily.

"They could be extremely influential. Cardinal Casey of Chicago, for example, has for years sent generous donations to many dioceses throughout the world. Perhaps his word would have considerable weight among those who have been his beneficiaries."

"Perhaps . . ." Kiejson bumped his battered cigar box against his snow-crystal paperweight as he dragged it to his side of the table.

"As I see things," Wingate continued, opening wide the briefcase, "it is really a matter of numbers." He removed a glassine folder, held it in his hand. "Two thirds plus one. Presently 96 of the 114 living cardinals are eligible to vote. Sixty-five votes and the next pope is chosen, that's a fact. Ten United States votes, four from Canada, another five from Central America, add twenty-one from South America, and we have forty already."

Kiejson grunted neutrally, spread his hand across the top of the cigar box, watched Wingate steadily.

"The vast majority of the cardinals—holding the decisive votes—come from outside Europe. Still, they remain in need of a European as a candidate, almost surely not an Italian." He opened the folder carefully. Kiejson withdrew his hand from the cigar box. "Your Eminence, I have here a computer disk with pertinent excerpts from dossiers prepared by agencies of my government on the fifty most important cardinals." He removed the disk from the sleeve in the folder, handed it to the cardinal.

"May I say, Your Eminence, that this information may prove very useful in preparing for the forthcoming conclave." Wingate closed the jaws of his case, snapped its gold-toothed locks. "Did you know that the archbishop of Marseilles has been contributing to the education of a dancer?" He raised his eyebrows. "She dances, as I understand it, only for him . . ."

The Dutch cardinal lowered his head, placed the disk on the table, took a deep breath.

"You will find extremely interesting material on Cardinal Casey." Wingate smiled complacently. "He will certainly want to cooperate with you."

"He's *your* archbishop."

Wingate's expression did not change as he responded softly, "That's a fact . . ."

Kiejson narrowed his eyes, waiting for the ambassador to continue.

"Your record, Your Eminence . . ." Wingate paused.

"Yes?" Kiejson gazed up from beneath King Lear eyebrows directly into the ambassador's eyes.

"Your record . . ." The ambassador pulled the case onto his lap, ". . . is, of course, exemplary."

The Dutchman stared uncertainly at Wingate, rose slowly from his chair. "And now, Mr. Ambassador, if you will excuse me . . ."

Wingate stood up immediately. "Yes, Your Eminence, it was good of you to give me this time."

THREE

The door to the Da Vinci suite was opened by American Catholic book publisher Roger Tansey, a short, freckled man of sixty-five on whose brow lay a turned-down coverlet of fading red hair. He had stopped speaking to Michael a few years before to punish him for giving one of his theological commentaries to a rival publisher. Classic Bicycle Irish, Michael thought, the kind that make your ass sore. Tansey turned away huffily as Josef Beck grinned behind him, teeth and tan right off a Third Reich poster. *"Ja, ja,* Michael, and how are you?" *Ja, ja,* Josef, how's the master race these days?

Monsignor Tracy greeted a buzzing group of old acquaintances, European theologians, arms folded, eyes bright, discussing a strange mixture of Dead Sea scrolls, Aramaic verbs, and naive papal politics, an uncertain soufflé of a conversation. Stand this crowd on the third rail, Michael thought, and they wouldn't feel a thing. Unless they fall in love, he added, and then, of course, they wouldn't be in here at all. A French Scripture professor weepily mourned Pope Jean, wagging his quill beard above a food-stained clerical vest. A sprinkling of editors of Catholic papers stood next to two Catholic college presidents, all of them with the shanghaied look brought on by overdoses of just such events. Beck gestured them toward the large adjacent living room. As the clusters of men floated past on their bubbling stream of talk, Michael touched Beck's arm. "What can you tell me about Mother Hilda?"

"*Ja, ja,* she keeps her finger in the dike," the German replied, waving the guests forward, "she stands against the modern tide." Beck looked beyond Tracy, willing the group to move along, speaking mechanically. "Hilda represents the strength of the Catholic mystical tradition. It is more radical for our present culture than it was even a thousand years ago."

So you call her Hilda, do you? Michael was distracted by a heavyset priest's noisy entrance into the suite. "You know Jack Parker, don't you? From San Francisco." Sure, everybody knew Jack Parker, church historian, seminary rector, general raconteur, and often, as at the moment, half bombed on important occasions. "Hey, Mike," Parker called out, "I hear you're a good friend of Monsignor Lanza's . . ."

"We know each other . . ."

"Good old modest Michael. Self-effacement! One of the noblest of virtues! Ideal in future members of the hierarchy." He laughed merrily, coughing himself to a spluttering stop. "Mike, you can do me a big favor. Put a word in with Lanza for me, will you? I'm postulator of the cause for Francisco Montoya's canonization. You know, the apostle of the Pacific. Should have been made a saint years ago. Lanza has been stiffing us. But if *you* . . ." Beck interrupted, assured Parker that he could talk to Michael later, directed him into the living room.

Michael nodded as Parker moved off, then turned to Beck. "What do you know about Mother Hilda personally, Josef?"

"Have you been to Munich, Michael? Have you been to her house? You should go to Munich . . ." He half pulled away, surveyed the living room. Michael followed Beck, taking the seat closest to the door.

"Fellow members of the committee," the German theologian intoned above the settling-down noises of the group, "this afternoon we have serious business. We intend not only to influence but to determine the outcome of the forthcoming papal election." He ticked off the number of cardinals from each quadrant of the globe, reviewed the conclave voting rules, Two thirds plus one, sixty-five votes, gentlemen, *only* sixty-five votes. Inside Michael's imagination Mother Hilda floated mystically into the Sistine Chapel, I have a message for you, princes of the church . . .

Germans, Michael thought as Beck droned on, need beer halls for real *putsches*. Beer halls. Munich. Mother Hilda. Michael shook her out of his head as the bearded French Scripture scholar bolted out of his chair, waving his hands.

"Father Josef!" The Frenchman shouted angrily. This, Michael mused, is how world wars get started. "I feel in conscience," the Frenchman went on, "that I must bring up a matter—it is theological, yes—that we have not discussed yet. We have *no women* on this commission. So, you see, we are guilty, yes, we are *all* guilty of what we accuse the cardinals of, being an all-male group electing the pope."

The room exploded in argument. Beck demanded quiet, spoke acidly. "We *cannot* discuss this now. This is an *action* committee, it is not a cell in which to discuss feminist theory. Let us discuss it *later.*"

"You Germans are good at not thinking about painful issues!"

Beck's handsome face turned purplish. "Good order," he said sharply, "is preferable to decadence." Shouts from all sides.

"Yes," Parker responded, "and Goethe said that if Germans had a choice between injustice and disorder they would choose injustice every time."

Beck scowled at the grinning Parker, pounded on a table as the Frenchman declaimed vehemently, "We cannot, my brothers, ignore half the human race, it cannot be done, *cherchez la femme.*"

"*Vive la France,*" Michael muttered. He rose and headed for the foyer as the committee members began to argue violently. Nothing, he reflected, is quiet on the Western front. Roger Tansey got out of his chair, hurried to leave before Michael.

Beck rushed after Tracy. "Michael, Michael, please. Prima donnas, they will settle down. Please remain, we need you."

"Me, or my contacts at the *New York Times?*"

"The latter? Well, yes, but only in part." He looked past Michael, trying to flag Tansey down, but the publisher was just closing the door. Beck turned his gaze back to Michael. "We are preparing our own film, a guide to the candidates. Michael," the German said urgently against the fractious voices in the adjoining room, "half these men are fools. And I can do without Tansey's sarcasm. But you, don't you see why we need you? The numbers we need to influence are so small, the cause is so great . . ."

Michael made a peace signal with his left hand. "Let me know when your film comes out, or the bark of Peter comes in." He winked, turned, closed the door against the angry debate. Tansey, his back turned, stood at the elevator halfway down the hall. Everybody's mad at somebody here, the whole scheme is falling apart. Mother Hilda would love it.

Michael stopped suddenly in the middle of the corridor. Mother Hilda. He glanced down at his injured hand. Strangled sounds drifted out of the Da Vinci suite. Of course, that's *exactly* what she'd love. And I'm going to Munich to talk to her about it.

FOUR

Monsignor Tracy heard about the latest bombing from a man in the elevator. In E.U.R., Mussolini's Art Deco section of new Rome, the police station, he didn't know about casualties, he had just learned about it himself, everybody in the lobby talking . . .

"Annie? Is this a bad time to call?"

"I'm between patients, it's okay. How *are* you?"

"Coming along." He explained about his hand and Mother Hilda's diagnostic prophecy, the reverse Lourdes effect, he called it.

"She said *what?*"

"It won't heal while I'm in conflict, something like that."

"You sound like you believe her."

Mike dragged out a skeptic's groan.

"But she has you upset, I can tell that much from here."

"I think I've got her number in one way. She enjoys upsetting men, there's nothing she likes better than men fighting with each other."

"It sounds like the conflict is more in her than in you."

"I'm going to Munich to talk to her about it. My hand feels better already."

"Munich?"

"Now, don't get upset, I'll only be gone a day or so. Part of getting the story on her, she's the key to unlocking the mystery of how the pope died. I inherited a cop's instincts from my father. I know I'm right."

Ann sighed. Michael grimaced as a wave of longing big enough to surf on rushed across his heart. "What is it?"

"Mike, don't you see, going to Munich just gets you more involved, it doesn't . . ."

"If I find out how the pope died, they'll have to give me the permission."

Another pause. "Mike, you said yourself once that you were an Eagle Scout in priest's clothing. Don't you see, they're *not* going to give us permission? I thought they would when I got permission to leave the convent. But I don't believe it now."

"It can't be much longer . . ."

"You say that, Mike, but nothing's happened. You didn't get any good news from Monsignor Lanza, did you?"

"Only some advice I can't follow. But I'm going to see Cardinal Casey about it before he goes into the conclave."

"They're never going to let you go, don't you see that?"

Michael's turn to pause. She's right, he thought, I felt it for sure the minute I said good-bye to Lanza. *He* knew it, he knew that even good guys catch something if they work in the bureaucracy long enough, it's like miner's lung, the lethal breath of undertakers, tax auditors, bank loan officers, what a brotherhood of killers. And I believed them, I really thought they were taking Ann and me seriously. The old man used to say that people with no principles had a terrific edge on people who did.

"Mike, Mike, you're lost in one of your distractions . . ." Ann's voice brought him back to reality.

"Look, Annie, I've got to give this one more try. I think Casey may be able to help. We've planned it this way, we've waited this long, a few more days won't make that much difference. If, after everything I've done, they still say no, we'll switch to plan B."

"Plan B?"

"We'll go ahead and get married anyway, whether the official church lets us do it or not."

"Mike . . ."

"By a priest, of course. I'm sure we can get one of my old friends to marry us, they're not all as worried about their careers as people in the bureaucracy. Besides, the man and woman confer the sacrament on each other. The priest is just a witness."

A long quiet pause. "Do you really mean that?"

"Yes, I really do."

FIVE

"Yes, Missy, I think it's all settled." Cardinal Casey glared at the glass of medicine on the side table.

"Well, either it is, or it isn't. Which is it now?"

"Franz tells me it's a closed matter."

"*Franz,* that one . . ."

"Now, Missy, he's one of the most important men in the church right now."

"Thick paste never sticks."

"Missy . . ."

"Is there something wrong, Tom? You sound down or something."

"No, everything's fine. I just wanted to check in with you, see how everything is. How's your son Ed doing?"

"Ed is just fine. He's on a business trip with Eileen. They took the kids. He was going to be in Orlando and . . ."

"Yes?"

"Are you sure you're alright?"

"Fine. Little Mary okay? And Kevin?"

"The kids are fine. They always ask for you, want to know if you're going to be pope . . ."

"Well," Casey cut in, "they may not be far off the mark."

"Tom!"

"I think I might just be . . . Well, Franz says there's every reason to think the other cardinals would turn to me . . ."

"Oh, Tom, wouldn't Momma be pleased! I just can't wait to call Ed . . ."

"No, Missy, please. I'd rather you didn't talk about this to anyone. But it would be awfully nice if you could come over here."

"I'll get there, don't worry. Wouldn't Momma be proud, though! She's smiling about it in heaven right now."

"Yes . . ." Casey picked up his glass of Maalox, replaced it on the table. "You know, I've been thinking a lot about Momma . . ."

"You thinking about when Momma died? Now I know why you sound so low."

"Well . . ."

"You did the right thing, Tom, we thought so then and we think so now. The old cardinal was dying, the flights weren't as easy then as they are today. You did your duty, Tom, and it was hard, I know it was hard. Momma understood. She'd given you to the church, she said that to me just before she died, she said your place was at the cardinal's deathbed rather than hers, she prayed that you would stay, honest to God. Know your place and you'll find your place, she always said that. And she felt that if you left the old cardinal someone else would take your place quick enough. She knew those foreigners alright. Now, I don't want you thinking about the past. Past is past. And if you hadn't stayed, well, maybe what's happening now would never have come about. God has His ways! Now, don't you worry, and I'll get over as soon as I possibly can."

Casey held the phone for a while after he and Florence Roberts said good-bye. Missy and Tom, the Chicago cardinal reflected, we've called each other that for as many years as I can remember. Ever since Aunt Mae died so young and Uncle Matt sent Missy to our family to be raised. Young Irishmen who lost their wives did that all the time then. It seems such a long time ago, such a long, long time ago . . .

SIX

Jimbo had learned of Angelica Tomai, Rafallo's mistress, from Professor Lambertini, the Einstein-haired doctor who had preceded the count as the papal physician. It was about all he had learned from Lambertini, who wouldn't discuss the late pope's health or how he treated him. But Lambertini had not exactly spoken of Rafallo as if he were in the same league with Dr. Jonas Salk. "His training," Lambertini had snorted, "was in ophthalmology." And, he added, Pope Jean did not have eye trouble. "The only one who knows Rafallo well," Lambertini had said, concluding his brief interview, "is Angelica Tomai, the actress." It had not been difficult to make an appointment with the beautiful Italian movie star. Jimbo lay in her bed, in the grip of Irish–Catholic regret.

Play me those postcoital blues, the broken-down bar singer crooned inside Jimbo's smoky nightclub of a soul, just as blue as I can be. The journalist surveyed Angelica Tomai's contours in the semidarkness, lines and shadows fine and deep and soft, a wonderful stretch of the desert by moonlight, sheiks would kill for the oil reserves, a man could die here, drown himself, imagine drowning in this mother-of-pearl desert. Still, for him, this was the relief that was no relief at all, like the way the priest described the flames of hell when he was a kid, the fire that burns but does not consume . . .

Jimbo sighed. "Ah, shit," he muttered.

"What?" Angelica asked softly.

"Ah, shit, the famous Chinese philosopher . . ."

It hadn't been difficult to get into bed with the actress. The journalist wished it had been, it would have been more satisfying in every way. With her, yes, and as a way of getting at Michael, conquering her was a way of conquering him. And at Maureen, too, he felt that every time he took a new woman. But it hardly ever worked, not for long anyway. Angelica had received Jimbo as Mother Earth did the rain, she had taken him over, swallowed him up, absorbed him and his mixed feelings effortlessly, and he felt depressed. And guilty. That's part of why I'm mad at Michael, he thought. The good boy monsignor chucks his sense of sin like an old coat, while mine's painted on. Jimbo had even lost the edge off his enthusiasm for investigating Umberto Rafallo. He had entered Rafallo's intimate world, nibbled at the lush vegetation, and what, he wondered, have I learned, or proved, for that matter? That I'm mad at my brother, and Maureen, that I still have a Catholic conscience. Ah, shit, indeed.

"Jimmy . . ." Her heavy accent transformed his name, made it sound fresh and magical.

"Yes?"

"Would you get me a cigarette?"

He fumbled on the night table, retrieved a cigarette, watched her face in the matchlight, remained crooked on one arm. The rouged and powdered pope, stiff on his catafalque, slipped over the misty falls at the far edge of his attention, the hell with it . . .

"Jimmy, I have just finished the most wonderful movie."

"I'll bet."

"It is called *Pietro*. A wonderful script." Jimbo touched the skin of her face in the small bright halo that spread across it when she inhaled her cigarette. "By Torelli, who also directed. The story of an artist and the model who brings him greatness." She leaned away from the journalist, quashed the cigarette in an ashtray, rolled back. "I play the model, Maria. Maria is under his spell, feels that he loves her for herself . . ." The actress sighed. "But she comes to realize that he loves her only for what he can get from her. Maria kills him, finally. It is very tragic, yes?"

"Oh . . ."

"Yes, after they make love in his studio for the last time."

"That sounds . . ."

"Then she kills herself as well." She hunched closer to the inching-away reporter. "Jimmy?" She touched his shoulder. "Jimmy, you said you wanted to interview me about the movie. But . . ."

"But what?"

"I don't think that's why you came to see me at all." Her tone was confident, acidic. "You're a child," she continued, "like most men."

"And you didn't take me to bed for nothing, either. You want a story in *Time.* That's it, isn't it?"

"And you want to know about Tootie."

"Tootie?"

"Umberto. The count. The pope's doctor. Tootie. He warned me that reporters might be contacting me. And that they would want to know about him. Tootie is also a child."

The great Angelica, Jimbo sighed, my Mother Hilda. "Did Count Tootie kill the pope?"

"Tootie? He would never talk of his work with me." Angelica pulled Jimbo closer to her, kissed him again. "He is sweet-natured. That is what I like about him."

"That and the drugs," Jimbo said wearily. "He *does* get you drugs, doesn't he?" Jimbo swung his legs out over the edge of the bed.

Angelica was silent for a moment, then spoke flatly.

"You want to know something about Tootie. I am interested in publicity. It is a fair exchange."

Jimbo shook his head, reached for his clothes, Why do I get into these things? "Okay. You tell me your dream and I'll tell you mine."

"You are a very unhappy man, aren't you?" Angelica propped herself up on one arm. "I could feel the troubles in you."

"Good-bye, Angelica." Jimbo slipped into his shirt, started to button it, felt his hands trembling.

"You are a real American, Jimmy, you all think you are Bogart. Tootie has a heart, he does not pretend not to. He is a gambler in money and romance, and if he does a little business, at least he admits it. We learned this from our parents who learned it in the war. You do the business you must do in order to stay alive."

Jimbo put on his jacket, paused, feeling his own frustration. "What do you mean, he's a gambler?"

Angelica pulled the sheets up over herself. "I've told you enough already." She let a smile break slowly across her face. "But he *is* a gambler, he always needs money."

Jimbo studied the actress for a moment. "Okay. I'll see what I can do about a story." Then he hurried toward the door.

"You are an unhappy man, aren't you, Jimmy?"

He turned around, opened his mouth, closed it, and left the room.

SEVEN

Munich was like Milwaukee multiplied by some unfathomable Teutonic factor with the whole Fatherland guzzling beer from its Zeppelin breasts. Michael felt lighter despite the heaviness of the city whose towers, belfries, and arches pressed down on him from every direction. He took a cab to Mother Hilda's place, Hilfen Haus, sensing that it was the right thing to do but growing more uneasy as each gingerbread house flashed by the window.

The seedy square in front of the three-story house was filled with people of every age, some in wheelchairs, others with crutches or canes. Michael walked slowly through the subdued crowd. A young American woman looked down at a man about her own age, nodded her head eagerly at the slurred growls that came from his stroke-twisted mouth. Yes, yes, she flashed with her eyes, hugging him gently, adjusting him in his chair as one would a delicate figurine in a nest of tissue. Next to them, a middle-aged couple sat on either side of a smaller wheelchair in which a crippled girl of five or six laughed joyfully. A murmur of prayer in a language Michael couldn't name rose like plainchant from a family huddled on a bench just outside Hilda's door. An old priest in a patched cassock knelt on the worn sidewalk.

Pilgrims crowded the old-fashioned foyer, lined the hallway leading to the back of the building. Michael edged into a corner, observed the tranquil men and women as they stood praying or chatting softly. The mood was gentle, effervescent, expectant. An old woman asked for his blessing. He noticed a fresh seepage of blood on his bandage as he raised his right hand.

The room stirred, *Die Mutter kommt.* The message echoed in half a dozen languages, shaded off into a tense quiet. A door opened somewhere out of sight, soft happy sounds of greeting built up. Mother Hilda appeared in the hallway as if summoned by a medium. She was flanked by four young women in blue smock-like dresses. They must be the ladies of the night, Michael thought, working their way back into the sunshine. The seeress smiled as sweetly as her tightly drawn features allowed, looked into each visitor's eyes, touched each one's shoulders with her gauze-trussed hands, moved just beyond their reach like an astronaut floating through a weightless chamber. She entered the foyer, circled through the crowd, paused an extra beat as she reached Tracy, locked her eyes on his, steadied herself, arresting her flowing motion. She glanced down, lifted his right hand, held it between her palms, released it slowly. She looked up, her expression unreadable, although it gave off the slightest crackling electrical discharge, and moved away.

He followed her out the front door. She stooped to say something to the old priest kneeling on the sidewalk. He listened carefully, his mouth half open, his eyes welling with tears. She moved on, smiling and touching each visitor, then looped back to the entrance of her house. Those who had been inside now clustered near her entourage, overflowing the curb. Dead silence except for traffic sounds in the distance. The seeress began to sing in a sweet low voice. *Ave, ave,* the Lourdes hymn. The crowd joined in, tentatively at first, then wholeheartedly. As the last affirming notes drifted away Mother Hilda turned and went inside. The sojourners remained in tight formation for a prolonged moment, then slowly began to disperse.

"Did you come here for a miracle?" Michael asked the young woman wheeling the stroke victim out of the square. The man looked up awkwardly, eyes alight in the gnarled leaning tower of his body.

"No, Father," the calm, self-possessed woman replied, reaching down to caress the man's lolling head. "My husband and I come every year." He made a gagging sound of agreement, saliva unstringing down his chin. "We get great strength and hope from coming here." She smiled easily at Michael. She's the real thing, he thought, peace and contentment in a world of fear and loathing. "We try to visit Lourdes every year, too." She kept her hand on her husband's shoulder. "Are you from America, Father?" "Yes, yes, Chicago." They were the O'Connors from Philadelphia. Ted graduated from Villanova, she from Rosemont; they could never have gotten through his stroke without their faith. Ted was only twenty-nine when it happened.

The smaller wheelchair with the smiling child trundled by, the woman greeted the parents, an older couple. Michael wondered if he had been a priest once, and she a nun. A cerebral-palsied child from their union. Monsignor Tracy stepped back as the couples bent toward each other as comfortably as old friends, the little girl joining in unself-consciously, an angelic cripple in a Victorian drama. "Would you give us your blessing, Father?"

Michael felt on the outside of this intense group, whose members were bonded so strongly by misfortune and faith. Is this the peace, he asked himself, that surpasses understanding?

"Your blessing, Father?"

Michael shook free of his thoughts, raised his bound hand. "May the blessing of Almighty God, the Father, Son, and Holy Spirit, descend upon you and remain with you forever . . ." The people moved off resolutely, strongly. Still, Michael felt, something doesn't fit here, what is it that doesn't fit?

During the afternoon Michael walked for miles through the old city. His hand felt warm and tingly. Had Mother Hilda cured it, he wondered, or beamed up an infection? His good humor faded as the seeress re-entered his imagination, followed by her quiet, obedient array of reformed prostitutes. Michael sighed. We get great strength and hope from coming here . . .

He visited the old cathedral, the twin-towered Frauenkirche, tried to say some prayers, inspected Emperor Ludwig's tomb, rode the elevator in the north tower, viewed the finely engraved die of the city, with Alpine peaks set boldly against the distant palimpsest sky. He watched a long time, trying to identify the slight gap in the reality of Hilfen Haus that had registered inside him. This isn't, he mused, the kind of spiritual crisis they warned us about in the seminary. The seeress of Munich, she *knows* how the pope died, and she knows that I know.

From a bench on the far side of the square he watched Mother Hilda and her blue-clad helpers glide through the late afternoon shift of visitors in front of Hilfen Haus. The evening star rose in the navy blue summer sky, friendly yellow lights went on gradually in the quaint old houses. The square was quiet and vacant except for a solitary cyclist. He rose and walked toward the seeress's headquarters. He paused, pushed through the unlocked door, stood absolutely still in the empty foyer, listened to the nuns singing their night prayers somewhere upstairs. He turned, looked out the front window into the rapidly darkening square. There was a noise down the corridor behind him.

Michael whirled. Nobody there. Light splayed from beneath a door at the far end of the murky hallway. He waited, listening to the house recite its history of complaints, two centuries of aches and groans counterpointing the muffled choir. The noises down the hallway were contemporary everyday household sounds. He stepped carefully on the old boards, hesitated as he put his left hand on the knob, took a deep breath, slowly opened the door.

Mother Hilda, iron-gray hair cascading down her shoulders, stood in the middle of the kitchen, busily chewing on a chicken breast. Platters of vegetables, meat, and bread lay on the table at her side. A glass of dark fluid stood next to an open jar. Her eyes were fierce above her grease-splotched cheeks, her gleaming lips and chin.

They froze, staring at each other, the hunter and the famished animal. In a pause in the upstairs singing, Michael could hear Mother Hilda's breathing, the drip of water in the old stone sink behind her. Jesus, Mary, and Joseph. She glared at him, half groaned, half sobbed, "Go away, go away . . ." The shredded piece of meat trembled in her bandage-strung hand. She raised it to her mouth and tore at it greedily.

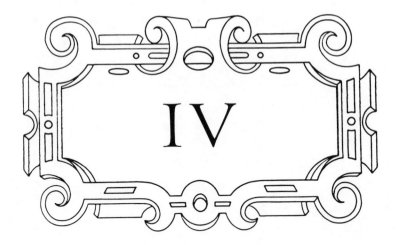

IV

LAMENTATIONS

ONE

Michael braced his back flat against the door. Mother Hilda gnawed almost violently, one eye flashing above a bobbing flap of chicken skin, nothing but the small sad sounds of the house, the dulled, cadenced singing somewhere above them, the walls were closing in. He inhaled deeply, intimidated, feeling a sense of danger pressing down on them, God's hand, maybe, let it be God's hand and not the devil's hoof. The seeress's neatly folded headpiece lay on the sideboard, the bandages on her swiftly working hands were stained with food. She dropped the tattered remains of what she had been eating, eagerly drank some liquid, put the glass down hard, making a scratchy thud on the chipped enamel surface of the table. Her frail body heaved beneath her habit as she gasped at the priest.

"Go away!"

"Mother Hilda, what . . . ?"

"Go away . . ." She slumped slightly, like a sail losing the wind, reached for a piece of crusty bread, bit into it, swallowed, drank again, a trickle of fluid running crookedly down the side of her chin. "You do not know what you are seeing. You are doing the devil's work. Go away."

Michael took a step toward her, easy, easy now. "I want to help you." Another step, sideways. "And I want you to help me."

"Father, Father," she cried plaintively, "you do not know what you are talking about. You should help yourself, yes, *you* are the one in need."

"Mother Hilda, I know what this is, what you're doing here."

"You are only wise as the world is wise, that is all."

"Maybe." He took one more step, stood directly opposite her. "Mother Hilda, I don't care what you eat, where, or even how much . . ."

"You are blind. You have eyes but you do not know what you see." She leaned on her hands, drilling into him with her diamond-bit eyes. "You are a child of the world, not of the spirit."

Michael's right hand began to throb. He clenched and unclenched it slowly. "Look, Mother, having a food binge while the other nuns are praying isn't exactly the work of the spirit either." He spoke gently. "We're both of the flesh, Mother, you know that, don't you?"

"You are not my judge."

"I'm not judging you."

"Yes, yes, you do." Her breathing became strained, hauling up something heavy, bumping on every step all the way, out of her soul. "I see . . . it . . . in your . . . eyes." She slumped, a wave of charcoal-ash hair rolled forward in slow motion as she sagged, struggled to keep herself upright. Michael hurried around to catch her. She pulled away as he reached toward her arm, dragged herself painfully along to the far end of the table, raised her head, shook away the aureole of hair. *Do not touch me . . ."*

"Mother Hilda . . ." Michael was surprised at the calmness of his voice. "I think you'd better sit down. Let me get a chair . . ."

"No!" She lowered her head again, steadied herself, working hard to get the bellows working again. Michael could feel her struggle shudder throughout his own body.

"How did the pope die?"

"I do not know."

"Yes, you do. You know that you do."

She shook her head, half turned away, contorted her features, clenched her teeth, held on against some internal Waterloo. "No, no, you misunderstood . . ."

"No. I want the truth. I don't know why you left Rome so suddenly. My guess is that it suited you just right."

"Stop it, you are doing the devil's work for him . . ."

"You left Rome with everything in an uproar. Terrorists, killers, men turned against each other, men ready to fight about who the next pope will be, they were fighting already."

Mother Hilda breathed more regularly, she was cutting loose, pushing her skiff away from the shore, good-bye, Father.

"I know you're good at it because you've had me plenty upset. Maybe it's for revenge on men for what they do to these women you work with, I don't know . . ."

"You are a blasphemer," she said distantly, "the devil has you in his grasp and you do not even know it." The seeress was floating downstream, getting beyond his call. "*You* come here and dare to say such things! The people who come here find peace, God comforts them, they have the strength to go ahead with lives that are unbearable. And *you!* You are leaving the priesthood because you have neither their faith nor their courage. You give up on the unbearable. What do you know of my work? May God forgive you for misunderstanding it so! May God forgive you for surrendering your soul to the world."

"Mother Hilda, I'm not passing myself off as a saint."

"How dare you! God speaks a language you cannot hear, much less understand."

"Mother Hilda, your reputation is for healing, but you only deal with people who are upset. That's why you can calm down these poor broken people who come to see you. Although my hunch is that they've won their battles before they come here. They've all been broken in some way or other. That's the condition they have to meet to get a smile out of you. You're comfortable with hurt people, in a way you dominate them through their hurt . . ."

"Lies, lies, the devil is the father of all lies."

"I understood it when I looked at the Alps in the distance today. They're broken, but strong at the same time. And mysterious. You do lots of good. But you have to dominate others in order to do it. You try to dominate me because I'm a broken priest, and because my hand was wounded. That's so, isn't it?"

"You were struck by God. You will not be healed if you work against Him."

"And this not eating of yours, that's part of it. The world calls it anorexia. You get control over others by controlling yourself in this extreme way. You starve and nobody, nobody in the church or anywhere else can stop you." Michael began to feel faint, leaned on the table with his good hand. "Everybody," he said hoarsely, "has to stand back, let you have your way. Even the pope. He's never been able to get you to do anything you didn't want to do. You understand that, don't you? You know the kind of power you have. Your power over others comes from your power over yourself. You've got everybody bullied, spiritually bullied. And you punish yourself at the same time. You hate yourself because you know how you lead people on, yes, *lead* them on." Michael took a deep breath, tried to steady himself as his field of vision darkened, a sickening dizziness settled on him. "And you know you have to eat, that it builds up, and builds up, that right, isn't it? Finally, you'll eat anything . . ." He swept his bandaged hand in a gesture over the table.

"You are an evil man. The church will be better off without you."

"You may be right about that, too." Mother Hilda was coming in and out of focus. Michael struggled to get his words out. "Behind all this, behind everything, you're hiding some secret. And that secret is connected with the way the pope died."

"You *are* evil, you resist God's ways. He has deceived you into thinking you see me, when you only see the devil's image of me . . ." The singing stopped, the silence had a high-tension buzz in it. Mother Hilda's image turned liquid as she took a step toward Michael. He could see her eyes, those piercing eyes, swaying like lanterns in the night. He felt nauseated, began to fall, knew he was falling, falling backward, away from her, knew he was sinking into a swampy darkness.

Someone placed a warm wet towel on Michael's face while another person supported him from behind. He shook his head, opened his eyes on two blue-clad women holding him. They must have come down after night prayers ended. His hand seemed to expand and contract with waves of pain.

"The devil has deceived you." A cool, clear, slightly accented voice. He looked up at a tall, thin nun of Mother Hilda's order framed in the doorway. "Yes, Father, you have been deceived by the devil." Michael glanced slowly around the room. No steely seeress, no headpiece on the sideboard. He looked back at the nun.

"Mother Hilda has been in chapel the whole time, singing vespers and compline with the community."

"What?"

"You, Father, have seen only an image created by the devil. It has happened before."

The women in blue finished wiping his face, helped him to his feet, and scurried out. The tall nun observed him calmly. "You have had a very upsetting experience. It happens to people who underestimate the power of the devil. I am Sister Matilde. Come with me, please."

Rubber-legged, Michael followed her out into the corridor, up a flight of stairs, down a short hallway. Sister Matilde opened the chapel door, blessed herself with holy water, offered it on the tip of her fingers to the priest, follow me. Near the front of the chapel Mother Hilda in full habit sat serenely on a simple wooden chair, a Bible open on her lap. She looked up. Her face was dry, clean, dead calm.

TWO

"Yes, Father?" The seeress's voice was soft and natural. She seemed afloat on a thousand years of monastic self-possession, the contemplative moored securely in some divine cove, let the storms howl, I will ride them out.

"With all respect, Mother, I think we just talked down in the kitchen."

She wrinkled her brow in puzzlement, and concern, as if he were a small boy who had just skinned his knee tumbling off his bicycle by the convent door. "I have been here all evening."

The seeress looked past the priest at Sister Matilde. Michael could hear the nun's retreating footsteps, the gentlest closing of the chapel door.

"Sit down, Father." She nodded toward the plain chair just across the aisle from her own, her voice as flat and level as the nearby altar. "You speak of some conversation with me."

A devotional candle hissed, drowning in its own molten wax as Michael scraped his chair into better position, holding the unmoving seeress with his eyes. "Mother, just what did you mean when you told the Holy Father that you saw death riding into the streets of Rome?"

"I? I do not recall anything like that."

"Come on, Mother, I *heard* you say something like that when the bells started tolling the death of the Holy Father."

"You poor man, you were injured in the explosion." Her eyes focused on the blood-stained gauze bunched on his right hand. "Yes, I remember now, Father. You must have a fever from the infection."

Michael scanned her features, noticed a tuck of steel-wool hair peeking out of her headpiece. The chapel seemed overwhelmingly quiet and hot, as if they were sitting hard by the coals in some paralyzing sauna. The priest stood up, felt his pants legs clinging damply to the backs of his knees, inspected the front of her habit—not a stain on it—examined again the large Bible spread on her lap, what book is she reading? Lamentations.

Your hands, Michael thought, you're hiding your hands, you didn't have time to change the bandages with the food stains on them. You know what I'm thinking, don't you? Mother Hilda's face reddened under the indictment of his look. "Father," she said serenely, "I would like to go to confession."

Mother Hilda rose, her eyes keen as augers, clutching the Bible in hands hidden by the folds of her habit. "You are still a priest, Father. I would like to go to confession."

A hint of dizziness returned as Michael stared at her. "There are plenty of other priests in Munich besides me." He turned, walked up the aisle.

"You cannot refuse to hear a suffering person's confession." She placed the Bible on a kneeler, kept her hands beneath the shield of fabric. "No wonder you do not wish to be a priest anymore . . ."

He stopped dead in front of the heavily draped, wooden stall confessional recessed in the back wall. It gave off ghostly emananations, the carbon traces of old trapped sins clacking faintly in their diminishing half-lives. He hesitated for a moment, pulled aside the drape, sat down on the hard bench, pushed the slide open.

"Bless me, Father, for I have sinned." He could make out Hilda's shadow behind the screen. Her voice was steady, knowing, unnerving. "I went to confession last week."

"Yes?"

"I have been negligent in caring for the young girls on several occasions. I have been angry with them and I have been harsh in my judgments of the sisters."

Michael leaned his head closer to the sheer mesh filament between them. "Is that all?"

A long pause, a sibilant release of breath. "I . . . I have had great temptations of the flesh. I have done everything that I can to ward them off. I may have dwelt on them longer than I should . . ."

"Yes . . ."

"I am the bride of Jesus, who loves me like a husband. Yes, He fills me, He ravishes me as no man could . . . But I am drawn to other men, men who would make me unfaithful to Jesus." A strained pause. "I am attracted to you, Father. I dream of you, yes, and of your coming to my cell . . ."

Michael shifted uneasily on the bench.

"But it is worse knowing that you are now leaving the priesthood. I do not want some other woman to have you. I must stand against the devil for he wishes to destroy my marriage to the Lord. And I feel that you, then— yes, these are my thoughts—that *you* are the devil's agent, that he has succeeded in taking you over. I confess and ask forgiveness if I judge you harshly. But I do not think that I do. You have allowed the devil to use you, it is your fault, and so he has wounded you, put his mark on you. Now he has brought you here to tempt me and to deceive you."

Michael felt her breath, scented with chicken and wine, on the side of his face. She spoke again, intensely. "You must not look into the pope's death any further. It is the devil inviting you to eat from the tree of the knowledge of good and evil."

He sighed, readjusted himself. He could make out the seeress's pale taut face just beyond the screen. Her voice sounded worn and urgent. "You must *not* seek further explanations of the pope's death."

"Confession is for telling your sins, not threatening the confessor who hears them."

"Give this quest up," she said slowly, deliberately. "Return to the altar. Be obedient and give yourself back to Jesus as His priest. You must stop this effort to seduce me. Yes, *that* is what you want. You want me. I feel it."

A long pause. "For these and all my sins, I ask God's forgiveness."

Michael sounded weary to himself as he spoke. "Whatever mystery there is in your life, God understands, just as He forgives whatever sin may be there. Say one rosary for your penance and make a good act of contrition."

He raised his still smarting hand, made the sign of the cross, uttered the words of absolution. He sat perfectly still, oppressed by the sudden, strange silence. He peered through the confessional screen. Nobody there. He rose, yanked the curtain aside. The chapel was empty and, except for the winking scarlet flame of the sanctuary lamp, completely dark.

THREE

"I'd like to talk to you." Jimbo Tracy, in his military attaché's uniform again, pressed his index finger into the small of Count Rafallo's back. "Smile at me, Tootie," the journalist whispered, "and when you turn around, act like you know me, people are watching." Rafallo forced a headwaiter's nod, cleared his throat, fell in step with the journalist, glanced back over his shoulder to check the retouching he had just performed on the dead pope's features. Their footsteps sounded on the marble floor as Jimbo led him away from the candlelit bier in front of the main altar of St. Peter's. The great glittering vault of the basilica had been cleared of mourners and closed for fifteen minutes in order to allow the papal physician to knit up the unraveling veil of the pontiff's remains. "Where did you get your start, silent movies or Kabuki?" Jimbo asked tightly. "Maybe paint-by-the-numbers?" Rafallo growled through his beard as they marched toward his Vatican office, Swiss Guards' halberds clanking as they parted for them at every juncture.

"Who *are* you?" Rafallo dropped his bag on his desk, sat down.

"Anybody ever tell you that you look a little like Pavarotti?" Jimbo perched on the edge of the desk, plopped an envelope onto its smooth surface. Rafallo glared at him. "I mean that strictly as a compliment, Count. Of course, if *you* promise not to sing, *he* won't practice medicine." Jimbo leaned forward, opened the flap on the envelope. "Or try to sell pictures of the dead pope to *People* magazine."

Rafallo inhaled sharply as the reporter shook a dozen prints of the dead pope onto the desk in front of him. Pope Jean stretched out in his soiled cassock. Profile shots, head-on pictures, the Holy Father, his mouth fallen open like Marat's in the bathtub, a sheet pulled up to his chin on the count's work table, views of various stages of shoring up and tinting his features. "Not your usual holy card stuff," Jimbo said. "Nothing you'd want pasted on your papal blessing."

Rafallo surged out of his chair. Jimbo pushed a hand against his chest and he sat down again. "I should have guessed," the journalist continued, "when I saw the camera and the empty boxes of film in your laboratory. And these are just the teasers. You told them you had plenty more to sell. Well, you saw a business opportunity and took it. Insider trading, as they say."

Rafallo fumed, swept the pictures aside with one hand. "How . . . ?"

"Well, Count, when you decided on *People,* you forgot that *Time* is part of the same company. Dumb, very fucking dumb of you. When you offered them these samples this afternoon, they asked me to check it out. And just when I had almost lost interest in you."

The papal physician's face brightened. *"You* are negotiating for them?"

"They think so. And I have to admit, the bastards may make you an offer. And, of course, you can try someplace else. The *Enquirer,* for example, they're your kind of people." Jimbo lit a cigarette. "On the other hand, I think you may just want to withdraw these from the market . . ."

Rafallo gazed steadily at him, fingered the edge of one of the scattered pictures.

"You're enterprising, Tootie."

The count bolted completely out of his chair, grabbed Jimbo by his coat lapels. "Don't you dare call me that again!"

"Easy, easy," Jimbo said, pushing him away, "your secrets are safe with me. I just want the truth from you." Rafallo pulled back, breathing hard, pushed his chair aside, rubbed his hands anxiously.

"I don't know how he died . . ." He shook his head, turned away, turned back, as if truth were some alien mass of cells multiplying inside him, pressuring, choking him, threatening to erupt. Jimbo quashed his cigarette, straightened up. "I guess I'll have to title my story, *The Selling of the Papal Remains.*"

"What are you talking about?"

"I forgot that you didn't know I was there. In the papal apartments, just after you finished your work. And I wondered what was in that steel canister. I think I know. You removed his vital organs. I'm right about that, yes or no?"

Rafallo's expression passed through stages of surprise, shock, and alarm, then collapsed slowly like a barn with too much snow on the roof. He studied the floor for a moment, then raised his head and looked directly at the journalist. "I had the pope on a medication," he began reluctantly. "Quinidine. He had responded well to it. I watched him closely, let him eat more, permitted him to smoke his pipe in the evening. A sweet man but forgetful. Absent-minded, the professor in him. So I had him on a regular routine. He became very good at it. You must understand that Pope Jean *did* have heart problems. We did not publicize it, the Holy Father deserves some privacy, his condition did not seem immediately life-threatening . . ."

"Yes?"

"As soon as he was anointed and the cardinals and the nuns left, I searched his cassock pocket and his pants, too, for his pills. They were not there. So I went through his medicine cabinet. They were not there either. That is the place I insisted he keep them. It was part of the routine." The count paused, drew a breath. "I searched everywhere in his apartment. I was alone but I am sure that I did a thorough job. I went through his desk, checked the seat cushions of his office chairs. Nowhere."

"Taking pictures all the while."

"For your information, I started taking the pictures to have an inventory of his closets, drawers, medicine chest, everything. I wanted to cover myself in what I thought was a situation that I could not explain. His most important heart-regulating medicine was nowhere to be found. I took photographs of everything."

"And then you had the bright idea of taking pictures of him, too."

Rafallo shrugged, rubbed his beard with the sleeve of his jacket. "All the while, the cardinals were disputing about whether there should be an autopsy or not. Maestrini was firmly against it. I had to meet with a group of them the very next morning, including Maestrini. But they overruled my recommendation for an autopsy and embalming."

"Didn't they ask you how he died?"

"They presumed he had a heart attack. I said that all indications were in that direction."

"Nobody asked about the medicine?"

"Maestrini wouldn't allow any talk about the pope's health. He also ordered that the papal apartments be cleared out immediately, that all his effects be removed, even his books and papers. I don't know where it all went. Sealed in storage, I suppose."

"Well, what about the medicine? What did you call it?"

"Quinidine." He sighed. *"That* is the mystery. Medicine doesn't just disappear. Somebody took it, I am afraid, so that the pope did not have it when he needed it. His left hand was jammed into his cassock pocket when I first examined him on the floor of his chapel. He had been trying to get his medicine. That was obvious to me."

"You're sure of all this? Couldn't one of those nuns have picked it up? Maybe a Swiss Guard?"

Rafallo made a dismissive gesture, shook his head. "Now do you understand why I did everything I could to preserve the appearances of things in the circumstances? My own personal problems had nothing to do with it."

"But you're suggesting . . ."

"That someone arranged for the pope to die Cleverly. With calculation. Someone who knew his habits well." Rafallo sighed again. "I am suggesting murder. And all the evidence is gone."

FOUR

Michael Tracy stepped wearily into the elevator at the Hilton, Mother Hilda clattering a flamenco on the tiles of his imagination. Pilgrims usually get cured, he thought, but I catch the disease, there's a lot of it going around. Is this holiness or madness? Maybe they go together, conventional ideas about life don't seem to persuade anybody anymore. The kingdom of heaven suffers violence, and the violent bear it away. I never understood what that meant. Until now. Maybe.

Jimbo was lying on his bed when he entered his hotel room. "Michael, *mon père, mon frère* . . ." He hopped up, electricity streaming off him, put his arm around Michael's shoulder. "Have I got a story for you!"

"You'll never top mine." The priest slipped carefully out of his suit jacket, eased it over his hand, dropped it onto a chair, began to loosen the grimy blood-daubed bandage. His brother stepped closer, pinching off the first bloom of his Rafallo story, took over unlooping the strands of gauze. "What the hell have you been doing, anyway?"

"On pilgrimage," Michael said in a drained voice. "I didn't duck when a guy threw his crutch away."

"Very funny." They edged into the bathroom. Jimbo cleaned and re-bandaged the wound, excitedly rattled off his story of the papal physician, the pictures, the cardinals' inquiry, the missing bottle of heart medicine. He finished, looked up into his brother's vaguely staring eyes. "For a professional confessor, you're not listening very closely, Father. Don't you understand what I've been telling you? I've got the first evidence that somebody may have knocked the pope off." He leaned over the sink, rinsed off his own hands, called after Michael, who had walked back into his room. "Your boss, that is to say, your *late* boss . . ." He followed the priest, drying his hands energetically. "Mike, don't you understand? We may be talking the sorrowful mysteries here, also known as murder one."

"Yes, yes . . ." The priest slipped out of his clerical shirt, tossed it on top of his discarded jacket, pulled a fresh one out of his open-jawed suitcase, put it on slowly.

Jimbo stared at his priest brother, followed him as he walked out onto the balcony and gazed absently across the dead calm sea of Roman buildings, colored like *café au lait.*

"Well?"

Michael grunted, a snort of whalesong from the absorbing depths.

Jimbo studied him for a long moment. "What, you lovesick or something? Having sweet thoughts about your nun friend, the doctor?"

Michael glared at him, irritation sprouting like mold on his tone. "She's not a nun anymore . . ."

"Uh-huh," Jimbo responded, check-mark fashion. "I see. Well, let me approach this a different way. Maybe the pope's been murdered. Who the hell knows what else is going on here? You're one of the few people who might be able to help me get to the bottom of this. *That's* got to come first, this time."

The priest sighed, turned his head away.

"Listen to me, Mike. Love is a pill, a lot like cyanide. Don't swallow it, not yet. It doesn't work, it doesn't end the pain, it just recycles it." He took a breath, edged closer. "You can't run out on this. You owe something to the world right now. Goddammit, you owe something to . . ." He broke off, shook his head disgustedly. The brothers looked at each other hard, like duelists through locked swords.

"What *were* you going to say, Jimbo? I owe it to *you*, that's it, isn't it? You want to call in all your big-brother chits, how you wiped my nose and cleaned my bottom, and now I owe you something, like helping you win the Pulitzer Prize."

"I was *going* to say you owe something to Mom. You're about to break her heart by leaving, you know that, don't you? Have you even told her yet? Who the hell sacrificed for you, so you could stay in the seminary after Denny dropped dead? She made it look easy, didn't want you to worry. You probably didn't even notice it. Don't you think you could stop worrying about yourself, don't you think, for once in your life, you could step down from your pedestal?"

Michael's glance softened, he lowered his head.

"Mike, why don't you break your own heart for a change . . ." Jimbo turned abruptly, walked back into the room, smacked one fist into the palm of the other. Michael followed. "Jimbo," he said in a voice burnished by fatigue, "I'm sorry you resent me so much . . ."

The journalist brother inhaled, bit his lower lip lightly, took a few steps toward the door. "What the hell is wrong with my calling in a few markers? I damn well *do* think you ought to try to help me. Sure I do. Maybe you don't even realize how much you've ignored me over the years. You haven't really answered me because you never really do listen to me. *Never.* You look down on me. You don't mean to, but you do. That's why I think you're making a mistake getting married. You don't know how much room you take up in a relationship."

"Jimbo, I . . ."

"Forget it." The reporter put his hand on the doorknob.

"Look," the priest said, drawing on his energy reserves, "you're not listening to me either. You've always acted like a big brother, like I never learned to blow my nose. I'm not thinking just about getting married, I'm thinking about this whole strange church I've been involved with. Hardly anything is really the way it looks on the surface. Too much is made to look good, like the pope over in St. Peter's right now, just put another coat of paint on, doesn't he look natural? And I've done my part in these kinds of things over the years. But I see through myself much better now. Keep up appearances, don't face the implications of all the screwups that occur. That's how to become a monsignor. Anything goes in order to keep things under control. The pope's death is just the latest on a long list of screwups that turn into cover-ups. All for the best of reasons, of course. *That's* what I'm really thinking about. And I've been waiting two years for *these* people to tell me whether it's okay to get married or not!"

He turned away as his hand tingled with pain, carefully clenched and unclenched it, shifted around toward his brother again. "The bureaucratic church survives because it's on a permanent bias, it fits the hole in the world perfectly. They were made for each other. Some of these cardinals and bishops live in frosted-glass houses, otherwise they couldn't keep getting up in the morning." He paused, took a deep breath. "And you're more like them than I am, you think being in love and getting married are unhealthy, what's personal must yield to the good of the organization, so help you, Henry R. Luce. You're a company man at heart, anything for the company, *you're* the Tracy who should have been a priest. You're a closet bureaucrat pretending to be Sam Spade. No wonder you work for *Time*. That's why you could track down Rafallo, you understand rouge jobs on the dead, you have the instincts for that world alright. Well, it's not mine anymore, I'm choosing what's healthy. You can't keep health under control. Let the dead bury the dead."

Jimbo pulled back a step, ran his tongue around the inside of his mouth, spoke in a calm-down-now tone. "What the hell happened to you in Munich anyway? What did the red baroness do, dive-bomb you in her mystical Stuka?"

Michael shook his head imperceptibly. "I'm not going to talk about Munich."

Jimbo kept his doubting expression in place. "You just want out of the corps, that it?"

"That's it."

"Yeah, well while you're going through your Martin Luther phase, I'm still going to try to find out what happened to the pope and his medicine. In case you're interested, *somebody* has to care about the institutions that keep this goddam civilization running. There's damn little that does. You're just like all the priests I've met with the hots, you don't know the difference between the burning bush and a damp crotch."

"I've had it, Jimbo, I've had it with everything, including you, for a while . . ."

"No, Mike, you're just growing up, is all."

Their eyes collided like dirt-game marbles. "Look, Jimbo, you all sacrificed for me, I know that, but I'm not a trophy for the Tracy clan. Or for the church bureaucracy. I'm going to live my own life my own way."

"Pop Psychology 101." Jimbo turned the knob. "Insight on the cheap. Unworthy of you. You'll be into est, the next I hear. Denny would just tell you to cut the bullshit, that's what he'd say, the old man."

"He'd also tell me to do what I thought was right."

"Maybe."

"You're on your own, Jimbo."

"Good luck, kid." Jimbo turned the knob just as a muffled roar rose from the city beyond the open balcony door.

FIVE

Cardinal Kiejson shook his head slowly as he read the report on the explosion near the school below Monte Mario. Twenty children injured, four critically, the New Century Movement claimed credit for it. The cardinal's face was white and taut as he walked slowly across the room. The papal funeral tomorrow, it is time to take action . . .

Kiejson placed the report on the coffee table, unclipped his scarlet cincture, dropped it onto his leather chair, reached over and switched on his computer. He programmed it, paced back and forth while it ground itself into working order. He slipped the disk Ambassador Wingate had given him into the machine, sat down, entered the access code, RED HAT, touched the keys. A list of his brother princes of the church rose on the screen before him.

He paused, compressed his lips, tapped the scroll away, contemplated the cleansed screen solemnly, rubbed his hands together, typed in his own name. His dossier glided silently up before him. KIEJSON, FRANZ JOSEF. BORN SEPTEMBER I, I927, UTRECHT, THE NETHERLANDS . . . He read the single-spaced listings intently, frowned as he called up another page, then another, seven in all. The Dutch cardinal tapped the OUT key, sat without moving in the glow of the clear screen for several moments. *Mene, Mene, Tekel, Upharsin.* The moving finger writes . . .

He touched the keys again. BOUYER, HENRI CLAUDE PHILIPPE. ARCHBISHOP OF MARSEILLES. BORN APRIL 9, 1938, PARIS, FRANCE. Kiejson leaned closer to the screen as a subordinate file came into view. BREMOND, MARIE. TWENTY-SIX YEARS OF AGE. "FOR SEVERAL YEARS CARDINAL BOUYER HAS MAINTAINED A CLOSE RELATIONSHIP WITH THIS WOMAN, PRESENTLY A MEMBER OF THE FRENCH NATIONAL BALLET. HE HAS DESCRIBED HER AS HIS NIECE, HAS PAID FOR HER EDUCATION AND HER TRAVELS SINCE SHE WAS FOURTEEN. BEFORE HE BECAME A BISHOP, SHE LIVED DURING THE SUMMERS IN HIS RECTORY IN NANCY. SHE MOVED TO TOULOUSE UPON HIS APPOINTMENT AS ARCHBISHOP FOUR YEARS AGO AND WAS PART OF THE LARGE PARTY THAT JOURNEYED TO ROME WHEN HE WAS MADE A CARDINAL TWO YEARS AGO. OUR INVESTIGATION CONFIRMS THAT HE HAS MISREPRESENTED HER AS A RELATIVE, THAT, IN FACT, HE MET HER WHEN SHE WAS A STUDENT IN THE SACRED HEART ACADEMY NEAR NANCY WHERE HE SERVED AS CHAPLAIN . . ."

Kiejson finished reading the account of meetings, photos, videotapes, recordings, the accumulated evidence that Marie Bremond was Bouyer's mistress. He studied the paragraphs about the archbishop's relationship with Marxist labor leaders, his involvement in the anti-nuclear movement, his remarkable popularity among the people. The Dutch cardinal raised his eyes, gave his typist's chair half a spin, gazed at the narrow corner window, gilded by the summer evening sun. The hum of the computer was the only sound in the room.

He swiveled back, typed in another name. BREITFELTDER, FRIEDRICH JOHANNES, archbishop of Berlin. Twenty minutes later he read the file of CALDWELL, JOSEPH PATRICK, archbishop of Boston. He then inspected the pages on TOSTA DE SA, TOMAS, of Rio de Janeiro and MELLA, ANTHONY FRANCIS, of Bombay. Kiejson picked up the scarred crystal, watched the snow settle like information inside his head. He grunted, adjusted his glasses, and typed again. CASEY, THOMAS JOSEPH, archbishop of Chicago.

SIX

Monsignor Tracy's hand was worse the next day. An Italian doctor clucked at him from behind enormous eye-distorting glasses, treated the wound, wrote a prescription for antibiotics. I guess I ought to stay off it a few days, Mike had said, but the Italian doctor didn't get it, just shrugged and sent him off with a warning. "You need some rest. Is something else bothering you?"

Is something else bothering me? My hand, my brother, Mother Church, Mother Hilda, a.k.a. the vanishing penitent. My heart, how about my heart? He called Ann at noon, felt the intervening time zones strapped together, weighing him down like a piano on a moving man's back. "Annie, I'm going to see Cardinal Casey, yes, before the pope's funeral, this evening. I got an appointment through his secretary, Monsignor Hawkins, an old classmate."

"Mike, do you really think that will do any good?"

"Casey is a very influential man, in his own way. He understands the Italian temperament, you call on truth only when everything else fails. I think he can get the permission through during these general meetings the cardinals are going to have. It's worth trying . . ."

Ann didn't respond.

"It means a lot to me to try this . . ."

"You've been hurt enough by these people . . ."

He rang off, wondering at himself, trying to arrange his departure from the priesthood on the very day the pope was being buried. That's me, the contrary pilgrim, heading out when everybody else is heading in, the Irish poet more than the curial official, I would have made a lousy bishop. His hand smarted and he thought of the children hurt in the latest bombing.

As the cab passed through the Borghese Gardens Michael thought of the waiting Casey, a cunning pharaoh deep in the pyramid of the Excelsior Hotel. In the priest's fantasy it was old times. Cardinal Casey was standing next to Mayor Daley on the reviewing stand of Chicago's St. Patrick's Day parade, powerful men in bulky overcoats, thick as trees all around, it could have been May Day on the Kremlin wall. "Shake hands with the cardinal," the twinkly-eyed Daley said to every homburged politician who climbed onto the stand for the mayoral blessing. What an easy move old Daley had, the smoothest hand-off play Michael had ever seen.

After the final pipe band had squealed into the chill dusk, the cardinal had invited Tracy to ride back to his residence with him. I'd like to talk to you, Father. Within twenty minutes Michael was sitting in the archbishop's out-sized calliope of a house on the edge of Lincoln Park. While Casey was upstairs Michael studied the yellowing souvenir papal skullcap mounted under a ticker-tapelike glass bell in the front parlor. The stuffy silent house seemed under glass, too. A clock chimed in a nearby room and Casey descended the stairs carrying a tray with two pony glasses and a bottle of sherry. Some Protestant divine, Michael thought, must have given him a case, very ecumenical, but it didn't turn the cardinal into an Agatha Christie vicar coming in from the garden for fellowship.

"I wonder," Casey had said, grasping the bottle in his strong hand, "whether you would like to take on a writing job for me?"

He asked the question again but now his brown-spotted hand clutched a glass filled with milky-looking medicine and his features had the hard-rubbed gray look of driftwood. Michael needed a moment to sort out his déjà vu and to locate himself properly in Casey's Roman hotel suite. "Yes, I wonder, Mike," the cardinal said, "especially since I understand that you're doing something for the *New York Times*."

"The magazine."

"Yes, well, what difference does it make?"

"I really wanted to talk to you about something else."

"Oh?" Casey swigged his medicine, spoke good-naturedly, a little push in the joviality, the false heartiness men affect in white-skinned intimacy after golf games. "You've gotten over that idea of leaving the priesthood, haven't you? I told you it would pass."

Michael noticed a high-wire quiver in his own voice as he answered. "It hasn't really passed, Your Eminence. I don't think that it will. I'd like your help to get my final papers processed."

Casey laughed gently. "We can't really be concerned about these personal things right now, can we?" He lowered his glass to the table next to his chair. "Now, I'd like you to suggest an article to the *Times* . . ."

"They prefer to think up their own ideas."

"Yes, but suppose you were writing about a cardinal who might just be the next pope . . ."

Michael throttled an impulse to protest. Who, where is this person, did somebody put something in your medicine? He held on; a wild horse of laughter bucked furiously inside him.

Casey pursed his lips, appraising the situation. "Do you think there's something amusing in this?" He looked intently at Michael Tracy. "There are many signs that the cardinals may turn to me as the next Holy Father."

Yes, Michael thought, and I can fly, open the window, I'll show you. Mother Hilda buzzed under Michael's skull plate like a stunt pilot beneath a big-city bridge. What a week this has been! How do I get out of here?

"Suppose," the cardinal said slowly, "just suppose that you had information about the conclave that nobody else had. That would make for an interesting article. One from the viewpoint of the newly elected pope." He paused. "An American pope."

"I'm sorry, I came to ask for your help about my rescript . . ."

Casey smiled indulgently. "You must realize that in my position I can't approve anybody's leaving the priesthood." He lowered his eyes, flicked a mote of dust from the arm of his chair. "It wouldn't look right."

"In that case, Your Eminence, I'm afraid I can't help you. And you can't help me."

"Mike, you're mature enough to understand that duty comes before anything else, or you should be." Casey's voice grew preacherly, testy, and self-righteous. "I presume that you will come to your senses. And I presume, as one of my priests, that you will do what I want when I ask you to write an article about me." He cleared his throat. "It's a great opportunity for you, too."

Michael blinked, started to rise. This, he thought, is a classic Chicago arrangement, it's like having a drawbridge close on you, it doesn't make much difference which side comes down on you first, you're just pavement to be walked on afterward.

The cardinal adjusted his glasses, picked up a brown envelope. "Here's some background material that may be useful."

This, Michael sighed inwardly, this is what drives people into Unitarianism. "Your Eminence, I can't speak for the *Times*. I really have to say no. My father told me never to get into cars with strangers who make you feel uncomfortable."

Casey frowned. "What are you talking about, anyway? You have delusions of being Thomas More. You're in a temporary low period. You'll snap out of it." The cardinal rose slowly from his chair, handed the envelope to Michael, took a few steps toward the door. Michael kept a few feet between them as they walked across the room.

"I know you'll think about this," the cardinal said unctuously. "And you'll get over this idea about getting married. Don't you realize that if you keep talking that way, you'll never be a bishop? And a young man like you has a great future in the church . . ." He paused in the entrance foyer of the suite, tugged at the chain of his episcopal cross. "You'll come around. The church expects it of you." He smiled icily. "And so do I."

Michael looked into Casey's composed face. The eyes were serene, welling with rectitude, steady beacons of a soul that entertained no doubts, the running lights of a man who considered himself hooked into the divine pipeline. He's like Hilda, traveling in his own divine Lear jet.

"Good boy, Mike," Casey said, chucking Tracy on the shoulder, "good boy." He opened the door and Michael found himself suddenly in the hallway. Would Casey have noticed if I fell off the edge of the world?

SEVEN

The pope's funeral, T minus fifteen minutes. Tanks and armored troop carriers ringed the great space in front of St. Peter's, on its statued roof the drawn submachine guns of the *carabinieri* glinted in the harsh afternoon light, soldiers wearing futuristic helmets crowded the balconies above the great entrance doors and lined the worn and ancient steps, shoot-first scowls on Latin-lover faces everywhere, it generated biblical jitters, the sun might stick in the sky, the earth might open up.

Michael's red-piped cassock, combined with his press credentials, gave him license to circulate more freely than other journalists. Jimbo would be mad again, accuse him of pulling clerical rank. A grave Dan Rather looked up, crinkly-eyed, from the television platform at a pair of sharpshooters lolling in the cupola on top of the basilica's dome.

Michael hurried inside, watched as they lifted the pope's moldering body, as light as a Styrofoam shell, and lowered it into the plain pine box the pontiff had requested in his will, fixed the lid in place, shielding him at last from the inspection of the devout and the curious. This can't be accidental,

Michael thought, these garish lessons in mortality, this grisly *memento mori* of letting deceased popes disintegrate like the Gettysburg dead. Powerful bureaucrats playing eternity chicken, Michael mused grimly, to see who'll back away first from wanting to be pope. *Dies irae, dies illa.* And now they're going to lay him out in the sun for a couple of hours during the funeral mass, he'll be glad to get into the cool tomb down in the grotto alright. Still, Michael was moved by the sight of the packing-case coffin bobbing on the shoulders of Swiss Guards as they transferred it to a hinge-gated, rubber-tired catafalque until the procession started. Me and the pope, we're both having trouble making our getaways.

In the sacristy the lowest buzz of conversation mingled with the rustle of scarlet silk robes as the cardinals waited for the signal to line up. The papal master of ceremonies, Monsignor Testagrossa, cleared his throat and inspected one last time a yard-high red leather missal that would be used in the ceremony. Thomas Cardinal Casey eyed Cardinal Kiejson twenty feet away speaking almost literally into the ear of André Cardinal Menier, archbishop of Paris, the "popemaker" as he was known, the subtlest ecclesiastical wheeler-dealer since Cardinal Spellman. As Casey moved toward them, Bryce Cardinal Nishimura of Tokyo, all bows and smiles and no bigger than an ornamental jockey, intercepted him, thanked the Chicagoan for his generous Christmas gift. Casey bowed, chatted briefly with the Japanese prelate. One vote from the Pacific rim, Casey judged, but hardly any power to deliver others. The Chicago cardinal pulled away, reached Kiejson just as the archbishop of Paris stepped away from him.

"What," Casey asked in a voice just above a whisper, "does Paris think of things?"

Kiejson nodded toward a Spanish cardinal, did not look directly at Casey. "Oh, we were just reminiscing about the war. Nothing really . . ." The two cardinals moved slowly through the knots of subdued confreres. Casey sensed that everybody was watching them, Chicago and Amsterdam, princes to be reckoned with, attention must be paid, Casey liked the reaction, it was respectful, admiring, yes, he liked it very much. "Our friend Maestrini," Kiejson said out of the side of his mouth, "plans to move the conclave up. It will start in three days."

Before Casey could respond, a short, elderly Italian cardinal touched him on the arm, beamed a smile at the American and the Dutchman. "You are two of the few cardinals I have actually met before. I have not met many of the others yet." This in a low, pleasant voice. "I am Angelo Solieri."

"Yes, yes, of course," Kiejson said quickly, "you were just made a cardinal last year, no? In recognition of your half century of work as Vatican archivist."

"We met," Solieri said softly, "on that sad day of the Holy Father's death."

"Yes, *Eminenza,*" Casey added benignly, "you anointed him."

The plump Italian nodded his head as Casey shook his hand. "Nobody knows me," Solieri said brightly, "because I have always been either in the church's attic or in her basement." He chuckled. "It is very pleasant to be in the fresh air again."

Casey stole a look at his Dutch comrade who had detached himself and was greeting a line of prelates with low-key assurance. The archbishop of Chicago glanced at his watch, raised his eyes into those of the archivist, this man is hard to shake off, he doesn't know how to act in the real world.

"Don't worry. I'm not going to ask you for money," Solieri said genially. "I have always been grateful to you Americans. Your generosity meant much to me during and immediately after the war. I do not think I would be alive today except for you Americans."

Casey nodded, forced a smile, who is Kiejson talking to now? Somehow he could not win release from the older man's gaze.

"You, Cardinal Casey, have always been of interest to me," Solieri said in a disarming tone. "I know of your benefactions to the Vatican archives. My life work, you might say, is the bread that you cast on the waters."

Casey smiled in acknowledgment, tried to swing away. Solieri stood his ground, stepped a few inches closer to him. "I should very much like to speak with you, my American friend." He gripped Casey's arm tightly. "I would very much like to show you the archives while you are here."

"Yes, well . . ."

"You would be surprised at what we have there."

The master of ceremonies gave a signal, a pure and cleansing tide of Gregorian chant washed through the great church, and the cardinals quickly took their places and began to move out of the sacristy.

Michael had gone outside again to watch the princes of the church as they came squinting out of the center door into the sunlight. The older ones were a compendium of orthopedic problems, limps, hitches, and hobbled gaits; the younger, with pious attitudes toning down their sure-footedness, moved along smoothly, masters of the art of seeming not to hurry. Michael thought he could smell the odor of fresh yellow pine as the papal coffin was borne tenderly out onto the piazza and lowered onto a stand halfway to the obelisk.

As the cardinals spread like a crimson mantle along the landing of the broad stairway, the *camerlengo* Maestrini, almost obscured by flanking ministers, climbed the steps of the outside altar to begin the Mass. The smoke from the incense drifted sluggishly in the muggy air, the Latin phrases echoed from the loudspeakers like ball-park announcements, in the distance the waters of the ornamental fountains splashed gouts of silver in the sunlight. The music soared and a strange and moving peace settled on the area hemmed in by military hardware, nobody's going to get killed here today.

Michael turned to see Jimbo advancing toward him in his uniform. "How you doing?"

"Okay."

"You sure?" The Vatican buildings seemed to envelop them like a great muffling tent, shutting out the spectacle and noise around them.

"You been called up to active duty again? Or do you have the ice cream concession?"

"You're wearing a uniform you have questionable title to yourself. As it happens, I'm meeting with the head of the Rome police when this is over. You?"

"Just on my way out."

They sized each other up tensely. "I hope you've told our mother about your plans." Jimbo punched the phrase like a time clock. "Be a hell of a thing for her to read in the newspapers." He lowered his head, slipped quickly past his brother.

Michael Tracy stood perfectly still for a moment as the sound and color of the funeral tuned up again around him. He skirted around the quadrants of chairs that had been arranged for the official mourners. Behind the diplomats sat church dignitaries and a Joseph's coat of delegations in native costumes. In the last row of the VIP section, Count Rafallo leaned close to a dark-haired woman wearing enormous sunglasses, his paintbrush beard stroking her bosom, kind of a pre-mortem exam going on. Forget it, Michael said to himself, I don't even know the man.

The editor of the *New York Times Magazine* had been very understanding on the phone, but he wanted Tracy to cover the funeral and election and to downplay Mother Hilda. Fine, Michael had said. Mother Hilda stared up directly into Michael's eyes from a rigid kneeling position on the pavement next to a section for religious women. Her face was as hard as an image in a lightning-split rock, her eyes iridescent, compelling, demanding. Michael looked away, hesitated, wondered if he should say something, decided against it. So long to you too, Hilda.

As Michael passed her, his hand tingled as if he'd gone too close to a stove. He circled the bier to get a better view of things. Josef Beck, his wood-shaving hair glistening in the sun, stood stolidly with a throng of German pilgrims. Tomorrow the world, Michael thought involuntarily. Various members of Beck's committee were scattered throughout the crowd, here comes everybody. Somewhere on the cobbled expanse Michael had crossed a boundary line, he felt uncomfortably but decisively estranged, his visa had expired, he had run out of sympathy for everybody but the falling-apart pope out in his sunny daub of a coffin. I love it, he said half aloud, but I've got to pull out of the dead man's grasp of this spectacular church. The church likes mysteries, fine, it can add the pope's death to its collection.

He moved slowly across the plaza toward the blue fencing at the open mouth of the Bernini colonnade, struggling with every step against Rome's resistant mood, that undertow of death that ran swiftly through the city even on its best days. The Gregorian chant rose and fell majestically behind him, farewell to that, too. Michael looked back, craned his head for one last view of the pope's coffin, a tiny yellow dinghy, a skimpy life raft floating on the vast sea of ancient ceremony with Dan Rather whispering a description as if it were a golf match. Good-bye to all that.

Michael ducked under a wooden hurdle, made his way through the line of sullen soldiers standing by armored cars, passed through the milling crowds of mourners, some praying, others chatting and laughing lightly. A young man with a bandit moustache was selling souvenir fans with Pope Jean's picture on them, Coca-Cola, too. Beyond him, a news vendor hawked papers. As Michael passed, he read the headline: TWO CHILDREN DIE FROM BOMB INJURIES.

CHRONICLES

ONE

"Ambassador Wingate will see you now."

Jimbo rose from the waiting-room chair at the United States Embassy, nodded to the blond receptionist, followed her down the corridor, noting the metronomic swing of her backside, sheathed in a skirt of white and gold. Papal colors, he thought. How fitting, how tightly fitting. He was reevaluating the temporary vow of celibacy he had so ruefully taken after visiting Angelica Tomai when they reached Owen Wingate's outer office. Jimbo smiled at himself, the flesh cares little for the mind's promises, he thought, that's why I want Michael to keep his vows, I need him to be pure. A middle-aged secretary with chestnut hair coughed and ushered him into Wingate's office.

"Jim, Jim, how have you been?" Ambassador Wingate rose from behind his large, miniature-flagged desk, moved as smoothly as he had when he and the journalist had played on the same high school football team almost thirty years before. He was a man who took delight in himself, luxuriating in his fitness, and drawing strength from the reassuring odors that rose from his carefully constructed self—fine cigars, a manly scent, a subtle deodorant, expensive leather. "Did you pick up the atmosphere you were looking for in the Vatican?" Wingate spoke genially as he directed his visitor to a comfortable leather chair placed at an angle to his desk. Jimbo nodded, sat down slowly, studied the chinks of gold that glowed numbly at the joints and casings of the rich-men's-club decor of the spacious office, inspected the framed document of ambassadorial appointment hanging just above Wingate's head.

"F. Owen Wingate," Jimbo said in mock appreciation, "you ought to hang lace curtains in here to go with using your initial and your fancy middle name. What happened, Ownie? I thought only undertakers and judges did that. Like J. Miles Plunkett, Chicago's pioneer of the prepaid funeral, or F. Lanning Curry, the famous jurist now in the slammer, if memory serves."

Wingate let his smile fade as he took his own chair. "You did get the feeling for things inside, I presume."

"A long time since we went to Ignatius together. Remember Father Reardon, he could hit you in the back of the room with a piece of chalk from a seated position, like a catcher with a great throw to second base."

The ambassador flashed a quirky smile. Jimbo cleared his throat. "No Proust in your soul, I guess, Ownie."

"Well," Wingate responded easily, "I'm all for old-time recollections but the papal funeral has kept me quite busy. Maybe you haven't had quite as much to do."

"Oh, I've managed."

"And," Wingate continued, "I really don't have much time now. The city is very tense. I've just had a call that it's gone into a major alert mode. They're beginning the conclave early for security reasons. I don't have time to swap baseball cards today."

"Good old Ownie. Despite the manicure, you've still got that shit-eating smile you had when you first started turning odometers back. And, yes, the inside mood was very helpful, *very* helpful. The uniform, well, I'd like to get it cleaned and then I'll get it back to you."

Wingate's face hardened. "You've always been like this, Jim, as far back as I can remember. You like to insult people, especially those who've been nice to you, show them you don't need them, never did."

"That's about right," Jimbo said. "It gets their attention when I've got something important to tell them. And I haven't had much luck telling people what I've found out so far. I have information—the only real information around—that the pope's death was not natural at all."

Wingate rearranged a pad and pencil on his unspotted desk blotter, lowered his eyes, spoke in a polite, dry voice. "I've heard these rumors." He paused, smiled again. "About the uniform, no need to have it cleaned, I'll send somebody to pick it up."

Jimbo felt the stitch of healing flesh as he wrinkled his forehead, described his adventures with Rafallo in a controlled tone. The ambassador's expression did not change.

"You know, Ownie, I remember you were an A student and all that, but I've seen automated bank tellers more responsive to me than you are."

"Jim," Wingate replied calmly, "you're not using good judgment. You're trusting Rafallo too much. So did the pope. That's a fact. Father Reardon, as you will recall, was a great shot except that he often hit the wrong kid." The ambassador leaned back in his chair. "Rafallo didn't take care of the pope properly. That's all. Malpractice, we'd call it back in the States. It's as simple—and as sad—as that."

"You don't believe that, Ownie, not for a minute."

"Look, Jimbo, I don't have a lot of time but you ought to see things in perspective. Glasnost has been a very successful smoke screen. The Russians are extremely shrewd adversaries. They aim at the soft areas—culture, sports, and religion—areas that are, as they say in their reports, belief intensive. The Russkies know they can make headway if they introduce doubt into these influential aspects of life. Behind this smoke screen . . ." Wingate's tone stiffened. "They're raising all kinds of hell. There is nothing the Communists would like better than to disrupt the papal election. You must realize that the late pope was *not* perceived as an ardent anti-Communist. He trusted them. 'The host of glasnost,' that's what he was called. Let's face it, Jimmy, Pope Jean was naive, naive about the Russians, naive about his doctor."

Wingate's brief fusillade of laughter was harsh and derisive. "The Communists are interested in seeing that a cardinal of Pope Jean's liberal persuasion succeeds him. How better than by heaping sympathy on Pope Jean, creating doubts about his death, making him a martyr to reactionary forces, by capitalizing on the very ambiguity that the world found interesting in him."

Jimbo lowered his head, spoke to his shoes. "Do you guys take lessons in this, what is it, anyway, that . . ."

"Jimmy, you're playing into their hands. Our real concern is the terrorists. The members of the New Century Movement are literally heralding a new century of revolution. They want to strike the world's greatest bastion of anti-communism, the Vatican. *They* are the number one intelligence and tactical problem in Rome right now. As ambassador to the Holy See, I must be concerned about that, *not* about the pope's death. The way he died doesn't matter, he's *dead*. You would do his memory a disservice by trying to play detective right now."

The journalist slowly rose from his chair. "Why is it, F. Owen, old pal, that for a kid whose old man worked for the Chicago machine, you come at me like some sort of reform politician, all high-mindedness and patriotism. I never met a reformer who didn't have something else in mind. Don't you think I know when people are squeezing me?"

Wingate raised his eyebrows slightly, shrugged his shoulders dismissively.

Jimbo swept a gesture toward the windows. "Ownie, I've talked to the chief of police, Freddie Montuori. Like talking to an iceberg floating off Newfoundland, fucking snow-blind, he hasn't seen anything at all. Well, yes, the *Titanic* did scrape by a little while ago but it didn't amount to much . . ."

The ambassador fiddled impatiently with the pad before him as Jimbo walked slowly back and forth in front of his desk.

"So then I went to see Bert Hickey of the CIA. I know, I know, he's operating under cover as an art dealer. What a joke, he cries at Norman Rockwell covers, Bert does. Hell of a lot of middle-aged Micks like you and Bert doing the bidding of the U.S. government around the world, did you know that? Of course, they've turned to Mormons for their straight-arrow supply now, Irish Catholics not being what they once were . . ." The journalist paused, looked down at the ambassador. "Bert Hickey and I went to Notre Dame together on scholarship. I didn't think he'd bullshit me, didn't think you would either. So I ask him how come he doesn't check the pharmacy records about the pope's medicine. He gives me this line, you'd think it was Chicago, medicine for public figures is never prescribed in their real names, not in the Vatican, the poisoning of churchmen having a long history there. There are no records, for security reasons, that's what the head of station tells me."

"Jimbo, Jimbo . . ." This in a slightly whining, come-back-to-your-senses, tone.

Jimbo leaned forward, spread his hands on the desk in front of Wingate. "Let's come back to that. What of the terrorists you're so worried about, the New Century Movement? All we've got are the bombings and the reports of a few phone calls. Nobody can even remember the names of the people who actually took the phone calls . . ." The reporter straightened up. "And I've made a computer search and a lot of phone calls about terrorist organizations. This New Century Movement seems to have come out of nowhere. Nobody, I mean *nobody,* has ever heard of them, knows of any connection to any other group, nobody can even say what their cause is."

Wingate glanced at his desk calendar, then at his watch. "What's this I hear about your brother, the famous Monsignor Tracy?"

Jimbo bristled. "What the hell are you . . ."

"It's just, Jimmy, you've been giving me a half-time pep talk, as if we didn't know anything here, as if *my* loyalties were somehow amiss. You're buying Communist propaganda on the one hand, and your brother's deserting the priesthood on the other—especially now—well, those aren't exactly signs of loyalty either."

"Who said Mike's leaving," Jimbo asked angrily, "who told you that?"

Wingate picked up the pencil from his desk, flexed it between his balled fists. "I don't think it helps to have one of our best-known priests checking out just at the moment when we should all be closing ranks." He held the pencil like a javelin, pierced the air. "Armageddon's out there, not just a good story, don't you realize that?" He dropped the pencil, opened the top desk drawer, removed a folder, held it in his right hand. "Our reports suggest that you two—you and your brother—have a deal going, a million-dollar deal. Monsignor's supplying you with inside Vatican information, you're working the street, that you've already got a book contract, that you're working on movie rights, that you two Micks from Chicago stand to do very well, trading on the pope's death . . ." He paused, caught his breath. "*I* arranged for you to get inside the Vatican. For the *atmosphere,* you said. Sure, you'd done me favors, but they're all paid up now. I warned you that if you fucked around, you'd get fucked. And that's a fact."

Wingate hunched forward. "Don't you think we know you two have been chasing all over town on this story? That you've been laying Angelica Tomai on the side, you think we don't hear about these things? And your brother, Saint Michael, has learned plenty of confidential things over the years, now he's mixed up with some bunch of left-wing priests, trying to fix the papal election. You think we're not interested in him, in his visits to Monsignor Lanza, who's in charge of saints but doesn't believe in the devil anymore, and his friendship with that heretic Josef Beck and his lame-brained crowd of conspirators, you think we don't follow these things?"

Jimbo grimaced, spoke in a tight voice. "You're looking at the wrong things, Ownie. Rome is burning and you're tracking the Tracy brothers. You can't be serious . . ."

Wingate suddenly stood up. "About that uniform."

"Fuck the uniform, Ownie." Jimbo straightened up. "You know what this reminds me of? The time they set up my old man. You remember. Hell, everybody in town knew Alderman Horowitz was banging that black secretary. Then this dude using her to run cocaine deals in City Hall—hell, she delivered it with the mail—well, the dude shows up the wrong night, things get out of hand, enter Horowitz with his little nickel-plated pistol, he shoots them both. The fix is put in up and down and sideways, evidence disappears, murder and suicide the coroner calls it. And there was a bullet hole in the back of the dude's head you could drop a golf ball in. They needed a patsy to give Horowitz time to walk away. And they picked Captain Denny Tracy because he had supervised the case. The sacrificial lamb, the fall guy. The evidence disappeared and they accused Denny of manufacturing it in the first place, of false arrest because he called Horowitz in for questioning, of violating rules and disobeying orders. Just like *you're* trying to make me and my brother your case, *they* made our old man the case instead of Horowitz. The book they threw at him was so fucking heavy, they had to roll it downhill."

Wingate's voice was soft, conciliatory, patronizing. "Everybody felt bad about your father. But that has no connection with the pope, that's old-time stuff, a score you haven't settled yet. That's what's got you off base . . ."

Jimbo ignored him, spoke intensely. "They sprung the gallows trap under my old man before he knew what happened. Down he went into the darkness . . ." The journalist paused. "But that's not what killed him. They let him resign with no charges pressed. And during that whole time, *nobody* spoke up for him. *That's* what killed him, all these honest guys looking the other way, great Mass and Communion men, marching with the Holy Name Society, had to think of the wives and kids, the pension, too. And

Horowitz, he went on to become head of the City Council finance committee. *He* made money the Chicago way, he stole it. And his son, for God's sake, went to Harvard, changed his name to Hampton, became an Episcopalian, then a Catholic, giving us all a bad name. And the son of a bitch is the cardinal's lawyer now. And your old man . . ."

"Look, your father was a good man, my old man was too. But Denny's dead, let him have some peace. You can't get revenge for what happened to him by trying to solve an imaginary murder of the pope."

"You finished, Mister Ambassador?" Tracy exhaled, set himself squarely. "You've mentioned all the Tracys but my mother. Anything you want to say about her before I go? Arrange a strip search, maybe a court-martial?"

Wingate pursed his lips, shook his head as if at a misbehaving child. "You're just proving my case with this nonsense . . ."

Jimbo slashed the air with his hand, spoke in low, even tones. "Denny used to say that there was nothing in the world worse than a cozy Irishman. I never knew exactly what he meant. Until now, that is. And he was right. And I'll thank you, Ownie, not to give me any wiser-than-thou advice about him. Or about my brother. I'm sure you're looking out for me. That means I've got you worried. And your whole staff. That means I'm picking up the edge of the right blanket, that there's somebody sleeping under it who shouldn't be. Now, I'm going back to work." He turned, stopped by the door. "And, Mister Ambassador, I'll thank you to take your nose the hell out of my brother's life." He turned the knob. "And mine."

"The uniform, Jim, I wouldn't want to hear that you've been detained for possession of a uniform to which you had no right."

Jimbo smiled. "That's a fact." And closed the door softly.

TWO

Monsignor Tracy had returned to the square to watch the pope's funeral until the last cloud of incense shredded apart on the battlement-like facade of St. Peter's. He had then walked for miles, wrapped in silence, and cabbed the rest of the way back to his hotel. He did not sleep well. Two small children kept appearing in his lightning-flash dreams, the innocent victims of the terrorists at his door, silent trick-or-treaters visiting from eternity, drifting and climbing through his head like biblical angels.

He took the crumpled newspaper with the story of their deaths out onto the balcony, inhaled the summer morning air, inspected St. Peter's, squatting like a sumo wrestler in the middle of Rome, indifferent to time, to your troubles and mine, immovable despite the steady prodding of two thousand years of individual concerns, a force more powerful than the popes withered like dead grass deep inside it.

Michael had stayed up late and called his mother before he had gone to bed. She had listened quietly as he explained that he was seeking permission to marry the woman she had known as Sister Ann. "Oh . . ." was all she said, sorrowfully, fatalistically, as if she had long expected to hear this, that her prayers couldn't hold it off forever. Her sadness rattled the vacuum of quiet the way a hot stove does an empty pot. Michael probed the resistant silence hesitantly. "I don't want to hurt or disappoint you but I just can't go on this way any longer . . ."

"Oh, Michael," she finally said, "I've always been so proud of you. When I think of you on the altar, wearing the vestments, saying Mass . . ."

"I . . ."

"Can you think about this, can you do that for me, pray about it while you're there?"

"I *have* prayed about it. They say they'll give me permission if I'm crazy or if I say that you forced me to become a priest in the first place."

"That's not true, that's not true at all . . ." She paused. "Are those men trying to hurt you, Michael? What they say isn't true. You wanted to be a priest when you were a little boy."

Mike swallowed hard. "They can't hurt me, not any longer." He sighed, went on to explain as much as he could. She kept asking if he was alright, as if he had been explaining an accident he had survived with minor injuries, and would be home soon. There was a long pause. "Maybe," she said slowly, "maybe we were too close to each other . . ."

Monsignor Tracy finished replaying the conversation internally, walked back inside his room, subdued, thinking about Jimbo. Why don't you break your own heart for a change? He inspected the messages he had ignored the night before, two from Josef Beck, *Urgent meeting, please come.* He dropped them into the waste basket, dressed, and headed for the Vatican.

His press credentials gained Michael access to sections of the Vatican barred to the public because of preparations for the conclave. The Sistine Chapel and the surrounding area swarmed with workmen, rang and buzzed with the sounds of hammers and drills. He gazed up at Michelangelo's ceiling, its colors cartoon-bright from the recent restoration, moved out of the way as a foreman shouted instructions about the placement of the lumber for the temporary raising of the chapel floor. Here, he mused, in this strange mixture of now and then, the cardinals would gather shortly to select a successor to Pope Jean. Michael watched a security man sweeping the ancient walls with a device to detect electronic bugs, a post-modern exterminator. He sniffed the odor of freshly cut wood, thought of the pope's mean coffin, left as a group of European journalists entered to inspect the chapel.

He angled slowly across the great basilica, oblivious of the crowds, was allowed, thanks to his press card, to descend to the grotto whose alcoves held the tombs of the popes. It was quiet, empty, rich with the smell of flowers heaped on the just sealed vault of Pope Jean. Michael peered down through the dim light, *what did I come here for anyway? My heart is made up, I can't change my heart, you have to follow your heart and test it against your conscience. I've told people that all my life, my conscience is made up.*

Mike knelt down, slowly became aware of another figure on its knees at the edge of the niche, an old priest, his silver-fringed bald head bowed in prayer. Tracy turned his gaze back to the mass of flowers. The dead children played silently in the tangled sprays and blossoms. *Why don't you break your own heart for a change?* He felt a pang of love for Ann, a cello quartet began playing bittersweet melodies inside his chest so loudly he thought they would disturb the old priest's prayers.

Between the throb in his chest and the one in his hand, he couldn't concentrate, *Pope Jean, you're a Frenchman, you understand.* Michael rose carefully, looked at the aged priest lost in prayer, *you don't see that much anymore, he must be one of the confessors for St. Peter's.* He waited a moment, stepped over and touched the old man's shoulder. The priest looked up at him from a bright, sad face, dryly and wonderfully weathered, his prominent brow lined fine as old china above lively brown eyes. "Would you," Michael asked softly, "hear my confession?"

The old priest nodded wordlessly, steadied himself with one hand against the wall as he rose, walked knowingly down the pillared corridor past the darkened, chained-off spaces where other popes lay under statues and within sarcophagi, *requiescant in pace.* The stout elderly priest floated confidently along, *maybe he's another angel, maybe I've fallen in with them, gypsy underground angels, maybe we're all dead . . .*

The old man turned suddenly, gestured to a prie-dieu next to a chair barely visible in the darkness below a winged and fluted ossuary. Michael knelt as the old man draped a small violet stole over his shoulders, settled himself in the chair, made a sign of the cross, mumbled the beginning phrase of the confessional ritual.

"Bless me, Father, for I have sinned . . ." Michael paused, looked at the chunky silhouette of the old priest. "I don't know if I've sinned or not. I know that I've been selfish . . ." He sighed. "I don't know what God expects me to do . . ."

The whole story tumbled out in the eerie silence of the grotto, Mike's love for Ann, his desire to receive the church's permission to marry, the long delay, and now the suggestion that he would have to accuse himself of being crazy in order to be free, it didn't make sense, it wasn't the truth, it wasn't as true as the love he felt, he had to follow what was truest . . .

Michael hesitated.

"Yes?" the old man inquired gently.

The younger priest told him about Mother Hilda, of his brother's pressure on him to help solve the mystery of the pope's death, of Cardinal Casey's expectations. "Maybe I've lost my faith, I don't know. I don't want to be involved in making things look good anymore. I just don't want any part of that anymore. The only thing I can seem to trust is love, the thing they always said wasn't to be trusted at all. I don't really feel that I'm betraying the gospel by loving another person. Then I say to myself, you're making yourself sound too noble, you're making it easy for yourself. But I've learned there's nothing easy about loving somebody . . ." He paused. "I am bothered by the death of those children from the bomb. They haunt me, make me feel I have to respond to them, that I can't let go of their hands, that they're asking me for something the way kids did in parish work, kids who were sick or poor or had bad luck . . ."

Michael lowered his head, his voice cracked slightly. "For however I've sinned in thought and deed, and for all the sins of my past life, I am heartily sorry . . ."

The old priest remained silent for a moment, allowing Michael's anguish to disperse in the cool darkness. "God understands the human heart, Father," he said softly, "and He understands yours, too. You are not the first priest to feel the way you do." He shifted slightly in his chair. "The true church is not that of the men who make mistakes and hide them rather than admit them. It is the church of Peter who said that he did not understand spiritual things and who wept for his sins, and the church of Paul, who persecuted believers and thought himself the least of all the apostles. The church belongs to those who can say from their hearts, 'Forgive me, for I am a sinful man.' That is the church of Jesus and of those who take His words to heart and try to live as He teaches . . ."

The old priest let his words trail off. "So I cannot counsel you to leave the priesthood. No, I cannot in conscience do that. The church needs good priests. For myself, I would like you to remain as a priest. I pray that you will." He paused again. "But I cannot counsel you to go against your own conscience either."

The confessor reached over, fumbling in the shadows, gently touched Michael's bandaged hand, spoke as a father would to a stricken child. "You must not believe that the devil has taken you over, or that it was he who wounded you. Nobody, no matter who they are, can say that. No, God would not allow that. He knows that you want to do the right thing. I think your hand won't heal because you are so upset, but I think your upset comes from wanting to do what is right. God does not ask for anything more. But you cannot do everything, you cannot please everyone. Peace will come to your heart, and healing to your hand, when you choose what you really believe God wants of you and put other things aside."

The old man was quiet for a long moment as he looked toward Michael in the darkness. "No matter what anyone else thinks, you must follow what is deepest and truest in your own heart. That is put there by God Himself, God's truth has a sound and feel like no other, that is how we can tell it from all that is false . . ."

He removed his hand, turned away. "Whatever truth you decide is yours, whatever path you follow, will not be easy. We must follow true love, yes, but the path is harsh and uphill. Only love lets you climb it. Remember that." He paused deliberately, peacefully. "For your penance, say the Our Father and the Hail Mary, say them for these dear dead and suffering children, and pray for the church, too, that it may find a good Holy Father who will, despite his human frailty, lead it wisely. And do not be angry with the church in your heart. Now make a good act of contrition."

There was a noise beyond them of a door opening, of switches being thrown. As the old priest raised his hand to make the sign of the cross, a simple bishop's ring gleamed in the light that filtered down the gallery of chess-piece tombs.

THREE

A preoccupied Cardinal Bouyer of Marseilles closed the office door of the prefect of the Congregation for the Doctrine of the Faith and walked slowly down the hallway to the old-fashioned birdcage elevator. Joseph Cardinal Caldwell of Boston had seemed totally absorbed when he departed an hour earlier. Inside, Cardinal Kiejson was concluding a clipped, monsyllabic telephone conversation with Ambassador Wingate as his secretary, Monsignor Fina, handed him a folder. He read the note pinned to it as he hung up. "You say that Monsignor Lanza asked me to review this? And that Cardinal Casey has already approved this?"

"When Monsignor Tracy's petition was first submitted," the aide responded, "almost two years ago."

Cardinal Kiejson's eyes dropped to the *International Herald Tribune* that lay on his desk. DUTCH AND AMERICAN CARDINALS THOUGHT CHOICES IN CONCLAVE, the headline read above their pictures, Casey's by Bachrach, ten years old and a shade too formal. Kiejson's was one of his favorites, outdoors, the wind ruffling his hair, lifting his cape dramatically. The Dutch cardinal scanned the text. Casey was described as "traditional, financially able, shrewd, controversial," while he was called "a strong orthodox leader whose agenda is dominated by plans for the Catholic Church to emerge strong and unified in the twenty-first century." Kiejson checked his watch, eleven thirty, he was due at the first general meeting of the cardinals in half an hour. "Is there anything else, Monsignor?" Kiejson glanced down again at the newspaper.

"The meeting, Your Eminence, at twelve."

"Mmm." The Dutchman pushed the thin paper to the corner of his desk, removed his glasses, rubbed his eyes. "It is very important to know exactly *how* to read things." He replaced his glasses, looked up at his assistant. "Tell me something, Monsignor," Kiejson said, leaning back in his chair. "You know many American priests and bishops. What do they really think of Cardinal Casey?"

"Your Eminence, I've had only limited contact with Americans in my work."

The cardinal examined his secretary, turning him slowly in the CAT scanner of his observer's shrewdness, smiled appreciatively. "That is a careful answer, Monsignor."

"I don't think I *can* answer your question."

"On the contrary, your caution *is* the answer." The cardinal pushed his chair back, stood up.

"Your Eminence, Monsignor Tracy's file. Monsignor Lanza asked if . . ."

"I will go back to the apartment during the afternoon break," Kiejson said, moving around his desk toward the door. "Please bring any important messages or mail over there."

Across the city at the Hilton, Michael had just awakened Ann back in Chicago. "Yes, I *am* sure . . ."

"I have some patients this morning, then I'm supposed to go to this heart seminar."

"Think of *this* as a heart seminar. Ours. I'm decided, absolutely, once and for all." He took a deep breath. "Come right away. I'll get a priest to marry us; we've waited long enough."

Ann paused, excited, unbelieving, uncertain that she could trust this sudden resolution of their long frustration.

"Annie, it's the *right* thing to do. It's the truest thing."

"Are you sure you can really leave the priesthood? Are you sure you'll be happy? Doing it this way, I mean?"

"This is straightforward, that's what I suddenly realized. That's why it's right. It doesn't involve any deception, no tricks, no complicated treasure maps telling you to take three steps forward, two back, wait for the full moon and dig under the fourth tree from the left. I know this is right because there's nothing complicated about it. I should have realized that a long time ago."

"Mike, do you *really* know what you're doing?"

"Why do you keep asking that?"

"You're such an idealist. And a romantic, too. You've idealized the church, you've romanticized the priesthood . . ."

"I know what I'm doing."

"You've romanticized our love . . ."

"What's wrong with that?"

"Nothing, it's wonderful. But you have to be sure that now you're not romanticizing leaving the priesthood. I couldn't take it—do you understand how I feel?—if you woke up some morning thinking you made a mistake, that . . ."

"Ann," Mike cut in, "I'm asking for your hand in marriage. Will you be my wife?"

"Yes, yes."

"I love you more than anything else. I'm not just escaping my old life, I want to begin one with you . . ."

"I love you, too, Mike. I guess I just can't believe we'll actually be married after all the delays."

"I'll get one of my priest friends to marry us. That's Catholic enough for me. Now you've got to catch the plane tonight. It's hard to get reservations because of all the excitement, so I made them for you through Jimbo's office, they have a contact at TWA."

"*Jimbo's* office?"

"Now get packed, and I'll pick you up in the morning."

"Was there anything in the Chicago paper?"

"Yes, Tom, your picture on the front page, a big story. They say you and that Dutch friend of yours are the likely candidates."

Cardinal Casey waved his secretary, Monsignor Hawkins, away from the door to his bedroom. The young man made a hand signal. The meeting begins in twenty minutes.

The cardinal held his hand over the telephone. "Wait for me at the car."

"What's that?"

"Nothing, just Monsignor Hawkins. The cardinals are meeting at noon today. I have to be there, of course. I told Boston we'd pick him up, Cardinal Caldwell, that is."

"Is he for you?"

"He told me so the other night. I'm counting on him to talk to the other Americans. He has good friends in France and Spain."

"What about this Dutchman?"

"Franz? Oh, I think he knows that it's time to elect an American."

"I wonder. Just looking at his picture in the paper makes me nervous."

"Oh, Missy."

"I'm serious. Little things tell a lot. Well, when you had this Dutchman visiting your house in Chicago the year before last, I was waiting for you down in the main hallway. His nibs was in the parlor, didn't know anybody was watching. And he was looking for a mirror, needed to comb that silver hair of his, oh, just right. I watched him primping there for five minutes."

"Missy, that's an exaggeration."

"Not much, I'll tell you."

"It's the Irish in you, Missy, you're always looking for something to criticize, something to worry about."

"You'll see."

"Look, Missy, I'd like you to be here."

"I'm planning on it. I wouldn't miss it. I got the ticket you had the chancery office send."

"You'll be here in the morning, then?"

"Yes, Tom. I can't miss the day you become pope."

"Yes, Missy, I . . ."

"Yes?"

"I . . . I'll have you picked up."

FOUR

"Josef, this looks like a bookie parlor."

"A *bookie* parlor?" Beck surveyed the machine- and paper-cluttered Da Vinci suite. "I do not understand."

"American talk, Chicago talk, it doesn't matter."

"I'm glad you came down, Michael," the German theologian said, running his hand through his tousled hair. "The time is short. We need a good article in the American press, yes?"

"I've come here to ask you about some other matters."

"Yes, yes." The Rhine gurgled in Beck's voice as he cleared a stack of magazines and position papers off the living room couch. "To sit, please." Mike checked the corners of the room as he sat down. There was a computer, a Xerox machine, a pile of news releases spilling off a card table. Beck seemed suddenly a noble, if misled, warrior, the kind of romantic reformer Michael had encountered on fruitless missions in a number of settings—the wistful scripture scholar at Catholic University in Washington who had led an attempted coup against the then bishop rector only to be ousted from the faculty himself, the seminary professor who tried to expose the mishandled finances at his institution and ended up in a country parish. Michael thought of Dollfuss and Dubček, of the Hungarian Freedom Fighters, of doomed efforts at nobility in Iron Curtain countries. He thought of Chicago and of his own father's sturdy innocence in the face of forces that didn't care about it at all. Michael felt sorry for the German theologian about to be overwhelmed and made to look foolish, to lose more than he could ever gain by this quixotic effort. Humor and sarcasm would never convince Beck that he was taking on the biggest windmill of them all.

"I'm glad you are here," Beck said airily, confidently. "We are ready for the big push. There is a news conference tomorrow, our papers are being distributed to each cardinal, we have made valuable contacts with the Third World . . ."

"Hold on," Michael said, raising his bandaged hand. "If I can't talk you out of this adventure, maybe you can help me."

"But surely you will join our cause. The thought that either Kiejson or Casey should become pope, well, a just God would not allow it."

"Ironic observation won't have any real effect, Josef."

"What?"

"Being right, even stylishly right, theologically right, won't help your cause. It seldom does."

"We shall see . . ."

"Now I have some other matters to discuss with you."

Beck nodded. "Yes?"

"First of all, I'd like some more information about Mother Hilda."

The lines in Beck's good boy face softened as his expression went slack. "Yes . . ."

"What do you really know about her? Where did she come from? What is she up to?"

Beck pursed his lips, lowered his head, spoke in a grave voice. "I cannot speak of Mother Hilda, please excuse me."

"What's the matter, Josef? I'll keep it all off the record."

"Mother Hilda, this very morning, came by, that is all I can say."

"Come on, Josef, no need to dodge, this isn't Nuremberg." Michael regretted the wisecrack immediately.

Beck sat motionlessly, in the grip of some enormous Germanic gravity field. "I can't talk, Michael. Please."

Michael rose, walked around the couch, looked down at Beck, marveling at feeling sympathy for him twice in less than ten minutes. What had happened? He paused, thinking of his own experience with the seeress. Of course! Mother Hilda's been to confession to Josef here, that's why he can't talk, she's got him tied up under the seal of the sacrament, she's cornering the market on forgiveness. And closing the mouths, including my own, of anybody who knows anything about her.

Beck raised his eyes to Michael's. "Can we talk now, perhaps, about the news conference?"

Michael didn't know what to say. Everything that came to his mind would make things worse. He smiled. "I was going to ask you to marry me but this doesn't seem to be the moment for that." He laughed. Beck joined in uneasily, "*Ja, ja,* Michael, always the one for humor at a hard moment . . ."

Michael flashed a peace sign with the fingers of his left hand and hurried out of the suite.

Joseph Cardinal Caldwell, fifty-two, dark-haired, his handsome features chiseled by jogging into spurious ascetic leanness, climbed into the backseat of Casey's Mercedes, threw up a smile thin as a movie storefront. "Good of you to pick me up, Tom."

"You look good, Joe. How's your mother?"

"Eighty-two," Caldwell said as the car oozed into the traffic, "but she's at the eight o'clock Mass every morning."

"The nuns take good care of her, I suppose."

"It's a comfort . . ." Caldwell glanced out the window at the city, heavy-looking, sepia-tinted, a stereopticon slide of sights peered at by linen-suited travelers a century before.

"Have you," Casey asked, looking straight ahead, one fan to another at the ballpark, not wanting to miss a play, "talked to our friends yet?"

"How long," Caldwell asked, turning toward Casey, "is it, your mother's been dead now?"

"Joe, is there something bothering you?"

Caldwell rearranged himself on the hearselike cushions, explored the inside of his hollowed cheek with his tongue. "Let me ask you a question, Tom."

Casey raised his eyebrows. "Yes?"

"I hate to bring this up. It isn't that *I'm* curious or uncertain, but, well, it's the kind of question I've been getting from other . . . well, *other* people. They want to know about this Vatican Bank business. What with the collapse of DioGuardia's empire, and his shooting himself, and the rumors . . ."

"The rumors that I endorsed the investments in DioGuardia's Transalpine Investing? Is that what, as you call them, *other people* want to know about?"

Caldwell ran a finger inside his Roman collar, nodded.

"I'm glad you brought that up, Joe. It should be brought out into the open before the conclave begins. Left in the dark, it's a *very* dangerous rumor, it could be very harmful. The truth is simple. I had nothing to do with it, I had no role in supporting DioGuardia's empire or those holding companies that went down like a house of cards when his paper was called in."

Caldwell's eyes brightened as he looked directly at the Chicago archbishop. "Is there *anything*—not that *I* doubt your word, but you know how these people are—is there any way to back that up?"

"Okay. What would they think if they knew that the *pope* vindicated me, that he was to sign the papers that cleared me the afternoon he died?"

Caldwell held his eyes on Casey.

"Ask Franz," Casey said almost jovially, "he can tell you, *he* was there, *he* had the papers."

The archbishop of Boston wrinkled his forehead, rubbed his chin.

"Franz," Casey boomed, chasing a ghost, "can tell you everything."

Caldwell turned his head, looked out the window, frowning.

As carefully as if he were working adhesive tape loose, Franz Josef Cardinal Kiejson pulled himself away from a circle of confreres, peered between and above their nodding heads, arched himself slightly, not quite tiptoe, scanned the murmuring hall, checked the entrance. Cardinal Maestrini fussily rearranged the bottle of mineral water before him on the dais-like head table, gestured impatiently, operatically, for order. Cardinals, however, constituted a difficult crowd to seat. They were accustomed to take their places only when they felt like it, mostly before or after everybody else. Della Femina, the cardinal archbishop of Naples, bent toward two fellow princes below the dais, smiled broadly as he told a joke, chauvinistic and almost as old as the city, listing the three jobs even Jesus wouldn't take on: to hear children's confessions, to preach a retreat to nuns, and to arrange a procession of bishops. The cardinals parted reluctantly, hands extended, almost touching, it was hard to get down to business.

Kiejson paid a tithe of *abstracted* attention to the archbishop of Lima at his side, keeping his eyes fixed on the door. Casey and Caldwell entered, the archbishop of Boston, eyes lowered, maybe a step behind, in the furtive style of lovers leaving a hotel, you couldn't really tell what had passed between them. The buzz trailed off and the cardinals began to sit in slow motion, chatting, sending greetings, tag-end messages, exchanging the smiles and winks of high order male bonding, slowly, slowly, all the way down to the brocaded seats of their chairs. Cardinal Solieri touched Kiejson's arm. The startled Dutch cardinal forced a smile. "How good to see you, *Eminenza.*"

"I would like to talk to you," Solieri whispered, the last cardinal standing in the settling-down hall.

"Of course, of course, but . . ."

"After this general meeting, yes?"

"Well . . ."

"It is very important . . ."

Maestrini pointed toward Solieri from his position of command, murmured a joke in Italian. Our archivist has been in the library too long, *va bene.* Laughter rippled as the princes turned their attention toward the old man. Solieri's face reddened, he backed haltingly away from Kiejson, bumping other cardinals as he moved toward his own chair. Maestrini, his face turning expressionless, plain and white as plaster, signed himself, recited a brief prayer in Latin above the lowered heads of the College of Cardinals, at last, and variously, convened.

Church historian Jack Parker had agreed to have lunch with Monsignor Tracy. The Californian, forty years old and built like a lineman who had moved to the announcer's booth, grinned from a puffy tanned face, waved a Bloody Mary at Tracy, urging him toward a corner table in the trattoria. "Did you hear that Obergruppenführer Beck is having a preliminary press conference, kind of a teaser, this afternoon?"

"So that's why there are so many reporters and television crews around," Tracy replied, snapping open the flag of his napkin as he sat down.

"Herr Josef knows how to draw a crowd. I'm surprised he isn't holding it at night in a stadium with searchlights and free beer for pure-blooded Aryans." Parker chuckled, signaled for the waiter.

"Jack," Tracy began hesitantly, "I wanted to ask you for a favor . . ."

Parker nodded, handed his empty glass to the waiter, ordered another Bloody Mary and lunch for both of them. "What is it?"

Michael bent forward slightly, swiftly explained his plans to leave the priesthood, his two years of frustration in getting his rescript approved, his decision to get married anyway. Would Jack Parker officiate, as a pastor might in a such a situation?

The waiter placed the fresh drink in front of Parker. The Californian lowered his eyes for a moment, then raised the glass, dipped it toward Tracy. "Sure I'll witness your marriage, why the hell wouldn't I? *Sacramenta propter homines.* The sacraments are for the people. Besides, I only *witness* it, the man and woman *marry* each other . . ."

Tracy felt suddenly lighter, the way he always did flopping heavy gold-threaded mass vestments back onto the sacristy case. "Jack," he said in a slightly chipped tone, "I, Ann and I, we'll always be grateful to you."

Parker winked, sipped his drink.

"I've talked to Brother Louie Faerber," Mike said, "he's the head of the Word of Mercy brothers, they have a house up here on Monte Mario. You probably know him. He said we could use the chapel there, tomorrow at noon. Louie's got a friend who's taking care of the civil papers."

"Great, I think it's great. Better than being part of this monkey shit committee trying to fix the papal election." Parker tasted his drink again as the waiter brought their lunches. "You know why Beck and his gang won't get anywhere? They're plenty naive, but they're not evil enough. That's their greatest weakness, insufficient evil."

Tracy eyed Parker uneasily. "Jack, it's really good of you to do this."

"That's what priests are for," Parker answered, a slur rising from his sentence like a shark fin out of the water. The Californian crimped his brow. "You're lucky, Jack, you know that, don't you? You're lucky if you love somebody, and if they love you back. Damn lucky . . ." He attacked his lunch.

"Would you mind if I ducked out of here? Lunch is on me, but I've got a lot of things to do."

"I understand," Parker said, draining his glass, "and lunch is on me, I mean, on the archdiocese of San Francisco. I'll see you tomorrow. Word of Mercy House, twelve noon, right up the street."

Michael hurried across the lobby. The reporters were leaving too. Another explosion, he heard one of them say.

"Jimbo?"

"Yeah?"

"Catch your murderer yet?"

"There's all kinds of killers, little brother, some people I know actually use heartbreak as a weapon." The journalist brother paused, leaned forward on both elbows, pitching himself above the front-running cardinals staring at him from the *International Trib* on his desk. "You talked to our mother, I understand . . ."

"I explained everything as well as I could. It wasn't easy."

"What do you want, the Purple Heart? Can't you even hear yourself *now?* The only thing you can talk about is how hard it was for *you.* How about her?"

"The reason it was hard, Jimbo, was because I *knew* I was hurting her. Maybe you did, too, when you left Maureen."

Jimbo Tracy sighed, crooked the phone receiver between his chin and his right shoulder, he felt sour inside, nothing Alka-Seltzer could fix.

"Jimbo, Ann and I are getting married tomorrow. Father Jack Parker from San Francisco is going to officiate. Noon at the Word of Mercy House chapel, on Monte Mario. I'd like you to come."

The journalist swallowed hard, goddam, goddamit anyway, rubbed his eyes with his left hand, felt a twitch of pain in his forehead. "Why don't you just go off and do this somewhere else? Somewhere where I won't have to know anything about it?"

"I'd like you to be best man." Michael's voice cracked. "You're still the best man I know . . ."

"Mike, what are you trying to do, kill me?" Jimbo plucked the phone from his shoulder, stood up, circled his chair, took a deep breath. "For Christ's sake, I *can't* go, don't ask me to."

"Jimbo . . ."

"I *can't.* You go ahead, do what you have to, okay?" He took another deep breath. "I just don't want to know anything about it . . ." Jimbo Tracy hung up, stood for a long moment, sent his chair spinning with a kick, stalked into the outer office, silencing the banter of the staff, what's eating him now, slammed the door explosively.

FIVE

Cardinal Kiejson made a choppy gesture, commanding as much as inviting Ambassador Wingate to sit down. The Dutchman gave off electricity, his white hair bristled alertly. "What," he asked sharply, "what in God's name is happening? Another bombing this very afternoon as the cardinals were holding their general meeting . . ." He stood, held by some inner vision, one hand on his chair. "In the Borghese Gardens . . ."

"Nobody was injured," Wingate replied dryly, "and let me assure you that my government is duly concerned."

"As well they should be. This is monstrous, these bombings *must* be brought under control." Kiejson lowered himself stiffly into his chair.

"Terrorism, Your Eminence, does not turn on and off as the water tap does."

"What is that supposed to mean?"

"We cannot, Your Eminence, with all respect, solve the problem this afternoon. I can, however, give you assurances that the matter will be taken care of. There will be no bombing during the conclave. It is, if I may say so, *our* business."

"And the conclave is *mine.*"

Wingate flashed a card-player's smile. "Not quite, not quite. We are interested in your election, you must remember, and feel that we can exercise considerable influence, subtly of course, on your behalf. Indeed, we are prepared to do whatever you ask of us."

"Which is simple. Stay out of it."

"But, Your Eminence," Wingate replied calmly, "we are already in it."

Kiejson flushed, accenting the scar on his jaw, remained silent.

"Have you, Your Eminence, spoken with the archbishop of Chicago?"

"Not yet," Kiejson responded, gutturally. "I was hoping . . ."

"Hope, of course, is part of your business. It does not, however, play much of a role in that of the United States Attorney for the Northern District of Illinois in America. He has been authorized by the Attorney General to proceed with his inquiry into the failure of Lincolnland National in Chicago, a unit of DioGuardia's empire. The Vatican Bank, of which Cardinal Casey was a director and adviser, was apparently negligent in not spotting this fraud and doing something about it. The investors lost over two hundred million dollars. The inquiry will, of course, focus directly on Cardinal Casey. Unless . . ."

Kiejson looked darkly at the ambassador, inflected a grunt into a question.

"Unless Casey withdraws as a candidate, unequivocally and irrevocably, in the conclave. This is unconditional, no bargaining is possible." Wingate glanced at his watch. "Even as we speak, the U.S. Attorney is briefing the archdiocesan lawyer, a Mr. Hampton, who will fly to Rome tonight to explain the situation to the cardinal. You go into conclave the day after tomorrow. Cardinal Casey, who has considerable Third World support, must withdraw and shift his votes to you. I suggest that you speak to him as soon as possible about this."

Kiejson's eyes trailed Wingate rising from his chair. "I . . . I will speak to him this evening."

"May I say that I am amazed, Your Eminence, that you seem surprised by what I have said? You knew very well that it might come to this, that at the point where our visions converged—the need for a new crusade, to forge a spiritual and armored phalanx to destroy communism for good—you appeared to understand that it was a mission that was not without ambiguity, that, once initiated, there would be no allowances for reconsiderations, no, shall we say, retreat into sanctuary. We expect *all* partners to honor their commitments. You do understand?"

"Yes, yes." Kiejson got up slowly. "It is just that these bombings, I did not anticipate anything like this . . ." He walked slowly at Wingate's side to the door of his apartment.

The American bowed, as if to kiss the cardinal's ring. Kiejson withdrew his hand swiftly. Wingate smiled, a hard-to-figure smile. "Good evening, Your Eminence." He hurried down the creaking, shadowed stairway, ignored the attendant in the lobby, pushed open the entrance door, almost bowling over Kiejson's just arriving secretary, Monsignor Fina, stepped without a backward glance into his waiting car.

Cardinal Kiejson stood tensely in front of his computer, bit his lower lip lightly as he switched the machine on, gazed without focus until it beeped, reached for and inserted the program disk. The sound of a key in the door. Kiejson turned as it opened. "Ah, Monsignor . . ."

"The mail, Your Eminence, and a great many messages," Monsignor Fina said, angling a load of envelopes and packages through the door, kicking it not quite closed with his foot. He emptied two bulging brown envelopes onto the coffee table as the cardinal searched for the disk he wanted.

"Everybody wants to interview you."

"Oh?" Kiejson turned toward his secretary, holding a disk between the thumb and forefinger of his ring hand. "Who exactly?"

"Well, to start with, the *Times* of every place, New York, London, Singapore . . ."

Kiejson raised his eyebrows appreciatively, slipped the disk into the computer, bent slightly, tapped RED HAT on the keyboard.

"And Mother Hilda wants to see you this afternoon."

The Dutch cardinal whirled abruptly, his shadow falling across the pale bloom of the computer screen. *"What?"* Kiejson scowled. "Of course you told her that it was impossible . . ."

"May I say, Your Eminence, she did not ask me for permission. I told her it was really out of the question, but she didn't pay much attention to me."

"She," the distressed Kiejson snapped, "she *cannot* come *here*. We do not have women here, *never*, except the nuns in the kitchen. No, *no* . . ."

"She told me to tell you that 'The visited are blessed more than the visitor.' "

Kiejson threw up his hands, shook his head. "I simply do not have time . . ."

An insistent rap on the almost closed door; Kiejson stared at it, then at his aide. The rap grew louder. "Monsignor," the cardinal said, "I am going to use your rooms for a while. I expect you to handle, uh, to treat Mother Hilda courteously but to postpone her visit."

The door opened, freezing the cardinal's hand just as he reached for the door leading to his aide's quarters. Mother Hilda, arms folded beneath her mantle, stood, slender and intense, in the doorframe. "Go," she snapped, to two nun companions who dropped from sight like felled birds, a sound like fluttering wings rising up the stairwell behind them. "Your Eminence," Hilda intoned, drifting across the threshold, "I beg of you, may I have your blessing?"

Kiejson pulled his hand, reluctantly, painfully, away from the door, that awful expression of almost escaping on his face as the seeress slid to the floor in front of him. He stared down at her bowed head, looked at his secretary, Do something, monsignor, anything . . .

"Your blessing for my poor soul and my work."

Kiejson took a deep breath, traced a cross in the air, muttered the Latin words hurriedly, edged away as Mother Hilda rose to her feet. She looked at Monsignor Fina, no mistaking that expression, You will leave, please. The priest half nodded, slipped through the door, and closed it softly.

The Dutch cardinal moved swiftly to the far side of the piled-high coffee table, stood behind his easy chair, the screen of his computer glowing dully, expectantly, at his side. His voice was constricted. "You asked to see me?"

"No, Your Eminence, it is the Lord who wished you to see me."

"I am not as confident as you of His wishes."

The seeress moved slowly across the room, her eyes clouded, remote as a distant galaxy, fixed on Kiejson. "Do you know what I told the Holy Father?"

The cardinal nodded, felt cracked leather on his perspiring hands as he grasped the top of his chair.

"I warned the Holy Father. I felt . . ." She lowered her head, as if stabbed by pain, pointed to her heart. "I felt *in here* that he was in danger, that death, death would come in disguise, that I had seen it ride into a city once before, that the danger was greatest if . . ."

"He died a *natural* death," Kiejson said firmly. "The Lord called him home. Surely you can accept that."

She raised her head, looked around the room, then at the coffee table. Her eyes stopped at the snow crystal, half hidden in the papers. Her tone became dreamy. "The snow, yes . . ." She looked around the room again. "This place, so plain . . ."

Kiejson watched her as she turned slowly, taking in the details of his apartment.

"Yes," she said softly, "it is very much like . . ." She broke off in mid-sentence, gazed at Kiejson again.

"What is it you want, Mother?"

She broke her reverie, spoke huskily. "The great mystery of life is discovered in waiting." She paused, lowered her head slightly. "The world rejects waiting, is that not so, Your Eminence?"

Kiejson nodded, watched her, energetically willing her not to come closer.

She raised her head, spoke in a more familiar tone. "If we understand waiting, we understand all of life. The problem, Your Eminence, is that some people wait too little." She looked directly into his face, let his eyes find hers. "And some people wait too long."

"If you will excuse me, Mother Hilda, I am very busy these days. What do you want to talk to me about?"

The seeress shifted her arms beneath the folds of her habit, firmed up her voice, telling, not asking. "You, Your Eminence, although you are expected by others to be chosen, *you* must not try to become pope." She glided forward, stood directly across the table from Kiejson.

He stood his ground. "Nobody *tries* to become pope . . ."

She stared silently, intensely, at the half sphere of the snow crystal visible in the clutter of the table that separated them, as if to set the papers and books ablaze or conjure up a presence, burrowing it up out of some other time. The cardinal dug his fingers into the back of the chair, held his ground.

"Franz," she said softly, sadly, "Franz, have you forgotten?"

"You are upset today, Jimmy . . ."

"Forget it, will you?"

Angelica Tomai crooked herself up on one arm, looked down at Jimbo's set, staring face, tiptoed with her fingers on his chest, fashioned a whorl of hair.

"Stop it. It doesn't help." He rolled away from her, reached for a cigarette, lit it, lay back on the pillow as he inhaled.

"You are very angry today, Jimmy. Or very guilty."

"You're a mind reader," he said acidly, "you can take it up when you get older, dress like a gypsy, con the rich and famous . . ."

"Jimmy," she said with sudden firmness, "Jimmy, do you come here just to make a fool of me?"

"Let's not get philosophical. One thing I didn't come here for is philosophy." He reached over, flicked ashes into a glass ashtray on the night table.

"I mean it. You must treat all women the way you treat me. As some sort of lovely convenience."

Jimbo frowned, looked at her in genuine puzzlement. "Please, Angelica, no lines from your greatest scenes today. You're a great lady, I'm sorry if you don't like my style. You put everything on a business basis the other day . . ."

"A woman wants a man to hear the things not spoken. But you, you treat everything with a joke. Don't you know how that makes me feel?" She slipped out of bed, donned a robe, stared down at him. "You don't, do you? You don't have any concern for how I might feel right now. Why don't you just get out?"

Jimbo raised himself on one arm. "Get out? Fine." He swung his legs over the side of the bed, pressed his cigarette into the ashtray, reached silently for his clothes. "You want tenderness; I think there's a murderer loose in Rome. Can't you understand that? I thought the count might be public-spirited enough to give me some more help."

The actress sighed, stepped to her dresser, picked up a pearl-backed brush, tugged at her lustrous black hair. "I don't know anything about it."

"Come on, he wouldn't have warned you about reporters if you didn't know something."

"The only thing he's said to me lately," she replied in a tight voice, "is that there's nothing on paper, nobody put anything on paper . . ."

"More insights from Italy's foremost medical genius. No wonder you two get along; thought doesn't interfere with your relationship."

"You said you were leaving." Angelica studied Jimbo's broad back as he worked himself into his shorts. "That's *all* Tootie said. No paper, that's the whole problem."

"Where the hell *is* Tootie, anyway?" Jimbo picked up his shirt, plunged his right arm into a rumpled sleeve. "I've been trying to reach your friend all day, but there's no answer at his office, nobody knows where he is."

"If you ever come back, Jimmy, don't bring any work. Or any guilt, either. All you bring here is anger that has nothing to do with me."

"Ciao, Angie," the journalist said, picking up his coat and tie. "Ask your Latin lover if the missing paper happens to be the pope's prescription for Quinidine, will you?"

"On second thought, don't come back until . . ."

"Until what?"

"Until you grow up. Tootie, in many ways, is more grown-up than you are."

He turned by the door, stuffed his tie into his side pocket, shook his head. "I liked you better the last time." He closed the door just as she threw her hairbrush at him.

SIX

Cardinal Kiejson sat bolt upright during the late afternoon general congregation of the College of Cardinals, the perfect candidate right down to his battle-ribbon scar. He appeared to be peering out of the hatch of a submarine that had just broken through the ceiling of ocean above a sunken enemy fleet. This iron look was, however, a function of willpower. Kiejson wondered if the other cardinals, busily observing him, pretending not to, could read his thoughts, as he as a child supposed Dutch elders could by peering at the back of his blond, bowl-cut head. Can they possibly sense what has taken place this afternoon, he worried, are signals slipping through my grasp? Mother Hilda's face floated into his consciousness, Mother Hilda *now* . . .

The cardinals suddenly scraped their chairs back from the long tables, Maestrini rattled off a concluding prayer, *agimus tibi gratias,* the threads of Kiejson's absorption snapped abruptly, he rose solemnly, smiled as the archbishop of Lima made a friendly remark to him. His confreres crowded around him as he made his way slowly between the tables, nodding, smiling, Yes, yes, *Eminenza,* only one more full day of this before the conclave would begin.

Cardinal Casey chatted amiably with a knot of Third World cardinals, he felt better about things, the other red-clad colleagues seemed genuinely supportive, it was time for an American, what is Lima talking to Franz for? From the dais, Maestrini the *camerlengo* watched grimly as the two favorites were drawn toward each other by the converging tides of their colleagues near the back of the hall. Maestrini picked up his papers, sniffed, and walked stiffly but rapidly up a side aisle, avoiding the cardinals clustered at the entrance. Cardinal Solieri stood alone in the foyer of the old building. *"Eminenza,"* he called to the unheeding Maestrini as the *camerlengo*, surrounded now by aides, swept past him and out the front door. Solieri backed away as Casey and Kiejson, now almost side by side, floated slowly by on the crimson ecclesiastical river. He watched through the open doors as the Dutch and the American cardinals paused to exchange a few words in front of a purring limousine. How different they are, Solieri mused, and how alike . . .

Michael had talked again to Ann on the phone to tell her that everything was set, I can't believe it, she said, I never thought we'd really be able to have each other. Michael felt an extraordinary surge of longing, and, as he left his hotel room, a strange sense of divestment from his clerical persona, as if he were leaving a ghost behind who filled out, as the invisible man did, his black suit and collar, lounging about emptily in them, waiting for the defrockers to take away what remained of his ecclesiastical life.

Two reporters hailed him as he cut through the lobby, what can you tell us about Josef Beck's committee, he's promising big revelations tomorrow, maybe something on the inside story of Pope Jean's death, and that you have a message from Mother Hilda, what can you tell us? They pressed Michael despite his protestations, I'm innocent I tell you, and I don't have any messages from Hilda, Fatima, or anywhere else. It wasn't easy to break away from them, madness, Michael thought, was balling itself up like a tornado in the summer Roman air, tombs might split open and ancient saints and Caesars wander the streets, the shades of Garibaldi and Mussolini, perhaps the Borgias would show up, anything could happen in this brooding, straining, something-about-to-be-born atmosphere, it was definitely time to pass through the city gates and into a new life.

"Michael!" Josef Beck coming through the entrance door that was Michael's goal, "I must speak with you." Beck, his gold curls jangling, took Tracy's arm, waved the reporters away. "We must talk *in private,* yes?"

"Right here is the best I can do, if you don't mind those reporters trying to read lips."

"Michael," Beck almost hissed, "why didn't you *tell* me?" The German theologian maneuvered Mike to a couch against the far wall. "Why didn't you let me know that you were leaving the priesthood, that you are getting married *tomorrow?"*

"Your invitation must be in the mail."

"I'm serious. Have you thought of the impact of this on everything we're trying to do?"

"We? I'm not on your committee. Don't talk *we."*

"You are just as good as a member, you have the same sympathies, you were to write an article for the *Times,* yes?"

"No, I told you that several times. And who told you I was getting married?"

"It doesn't matter. Listen, we *counted* on you. How will it look, on the very day of our big public presentation, if the word gets out that you have left, that you are being married in Rome itself? It is a question of our credibility, the credibility of the whole cause . . ."

"It might enhance it."

"No, no, please, this is a grave matter. What will the cardinals say when they hear of our proposals for the conclave? They will point to *you* and say, *there, that's* the kind of committee this is, and they will write us off! After all this work! Michael, for the greater good, you must postpone this wedding. Please, for the cause of a reformed church, put this off . . ."

"I *have* put it off, Josef. For *too* long. You're making this too melodramatic. *Nobody* will pay any attention to my marriage. Not unless *you* make an issue out of it."

"Michael, I regard you highly, I have great respect for you and your work. If you postpone this, I will witness your marriage myself. Later on, that is. A little time, it is all I ask."

Michael stood up. "That's what I've been hearing for years. You Germans have funny ideas about time. A little time to you is three acts of *Parsifal,* a couple of World Wars . . ." He took a step away, looked back at the theologian. "Why don't you call in your fellow landsperson, Mother Hilda, have her speak up on your behalf, maybe whip up a miracle, she'll keep them distracted, nobody will give any thought to me."

"Michael," Beck said, plucking at Tracy's sleeve just above his bandaged right hand, "I'm very serious. I will not speak of Hilda. Besides, I do not think of her as a landsperson of mine. All I'm asking is that you wait until after the cardinals enter the conclave. Don't give me your final answer now, yes? Think about it, please."

Michael pulled his arm free. "Josef, old friend, I appreciate your concern. I would like you not to speak about my private life. It isn't a public matter anymore. *Verstehen Sie?*"

"Thank you, Michael, thank you very much."

Michael sighed, a German head is harder than paving stone, old Denny used to say, except you can't grow grass through it. And just when I was beginning to feel sorry for Josef. He turned and headed for the main entrance. Good old Jack Parker. Big heart. Big mouth, too.

"A long day, Thomas," Kiejson said, pointing toward the familiar battered chair opposite his own. The Chicago cardinal nodded, sat down carefully, waved off the silver cigar box proffered by the Dutchman. "Maestrini keeps his counsel well," Kiejson said, standing by his chair as he chose and lit his rationed cigar. "In public, anyway." He exhaled smoke into a dull, tense silence. Casey tugged the bunched pleating of his cassock free beneath him. "Is there something in particular you wanted to talk about, Franz?"

Kiejson circled his chair, glanced at his humming, blank-faced computer. He had forgotten it during Mother Hilda's visit and left it on when he hurried to the late afternoon general congregation. "What do you make of old Solieri?"

"I couldn't make any sense out of that little speech he gave this evening. What was that all about, going on about truth as our first commitment in the conclave?"

Kiejson shrugged. "He is like a soldier who has hidden in the hills for years, not knowing that the war is over, a man who hasn't talked to anybody but himself in a long time."

"But, of course, you didn't ask me here to talk about the archivist."

"No, no . . ." Kiejson cleared his throat, adjusted his tone. "But Solieri does illustrate the uninformed character of many of the electors." He spoke very slowly. "And we cannot enter this conclave uninformed." Casey touched the bridge of his glasses, looked attentively at the suddenly solemn, reluctant Dutchman. "It is very clear," Kiejson said in a low, urgent voice, "that there are only two serious candidates . . ." He flicked the ash from his cigar. "The *camerlengo* has even admitted as much to some of his old friends. He does not like it but he is a realist." He puffed on his cigar again. "That leaves the two leading candidates in a rather peculiar position." Casey sat perfectly still, his face impassive.

"Many cardinals have spoken to me about this. I suppose to you as well." Kiejson inspected Casey's eyes for reaction, nothing there. "I might say, Thomas, that I have had conversations with your good friend, *eminenza* of Boston, about this, too." He spoke earnestly in the now sticky quiet. "Our friends in the Sacred College are concerned, Thomas, that unless the choice between the two leaders is resolved promptly, we are headed for deadlock. I hardly need explain the disastrous possibilities that could follow from that. Some think that a compromise candidate would be necessary, and *that* opens up all manner of dangerous possibilities."

"Franz," Casey said calmly, coldly, "let me remind you of something. The time has come for an American to be pope. We've been paying all your bills for a hundred years, we are the strongest Catholic country in the world, and we're not even a Catholic country. Cardinals from all over the world understand that the church has done very well in America. The church will do well in the next century with an American leader. I will fight very hard for an American candidate. It means a great deal for my country."

"And for *yourself* too, Thomas?" Kiejson's scar jerked electrically. "You would like to be the pope, that is so, isn't it?"

"No less than you do. No more than you do."

"Thomas . . ." Kiejson sighed. "Believe me, this is not a *personal* matter. I would renounce my chances immediately if I thought you would then be elected." He balanced his cigar on the ashtray. "But *that* is the point. *You cannot be elected.*" He stepped toward the computer, sighed again. *"You cannot be elected.* I doubt that any American can be elected."

"You don't know what you're talking about . . ."

"Let us see," Kiejson said slowly, his right index finger poised above the computer RETURN key. "An American pope would, as I acknowledge, be a strong asset to the church. But, Thomas, there are factors that make your election highly unlikely." His tone was sad, final, surgical. "Would you be so kind as to look at this screen with me?"

Casey rose, moved next to Kiejson. The Dutch cardinal tapped the key and the dossier of the fifty most important cardinals rose before them. "Let me, old friend, bring up your entry . . ."

"Mike, Mike . . ." Jimbo, bubbling with Jack Daniel's, just what Michael Tracy didn't need. "Mike, I *know* you're getting married, I *know* that, I want to talk to you about it . . ." A pause as the journalist brother struggled, to tighten the line on his voice, thrashing and wriggling out there in the white water beyond him.

"Jimbo, I don't think this is a good time to talk."

"Sure is, sure is. Look, little brother, that's you, little brother. I just want to say—even though I understand, you know, one man to another—go ahead, get married, sure, why not, what the fuck . . ."

"Jimbo, this is no time to play Judge Hardy."

"That's pretty good, *pretty* good. But, look, seriously, you're my brother. And brothers have to stick together, right? So you want to get married. Okay. I just want to ask you one thing . . ."

"Please, Jimbo, tomorrow morning you're going to wish we didn't have this conversation."

"See what I mean? You never listen. Look . . ." Jimbo paused again, reached for his drink on the makeshift bar in his apartment, set the bottle of bourbon wobbling, grabbed and steadied it. "Look, Mike, I talked to that back-alley abortionist Rafallo again today. He's been lying low, at his country villa, I got his number from, from, shall we say, a mutual friend. He's still trying to sell those pictures of his. He knows more than he's telling. I think he has that prescription for the pope's medicine, but he's scared to death for some reason, scared to fucking death . . ."

"Big brother . . ."

"Look, kid, I'll get used to your marrying, even though I think this former nun kind of stole you away, sure she did, let's face it, she knew what she was doing, these women always do . . ."

"Look, Jimbo," Michael said, growing angry, not wanting another fight, "if you've got something to say, let's hear it."

"Oh, *excuse me.* You don't like what I'm saying, you know why? 'Cause it's true. Can't you face the truth a little? These women know what they're doing every minute. Their specialty is the *idea* of love, that's how they get us." Jimbo inhaled deeply. "Back to the point. How about postponing your wedding, put it off until we can work this out better, have a regular wedding back in the States? Mom could deal better with it then, you know what I mean?"

"It's all set, Jimbo. I'd still like you to be there . . ."

"That's the thing. I could attend it much easier back in the States. Home field advantage and all. Better for you, too. But . . ." He sipped his drink. "I can accept your marriage, I really can, and I'm grateful, I'm proud you want me to be best man, I am, really . . ."

"But?"

"But I don't think I can take it *yet*. I'm not ready to be part of it, not yet. That's how I think we all feel. So, why not postpone it? What difference will a few weeks make? For your family's sake, for the Tracys's sake, for my kids, for Maureen, for everybody, let them get used to the idea that St. Michael the archangel is turning in his halo, you understand what I'm saying?"

"Oh, Jimbo, I . . ." Mike hesitated. "I'll talk to you in the morning." And he hung up.

Cardinal Casey straightened up, stepped away from Cardinal Kiejson's computer, as Leeuwenhoek might have turned away from the tube of his microscope after his first look at the teeming, invisible, dangerous world it had revealed. As a Chicagoan, he felt there was always another way to play almost any game, all a man needed was time to figure out a few things: the lay of the game itself, the odds, and, most of all, the other players.

He walked slowly across the room, stood for a moment with his back to the Dutchman. Kiejson watched him uneasily. The Chicago archbishop had read the long entry about himself without comment. It documented his early career in Rome, how he had missed his own mother's funeral back in Chicago to stay at the bedside of his dying patron, Cardinal Matarazzo. Then his first appointment as bishop in Wichita, Kansas, and his tenure as archbishop of Indianapolis, followed by his successful plucking of the jewel from the crown, the archbishopric of Chicago. There was a detailed history of his friendship with his cousin, Florence Roberts, "raised together after her mother died, they have remained close, but the relationship has been largely a public one, and rumors of its having a sexual nature have never been confirmed." The dossier also included a list of unconfirmed rumors and gossip, rough, unprocessed intelligence, deep and rich as a garbage heap, put it on a barge, no port would accept it.

Casey remained perfectly still as he reviewed what he had just read about his role as adviser to the Vatican Bank. More rumors and gossip, but some facts were right. He had been a friend, insofar as such men had friends, of the Italian financier Giovanni DioGuardia, had dined on his yacht, had spoken often with him about Vatican finances, American market moves, the investments of his own and other dioceses in the United States, he wished he had known about the taps on DioGuardia's line, but Casey had been careful, very cautious about what he had said.

The file revealed that Casey had supported DioGuardia's advice on many questionable transactions, that Casey had withdrawn all archdiocesan funds from DioGuardia's Lincolnland Bank just six weeks before it collapsed. Threatened with indictment, DioGuardia had tried to plea bargain. There were excerpts of statements he had given to the Feds in which he accused Casey of fraud and deception. Then, on the eve of his trial, DioGuardia had put a blue-steel pistol barrel into his mouth and scattered the hemispheres of his brain, richly encoded with figures and secrets, across a sixteenth-century tapestry on the wall behind his desk.

"Franz," Casey finally said, turning slowly around, "Franz, you told me that this matter was all settled, that the Holy Father had accepted my word, that he was ready to sign the documents that would vindicate me." He glanced at the computer screen, a quivering, glittering panel of his life story. "Franz, *you* had the papers ready for his signature the very afternoon he died. I had an appointment with him. It was *you* who told me that it was all settled." Casey paused. "What *happened,* Franz? First of all, to those papers? Were they ever signed? And second of all, why is it that only now, only *now,* with barely a day separating us from the conclave—we enter tomorrow evening, Franz!—what happened that you should be showing me this information only *now?*"

"I did have the papers, they were on Pope Jean's desk. I don't know whether he had signed them or not. They must have been put in storage when Maestrini gave the order to seal everything."

"There must be copies."

"No, they were the originals, that's all there were. The pope never wanted copies floating around until something was final."

Casey shook his head slowly. "There must be a way to break the seal on whatever is in storage."

Kiejson shrugged. "With Maestrini as *camerlengo?*"

Casey pointed to the computer. "What about *this?*"

"This information was only just given to me. Along with it, very clear instructions, *very* clear. You were to withdraw or certain proceedings would be instituted against you in the United States. I had no choice . . ."

Casey inspected the Dutch cardinal skeptically. "My mother used to tell me to beware of the person who says he doesn't like being the first one to bring you the bad news . . ." He lowered his head, frowned, thought for a long moment, then spoke slowly. "Think again about all this, Franz, I urge you. It just makes it more important that an American become pope. Otherwise, this whole story will come out as an effort to manipulate the papal election. It'll be just like every bad story of recent years—some out-of-hand government operation against communism, with the involvement, wittingly or not, of a distinguished Dutch cardinal." He let that sink in. "You, Franz, have obviously entered into some agreement with the Republican administration in the United States. Being a European, you don't understand that a current administration isn't the same thing as the whole U.S. government. Do you appreciate what I'm talking about?"

"Thomas, I have told you this only to protect you."

"Yes, but you actually believe that the CIA, or whoever, will make this collection of rumors and accusations public, that they will really try to force me to excuse myself as a candidate." There was bite in Casey's tone as he continued. "And, of course, they wouldn't dare. It would be political suicide to interfere in a papal election. Nobody, not the Catholics, Jews, or Protestants, would stand for that in America. Any move against me by the American government on such flimsy evidence would guarantee sympathy for me among our brother cardinals and *increase* my chances of being elected." He paused, looked Kiejson up and down. "Tell them to publish it, Franz, and let's see which one of us is ready to live with the consequences."

"I only *received* the information, I did not seek it. I want to save you embarrassment, that is all. These people know what they are doing."

Casey made a gesture of rejection with both hands. "They'll abandon you too, you understand that, don't you?" Casey began to walk slowly toward the computer. "Let's just take a look at *your* dossier."

"That will not be necessary," Kiejson said, stepping in front of the machine. "As I was told, it is 'exemplary.'"

"Sounds like Ownie Wingate to me." Casey stopped, removed his glasses, polished them with a crisp white handkerchief. "Maybe you can show me the file on Joe Caldwell, *eminenza* of Boston. You must have something on him or he would never have acted the way he did earlier today." He grinned sardonically. "A little light, Joe C., and now he's got the people thinking he's holy when it's only the jogging that makes him look that way."

Kiejson moved away from the computer, picked up his now dead cigar, relighted it carefully. "Thomas, there is more to this than you understand."

"Oh? Tell me about it."

"Your lawyer, a Mr. Hampton, is on his way to Rome right now to give you the details of the situation."

Casey frowned. "What do you know about Hampton?"

"Thomas, I'm speaking to you as a friend. And as someone who, like me, thinks of the good of the church in general. You have always been a realist. This is not just a question of American politics."

The Chicagoan surveyed the Dutchman again, how did he know Max was coming to Rome? "Franz," he said carefully, "they say that important men never make unimportant mistakes . . ." He walked out, leaving the door open. Kiejson stood quietly for a moment, listening to Casey's descending steps on the squeaky stairs.

Michael Tracy hung up the phone. Monsignor Hawkins, Cardinal Casey's secretary, had called, the old man wanted Mike to come to his hotel first thing in the morning, something very significant was up, drop whatever you're doing, you've got to do some important writing for him. And, by the way, Mike, the cardinal received the official letter of resignation you sent over here. He says he won't accept it, that you'll have to put it off, that there are more significant things for you to take care of first. No, all I can say is that he's very, *very* quiet, which means he's very, *very* mad, and very, *very* determined, which means he's after something very, *very* important, you know how he is when he gets that way, like a Japanese banker outbidding everybody for a Picasso . . .

Michael had never noticed that Monsignor Hawkins had any talent for metaphor, it didn't help anyway, Casey was at the bat, as the waggish clerics used to say of their cardinal when he entered his William Randolph Hearst mood. Michael felt achy, what is this, God's voice, is that how it works, as in the Bible with burning bushes and locust-eating prophets, the latest divine bulletins always coming out of unexpected sources, God playing Candid Camera with us, whispering to us through mailboxes and old archbishops? A bag lady will stop me next and tell me to repent and call off marriage. They all have the great old Catholic line, sure-fire persuasion for obsessives, reject your best yearnings, your best instincts, what's healthy about yourself, and you'll be holy . . .

Or is this some crazy coincidence, Michael wondered, loonier than Mother Hilda at the kitchen table, everybody wanting me to postpone the wedding for their own selfish reasons, they could form a club, make a game show out of it, *Speak Now or Forever Hold Your Peace,* the program that breaks up your marriage before it starts, in front of a live studio audience, saves you the pain and expense of getting a divorce. Mike shook his head, glanced at his watch. Eight P.M. Trust what's in your heart, that's what the old priest said. He decided to visit St. Peter's, to get out, to find some street distraction, maybe to pray.

Josef Beck's frowning face, aureoled with Shirley Temple ringlets, appeared in his imagination during the cab ride, good old Josef, like Wagner, a little heavy-handed about romance. The "Liebestod" sang in Michael's head as he climbed out of the taxi. He examined his gauze-bound hand as he waited for change, this isn't a game show, it's an interminable German opera, and we're stuck between the acts. And this wound is right out of German opera, too, Tristan, what a code name . . .

"Monsignor Tracy," Monsignor Lanza called from somewhere behind Michael. They greeted each other and fell into step as they crossed the piazza in front of the gray, brooding mass of St. Peter's. Lanza's alert brown eyes were serene in his terra-cotta face, his voice pleasant and controlled. "Have you come to any conclusions about holiness?"

"Have you?"

Lanza arched his eyebrows. "There is more searching in my work than finding."

"I've had the same trouble," Mike answered through barely parted lips. They paused as if in the grip of the half-slouching city that seemed bent under mourning, wariness, uneasy gaiety, as if someone were playing the piano in a back room of the house of death. They were also in the grip of things neither of them would say.

"It is a great irony," Lanza said thoughtfully, "that the institution so filled with meanness and smallness, and the most raucous voices of man, can also preserve and embody transcendent expectations, can speak with God's own sweet, clear voice."

"The problem, of course, is knowing which is which."

"Ah," Lanza replied, smiling wryly, "that is where the search comes in."

Michael looked directly into his eyes. "What are you saying, exactly?"

"That discerning the right voice is *the* problem for many good persons. Is it that of the unique prophet who can be followed closely by only a few? Or is it that of the great institutions—the communities which, despite their imperfections, know and understand us, often better than we do ourselves? I mean the family, the church . . ."

"Marriage?"

Lanza made the slightest bow, a concession and a conclusion, for he could not speak of his own efforts to get Michael's permission, and he did not want to hear what alternative plans might have been made.

"At least you haven't asked me to postpone marriage. That helps."

"You must expect people to do that . . ." They fell into uncomfortable step again. Lanza's tone became self-mocking. "I, of all things, have been asked by the *camerlengo* to supervise security arrangements for the conclave. The man in charge of guarding the doors to sanctity must also guard those to the papal election. Did you know that the cardinals are not allowed to bring flashlights or mirrors with them, for fear that they will send signals with them to the outside?"

"Your neighbor Cardinal Kiejson must be delighted."

"Ah, yes," Lanza sighed, "he may be more than a cardinal in a few days."

They paused, shook hands. "Thanks," Michael said, "for being a friend in a city of strangers. I want you to know that I am at peace with the voice I hear."

They looked into each other's faces for a long moment. "I will," Lanza said evenly, "be seeing you again, my friend." Then he turned away. Michael watched him as he walked slowly across the dusk-filled plaza, then turned and entered the basilica.

St. Peter's was austerely quiet, above it all, accustomed to history, its mellow floating light must have been trapped inside its walls for centuries, the same light had once fallen on Galileo and Michelangelo. Now, Michael thought, its moody dimness covered the church's human blemishes, brushed out time's ravages, it was the kind of light used to photograph vain and aging celebrities, it provided a sublime fix for every contrary ecclesiastical reality. Still, St. Peter's cut the ordinary down to size, intimated that the truly holy existed and might yet be found. Tracy descended to the dim grotto where the dead popes lay. He found the alcove in which Pope Jean's nearly weightless remains had been interred. If they hadn't bricked him in quickly, Michael mused, he might have floated away, a modern resurrection.

Mike knelt down at the edge of the space. The heaps of flowers showed signs of withering but the dead children still played in the sprays, their images fading, their voices fainter. He closed his eyes, felt restless as the day replayed in the theater in his brain, felt something that, from within the storm of resistance to his marriage and outside the institution's claims for loyalty, blinked at him, something he had noticed but couldn't recall. He shook his head, saw the dead and gone children rounding a far distant corner of his imagination, their voices beyond hearing now . . .

He opened his eyes, looked to his right. The old priest who had heard his confession knelt motionless at the opposite end of the crypt area. He was deep in prayer, as a miner is deep in the earth, his hands sensing even in the dark the splayed seams of gold. Michael felt a longing to speak to the old man again and, just as clearly, a sense that to interrupt him would be sacrilegious. In this dark tunnel, under the stone spine that bore the weight of St. Peter's glory, under the burdens of the long day itself, Michael suddenly experienced the force of authentic spiritual reality. There was the grail of his journey—overwhelming, compelling, peaceful—simple goodness, holiness itself, radiating from the old priest kneeling a few feet away. Michael rose from his knees and moved away slowly, looking back down the crypt every few steps until the praying figure was one with shadows.

VI

REVELATIONS

ONE

Mike slept fitfully. He had told the desk not to put through any more phone calls but Josef Beck had knocked at his door at midnight, will you send a cable to the *Times* about the committee, we intend to demand a popular election for the papacy, and we are calling for the election of the people's cardinal, Bouyer, the archbishop of Marseilles. Good luck, Josef . . .

The dead children, utterly silent, their features blurred, sat at the corners of his dreams as angels did on the oldest maps, here be dragons. He awoke at five, excited, distracted, the roller coaster had clanked its way up the tracks, it was in that last, tense interval before the descent, there's no climbing out now. Michael shaved and dressed, thinking of Ann and of their long, old-fashioned wait to get married, here he had been imagining himself as at least mildly rebellious, and he was actually traditional, almost Victorian in manner, everything but vellum invitations with the nubbly feel of genuine engraving.

The Catholic publisher Roger Tansey stared straight ahead in the elevator. Somebody else mad at me, Michael thought, you'll have to take a number, Roger, and wait your turn. He studied Tansey a moment as the doors opened to let another passenger get on. Perhaps I should speak to him, the priest thought, try for some kind of reconciliation, Roger is basically a good man, he just needs to control everybody. The doors opened on the noisy lobby. Tansey stepped quickly out of the car, headed toward the front desk. Michael watched him. Next time, he thought, next time I run into him, I'll see if we can't touch gloves.

Two hours later, he embraced Ann for a long time after she emerged from the crowd of arriving travelers. They held each other closely, quietly, their questions overlapping, shredding into laughter. It didn't seem possible —after all the years and separation, after a thousand long-distance phone calls, having deferred their marriage as if they were characters in a Harlequin romance—that they were standing together at last for good, and neither would have to go home at the end of the day. They inhabited a sweet hollow together, a quiet haloed zone shut off from the buzzing airport crowds, the anything-might-happen mood, the intimidating looks of the soldiers and security guards.

"By the way, Mike," Ann said, pointing to a slim gray-haired lady in a flower-patterned summer dress peering down at the baggage rack about fifty feet away, "do you know who that is?"

"Can't say that I do," Mike said, his eyes making a quick fly-by of the woman, coming to rest again on Ann.

"Well, she knows who you are. That's Florence Roberts."

Mike looked again in her direction, his mouth slightly open.

"Yes, we sat next to each other on the plane. She's really an old shoe, told me she was coming to Rome as a guest of her cousin the cardinal, and that she thinks he may very well be elected pope."

"*You* sat next to Florence Roberts?" Mike watched the older woman signal confidently toward a man in a chauffeur's uniform who hurried forward, picked up her large, old-fashioned suitcase. "Their honeymoon bag, no doubt . . ."

"What?"

"Nothing. Did you tell her we were going to be married?"

"Yes. Wasn't it okay?"

"Sure, sure . . ."

"She was happy about it, at least she *seemed* happy about it. But she was so excited about Cardinal Casey's chances of becoming the first American pope she didn't really pay too much attention. She just kept saying, 'My, isn't that nice now, isn't that nice?' She remembered you when you were stationed at the cathedral. You gave lovely sermons, she said, a little long, but lovely."

Mike lifted Ann's bag off the rack. "I have left nothing but lovely memories behind me, I thought you knew that." He nudged her gently and they headed toward the exit.

Michael lowered Ann's bag onto the sun-washed curb. A troop carrier groaned by, filled with Italian soldiers, eyes flashing, hands on their carbines, show us to the shoot-up. A Mercedes limousine followed, pulled up, the back window slid down. "Dr. Coleman, Dr. Coleman!" Florence Roberts waved a white-gloved hand at Ann. Cardinal Casey's cousin looked tiny on the pearl-gray mass of the back seat. "Get in, you two, I'll be glad to take you to your hotel."

"We're not right downtown," Mike mumbled as Ann hurried to accept the offer. Florence Roberts smiled benignly, settled back on the cushions as the window, that thousand-year forged glass again, rose as smoothly as a cat against the back of your leg. The chauffeur hopped out, put Ann's bag in the trunk. As Ann climbed in, Mike looked across the gleaming car roof at a slight, uncoordinated man signaling for a cab. An irritated Max Hampton, carrying a suit bag over one shoulder, what is *he* doing here?

"Watch your head," Florence Roberts said sweetly as Michael ducked inside the car.

Jimbo viewed himself in his bathroom mirror, can't we be friends? He began to shave very carefully, letting the pieces of the previous day drift down like debris into some kind of order inside his person. Michael's marrying that ex-nun at noon. Angelica Tomai's face rose in the steamy glass, you don't like women, do you? Jimbo nicked himself, goddammit, applied the styptic pencil as a patina of vapor erased the actress's image.

He washed his face, boiled water for coffee, stared aimlessly. I wonder if Mike told Mom that it's today. The journalist groaned, another milestone for the Tracy family, funny about us Tracys, we always *look* good on the outside and we've been falling apart for years. Maybe that's the way it is with all families, people in the doghouse, skeletons in the closet, uncles raving in the attic, things buried in the cellar, what the hell. Jimbo blew his nose, squinted at the bottle of bourbon, two inches of courage at best. He reached for it, pulled his hand back.

Count Rafallo had been tight-lipped about everything when Jimbo had finally located him at his country villa outside Rome, no wonder he needed money, Jimbo thought as he dried his face, he keeps so many women and houses going all over the place, he's pimping for himself. It was clear to Jimbo from the phone calls the count made while he was with him that the physician was making a big deal with some magazine, pictures and story, the last hours of Pope Jean, EXCLUSIVE. He had *Life* and *New York* in a bidding war, maybe he was offering a couple of shots of Angelica's charleys, too. Jimbo had watched the physician whispering on the phone, silhouetted against a stand of willows ruffled by the summer wind beyond the villa's picture window. With his combination of forthrightness, venery, and polished crookedness, the journalist thought, the count would make a terrific judge back in Chicago, maybe even a governor of Illinois.

Nothing on paper, the words came back to Jimbo. Rafallo had insisted that it did not refer to the papal prescription records, it was just that everything had disappeared, that there were no records, there was nothing anybody could find in the way of evidence. Jimbo shook his head, tossed the towel onto the sink, walked into his living room. That *has* to mean something more than he told me, I could feel it, son of a bitch, I could feel it in him . . .

Jimbo dialed the American Embassy, was put through to Ambassador Wingate who offered him a clipped greeting, salted with threat. "Yes, what is it *now,* Jim?"

"Nothing's on paper, that's what I hear."

Silence, caught-off-guard variety, on Wingate's end of the line.

"You understand what I'm saying? Nothing's on paper."

Wingate spoke slowly, calculating a risk. "Who told you that?"

"Quinidine, Dr. Quinidine."

"I just might want to talk to you again, Jim, about not getting involved in something you don't understand . . ." But a grinning Jimbo had already hung up.

"What do you mean, Monsignor Tracy said he wouldn't come?" Cardinal Casey's words clunked like dry ice, gave off steam, too.

Monsignor Hawkins maintained his professional cardinal's secretary manner. "Is there anything else, *Eminenza?*"

Casey glared at him. "Not now. And where did you pick up this *eminenza* business? You make us both sound like damned fools."

After Hawkins left, the cardinal swept away the pile of notes and messages on the table by his chair, called the Dutchman. "Franz, I've thought over our conversation of last evening."

"Yes?" Kiejson pulled himself erect in his chair. "I am glad to hear that. Before you say anything, let me put a case to you. Are you listening?"

"Go ahead."

"Suppose, just suppose, that a new pope needed the most experienced secretary of state that he could find. He would undoubtedly choose an American. That would be a great recognition for the U.S. church and, I might add, for the individual cardinal. That would be the highest-ranking post, under the Holy Father, in the entire church."

"Yes . . ."

"And, as an incidental aspect of the appointment, the individual would become a citizen of the Vatican State, would carry its passport, and would, for example, be immune to extradition laws . . ."

Casey hunched in his hotel room chair, paused a beat. "That's very interesting." Another beat. "Why I called, Franz, was this. I want you to know that I have no intention of renouncing my candidacy. I have talked to cardinals from around the world and my support is very firm."

"You honestly believe that?"

"I *know* that. And let me tell you something, Franz, something my mother used to say. Don't hold a fire sale before you own the store. It's been good to talk to you." He hung up without hearing Kiejson's protests, "One moment, Thomas, one moment, please . . ."

TWO

"I'm sorry, Your Eminence, but Monsignor Tracy is not in his hotel room. And I cannot reach his brother, either."

"What you mean, Monsignor Hawkins, is that you have failed to find him." Casey cleared his throat. "Again."

"I would say that I haven't found him." Hawkins fingered inside his collar. "Yet."

Casey looked coldly at his secretary. "How long have you been with me now?"

"Two years, Your Eminence."

"Hmm." Casey looked away, closed his eyes.

"Is there anything else, Your Eminence?"

"I want you to see that Mrs. Roberts is properly settled. Then I'd like you to bring her here and see that some breakfast is served."

The young priest lowered his head, turned toward the foyer.

"Do you think you can find her by yourself?"

Hawkins tightened his jaw, reached for the door just as someone knocked on its other side. The diminutive Max Hampton—a ruff of sandy hair, eyes snapping above facial planes scarred by snowed-over ski trails of acne—stepped past Hawkins without a greeting. "I have to see the cardinal right away." Hawkins closed the door as the lawyer dropped his suit bag on a chair and hurried across the living room to greet Casey. The cardinal rose, pulled his ringed hand away from the lawyer's bending head. Cardinal Kiejson's face appeared fleetingly in Casey's imagination, your lawyer is on the way to Rome to explain this to you . . .

"Max," Casey said, backing away as the lawyer straightened up, "I didn't ask you to come here."

"I tried to call. But you were at meetings and I didn't want to leave any important message with what's-his-name." Hampton jerked a thumb in the direction of the departed secretary, began pacing the rug as the cardinal sat down. "Couldn't really talk about it on the phone even to you, anyway. So I decided to fly over right away."

Casey frowned. "I'm sorry you didn't reach me. I would have told you not to come."

Hampton stopped in front of the cardinal's chair. "I'm going to have to speak very frankly."

"Everybody seems to say that to me these days, Max."

"First of all, you know, I'm sure, that Florence Roberts is in Rome."

Casey nodded. "In this hotel, as a matter of fact."

"She couldn't be here, if you'll excuse me, at a worse possible time."

The cardinal opened and closed his ringed right hand. "She's my cousin, you know that, Max."

"Yes, and her son Ed has gotten us into a very difficult situation."

"What?"

"Thanks to Ed, the U.S. Attorney for the Northern District of Illinois is on the verge of investigating your finances, your connection with the Vatican Bank, your relationship with DioGuardia."

Casey tensed. *"Ed?* What has Ed got to do with this?"

"Your nephew called your office the other day. He must have known you were in Rome, what's the matter with him, anyway? And Ted Rawlings has been out with the flu, and his secretary in finance has been down with it, too. Seems your nephew was in Florida, met somebody who gave him an inside tip on a stock. Little Eddie has what he calls a cash flow problem—that's what he told me when I spoke to him—so he thought, if you can call the process that, to call the chancery office. Nobody much around but he insisted on speaking to somebody with authority. Some layman named Masters took the call. Nephew told him to purchase stock in this company through some account, little Eddie had the number. Masters said he couldn't do that without authorization, nephew insisted, said it was okay, that you set the account up for this purpose, that he should look it up, everything would be fine, you did it all the time for him."

"That's not true."

"So Masters went and, with a little checking, found this account. Sure enough, there was a record of stock and other transactions in little Eddie's name, all authorized by you."

"What, what did he do?"

"And he found the source of the account's funds, too. He's a scrupulous fellow, and he didn't understand . . ."

"Didn't understand *what?"*

Max Hampton looked pained, how could he put this? "He found what he construed as commingling of funds, what he believed to be diocesan and other church monies invested in an account that seemed at least partially to underwrite the financial activities of your nephew Edward Roberts. There was also information about DioGuardia, some notes, some transaction slips, a strip of calculator tape. Some notes supposedly initialed by you about getting deposits out of the Lincolnland Bank. Evidence, *evidence,* if looked on in a certain way, that you knew DioGuardia was engaging in shaky financial activity long before his empire collapsed, and that you got out, and got the diocese out, in time. But a lot of people got hurt, including the Vatican Bank."

"Max, that's nonsense . . ."

"No doubt, but the material in that file could easily be misinterpreted, believe me." Hampton walked to the window, gazed down at the bustling Via Veneto, turned away, biting the inside of his cheek before he spoke again. "Little Eddie, with his nickel-and-diming, led Masters directly to this DioGuardia material. He might as well have put it in the papers."

"What I do in my account," Casey responded confidently, "is my own business. I'm a corporation sole. I *am* the archdiocese, legally speaking. What's given to the diocese is given to me."

"I understand, Your Eminence."

Irritation rode a lightning-bolt of pain in the cardinal's chest. He shifted in his chair, eyed the medicine, to hell with it. "Are you suggesting that others might not understand?"

"This Masters, think about him for a minute. The reason *he* was hired in finance was because he was so conscientious, so careful in his work, so completely trustworthy. That's what made him so upset to find this out, his tender Catholic conscience. He's one of those, what do you call them?"

"Scrupes, over-scrupulous." Casey sighed. "Couldn't anybody explain the matter to him?"

"As I said, nobody was around. It preyed on this man's conscience over-night. It became *his* problem, he had to solve it . . ."

"At my expense? Come now."

"Trouble is, his brother's an assistant U.S. Attorney, a stickler just like him, and he went to him for advice. That's how things got out of hand. His brother felt bound in conscience to report the matter. That's where we stand in one aspect of this. The U.S. Attorney had already been in touch with me, telling me he was being pushed pretty hard by the Attorney General to investigate everybody's connections with DioGuardia, including yours. He was still resisting him but, when this information came to his attention, he couldn't put it off anymore. He said, well, he insisted that I personally tell you . . ." Hampton paused, moistened his lips.

Casey eyed him steadily, spoke evenly. "Because I am one of the leading candidates for the papacy. That's it, isn't it? He hinted that if I were to withdraw, that these things might just disappear."

Hampton appeared dumbfounded, gestured with his hands. "It came to that, yes . . ."

"Can't you see this is blackmail? Suppose I loaned Eddie a couple of thousand dollars or so. I put my own money in that fund, it came out of that. And I use that account to channel money to bishops and priests behind the Iron Curtain. You know that. Oh, no, there's more to this than the pursuit of justice. The administration is trying to pick the next pope, that's what this is all about."

"It isn't just that, Your Eminence. The material about your relationship with DioGuardia is serious. The Vatican Bank took a bath on that, lots of people were ruined, there have been suicides, stories of murder, even . . ."

Casey's expression did not change. "And this will all disappear if I be-come the next pope, you realize that, don't you?"

Hampton stared down at the cardinal. One of us, he thought, is right, one of us is crazy. "I . . ."

"Have you talked to Joe Rozalowski?" Casey's tone was businesslike, decisive. Whatever he knew, he was not backing down.

"He's supposed to be here today, part of the congressional delegation for the pope's funeral." Hampton's energy, his capacity to believe, was wearing down, he was beginning to wonder about his own involvement. When he became diocesan lawyer, he never thought it would come to this. "But, to answer your question, yes, I have talked to Congressman Rozalowski. His advice is to stonewall everybody right now."

"You don't sound as sure as I am about this, Max. What's the matter, are you worried about yourself?"

"Let's be frank, we can't expect this to stay under wraps. Too many people see folders at the U.S. Attorney's office, there's no telling where this may lead, we should expect a leak."

"That would be unethical."

"Well, yes . . ."

"Max, pull yourself together. I want you to get this under absolute control. There's nothing wrong in my loaning money to a nephew, and there's nothing wrong with my taking money out of Lincolnland Bank. That's a tribute to my good judgment. You seem to take the worst-case scenario."

"That's part of my job. This is big, Your Eminence, I mean . . ."

"Nobody can put on the pressure like you, Max. Why do you think I have you for a lawyer?"

Hampton frowned, pursed his lips. "This nephew of yours . . ." He shook his head. "Everything *was* under control until he stepped into this."

"His mother is here."

"Wonderful timing. She's in the file, too. *I* understand, you've got to think how others will look on this . . ."

"Max, what you don't understand is that I will emerge from this conclave either as the pope or as his secretary of state. In either case, these wild charges will have to be dropped."

Hampton opened his mouth, gaped at Casey. He had been through a lot with the cardinal. Casey was running true to form, he always got tougher as things got worse. But this time, the lawyer thought as a tremor of anxiety ran through him, this time . . .

Casey removed his glasses, closed his eyes, spoke calmly. "This Masters fellow, is he still working for us?"

"You can't very well fire him now."

"Well, what about him?"

"We have to leave him alone." Both men sat in silence for a long moment. Then Hampton spoke in a dry, tired voice. "That's what Catholic education got for you . . ."

THREE

Michael changed into a fresh shirt, glancing momentarily at his abandoned black clerical shirt front hanging limp as a war criminal in the closet. I'm an old Texas Ranger, he mused as he awkwardly knotted his tie, saying good-bye over the corral fence to Old Paint, our great adventures together are over. He slipped into a freshly pressed jacket, went to the room next door that he had reserved for Ann so that she could rest and change before the ceremony. He would never request separate quarters for her again. People would laugh, Michael thought, to learn that he had done it just for these last few hours before their marriage, they would snicker at his being out of date, a terminal romantic. Some people laughed at old-fashioned love, especially those who longed desperately for it, perhaps to protect themselves against its never coming at all, like making fun in advance of the guest who can hurt us most by not showing up. But this arrangement for Ann's privacy felt right no matter what anybody else thought, Michael had heard enough contrary opinions anyway.

Ann opened the door. She wore a light-blue dress, and radiated that subtle freshness of fine mist trailing off fountains at night. Michael gazed at her, overwhelmed, yearning to be dissolved, to break free of time's binding and to be with her simply and completely. They embraced, leaving the door ajar, alive as an electrical storm is in its branching light, dazzling and explosive, all at once, everywhere. Michael pinned a corsage on her dress and they embraced again. They felt peaceful in each other's arms and Rome, new and old, fell away from them. They belonged together, tumbling in the weight-lessness of love's sweet void.

As they separated, Ann adjusted her flower, asked, in her medical voice, "How is your hand?"

"Why am I marrying a doctor, full of practical questions at transcendent moments?"

"Just want to make sure the dressing is clean. Men worry a lot but don't know how to take care of themselves. I really should take a look at it."

"You'll want my Blue Cross card next." Michael glanced at his watch. "Later, Ann, you can check it out later. Right now we don't have much time. Jack Parker said he'd be down at about quarter of." He took her left hand in his as they went into his room, closed the door. They walked hand in hand toward the gauzy summer light that blurred the edges of the balcony door. Outside, they looked toward St. Peter's, immured in silence and summer haze. The phone rang and Michael went inside to answer. Ann gazed at the tree puffs below the great dome, felt the pull of the church, the polar magnetism of its traditions and teachings, wondered for a moment if Michael would miss it and become restless without its immediate presence in his life. He looked grim when he returned to her side.

"Roger Tansey has had some sort of attack. Heart, they think, but they're not sure. That was Josef Beck asking me to take his place at their press conference."

"What is it, Mike?"

"Don't worry, I'm not going to do it." He paused, took her hand again. "Roger stopped talking to me when I sent a book to another publisher and he's turned down a couple of my efforts to clear the matter up. I was going to speak to him this morning in the elevator and I didn't. I feel bad that I didn't . . ." He shook his head. "The Irish in me, I guess. It's unsettling, news like that . . ."

"Is he going to be okay?"

"They think so. It's not that. I just wish I *had* spoken to him, that's all. It wouldn't have cost me much."

"You're right, that *is* Irish of you."

"Well, we've got other things to think about." Michael inspected his watch. Five minutes to twelve. Where, he wondered, feeling another uneasy shiver, is Jack Parker?

Jimbo Tracy sat behind the wheel of his Fiat parked thirty yards from his apartment house. Three minutes to twelve. He lit a cigarette, felt the warm soft pulse of the empty street, noontime sun filtering down through the silent badgelike leaves. He shifted in his seat, remembered being sick as a kid one summer in Chicago—the same in-between moodiness of the neighborhood when the men had gone to work, wash hung stiffly on the backyard lines, the small sounds of the television sets and the babies seemed muted, and once in a while a stranger came up the alley and rapped lightly on some woman's back door. The spell was broken as a car entered the street behind him. Jimbo bent down as it passed, looked up to see a black limousine, flying miniature American flags, stop outside the entrance to his apartment house. A frowning Owen Wingate opened the left rear door before his driver reached it, stepped out, tugged the jacket vent of his canvas-colored summer suit, took the measure of the building, and walked briskly inside.

Son of a bitch, Jimbo whispered to himself, *son of a bitch,* Ownie has time on conclave day to pay *me* a visit. In a few moments Wingate came out, looked up and down the sun-dappled avenue. You know I'm here somewhere, you paranoid son of a bitch. The ambassador signaled to his driver, climbed back into the car. I'm making Ownie nervous, Jimbo thought, as the limousine glided away, or he'd never come looking for me personally, never. Heading for my office now. Jimbo slapped the steering wheel with his right hand, sent a shower of ashes down into his lap. Ownie wants to find out what I know about the pope's death. Jimbo crinkled his brow, setting off a stinging alarm in his injury, but *what* the hell do I know? Nothing on paper and Quinidine, that's it. And yet *this* brings the U.S. ambassador to the Vatican out to pay a call on me?

He felt a sudden slight loss of bravado, what, he asked himself, do I do now, what's my next move? He dismissed the possibility of visiting Angelica Tomai, masochism had its limits. Not Rafallo, either. Then he thought of his brother Mike. Jesus, Mike's getting married *right now* a couple of blocks from here. Twin waves, one of guilt, the other of affection, converged inside his chest. Jimbo flicked the cigarette out the window, started the car, what the hell, I don't have to approve of the marriage in order to go to it, half the parents in the world wouldn't show up if approving the marriage was a condition for showing up. Besides, Ownie will never think of looking for me there . . .

At the Holy Office, Franz Cardinal Kiejson sat motionless, gazing at but not seeing the piles of correspondence, messages, telegrams, and telephone call slips piled on his desk. He touched his broad, strong hand to the jigsaw scar, like a graft of fish belly, on his cheek, silently reviewed the forty years of service to the church that had brought him to this extraordinary high noon of conclave day. His destiny, he felt certain, was to enter it as a cardinal and to emerge as pope. His beringed hand trembled as he lowered it to the desk. I have been called to this, he thought, it has been God's plan, everything, yes, *everything* that has happened in my life has prepared me for this moment. *Non nobis, Domine,* he recited urgently, *non nobis, sed nomini tuo da gloriam,* do not give the glory to me, O Lord, but to your own name.

The telephone rang as it had several times during the last half hour. Kiejson ignored it, glanced at his own image staring up from the newspaper at the corner of his desk. He crumpled and dropped it into the wastebasket, watched it blossom stiffly open again, then turned and walked to the prie-dieu set against the wall beneath a charred wooden crucifix. A scorched figure of Christ hung on it, his right arm broken off. Kiejson looked at it, remembered that night he had rescued it, heard once more the drone of German bombers, the thuds and heavy explosive cracks, the throaty growl of buildings as they gave way, the splatter of debris; he saw eyelets and tongues of flame everywhere, the sashes of fire that girded the city; he inhaled again the acrid smell of Rotterdam burning. Tears welled in his eyes as he lowered himself onto the hard kneeler. So long ago, he thought, such a long time ago . . .

Across Rome, in the starch-white chapel on the house on Via Remalda, Mother Hilda knelt before the simple wooden tabernacle, her arms extended. Her gaunt face was streaked with tears and her lips moved almost mechanically. *"Have mercy,"* she repeated with great effort, as if trying to fuse memory and will, "have mercy on me, have mercy on all of us . . ."

In Vatican City, Father Paul, Cardinal Solieri's assistant, studied the dusty-faced clock in the archivist's paper-strewn office. Past noon already, the young priest fretted, and the conclave is opening this evening, and the cardinals have another important meeting before that. He left the office, thinking of the old archivist's habits, it would be just like him to become absorbed in some ancient document and forget time and place, just like him. Father Paul smiled, it was not the first time he had gone searching for his chief on a significant occasion, he knew where to look. He moved confidently through the stacks, walking, as he thought, through centuries of church history with each step. He made a left turn into a vaulted corridor, passed carrels and cubicles, made another left turn, entered another area of stacks, hurried toward the lamp glow reflected on the ceiling in the far corner of the dimly lit room.

Cardinal Solieri sat at a tiny desk piled with folders and note cards. He wore a tattered, misbuttoned cassock and, bent over a file, did not hear his assistant at first. *"Eminenza,"* Father Paul repeated, *"Eminenza,* have you forgotten the time?"

"No," the old man answered sadly, barely looking up, "no, I am well aware of the time." He removed his wire-rimmed glasses, placed them on the papers in front of him.

"Have you found what you want?"

"Yes," Solieri said softly as he rose from his chair, "that is the pity. I have found it, and I have run out of time."

"Why do you keep asking me about Ed?" Florence Roberts lowered her cup of tea to the silver-strewn linen cloth of the room service table. "Is there something bothering you about him, Tom?"

Cardinal Casey compressed his lips, hesitated momentarily, placed his napkin on the table as if he were putting a liturgical cloth on an altar. "I feel very close to Ed," the cardinal said slowly, searching for the right words.

"I know that," Florence answered, invoking a thousand memories with her tone, "you really have been a father to him . . ."

"I'm just concerned that he's okay."

"How do you mean, *okay?*"

"Well, his business. After all, his children are still quite young. I hope he's successful, that's all."

"You mean more than that, Tom." She rose, came around the table, put her arm gently on his shoulder. "I've known you all my life. Don't you think I can tell when something is bothering you?" She massaged the back of his neck in easy, familiar movements. "What is it, Tom, what is it that's really bothering you?"

Michael forced a smile. "Just like a priest to be late. Did I ever tell you about Father Joe Tomkins, wonderful guy, the 'late' Father Tomkins, they called him. They'd schedule him for the eleven o'clock Mass but tell him he was due for the ten. That way, he'd be half an hour early in the sacristy instead of a half hour late."

"Mike," Ann intoned with the terrible sureness of certain domestic intuitions—the broken water pipe is on your property, the baby has the measles, daddy will be home late, tipsy— "Mike, it's ten after . . ."

"Early for some priests is ten minutes late for everybody else." He could hear his own false heartiness—Nixonian, flat, trailing away. "Jack's probably got his time mixed up, probably hasn't changed his watch since he left San Francisco."

"Why doesn't he answer his phone?"

"He's on his way here, that's why."

"Do you think you should call Brother Louis again?"

"Lou will call if Jack shows up there. I don't want to tie up the phone in case . . ."

Their eyes met, they recognized that they shared the same foreboding. The firmament was cracking, the road to Camelot might be closed at any moment. The ringing telephone jolted them out of their melancholy thoughts.

"*Yes.*" Mike blurted into the mouthpiece, "Oh. Yes, yes. No, I didn't expect to hear your voice. What? Okay, we'll be right down." Michael looked numbly at Ann as he hung up slowly. "That was Monsignor Lanza. He's in Jack Parker's room." He touched Ann's shoulder gently. "He asked if we'd come down."

The suave, black-suited Lanza, a notch of purple below his Roman collar, opened the door and stepped into the hallway. He bowed, smiled tightly, shook Ann's hand as Mike introduced her, murmured an appreciative Italian phrase, turned grave as a surgeon in blood-flecked greens, I have bad news for you . . .

He opened the door on a tumbled room. Papers and dirty clothes were scattered on the floor. A lumpy suitcase lay open on the desk, its straps dangling like a dead man's arms. The bedclothes were tangled like sheets just out of the dryer. A sound of retching came from the bathroom. Michael and Ann stepped inside warily, stayed close to the wall as if barred by the yellow ribbons fluttering at a crime scene. Lanza closed the door, made his way across the floor so that his gleaming shoes did not come into contact with any of the discarded clothes. He poked his head inside the bathroom. "Are you alright, Father?"

The toilet flushed, Lanza backed away from the door. A few seconds later, a disheveled, unshaven Father Jack Parker eased himself out of the bathroom. He wore a summer robe whose stripes were a variation on the flushed color of his puffy face. "Oh, Mike," he groaned as he ran a shaky hand through his uncombed hair. He looked at Ann. "Is this . . . ?"

"This is Ann," Mike said slowly. "We expected you to . . ."

"Yeah," Parker half sighed, half sobbed, "I know. I . . . I . . ." He sat down suddenly on the edge of the bed. "I'm sorry, Mike, I really am . . ."

Michael glanced at Lanza, stepped closer to the bed, felt his emotions imploding. He looked back at Ann, white-faced, motioned her to his side. He discovered that his mouth dried out as he tried to speak. "Jack, what happened?"

Parker wet his lips, searched the faces around him. "I'm sorry, Mike, I've been sick and . . ."

Lanza intervened gently. "Father Parker has had some unexpected news, bad news, in the last day or so. I was involved, I might add."

"I'll tell it, I'll tell it," Parker said, standing up, tightening the sash of his robe, winching the remnants of his dignity together. He took a deep breath. "I drank too much last night." His slitted eyes darted to Lanza, then fixed on the vague neutral zone of the far wall. "Monsignor Lanza here and I have had some business together. The apostle of the Pacific, Francisco Montoya, it wasn't going very well and I found out why yesterday. Monsignor gave me information, information that I can't take home with me." He paused, looked at Michael as if for understanding. "There's no chance for the canonization of Francisco Montoya, that's what he told me. He had, he said, uncovered irregularities in the process . . ." He broke off, his words congealed.

Lanza moved into the gap. "You must understand that Father Parker had nothing to do with this, he had no knowledge of it."

Michael took Ann's hand lightly in his, felt disappointment flooding through her. "No knowledge of *what?*"

"That somebody back in San Francisco has been tapping the funds collected for the canonization, that's what." Parker gestured with his hands. "I was given the assignment of getting his cause through the Roman bureaucracy." He paused again, swallowed hard. "You see, Mike, I needed a success. I've had some problems. I didn't resign from the seminary, I got canned for drinking too much, giving bad example. I've been trying to lick this and, when the archbishop asked me to take the Montoya thing, it was like a vote of confidence in me, a chance to get myself back on my feet, to be really respectable again. And it's the archbishop's favorite cause. We need a saint for San Francisco, he keeps saying, even tried to get Tony Bennett to record a song with those words . . ."

He ran his hand through his hair again. "I can't afford another failure, not now, and I can't afford to disappoint the arch, not with his favorite cause at stake. I had no idea that the distinguished lay treasurer—Frank Williams, the developer—has been milking the money, using it for seed money for a development named Montoya Mission. But I'm the one at the head of this thing. Did the archbishop give me this, knowing that it would blow up and that he could shift the blame to me? What would you expect from Jack Parker, they'd all say, he already blew the seminary . . ."

Lanza picked up the theme as Parker broke off. "It was a very difficult situation. We first became concerned when none of the small fees for services and research in our congregation had been paid. Then I began to look into it very discreetly. Father Parker knew nothing of it. I doubt that the archbishop really did until I spoke to him on the phone the other day. But Father Parker has been placed in a very difficult position."

"I need a success, Mike," Parker interjected, "I can't risk doing anything else that may draw attention to me right now, not while ninety thousand dollars is missing. I've got to ease myself out of this. I haven't got anything else going for me right now. I've got to straighten this out. I mean, I still have to help support my mother. You understand, Mike, don't you?"

Lanza looked on impassively as Parker recounted his drinking bout, his calls to Lanza this morning, the monsignor's kindness in trying to help him.

Then the priest went swiftly into the bathroom, closed the door. Michael caressed Ann. "I'm sorry, Annie. I'd better call Brother Louis."

"What are we going to do, Mike?"

"I don't know. I'll get somebody to marry us. I'll see if Louie knows a magistrate somewhere, some judge. Don't worry, we'll get married some-how today . . ."

Lanza lowered his eyes as Michael spoke, he did not want to hear any-thing more about it, the scandal over Montoya was enough for one day. "I must leave," he said evenly as Michael placed his call, "you understand. I do have to look after security for the conclave as well." He opened the door, turned back before stepping into the hallway.

"Yes," Michael said, covering the mouthpiece with his hand as he ad-dressed the departing Lanza, "that's what I've been doing for years, under-standing the screwups, fixing them up. I'm getting good at it."

As Lanza closed the door, Ann put her arms around Mike. He felt a sharp surge of protective need, of wanting to take care of her, make this situation right, find a happy ending to the ill-starred day somehow or other. He hurriedly explained the developments to Brother Louis, asked if some alter-native arrangements could be worked out.

Brother Louis said that he would see what he could do, that he would make some calls, and, by the way, Mike, your brother is here. Michael seemed stunned as he hung up. Jimbo is there. Jimbo came after all. The best man is there and we're not. Parker made the noises of a sick man from behind the closed door. Michael and Ann embraced. "It's going to be okay, Annie, believe me. I'm going to make this all up to you." He was afraid Ann was going to cry, what will I do, Mike wondered, if she cries? But Ann pulled away from him, dry-eyed, resolute, ready to make the best of their floundering day.

"Okay, Mike," she said, steadying him with her confident, emergency-room tone, "let's go."

"You won't mind if we have to be married by somebody other than a priest?"

"The important thing is that we go ahead, priest or not. God understands these things."

Lanza was standing a few paces down the hallway when they came out of the room. "I am truly sorry, my friend," he said to Michael, not quite to

Ann. Typical of priests, Mike thought, Lanza's just like the rest of them, they like you but they don't want to hear about your wife.

"Sometimes," Lanza said in a confessor's comforting tones, "these things happen for the best. We must read God's message in them."

"If God has sent a message by way of the Montoya cause, Jack Parker, and you," Michael said grimly, "I'm asking for it to be re-transmitted because it's too garbled to read."

"My friend . . ."

"Monsignor Lanza," Michael cut in, "I know you mean well. Sometimes things hurt too much for other people to say anything, even when they mean well. I'm asking *you* to understand this time."

Monsignor Lanza stepped back as they passed. He made a brief fluttering gesture, let his arm fall to his side, watched in silence as Michael and Ann hurried, hand in hand, down the corridor to the elevator.

Two miles away in a nondescript garage in a crowded back street, two men dressed in Italian Army uniforms loaded plastic explosive devices into the rear section of a buff-colored military van. The job completed, they nodded at each other and one of them climbed behind the wheel. The other opened a black valise, handed the driver an official identification card dangling from a chain. He placed one over his own head as the driver did the same. Then the first man removed a shield-shaped sticker, peeled away the backing, and affixed it to the lower left of the van's windshield. It read PASS, VATICAN CITY, ALL POINTS SECURITY. Then he opened the garage door, climbed in next to the driver, and the vehicle eased its way into the street.

FOUR

"Mother Church, Mother Hilda," Michael murmured to Ann as they hailed a cab, "one of them is laying hexes on us like an Amish barn painter . . ." He held her close as the taxi pulled away. She was silent, contained, filled with wondering. "What is it, Annie?"

"Nothing, Mike," she replied, nuzzling closer, "but there's something wrong about having an underground wedding. The church doesn't seem to want to let go, it doesn't seem right, it scares me a little."

"That's just the banshee in your soul. The Irish tempter, worse than the devil himself. We'll be on the other side of this in a little while." Mike suppressed his own uneasiness, pushed aside the morning's ominous foot-notes, Roger Tansey's heart attack, Jack Parker's collapse. "Believe me, I really think everything *is* going to work out." Ann didn't reply, just looked at Mike, then out the window in a kind of suspended silence until they arrived at the Word of Mercy House.

Jimbo Tracy stood near the far wall of the high-ceilinged, oak-paneled room, once the library of a member of the Italian royal family, now the office of Brother Louis, superior general of the Word of Mercy brothers who ran high schools and colleges all over the world. Louis matched the restrained, tasteful setting perfectly, a lithe, bespectacled, black-cassocked scholar at home with books, a man possessing the noiseless grace of a cat burglar. Jimbo Tracy held back as Mike and Ann entered the room, surveyed them uncertainly, uncomfortably, he wasn't here to bless their union as much as to hide out, he didn't want Mike to get the wrong idea.

"No luck yet," Brother Louis said apologetically, "but I should be hearing back from a magistrate I know. In the meanwhile, we can get these papers signed. I've got my secretary, a woman from the neighborhood, to be a witness. And we've got your brother . . ." He half turned, gestured toward Jimbo, ". . . for the other."

Mike smiled, thanked Brother Louis for whatever he could do, took Ann's arm lightly in his bandaged hand, led her eagerly toward Jimbo. Ann sensed Jimbo's truculence, its beeping signals growing louder with each step they took toward him. The phone rang, Brother Louis answered as Mike embraced Jimbo, "I can't tell you how glad I am to see you . . ."

Jimbo seemed to suffer the embrace as an adolescent boy endures a mother's public kiss. He lowered his eyes, put his hand out automatically as Mike introduced Ann. "You've met before, of course."

"At our mother's house," Jimbo responded diffidently, "a year or so ago. It's too bad she can't be here today."

Ann smiled, shook Jimbo's hand. "I really wish she were here, too."

"Well," Mike interposed, "we'd like Ann's folks, too, but we'll see everybody back in the States as soon as possible. The big thing, Jimbo, is that *you're* here."

"That," Brother Louis cut in half hopefully, "was the magistrate's secretary. He expects him to be in within the hour." He broke off, snagged on the frosty edge of the tableau of the Tracy brothers in ambivalent reunion. "Why don't we get the paperwork done?" He gestured them toward his desk. Jimbo stayed behind. "You, too," Brother Louis said. "We can't do this without the best man."

Mike and Ann walked the few steps to the ornate desk that the Brothers of Mercy had purchased along with the stately old residence. As Brother Louis checked the documents, Mike put his arm more tightly around Ann and they looked into each other's eyes. Jimbo watched them, thought fleetingly of when he and Maureen used to look at each other that way. What, the journalist wondered, happens to love like that, where does it go? Mike and Ann seemed unaware of his appraisal, of Brother Louis's shuffling papers, of the once royal house in whose library they now stood like museum visitors. Michael, Michael, Jimbo asked, why don't I want you to be in love? His inner tension subsided slightly, he moved grudgingly toward the desk.

"After we're married," Michael said, pulling away from Ann's eyes like a man breaking the surface of clear water, "I'll take better care of you."

"Michael," she said tartly, "all I want you to do is love me. We'll take care of each other."

Michael turned silent. Little brother has been checkmated, Jimbo thought, I haven't seen this happen much. Monsignor Infallibility without the last word, Michael put in his place. The journalist inspected Ann again, by God, I've never been able to do that, how did she?

Ten minutes oozed by. Jimbo made small talk with Brother Louis, asking about the regal inventory that came with the house, "Sort of like Cracker Jack, eh, Bro?" As Louis nodded somewhat dubiously, the journalist looked past him at Mike and Ann sitting peacefully hand in hand on a leather couch. They did not seem to be affected by the gluelike atmosphere, too thick to slog through, too dense to carry sounds. Love, Jimbo mused, trying to master the tender spot in his heart before it grew any larger, how little lovers know what time has in store for them . . .

The phone rang. Brother Louis snatched up the receiver, listened a moment as Mike and Ann rose from the couch, then passed the phone across the desk. Michael took it gingerly in his injured hand.

"This is Monsignor Lanza."

"Oh?" Michael answered uncertainly, awkwardly.

"I wanted to tell you that I am truly sorry that I can't be with you today. I wanted you to have my prayers and congratulations. I didn't want you to misunderstand . . ."

"Oh, I understand okay," Michael responded, keeping his voice in neutral, "only there's nothing to congratulate us on. We haven't got a magistrate yet."

Lanza spoke across Michael's final phrase. "Listen carefully, my friend. I am calling you from my rooms. As it happens, I have about forty-five minutes free. And none of my eminent neighbors is around. They're all at meetings this afternoon. If you will meet me at the private chapel here as soon as possible, I will be honored to witness your marriage on behalf of the church."

"*What?*"

"Please do not say anything," Lanza said calmly, "just meet me there. I have left word at the door."

Michael held the purring phone, explained excitedly what Lanza had just said, then hung up, embraced Ann. "Did you hear what I said? I can't believe it. Holy Mother Church just re-transmitted the message."

Everyone froze, uncertain for a split second about what to do next. Jimbo surprised himself by blurting out, "I've got a car. Let's go."

Everybody squeezed into Jimbo's Fiat. They were approaching Vatican City when Brother Louis clapped his hand to his head, he had forgotten to bring his secretary to be a witness, should he go back, should they stop and call? "Let's see what Monsignor Lanza can arrange," Michael said, "let's not turn back now." Jimbo turned into the street leading along the cinnamon wall of Vatican City, stopped at an intersection as a gaudily uniformed policeman waved and whistled through a military van bearing official stickers. "Follow that car, Jimbo," Michael said, his sense of humor returning, "and look important."

"My press credentials will get us to the door," Jimbo replied, "and if your friend has left word we shouldn't have any trouble." The journalist glanced back over his shoulder, saw Michael and Ann looking into each other's eyes like space travelers riding a beam of light. Jimbo turned away, tasted his emotions, a badly mixed cocktail, he judged, too much bitters. He made a face, focused his attention on the military vehicle moving ahead of them into the heart of the Vatican. The van's taillights blinked red as it halted, went black again as it slowly maneuvered over a traffic bump and under a moldering archway into a courtyard next to the building in which Lanza lived. "Here goes nothing," Jimbo said, following in its authoritative wake. A mustachioed guard in a downsized Napoleon hat bent forward, nodded when Jimbo mentioned Lanza's name, gestured theatrically as he stepped aside to let them enter. "By God," the journalist exclaimed, "your Monsignor Lanza does have influence after all."

"You forget, Jimbo, that he's the devil's advocate," Mike said as they pulled into a parking place. As they climbed out of the car they could see the van backing into a slot in the far corner of the noon-bright yard. They had not moved when a Mercedes limousine glided through the gates, passed within a few feet of them. Cardinal Casey's profile stood out sharply against the roan-colored wall beyond. "Did *you* invite him?" Mike asked, nudging Ann, "is he on your side of the family?"

Ann shushed him and the sleek car stopped halfway down the yard. They watched Casey ease himself out of the gleaming submarine of an automobile, shake his cassock skirt free, then walk toward an entrance to the building that seemed a twin to Lanza's. The cardinal did not acknowledge the greetings of the young clerics who hurried into the white sunlight to greet him, but passed, forlornly, Mike thought, like a soul entering purgatory, into the dark, cool passage beyond. Jimbo cleared his throat, cracking open Michael's reverie, and the small group hurried out of the parking area and across the sidewalk to the front door of Lanza's residence.

FIVE

Monsignor Lanza, his molten brown eyes brimming with light, welcomed the group warmly, his gestures deliberate, masking his inner feelings of working against the clock. He wasted no movement, however, as he quickly recruited a nun from the kitchen to serve as a witness, shepherded everybody into the private chapel at the opposite end of the dusky, silent hallway. "Cardinal Kiejson and the others are at general congregations and then go directly into the conclave," Lanza explained as he flicked on the lights in the small, bare chapel. "You see Amsterdam's taste," he said urbanely, "in our decor. *Eminenza* emphasizes the ascetic, the spare, penitential traditions of Christianity." He touched a match deftly to the candles on the altar. "Perhaps because of the climate in which he grew up. I," he continued as he beckoned the party closer to the altar, "I carry the warmth of the Mediterranean in my veins."

Michael took Ann's right hand in his own bandaged grasp, led her half a step closer to the altar platform as Jimbo, Brother Louis and a plump, black-eyed, white-habited nun lined up behind them. Michael removed two gold bands from his pocket with his left hand, gave them to Jimbo, turned back as Lanza pulled his head through the yoke of a lace surplice without disturbing a hair of his head. Jimbo stared down at the rings glinting in his lightly sweating palm, looked up as Ann gently moved Michael an inch or so, aligning their place as a couple directly in front of Monsignor Lanza. It was suddenly hushed as crowded churches become on muggy June days when the bride stands finally at her father's side, the organist's fingers stretch above the first chord of the bridal march, and everyone remembers that the risk of love is about to be taken again, that life is about to begin once more. This quiet of the heart was accented by the swishing sound of the white stole as Lanza draped it over his shoulders. Jimbo swallowed hard, felt agitation in his chest —something he had not anticipated—squeezed his eyes tightly together to hold off the surge of tears.

Lanza waited a moment, hefting a black leather prayer book with gold-edged pages. "My dear friends," he began gently, "I am sorry that we do not have time for Mass. But I am glad you are here for this joyous event. You who are about to wed must remember that stress and difficulty are the ordinary conditions of life, so that what has surrounded our gathering together may not be so unusual after all . . ." The mood lightened, Ann smiled up at Michael and the other members of the party relaxed. Jimbo bit his lower lip lightly, recalling images of his own wedding, caught a fleeting memory trace of what it was like to be in love.

"I could only find the pre-Vatican Two ritual," Lanza said, opening the book, "but you will not mind, I am sure . . ." He flipped a ribbon, began to read. "You are about to enter into a union that is most solemn and most sacred . . ."

Michael and Ann listened carefully, glancing at each other occasionally as Lanza read on ". . . sacrifice is always difficult and irksome. Only love can make it easy." Lanza paused, looked intently at them, "and perfect love can make it a joy." He concluded the introduction, came quickly to the vows, read them slowly. "Do you, Michael David Tracy, take Ann Frances Coleman as your wedded wife, to have and to hold, from this day forward, for richer, for poorer, in sickness and in health, as long as you both shall live?"

"I will," Michael replied almost inaudibly.

Lanza leaned closer to the couple. Something indefinable entered the air, a sense of promise and destiny, as he addressed the bride. "Do you, Ann Frances Coleman, take Michael David Tracy as your husband, to have and to hold, from this day forward, for richer, for poorer, in sickness and in health, as long as you both shall live?"

"I will," Ann responded firmly.

Jimbo kept his eyes lowered as he handed over the rings at the appropriate moment. He stepped back, glanced at Brother Louis and the stolid-looking nun. He needed to pull himself together before the end of the ceremony. Ghost-filled, that's what this is, Jimbo thought uncomfortably, who knew these spirits had lain in wait for him with their reminders of his own chances and failures? Those words "as long as you both shall live" made Jimbo uneasy, what the hell is going on, he complained to himself, cursing his Irishness, damning whatever had come unexpectedly and dangerously unstrung in his heart.

"You may kiss the bride," Lanza said genially, summoning Jimbo out of his deep well of introspection. The journalist watched as Michael and Ann embraced and kissed each other. Dear God, he sighed internally as another wave of mixed feeling rose inside him, *what* am I doing here anyway? Then Michael turned away from Ann, wrapped his arms around his brother, whispered as he hugged him, "Jimbo, I'm so glad you're here . . ." Jimbo coughed, shifted in embarrassment. "It's okay, kid," he said, "it's okay."

Lanza invited everyone back to his rooms in which, despite the short notice, he had arranged somehow for flowers, a small cake, and two bottles of champagne. "This may be the shortest reception on record," he announced to the group now enjoying an unexpectedly peaceful post-wedding buzz, "but it will not be an unworthy one."

The bride and groom moved closer to him. Michael embraced Lanza. "How can we ever thank you enough?"

Lanza shrugged, accepted a light kiss from Ann, stepped back, gestured for the now smiling nun to cut the cake. "Perhaps," Lanza said reflectively, "it is I who should thank you . . ."

"What do you mean? You've risked your career for us."

"Yes, my friend, and you have given up yours for the love of each other." He paused as he looked from Ann to Michael. "I am sure you will not put it in the papers that I witnessed your marriage. And my career, taking care of saints and Vatican security, will have to speak for itself."

"You seem very peaceful for a man taking a big risk . . ."

Lanza's eyes brightened, he smiled self-mockingly. "Perhaps you could call it *metanoia,* the conversion of heart we have spoken about. One of the few truly holy men I have ever met in my lifetime was, of all things, a labor leader. He used to say that the worst thing to get over was the fear that somebody could take away everything you had. The 'first fear,' he called it. Overcome that fear of losing everything, he said, and you would never be afraid of anything else." He looked beyond Michael and Ann into some world of memory. "This noon, when I watched you walk down the hall together, I could see that you were truly in love. And it spoke to me in a way that I cannot fully explain. Perhaps I remembered things that I had only seemed to forget . . ."

Michael nodded imperceptibly. Something familiar rang in the sweet bell of Lanza's voice, hints of things once glimpsed and given up, the same inflections of the heart he had heard in the dying old priest's last wide-eyed confession in that wind-battered prairie rectory. Lanza's eyes met Michael's, then Ann's, a wordless understanding flowed back and forth, something deeper than ambition, rules, or bureaucratic empires, something deep as life itself. They stood quietly together, joined in a spell they wanted to savor, hold on to even as it was slowly lifting away.

Jimbo shambled around the edge of things, seeming to chat with Brother Louis as he worked on restoring his own inner emotional balance. Something had gotten to him, what the hell is it, he wondered as he was offered a glass of champagne by Monsignor Lanza and encouraged to offer a toast. He blushed, felt the pinch of his forehead wound, looked into the bubbling wine. "Okay," he said turning toward Michael and Ann, "I didn't expect to be here today." Nervous laughter flashed across the group. "But, then, I guess none of you really expected to be here either." He paused, raised the glass. "I never expected my kid brother to get married. But I guess he didn't either . . ." Tension built around his unmoving figure. "Maybe I'd do this better in Gaelic . . ."

The room rocked violently, a wave of energy riding a muffled explosive tide rushed like apocalyptic wind through the apartment, staggering the guests, throwing them into each other and against the pitching, sliding furniture. The tray of freshly sliced cake toppled to the floor, the champagne bottles tottered, rolled off the table. Michael grabbed Ann, enfolded her in his arms, felt them both falling, glimpsed a crazy-angled view of Lanza's lamp dancing above the study desk as they hit the floor. A jagged ten-foot crack opened in the ceiling, releasing a shower of finely disintegrated plaster, dispersing memories sunk into it over hundreds of years. It eddied down on Lanza as he braced himself against the stout table at the center of the room. "Jesus Christ," Jimbo groaned on all fours, staring at the stem of the shattered champagne glass in his right hand, "what the fuck is going on here?"

SIX

The lights flickered, held fast, shining from fallen lamps through the cloud of dust like beacons at sea. Lanza, wearing a powdery mantle, still holding himself steady at the center table, coughed, shrugged, looked around the disordered room, coughed heavily again. The kitchen nun, her cheek bloodied, rose to her feet next to him, still holding the cake knife. Brother Louis fingered the broken lens of his glasses, shook himself, too stunned to speak, helped Jimbo, muttering in undifferentiated anger, to his feet. Mike assisted Ann, creased his dust-smeared features with a minstrel grin as she stood up. "Well, Mrs. Tracy . . ."

"How is everyone?" she asked, the calm professional. "Is anybody hurt?"

"I'm getting good at this," Jimbo murmured, glancing at the stem relic clenched in his right hand.

"Your head," Ann said. "I'll want to take a look at it."

Jimbo stared at her uncertainly, raised his left hand toward the Band-Aid on his forehead. Ann pulled it back. "I'll do that." She turned to Mike, who was inspecting his right hand. "Leave that alone, Mike," Ann said, "don't touch it." Lanza, coughing, nodded that he was all right. Ann inspected the nun's cheek, made her sit down, checked Brother Louis, who backed away, protesting wholeness. "Now," Ann said, sweeping the room with her eyes, "let's find how we stand, we may have to get out right away." She moved through the settling particle cloud toward the door.

As the group followed her, Jimbo muttered to himself, who the hell does she think she is, Florence Nightingale? A veil of pulverized lath and plaster hung in the hallway. The elevator cables still twanged in their shaft. Monsignor Lanza pressed a handkerchief to his face with one hand, extracted a set of keys from his cassock pocket with the other. He led them half a dozen steps down the hallway, unlocked Cardinal Kiejson's door, opened it on a surge of acrid fumes.

On the far side of the tumbled room the tall windows were shattered, a torn half mast of monk's cloth drapery smoldered in the casing. Mike and Jimbo tugged it down, stamped on it with their feet as another nun entered with a small fire extinguisher and sprayed it with foam. Ann and Brother Louis flanked Lanza at the window, looked down at the smoke-filled side yard, heard shouts, the C-sharp clarion of emergency vehicles, dissonant bells still sounding in a corner tower, soot-stained beneath its plumage of white vapor. Directly below it in the black-scorched far slot of the parking lot lay the fire-licked remains of the military van they had followed earlier. Pieces of it had landed on the adjoining wrecked and scattered cars. At the center, the Mercedes limousine lay on its back, a dead field marshal of German engineering, its wheels still spinning slowly. One of the old iron entrance gates had been blown off its hinges and the guard, his Napoleon's hat gone, his splendid uniform jacket tattered, stared uncomprehendingly at the scene.

Ann pulled at Monsignor Lanza's sleeve, asked him to use his Italian to see if any of the other nuns had been hurt. He turned, his brown eyes watering, made the inquiries, everyone was all right, nothing serious. The lights still worked, the water still ran, except for things being thrown about, the damage did not seem to be too severe. Lanza walked to the alcove. One of the battered leather chairs had pitched forward over the coffee table, strewing papers and magazines over the floor. The silver cigar box lay on its side, its contents scattered like miniature logs. The telephone nuzzled next to a crystal paperweight on the floor. Lanza retrieved the phone, picked up the paperweight, his obsessive instincts reasserting themselves. He dialed a number.

"I've got a tone," he announced to the group circling around him in the still hazy, burned-smelling atmosphere, "but I can't seem to make it work." He placed it on the table next to the pitted crystal sphere inside whose tiny universe the snowstorm had just ended. The trumpets of the emergency vehicles rose loudly through the shattered window space. "They will all know soon enough," Lanza said solemnly, "and I will have to attend to things . . ." He paused. In his silence he seemed to be contemplating his career, threatened now because of this security breach more than by the wedding. His eyes sent a message to Mike, perhaps I am not over that "first fear" after all.

Jimbo, blood oozing from beneath the small bandage on his forehead, surveyed the cardinalatial suite as the household nuns began to sweep and straighten things up. Mike picked up a black prayer book whose holy-card markers lay in a jumbled pattern around it. "Your hand," Ann said to him, "leave the cleaning up until later, first let's look at your hand." Mike lowered the breviary onto the table and followed Ann as Lanza led them out of the apartment, saying something about a medicine chest, he didn't think there was much in it.

Jimbo trailed behind, shaking off the paralysis of shock, looking at the computer which, wedged against the wall by stacks of heavy books on either side, had ridden out the blast without obvious damage. The modern machine, Jimbo thought, was saved by the ancient books, how do you like that? That's the Catholic Church for you, he muttered half aloud, the future surviving the present in the dead grip of history. Mike called to him. The church has the future and the past, Jimbo continued, it just doesn't react to the present. Mike called from the hallway. "Take it easy," Jimbo yelled back, "I'm having a poetic thought . . ."

The journalist shook his head, his story swirling like the tiny snowflakes in the crystal as he walked down the corridor. The New Century Movement, he thought as he stepped into the kitchenette, here I've been having an attack of sentiment, hanging around romantics, people with delusions of decency who think there's a happy ending out there somewhere, and all the while the New fucking Century Movement is out in the streets again. And Ownie, crooked old Ownie, I've got to get back to him, Rafallo too, my people, my fucking kind of people . . .

"Let's see now," Lanza said, reaching for the knob on the door of the cabinet above the sink as Ann daubed a cloth in water and cleaned the scratch on the kitchen nun's face. Mike felt a rhythmic pang in his hand, held it against his chest as Lanza cocked his head toward the sounds of voices and rubber-booted feet rising up the stairwell. "It might be better," he said hesitantly, "if you all went directly to an emergency room. Monsignor Fina may be coming any minute, and perhaps Cardinal Kiejson, too."

Ann looked up at him. "I could use a scissors and some bandages right now."

Lanza pulled at the knob, the medicine chest opened. Next to the lone glass sentinel of aspirin stood a small plastic bottle. The papal coat of arms was emblazoned on its label. The neatly typed inscription was in bold capital letters:

PP. JEAN   5/1/90
QUINIDEX EXTENTABS   300 mgm   #60
SIG: 2 TABS q 12 h.

SEVEN

"Jesus Christ," Jimbo said hoarsely, "Jesus Christ, the Quinidine . . . The pope's medicine . . ."

The room grew constricted, tight and airless, a world as closed on itself as that of the paperweight, except that nothing moved, neither mote nor speck drifted inside the choking static universe. Gravity pressed down on the onlookers as the mile-deep sea piled on divers contemplating a great pearl half born out of bottom sand.

"The grail," Jimbo added, haltingly, "it's the goddam grail . . ."

Lanza stared at the vial briefly, his ballroom-dancer calm shaken. His eyes flashed at the sound of men clumping down the hallway. He closed the door, his glance taking in the odd dust-streaked gathering—a sister cook, a former nun and ex-priest newly wed, a brother superior, and a *Time* bureau chief— the ages of the church recapitulated in surreal fashion. The prefect weighed odds and possibilities. Should he notify the *camerlengo* first, or Cardinal Kiejson? Lanza understood that, for himself and the church, much depended on his choice. Jimbo reached for the bottle. Mike barred the opening to the cabinet with his upraised bandaged hand. "Easy, Jimbo," he said, "let's just take it easy for a minute . . ."

Ann rinsed out the cloth, patted the kitchen nun on the shoulder. "You're alright, sister." The new Mrs. Tracy felt a quiver as she gazed at her husband, spellbound by the luminous white vessel of Quinidine. Was this, she wondered, another signal of the institutional church's unrelenting pursuit of Mike? The men who ran the institutional church always called it *she,* maybe they understood her capacity for jealousy, for possessiveness, for never letting go.

"Look," Jimbo said sharply, "I'm taking this bottle of medicine, whether anybody else likes it or not. It's *the only* clue to the biggest mystery of the century."

"I said to take it easy," Mike responded, putting his arm around Ann's shoulders. He whirled toward Lanza. "What about this, my friend?"

The prefect's sunless eyes locked on Michael's as he shook his head. The corridor noises counterpointed Lanza's silent gesture. He raised and spread his hands, resisting inquiry.

"You and your neighbors could get in here," Mike said evenly, "you told me so yourself."

Jimbo inhaled, stepped assertively forward. "Just *who* are these neighbors?"

"Stay out of this a minute, big brother."

Lanza pressed his lips together, spoke quietly. "Many people could have had access to this kitchenette. The nuns of the household staff, Monsignor Fina who is Cardinal Kiejson's secretary, and . . ."

"You," Mike said without accusation, "you took me here once yourself. And, of course, Cardinal Kiejson must know about it."

"Cardinal Kiejson, of course," Lanza responded, the smooth surface restored to his voice, "but snacks and coffee breaks are hardly his style. Many other people might easily have ways of getting in here. The room is never locked. Visitors come and go all the time. Cardinal Casey visited Cardinal Kiejson yesterday."

"Look," Jimbo interjected impatiently, "this Alphonse and Gaston act won't get us anywhere. We're not working out the pecking order of monsignors, we've got a clue that has to be brought to the proper authorities. If neither of you will do anything about it, *I* will."

The kitchen nun nervously fingered the rosary clacking at her side, looked anxiously at Lanza. Brother Louis wet his lips, shifted from one foot to another. Mike felt Ann's body pressing against him, pulsing with a message as clear as Morse code, *let's get away from here.* Lanza lowered his eyes briefly. "I will call Cardinal Kiejson at the general congregation and tell him what we have found."

The door burst open, a helmeted, rubber-coated fireman halted abruptly on the sill, lowered his ax as a diaphanous finger of smoke reached over his shoulder. Lanza spoke liquidly in Italian, the fireman backed out and clumped quickly down the hall. The prefect picked up his interrupted sentence effortlessly. "I will tell him that we have found the pope's medicine. First, however, I would like to restrain the rescue workers before they make things worse around here."

The prefect shook a crisp linen handkerchief loose, let it drop like a sacramental veil on the medicine, grasped it, plunged it into the pocket of his cassock. He closed the medicine cabinet, stepped into the clearing hallway, ordered the fire fighters to go downstairs and seal off the building, nobody in, nobody out, you understand? Mike looked tenderly into Ann's face. "Don't worry, Annie, we'll get out of here as quickly as possible." Jimbo, his imagination clanging like an old-fashioned radiator, searched his pockets for a cigarette, grumbled to a startled Brother Louis, "You saw all this, remember. I'm going to want to quote you unless this fucking monsignor puts us all under house arrest." The nun pulled a step away from Jimbo, her lips moving rapidly in silent prayer.

Lanza watched the last of the firemen retreat down the corridor, made some quick decisions as he surveyed the group, sent the nun to get the household sisters to clean up, starting with his own quarters, waved the others after him toward Kiejson's apartment.

EIGHT

The wedding party stood numb and quiet in the electric atmosphere of the Dutch cardinal's suite, the twin shocks of the last few minutes just penetrating their consciousness, eating through the Novocain layer of their regular defenses. What, they wondered, each in a different way, was happening to them in this pungent hazy aftermath?

Jimbo, released from good manners by the click of the lock as Lanza closed the door, spoke first, his unlit cigarette bouncing on his lips in time to his staccato sentences. "What the hell is going on here, Monsignor? You've got the clue, maybe to the crime of the century, in your pocket, we've had a bombing, there's a conclave scheduled to start, all this can't be *just happening,* a busy news day in the Eternal City." He snorted, punched the air with a violent gesture. "*We* tailgated the van that blew up, followed it right in here. You may be great making decisions on what dead people were really saints but you're sitting on all this as if you didn't want anybody to know about it. That's the feeling you give me."

"Jimbo," Mike cut in, "we're playing local rules here. Let's give Monsignor Lanza a chance. Monsignor Lanza *is* in charge of security."

"Yeah," Jimbo snarled, turning away, "well, he's been doing a swell job . . ."

"Thank you, Michael," Lanza interjected. "We are in a unique situation. I have to ask for your cooperation and your pledge of confidence."

"Count me out," Jimbo said quickly, "whatever you do, whatever you decide, whatever happens here, everything here is *on* the record."

Lanza studied him as the head of the Inquisition, unintimidated, might have evaluated a protesting barbarian witness, and spoke dryly. "We sometimes become involved in history in ways that we do not choose. Perhaps that is always the way. This, I believe, is certainly one of those times."

"Malarkey," Jimbo snapped, "it's easier to cover things up with talk like that." He strode across the room, his shoes crunching on the sparkling cloak of broken glass spread below the empty window casing. He grasped the ledge tensely, peered down into the parking area, smoldering under the white splashing fire hoses. A crew of men in military uniforms poked gingerly around the blast-darkened corner where the gutted, dismembered van lay. A crane squealed as it lifted the fallen gate away from the entrance. Nearby, a large piece of metal jutted out of the smashed windshield of Jimbo's Fiat. "Goddammit," he cried, whirling around, "you *know* this is connected with Pope Jean's death, admit it."

"Jimbo," Mike snapped, "knock it off."

"You," Jimbo shot back, walking toward his brother, *"you* know I'm right. Help me out, Mike. Can't you see what this is all about? You feel it, too, don't you, the way the old man did when he was on a case? There always came a time—remember?—when he'd say he had to let his instincts take over." Jimbo breathed heavily as he stood face to face with Mike. "You *can* feel it, can't you? Come on, Mike, come on." He swept a gesture around the littered room. "Who the hell killed the pope? And *why?* The answer is here somewhere, I can feel it, I can feel the goddam truth trying to get out . . ."

"I'm sorry, Jimbo," Mike said slowly, Ann's touch reminding him of their future, "that's all in the past, Jimbo. Our past, my past, too. You can solve this if you want. The explosion is where I came in." He hugged Ann. "Mrs. Tracy and I have more important matters to take care of. Come on, Annie."

Lanza frowned. "That may not be so easy, not yet." He picked up the phone, waited until the tone hummed, dialed a number, waited again, then spoke firmly. "This is Monsignor Lanza. Lanza, yes, *Lanza."* He pulled his head back from the crackling receiver, raised his voice, "There's something wrong with the phones so you must listen carefully. I must speak to Cardinal Kiejson. *Kiejson.* Yes, I know they are in a congregation. But this is a matter of the utmost importance." Everybody tensed, joined themselves to the prefect's effort to tease a reply out of the faltering connection. "No, I can't hear you. Tell Cardinal Kiejson that he *must* call his own apartment. Find Monsignor Fina. *Fina,* F-I-N-A, *Fina* . . ."

Jimbo ignored Mike and Ann, walked deliberately back across the room, Lanza's voice registering dimly on his consciousness as he scanned the floor, straining to read the tea-leaf debris. The journalist paused, inhaled deeply. Something was building inside himself as powerful and distinctively shaped as the need for a binge or a good lay. "The missing piece is here, it's talking to me," he said half aloud, flicking his unlit cigarette away, "it's *here,* the goddam thing is *here,* it's fucking *talking* to me . . ."

Lanza hung up the phone, looked warily at Jimbo. "There is nothing to do, nothing we should do, until the cardinal calls."

"Like hell," the journalist blurted out excitedly, "there's plenty to be learned. Come on, Mike, you must feel it in your Irish gut, the way the old man used to. I can tell by your expression, you *know* I'm right." He stepped rapidly across the space between himself and his brother. "Come *on,* little brother, help me out . . ."

Michael held Ann tightly as he faced his brother's intense gaze. He knew Jimbo was right, Jimbo *is* crazy, he thought wildly, he's Irish-poet crazy, sometimes paranoid crazy, but he *is* picking up something. Mike felt the fine edge of his brother's excitement, tribal energy flowing between them.

Ann looked from brother to brother, catching the invisible, static-ridden signals enveloping them. They were rising, she understood, from some primordial level of their Irish souls, a fragile but potent layer of Celtic intuition, the delicate vein that was the source of all the race's magic. Rising, too, from what the church, Mother Church, had made of them all, including herself, penetrating to their deepest nerves and fibers with an encompassing, irresistible presence. "Stop it, you two," Ann said, pulling on Mike's arm. "Come on, Mike, we can't help Jimbo."

Mike turned suddenly to her, like a man coming out of the deep, hungry for air. He shook his head, looked again into Jimbo's pale, tightly drawn face. "This is the Garden of Eden," Mike said, biting out the words, gesturing to include all of Rome, "the Garden of Eden, Jimbo. And whatever you think you're picking up on your Mick antenna, it's really the forbidden fruit that's tempting you. You want the knowledge of good and evil, you've always wanted it. It's your calling." He caressed Ann gently, kept his focus on Jimbo's eyes. "But it's not mine. Not anymore. And it's full of death, Jimbo, it's full of death . . ."

NINE

Brother Louis touched the absorbed Monsignor Lanza on the arm as Jimbo
stepped back from Michael and Ann. "I think I should go," the brother
whispered. Lanza broke free of his preoccupation, glanced at Jimbo and
Mike as they silently disentangled their Siamese-like souls from each other.
The prefect understood Brother Louis as a fellow bureaucrat, a good man
with duty as his sacramental star, Louis had not become head of an international religious order by being indiscreet, there would be no danger in
letting him go. Lanza scribbled a notation on a card, gave it to him, and
descended into his own thoughts again.

What, Lanza asked himself, is happening to me? The staid curial life—
with its serene, sanctified boredom, its noble works and petty intrigues, its
red-trimmed containment and preferment, as well as its promise of ultimate
ecclesiastical rewards—was riding the unpeeling crust of a dissolving world.
And this very day, the prefect thought, I counted myself brave for standing
for human love against institutionalism. But now the very soul of the
church, the light in its organizational darkness, is in my hands.

"Okay," Jimbo said softly, lowering his eyes, acknowledging defeat, Ann has Mike, he thought, marriage has him, I can't get him into the game anymore, not even when he knows I'm right, I felt that in him, something in each of us bubbling over, flowing together, things we knew without saying them out loud, maybe that's why I didn't want him to get married, we'll never be the same with each other again . . .

Ann embraced Mike, kissed him lightly on the cheek, trying to love him out of his sudden remoteness. Our childhood is finally ending, Mike thought, I'm not his little brother anymore. Mike shook his head, hugged Ann, felt overwhelmed as he looked into her eyes, yes, he thought, I'm growing up at last.

Jimbo walked slowly toward Cardinal Kiejson's alcove, grimacing at the taste of regret. Maybe, he thought, that's why Maureen and I had so much trouble, maybe I never really broke free of home, of being the police inspector's son, having the brother a priest, eternally pure and unconnected so you were always the same as you were as kids with each other, and now that's over for good . . .

"The hell with it," he muttered, punching one fist into the other, shoving his bitter musings as deep down inside himself as he could. "Dr. Quinidine," he said crisply, breaking into Lanza's preoccupations, "Dr. Quinidine, that's all I said to Ambassador Wingate, and he came after me as if I were Kim Philby."

"Yes," the prefect said absently, plunging back into his own unsettled thoughts, silently urging the phone to ring.

"Dr. Quinidine, I said to him," Jimbo continued, "Dr. Quinidine says there's nothing on paper." He circled past the blown-out window, listened for a moment to the sounds of machines and men's shouts, sniffed the burnt offerings of terrorism, paced back toward the alcove. "Dr. Quinidine says that there's nothing on paper . . ." He looked up into the pallid face of the computer screen, stopped abruptly, transfixed. "Nothing on paper," he said aloud, "nothing on paper." The journalist twisted toward Mike and Ann, shouted excitedly, *"That's* it! Son of a bitch, I knew the son of a bitch was here, I knew it." He gestured toward the computer. "Of course nothing's on paper. It's on a computer chip, like fuzz on a peach, it's on one of these goddam disks."

The others watched him for a split second as Jimbo searched the papers and folders scattered near the machine. "Easy," Mike said, "this isn't your business." Jimbo glared at him, riffled through pages, tossed them aside, snatched some from the floor.

"Please," Lanza urged, placing a restraining hand on Jimbo's shoulder, "leave everything as it is. These are Cardinal Kiejson's private papers."

"Yeah," Jimbo snorted, picking up one of the old books wedged next to the computer, "and in a few hours he may be a very public pope . . ." He leaned down, turned on the machine as he flipped the book open. A computer disk fell to the floor in the middle of the huddled circle. It was stamped in red TOP SECRET—CONFIDENTIAL. Nobody breathed for an instant as another wave of feeling washed over them, sending them tumbling again in time and space. "Son of a bitch," Jimbo muttered, "it's talking to me, son of a bitch if it isn't . . ."

TEN

The phone rang as Jimbo plucked the disk from the floor, stared at it momentarily, raised it as reverently as a priest elevating the host at Mass. Mike moved next to his brother as Lanza answered the phone.

"Monsignor Fina? Yes, this is Monsignor Lanza . . ." The prefect waved the brothers into silence as he pressed the earpiece closer to his head. "Listen, this phone line must have been damaged. You *must* get Cardinal Kiejson to come here at once."

"Let go," Jimbo said as Mike put his bandaged hand on his brother's arm, "let go, little brother." His tone was easy, quiet, as if there were nothing to struggle with Mike about anymore. The journalist slipped the program disk into the machine, stared at Mike silently as the computer groaned and Lanza repeated his message loudly in the background. Ann pressed close at Mike's left side. "Let go, Mike," Jimbo repeated softly, as if he had broken free of the room and was riding the whirling atoms in the keening machine. "This is the ball game," he whispered, "you're not playing today, nobody picked you for their team."

"Come on, Jimbo, I've got a bad hand but I think I can still take you . . ."

"That'll be the day," Jimbo snapped, removing the program disk, inserting the one with the confidential markings. Lanza shouted into the phone, *"Now, yes now,"* as Mike pulled at his brother's arm. Jimbo turned abruptly, the brothers fell together, clinched, pitted their weight against each other, grunting with the effort.

"Stop it," Ann said anxiously, "stop it, you two." She worked her hands between them as they staggered, bumping the coffee table, making the stacks of paper jump and avalanche over the edge. The crystal sphere rolled off the table, thudded onto the floor. *"Mike, Jim,"* Ann ordered as she moved in tandem with them, "you're not in the schoolyard anymore. You're not little boys . . ."

Mike relaxed suddenly, shook his stinging hand as Jimbo, puffing, backed away like a wobbling bottle. The journalist steadied himself, looked glassily at Mike and Ann, turned to the computer. Lanza hung up as Jimbo, breathing heavily, flipped through the old book in which the disk had been concealed.

"Cardinal Kiejson will be here in a few minutes," Lanza announced. "The line was very bad but I was finally able to speak directly to him."

"Does he know what's going on here?" Mike asked as Ann took his right hand gently in her own.

"Not in detail. He knows enough. He knows that it is urgent."

"Son of a bitch," Jimbo murmured as a file card fluttered out of the old volume. He picked the card up with his left hand, inspected a list of phrases, pecked out the first one, PRINCE, on the keys. He held his right hand above the keyboard, turned his eyes on his brother and Ann, then on Lanza frozen in place a few steps away. "If I'm not mistaken," Jimbo announced, lighting up, "this lady is very fat and ready to sing." He pressed the entry key, the screen jiggled, turned blank. He checked the card, entered the next notation, DOME. The screen remained blank.

"Jimbo," Mike implored, "let the police take care of this. This isn't the fat lady, it really *is* the knowledge of good and evil, it's not right, what you're doing . . ."

"Please," Lanza added, closing the circle around the journalist.

"You and Mrs. Tracy here," Jimbo responded, looking up from the card, "you get out of here before the next pope shows up." He jutted his chin at

Ann. "Mike is dead wrong. But where *you're* wrong is thinking we're still brothers fighting in the schoolyard. We're *not* little kids anymore, we're not brothers that way, not anymore. *You've* got him now. You're like twins, the two of you, so why don't you get the hell out if, as Michael the ex-monsignor here says, we're dealing with good and evil?"

The noises of the crane tugging at dead weight wreckage in the yard below filled the quiet as Jimbo carefully typed RED HAT. He tapped the entry key. A stylized American eagle rose on the screen, trailed by official symbols and numbers, a paragraph of codes and warnings, then a bold legend: ABSTRACTS: THE FIFTY MOST INFLUENTIAL MEMBERS OF THE COLLEGE OF CARDINALS.

The silence grew taut, expanded, threatened to burst. "Son of a *bitch*," Jimbo yiped, "she's about to sing the aria from *Carmen*."

Lanza moved to the phone, picked it up. "I'm afraid that I will have to call security."

"Wait," Jimbo called, scrolling the next lines up onto the screen, "this isn't *Casablanca,* and you're not Captain Renault."

The uncomprehending Lanza frowned, dialed a number, held his hand over the mouthpiece. "Michael is correct," the prefect said flatly, "you are dealing with the knowledge of good and evil."

"Look at this . . ."

Mike and Ann stepped back from the blossoming screen, kicking the Dutch cardinal's breviary, sending it skidding, a trail of bookmarks and holy cards in its wake. Michael leaned down, collected them quickly in his left hand, held them loosely as he spoke to Ann. "Mrs. Tracy, this is the second time I've done this. I'm taking it as a signal that we should definitely go."

A grim Lanza clutched the phone tightly as Mike nodded toward him. Jimbo tapped the keys again, watched as fresh information crowded onto the screen. "Ah," he cried, "the Rosetta stone on our own Cardinal Casey . . ."

The heavy machines in the yard growled, the lights flickered, once, twice, steadied briefly, went out. The computer screen turned as gray as the sea in front of the open-mouthed Jimbo. Lanza stared at the suddenly dead phone. The scattered fragments of glass winked brightly in the panel of afternoon sun that was now the room's only light.

"Now," Lanza said in a crackling voice, the well of his urbanity gone dry, "I advise you all to leave. God, it would seem, has again taken a hand in things. You can go down a back way through the kitchen. I will give you passes to get through." He removed some cards from his pocket, initialed and handed them to Mike. Jimbo tapped the keys vainly, angrily, turned away as a dazed medic does from a failed resuscitation effort, there was life there a minute ago. *"Son of a bitch,"* he repeated as Mike tucked his pass into his breast pocket, "son of a bitch."

"Is that your mantra?" Mike asked as they followed Lanza through a back hallway, down darkened stairs into the assaulting tumult of the crowded street.

Mike and Ann stood uncertainly on the roped-off sidewalk, showed their passes to a bristling security officer, gazed up at the building, a great husk of their molted institutional existence, silvered by the sun. It towered impassively above the surging crowds as complacent as a redwood, indifferent to the turmoil, aloof and demanding even in distress, like a queen giving orders to the policemen who arrest her. Still, Michael thought, stepping into the street, the Vatican is rich in secrets and stratagems and the building might suddenly reshape itself gelatinously, surround and repossess them. Mike edged Ann gently a few feet along the sidewalk. Despite the cascading sunlight, Rome seemed dark and mysterious as if the sharp odors had rekindled its deepest memories of fire and death.

Jimbo's Irish trickster's grin neutralized the brooding, reactive atmosphere. He patted his side pocket, winked.

"You didn't," Mike said, surprised, "you didn't . . ."

"The hell I didn't," Jimbo replied, immensely pleased with himself. "I palmed the disk as your friend Guido Sarducci was throwing us out."

"Jimbo," Ann said, "they'll be after you."

"They're already after me," he answered mischievously. "Ambassador Wingate's been looking for me all day. If he contacts you, tell him I didn't leave a forwarding address."

"What exactly," Mike asked, *"are* you going to do?"

"Well," the journalist replied, his eyes bright, "I'm sorry you won't come along. Be a hell of a honeymoon. I'm going to get this disk matched to some computer. Then I'm going to get it printed out. Not at *Time.* Wingate's hounds will be baying at the gates there. Then, when I figure the pieces out, I'm going to write the goddamndest story you ever read."

"Jimbo . . ." Mike broke off as a trumpeting police car, its lights flashing, parted the street crowds, pulled up imperially at the main entrance of the residence. An ashen-faced Cardinal Kiejson stepped out, surveyed the smoky, noisy scene as if memorizing it. Three police officers grouped about him, escorted him into the building.

"The Dutchman will be sore as a bastard when he finds this is gone." Jimbo touched his pocket again, looked up and down the street, then faced Mike and Ann, his bright, cold mugger's smile masking his churning feelings. "I," he said gruffly, "I have work to do." He averted his eyes. "Funny, Mike, this reminds me of the first day you went to school. I took you. You were just a runny-nosed little guy with black hair and blue eyes. I never told you this . . ." Jimbo sniffed, touched the blood-stained bandage on his forehead. "Ah, the hell with it." He suddenly hugged Mike, broke as if from a clinch. Jimbo felt a knot in his throat, composed his features. "You were a good kid." He made a quick nod at Ann, turned and hurried up the street.

Standing before the shattered window of his apartment, Kiejson spoke calmly. "If you don't have many possessions, Monsignor, then you can never lose very much." He seemed to let go of his disciplined posture, to float in meditation for a moment, then turned slowly. "You acted quite correctly in informing me about the medicine." The cardinal glanced at the darkened alcove, saw the glittering orb of paperweight on the floor, walked over, picked it up. "Now," he said, replacing it on the table, "now that we are alone, we must discuss the next step in this matter."

Lanza produced the fluted handkerchief that held the medicine. "Yes, Your Eminence, I presume that we should turn this over to the authorities."

Kiejson arched his right eyebrow, touched a hand to the pale scar on his jaw. "Let me say that I do not think that you failed as head of security because of this incident. Nor will I allow anyone else to think so. It is important that we make *no* changes in our plans right now. Nor would I trust anyone else."

Lanza nodded, said nothing.

Kiejson looked away from the prefect. "My judgment about this matter is that somebody found this medicine." He gestured toward it with his ringed hand. "Some good nun who was cleaning up the papal apartments put it in her apron pocket, then discovered it later and didn't know what to do with it." Kiejson paused, studied Lanza's eyes for reaction, continued. "And so she tried to return it. Probably too frightened to bring it to anyone. What more appropriate place could she put it in than a medicine cabinet? So I do not think that this discovery means much. I think, in fact, that the medicine is now irrelevant."

Lanza raised his eyebrows, opened his mouth to speak. Kiejson waved his hand, walked back to the glass-littered patch of light, spoke deliberately. "The last thing the church needs now is a new rumor that will have no foundation and that, on the eve of a papal election, can only disrupt things further."

Lanza swallowed. Kiejson, the silent prefect reminded himself, is almost the pope now.

"Since you have the medicine and nobody else knows about it . . ." The Dutch cardinal interrupted himself, looked inquiringly at Lanza. "Nobody *does* know, that is so, isn't it?"

"*I* know," Lanza replied dryly, "*you* know. Whoever put it there knows too."

"Yes, yes, of course, but you have the medicine and, lacking evidence, nobody could prove that it was ever found or, for that matter, lost." Kiejson fingered his pectoral cross, spoke as a man does when he does not expect an argument. "Its revelation could only gratify Moscow. I see no reason to accommodate the party chairman at our expense. We cannot afford further disruption in the church. We must stabilize matters. Do you understand?"

Lanza folded the handkerchief tightly around the medicine, placed it on the table in the alcove, stood back, thought that it looked like a napkin at an expensive restaurant. My duty, he ruminated, tasting ambivalence, my duty done again.

"For the good of the church, Monsignor," Kiejson said as if reading the prefect's mind. "You are a loyal son of the church."

"Yes," Lanza answered, his chest filled with the congested feelings of the day, "yes, I suppose I am."

ELEVEN

Michael smiled at Ann, patted her arm gently. They entered the hotel by looping around through the pool area to avoid emissaries from Ambassador Wingate or Josef Beck. A poster from the day's news conference still clung to the wall: A PEOPLE'S CHURCH NEEDS A PEOPLE'S POPE. Mike shook his head, turned to Ann, whispered as he hugged her, "This is the last of the cops and robbers, I promise."

Ann looked into his eyes, tried to penetrate their bright blue waters, as the elevator opened on their floor. Is there, she wondered, some Celtic ghost in those depths, some Tracy spirit that can never resist the temptation to plumb the knowledge of good and evil, some mysterious shade that will ultimately turn Mike restless in an ordinary life? "Are you really sure," she asked as they walked down the hallway, "that you'll be happy with me?"

"Mrs. Tracy," he said as they reached their door, "excitement is not happiness." He kissed her. "But happiness is exciting." He inserted the key with his left hand. "Why do you ask, Annie?"

"Something about you and your brother, something about the way you looked at each other back in the cardinal's apartment and then down in the street. He still doesn't want to let go of you."

"I'm sorry, Annie, I thought he was coming around."

"That's not the feeling he gives me. I began to wonder if I had married some combination of police captain, investigative reporter, priest perpetually on call, or a sweet gentle man who can be content in a quiet, uneventful life with me."

"And *I* wondered if I had married a woman who would stay at home with me or a doctor whose beeper will be going off at three A.M. every morning." Mike pushed the door open, grinned, and lifted her off her feet.

"Mike, your hand . . ."

"Mrs. Tracy, I really do love you. And it's only proper that I carry you over the threshold." He kissed her again, holding her tight, pressed his lips against hers, released them into joyous laughter. "And now, Mrs. Tracy, I bid you welcome to a very quiet life."

He angled her gently through the opening, kicked the piled-up messages deftly with one foot. "Hello the house, as the Irish say." He lowered her easily to her feet. "Well, Annie," Mike said, his eyes twinkling, "we're home at last."

"Mike," she said with a broad smile, "you'll get used to the beeper."

"*Extra omnes!*" The cry of the papal master of ceremonies grew louder inside the otherwise still and solemn area around the Sistine Chapel in which temporary cardinalatial quarters had been set up for the conclave. The late afternoon Mass in St. Peter's had concluded and the procession of cardinals had moved on a slow current of Gregorian chant through the great door into the famous chapel. Before the final bricks were mortared into place in an interior entrance, all but a few conclave officials were required to leave. Monsignor Lanza stood by the low exit through which the cardinals' secretaries ducked their heads as they passed. They are like paratroopers, the prefect mused, bailing out of this house of eternity back into time.

He glanced down at the security checklist handed to him by an aide as the ancient cry of dismissal, filtered through some warren of corridors, returned to him muffled and indistinct. Every wall had been swept for electronic eavesdropping devices, every sink, toilet, bed, and bricked-in window casing had been examined, the cardinal electors' own baggage had been searched, the foil on the candy bars brought in by the archbishop of St. Louis had set off the metal detectors.

Lanza looked up, let the document break like a wavelet over his hand, tried to listen to himself in the silence, accented only by footsteps and whispers. What, he wondered, am I making secure here? The new pope is almost a foregone conclusion, the voting should go quickly, the secrets of conclaves are actually very few, the intrigue is usually less relevant than the world supposes. But the *idea* of secrets, the sound of the Spirit's wings beating beneath Michelangelo's vast, intimidating ceiling, the promise of divine intervention in the world's all too human affairs, *that* is what I am making secure.

And what, he asked himself ironically, have I done today? Nobody inspecting me, in my fresh cassock and polished shoes, would suspect that this very day I have witnessed a marriage, been in a bombing, discovered the old pope's medicine and, at the bidding of the likely new pope, have decided to forget it. Is it always this way with sinners, he wondered ruefully, when they return to the commonplace world *after* the sin, sitting at their desks, making meals for their children, directing traffic in the streets, saying Mass? Cleaned up, we all look as if nothing had happened, as if we were righteous innocents, bystanders the whole time, no we didn't notice a thing. What am I to make of my intermittently noble life, Lanza asked himself, what does my life really mean? He shook his head. He had survived, he admitted grudgingly, uncomfortably, but he had not gotten over that first fear, not yet anyway . . .

The diminutive secretary of the archbishop of Tokyo approached the exit —no need to lower his black, finely barbered head—then stepped back to make room for Thomas Cardinal Casey, holding the bunched skirt of his cassock with one hand as he made his way cautiously into the conclave area. The Chicagoan turned, watched Franz Cardinal Kiejson edge his stooped nobleman's figure through the opening without touching any of the jutting bricks. Lanza compressed his lips as the two princes of the church walked past without seeming to notice him, their princely crimson robes covering their secrets elegantly.

"Extra omnes!" The diminished voice sounded again from within St. Peter's. A young priest approached Lanza. "All the cardinals are here now," he said, still swimming in the fresh excitement of his first conclave. Lanza nodded, guided the young assistant toward the opening, watched as the last

of the secretaries and other officials left, looked back for one last moment at the now empty space, had a flashing mental picture of the Quinidine, wrapped like Lazarus but as beyond recall from the tomb as Pope Jean himself.

Cardinal Kiejson stood next to Cardinal Casey outside the Chicagoan's room as two other princes of the church moved past them in the narrow corridor. "Thomas," the Dutch cardinal said quietly, "I *do* think that we should speak again. As soon as possible."

"There's not much more to discuss," Casey replied, grasping the doorknob, "especially this evening." He cracked the door, revealing an iron bedstead and a stand topped with an old-fashioned water pitcher.

"Is it the bombing," Kiejson asked calmly, "or something else?"

How much, Casey wondered, does Kiejson really know about my affairs? Casey had thought long and hard during the afternoon congregation, paying no attention to the discussion, watching Kiejson as he was called out, thinking, as thoroughly as he could, of what his strategy should be. During the Mass of the Holy Spirit, Casey had made his decision. He would stick with his candidacy, no matter what. His Third World support remained strong. He had nothing to lose. He would either become the pope or, at the right moment, become the grand elector for Kiejson and then become his secretary of state. Either way, the investigations of his affairs would be terminated. But he could not let Kiejson know what he was thinking, he only wanted the Dutchman to feel his resolve and understand that he didn't scare easily. Don't show your cards too soon, that's what Missy had said to him, invoking Mama, just before he kissed her good-bye at the hotel.

"Is it the bombing," Kiejson prompted Casey again, "or . . ."

"What else would it be?" Casey responded, poker-faced, as he opened the door and entered his quarters.

TWELVE

Unable to sleep, Angelo Cardinal Solieri had rolled off his lumpy cot shortly before four A.M. He padded in his old cassock and worn slippers to the Sistine Chapel and knelt in the broad empty area at its far end. He did not look up at the barely lighted glories of the ceiling as he pondered why God had made him a cardinal. Why, O Lord, the old man asked in the easy conversational style of his deepest prayer, why have you placed me here, as powerless and harmless as if I were at my cluttered desk in the archives? Am I here to be purified in my declining years for the sins of my youth, to learn sadly that I am hardly noticed by others, that, no matter what I have learned, I am just an old man whose time is running out, a librarian, a keeper of memory, better acquainted with the vast legions of the dead than with my living brothers in this college of cardinals? What can I do, Solieri pleaded from a groaning heart, why have you let me learn things when nobody pays any attention to me?

The old man opened his eyes, squinted in the semi-darkness at the two tiers of long cloth-covered tables that had been set up in the section of the chapel near the altar. Sentinel lines of hard, high-backed chairs stood stiffly behind the tables. So many electors, Solieri sighed, so many powerful and wise men who know so much more about the modern world than I do. I am almost too old to be here. How foolish, he thought, lecturing himself as he had all his life, how foolish and out of place I am. These men are surely guided by God, I must believe that. He rose slowly, creakily, from his knees. Other cardinals had now come to pray, gliding soundlessly in the cool darkness. I must, Solieri whispered, I must leave the future of the church to them.

As he moved slowly to an exit, he could make out Franz Cardinal Kiejson's heroic silver-crowned profile. Solieri hesitated momentarily, you will soon be the Holy Father, can you give a few moments to a troubled old man? Solieri shook his head, no, he said to himself, this is all temptation, the devil's work in me, I am only here, as Pope Jean appointed me, in an honorary position, I am not here to make history.

"Thanks, Freddie," Jimbo said, checking his watch. It was almost six A.M. "I knew I could count on you. Nothing like an old pal from Time Inc. in an emergency."

The ginger-haired, heavyset Fred Harshar rubbed his unshaven chin. "I like working for *Global Travel* a hell of a lot better. I don't usually come to the office before ten. Now just what is it you want to see on the computer?"

Jimbo handed him the disk, hurriedly but vaguely explained its importance as Harshar sleepily programmed his computer in the cramped office just off the Via Veneto. He inserted Jimbo's disk into the slot, turned toward him, smiling sardonically. "You don't mind my saying it, Jimbo, this is just like you . . ."

Jimbo's eyes flitted from Harshar's hand above the entry key to the blank screen. Harshar withdrew his hand, swiveled his chair toward Jimbo.

"You've always been like this, Jimbo, *always* . . ." Harshar stretched, scratched himself, opened a desk drawer, withdrew a wrung-out package of cigarettes. "There's nothing really wrong with *Time*'s computers, am I right?" He struck a match, lit his cigarette, inhaled. "It's woman trouble again, isn't it? Some little chippie down there at the office you don't want to run into, am I right?"

"Yes," Jimbo half shouted, "yes, women, boys, giraffes, anything you want to believe." He reached across Harshar's chest, tapped the entry key, ducked away from Harshar's coughed-out smoke. The official government insignia appeared on the screen, followed by the warnings and title. Harshar's mouth fell open, his cigarette dangling moistly, perilously, from his lower lip. "Holy Christ, Jimbo," he said slowly, "where the hell did you get this?"

Mike and Ann, tangled in each other's arms, were awakened at six A.M. by a phone call. Mike groaned, stirred, smiled at Ann as she shifted her head, opened her eyes—what eyes, he thought, have I ever seen them before? The phone rang again. "I told the operator not to disturb us . . ." He rolled across the bed, letting Ann's pleasantly tousled head move gently onto the crook of his arm, picked up the phone.

"This is Ambassador Wingate speaking."

"You must have the wrong number."

"No, no, you're Michael Tracy, the one who used to be a priest . . ."

"Well, actually I'm just getting into it . . ."

"Listen, *Mister* Tracy, this isn't a joking matter."

"You're entitled to your opinion."

"You're a lot like your brother. And, as a matter of fact, *he's* the one I'm looking for. This is an official matter."

Ann pulled closer to Mike as he raised his head. "Well, as you know, you've got the wrong Tracy. And I don't know where the other one is."

"That doesn't seem likely. We've learned that he was at the Word of Mercy House with you yesterday."

"Sorry . . ."

"That's the kind of attitude that got your father in trouble, Mister Tracy. Now, I'm very anxious to review his movements with you. We'd like to have a little talk with you this morning."

"Not this morning," Mike answered, but Wingate had already hung up. "Time to see the sights," he said teasingly, resting his bandaged hand lightly on Ann's shoulder.

"You're not having emergencies already, are you?" She rubbed her eyes, sat up next to him.

"No, and if Wingate can't find us, we won't have any."

Ann pulled Mike down close to her, hugged him, kissed his ear, the side of his neck, alternating her words with the light touches of her lips. "Let's play a little longer."

"I've got a better idea. Let's take the train to Florence, let's . . ."

"Let's not go anywhere."

"That's what G. K. Chesterton said. The best journey is the one that leads you back home."

"Oh Mike," Ann said in mock exasperation. "This is no time for quotations."

They fell into a laughing embrace. Mike pulled the covers up over them. "If you get used to my quotes, I'll get used to your beeper."

Twenty minutes later the phone rang again. Wingate's associate, a Mr. Hickey, would pick them up in an hour. They rose quickly, laughing like children as they showered and dressed, singing together lightly, feeling that they were finally free, that they had outrun the shadows of the institutional church and a new life, already happier than their long dreaming of it, had opened for them. They decided not to check out, to keep the room while they traveled for a few days.

"Never thought I could break away, did you?" Mike asked, slipping into his jacket, brushing it with his good hand.

"You continue to amaze me. I never thought you'd be willing to leave town during a papal election, especially not after yesterday. And that jacket is pretty dirty, Mike. You'd better change."

"I'm going to have some campaign ribbons struck for this experience. Meanwhile, Jimbo will carry on." He slipped off the coat, began to empty the pockets. "And on and on. I'm a little surprised at myself, happily surprised, of course. I haven't really been in on a good church mystery since the head usher at Holy Name skimmed a hundred grand off the collection baskets and blew it on the ponies—"

Mike broke off so suddenly that Ann turned away from the mirror, lipstick in hand, to look at him. He was staring at some holy cards and pictures he had discovered in the jacket pocket.

"Annie," he said softly, "Annie . . ."

"What is it, Mike?" Ann replied, her heart constricting, going icy.

"Look," Mike said, "look at this . . ." He held up a cracked and yellowed photograph, a bevel-edged print from an old Kodak Brownie camera. "I must have put these into my pocket in the midst of everything yesterday, after I picked up the cardinal's prayerbook."

Ann looked down at the faded picture of a young girl in a plain dress standing against a sun-washed brick wall. "What . . . *who* is it, Mike?"

Mike stared at it, recalling snatches of conversations that had nagged at the edges of his consciousness. "That's what Lanza was going to tell me," he said softly, "that's what Joe Beck *did* tell me . . ."

"What, *what* is it, Mike, what are you talking about?"

" 'I wouldn't call her a landsperson,' that's how Josef put it . . ."

"Mike . . ."

"This is a picture of Mother Hilda, that's who. A long time ago. Before she became the seeress of Munich, before she stopped eating, before she became a saint . . ."

"What are you talking about, Mike, tell me."

"Hilda's not German, that's what, Hilda's *not* German. She's Dutch. And the cardinal who may be elected pope today has carried her picture in his breviary for forty years."

"Let's get out of here, Mike."

Mike held his eyes on the photograph, felt its magnetic power, understood what Jimbo meant about clues, how mute objects talked to you, would swell up right before you, distorting themselves trying to break out of the mummy wrappings of their particularity. "Okay, Annie, okay . . ." His voice became hushed, he seemed to be staring beyond the old picture. The dead children, whose voices and faces had dimmed like those of carolers rounding a far corner, marched into his imagination again, the innocent dead, their faces white and smooth as bone. "Annie," Mike said slowly, "Annie, we have to see Mother Hilda before we leave."

Ann shivered, felt uneasy, frightened, and embraced Mike as much to protect as to be protected. The chill silhouette of St. Peter's fell across them like darkness from a racing cloud. They clung tightly to each other. The pale image of a girlish, pretty Mother Hilda looked out from a forty-year-long cavern of time, dank, smelling of good and evil. "Maybe you only get real love," Ann said quietly, "in order to give it back again."

THIRTEEN

Jimbo suddenly realized that he had not moved for almost an hour. He had read about half the dossiers on the cardinals with complete absorption. Fred Harshar had sat mesmerized as he called in the long sections of information, rumor, and appraisal. He turned wearily, anxiously, to Jimbo. "Did you steal this disk? Don't kid me, Jimbo, I don't want any beef with the government about secret files. *Global Travel,* this is the best racket I've ever had. I don't want to see or hear anymore about this stuff." He reached for the disk.

"Wait a minute, wait a minute," Jimbo said, placing his hand over the slot. "Look, Freddie, just one more favor. I need a printout of this material. You can do that, can't you?"

Harshar shook his head, fished a fresh cigarette out of his bedraggled pack. "Sorry, Jimbo, I've already seen more than I care to." He popped the disk out of the computer. "If nothing gets on paper, nothing will be on paper." He handed the disk to Jimbo.

"Great minds," Jimbo said, feeling no give in his stolid, nervous, one-time companion, "great minds often think in remarkably similar ways. But thanks

243

for the look-see." He dropped the disk into his coat pocket, stood, stretched, thought he could hear tiny cries coming from every joint. "Thanks, Fred. You, uh, you won't talk about this?"

"I don't know what you're talking about already."

Jimbo made a checkmark salute, nodded to the still humming computer, left the office. He hesitated on the landing outside, checked his watch: Seven-ten A.M. He walked down a few steps, felt the punch of a delayed reaction, leaned against the wall. He removed the disk from his pocket, inspected it, touched it, feeling its reassuring firmness, its slumbering power, as if he were a scientist crooking an unhatched dinosaur egg in his arm, dizzied and a little frightened by the possibilities of the information that it contained, jumpy as if, knowing its value better than anybody else on earth, he might the more easily drop it. Jimbo fumbled the disk in his trembling hands, slipped it back into his pocket. He took a deep breath. What, he wondered, do I do next?

Jimbo reviewed his situation rapidly. He had read perhaps half the material before Fred's feet got cold. What else is on there, he asked himself, and who *are* all these people I've been reading about? This is when I need Mike, Mike the ecclesiastical spotter. Maybe Tootie could help. No, Jimbo sighed, shaking the doctor out of his head, I've got to save him for the last minute. Maybe Brother Louis could help, maybe . . .

Jimbo took another deep breath as the front door opened, held it until a black-shawled cleaning woman shuffled in, climbed onerously up the complaining steps, glaring at him with yellow-brown rheumy eyes, fissured as finely as an insect's wing, gorged with sights of good and evil. Jimbo's heart beat faster as she looked away, continued up the steps, across the landing, up the next staircase. Jimbo patted the disk, descended the steps carefully, the red-stained Band-Aid on his forehead puckered by his inner concentration. I've got to stay calm, he declared encouragingly to himself, I've got to be logical.

There's enough on cardinals like Casey and the one from Marseilles, he thought, trying to find a starting point for his story, to ruin their chances at the conclave. But it's too late for that now, they're sealed in, and they wouldn't hear the news even if I broke it today. *Who* is this story about? Kiejson's summary was favorable—a heroic kid during the war, the personal asceticism, but news stories have little to do with good things. There's good in here, Jimbo said, touching the talisman disk again, and evil, maybe they always come mixed together, maybe Mike was right.

Jimbo stood inside the frosted-glass doors that opened on the side street off the Via Veneto. I've got the pieces, he muttered, the fizz of his original excitement almost gone now, the harsh difficulty of making something usable of his information asserting itself. How the hell does this fit together—the pope's medicine, the New Century Movement, the dossiers on the cardinals—what a hell of a time for Mike to get married. Jimbo walked up the alley to the Via Veneto, saw the Excelsior Hotel. Breakfast, he thought, couldn't hurt.

FOURTEEN

Ann nuzzled close to Mike as the cab squirmed through the schools of darting cars toward Mother Hilda's religious house on Via Remalda. Mike huddled close to Ann, his bandaged hand resting lightly in hers. "I don't want to do this, Annie," he said, staring straight ahead, "it's the same way I felt when I went to the seminary. It made my stomach turn over. I felt the same way every year when it was time to go back. I never thought I had a choice about it, that I had to go to the seminary whether I liked the idea or not. I thought that's how God did things, and the less you felt like doing them the more sure you were that God wanted them that way."

"I felt the same way about going to the convent, that it was a calling from God that, like it or not, you couldn't refuse."

"How Catholic of us . . ."

"My mother," Ann added in a dreamy, preoccupied voice, "was against it. She thought I had always gotten along so well with boys that it was a big mistake."

"*What* boys?" Mike grinned at her. "Just what boys are you talking about?" He kissed her on the forehead. "I wish," he said softly, "we had met then . . ." They lapsed into silence, the oppressive quiet of intervals in destined journeys, the uncomfortable reprieve mood of the ride behind the hearse, those stillborn moments in the last sunlight before everything is changed for good.

The frightened-looking nun opened the door, nodding as she dodged silently in front of them, whispering inaudibly as she led them into the severe chalk-colored room where the mournful, reproving Jesus still stared from the large crucifix. The nun hurriedly brought a companion chair, placed it next to the spindly one facing the plain table. Mike and Ann looked questioningly at each other, began to sit down when Mother Hilda entered the room as rigidly as a figure marching out of an old clock to announce the hour.

"Please," she said, nodding toward the chairs and seating herself, the folds of her habit billowing down into place around her. Her eyes burned like a fire above her worn features. "I expected to see you, Father," she said, looking only at Michael. "I knew that you would come."

"This is my . . ."

Mother Hilda closed her eyes as Mike spoke, lowered her head.

"I'm not Father anymore. This is my wife Ann. We were married yesterday."

The nun pressed her eyes shut, blocking out the information, waited a few seconds until Michael's words had evaporated in the air, then opened them.

"Mother Hilda," Mike said, taking Ann's hand, "I haven't come to ask your permission to marry. A priest in good standing witnessed our marriage."

"You cannot give up the title 'Father,' " the seeress replied quickly, acidly, still looking only at him, "no matter what you think. You have been called by the church and you cannot renounce her claims on you. But you still have a chance to repent, Father, yes, I see it clearly . . ." She gasped, breathing her intensity into the atmosphere, lowered her head. "Don't you understand," she asked in a tight, melancholy voice, "that you must not follow this path any further, that you can turn back even now?" She looked up. "You can still save yourself, you can renounce this so-called marriage, you can return to Jesus crucified . . ."

"That's enough," Ann cut in, surprising Mother Hilda with her firm voice, "that's enough."

"You are a *temptress,*" Mother Hilda shot back without removing her eyes from Michael, "can't you call yourself by your right name? Don't you know that Jesus is speaking through me, that He is trying to save you through me?"

"I don't believe that, no," Ann replied. "Michael and I love each other, whether you want to look at me or not. And you can't make anything evil out of it. Or out of me."

Mother Hilda smiled as if at misled children. "You do not know," she said in a drawn out cadence, "what love means. It is not the flesh."

"No," Mike interjected, "it isn't abstract or bloodless either. It's not *just* the flesh but it is that if it's love between human beings."

"Why," Mother Hilda asked in a sharp, despairing tone, "do you hate the church so? How has this happened?"

"I don't hate the church. Not the real church."

"The *real* church?"

"Yes, the real church, not the shadow church of bureaucrats trying to control people's lives. I love the church that Jesus founded, the church that comforts people, the church that holds up the symbols of life, the church of the sacraments . . ."

"The easy heresy of our time," Mother Hilda scoffed, "the church that lets you do what you want."

"Mother Hilda," Mike said, shifting his tone, "I didn't come here to justify myself or our love." He removed the old photograph from his inside coat pocket with his left hand. Mother Hilda's fierce eyes followed his movement. "Mother," Mike continued, "we came to talk about something else. And I think you sensed that. You're very good at sensing things, you're vigilant in a powerful way. And you always defend yourself by going on the attack."

"I will not listen to this," she said curtly, starting to rise from her chair. "I offer you the forgiveness of Jesus and you refuse it . . ."

"I'll take my chance with Jesus himself, if you don't mind." Mike leaned forward, his eyes locked on Hilda's. "You do protect yourself by attacking, don't you? We've been through this before, Mother, you and I."

"You cannot speak of confessional matters," she hissed, sitting down again, "you only increase your blasphemy, the shipwreck you have made of the priesthood . . ."

"I'm not speaking of confessional matters. I'm speaking of your kitchen at

Hilfen Haus, of our talk in your chapel, of the facts you didn't want to face about your need to control everybody around you, how they have to be dependent, broken in some way to get your help, and of how you'll help them just as long as you can stay in control."

"Stop this," Mother Hilda cut in sharply, "you must go."

"Not before you look at this," Michael responded, dropping the photograph onto the table in front of her. "That's you, Mother Hilda. A long time ago. And the man who may become pope today carried that picture in his prayerbook for forty years."

Mother Hilda inhaled sharply, studied the picture for an endless moment, raised her head, her eyes filled with the diamond-hard light of pain and remembrance. Her voice, as she spoke, was drained and distant. "I am no longer that person." She lowered her eyes again to the photograph, unable to look away from it.

"Mother Hilda, you *were* that person, you *are* that person." Mike touched her shoulder gently with his bandaged hand. She did not shrink back. "Mother Hilda, we'd like to hear the truth. It's not too late."

FIFTEEN

Cardinal Solieri examined the small white card on the green baize cloth before him. *Eligo in Summum Pontificem* was printed above a space for entering the name of the candidate. The concelebrated Mass was over, the cardinals had eaten hurriedly and lightly, and now, at last, they were in their places in the Sistine Chapel preparing to vote for a new Holy Father. The archivist thanked God that he was placed at the far end of one of the long tables. That's what old men get, he thought, when they are the most junior of all the cardinals. The Scripture verses of his earlier meditation fit him well, he concluded, for he was truly like St. Paul, a man born out of due time. Besides, his seat at the edge of things gave him more elbow room than his brother princes who were crowded as close together, he decided with a smile, as he himself had been as a child at table with his eight brothers and sisters.

Under the *camerlengo* Maestrini's watchful eye, the final preparations had been completed. Three cardinals had been chosen as *infirmarii,* whose duty was to collect the ballots of any of the electors who might be confined to their apartments by illness. Maestrini searched the tiers of prelates with his coal-fire eyes as other cardinals were selected to count, and still others to recount, the votes. The *camerlengo* watched the master of ceremonies and other functionaries leave, cleared his throat in the hush that followed the closing of the chapel door, gave the signal for the voting process to begin.

The princes bent over the tables like so many diligent schoolboys, some shielding their cards with their free hands as they inscribed their choices. Solieri continued to smile, marveling at the lightness and freedom he had felt since he had made peace with his helplessness and accepted his insignificant position outside the center of events. If God wants me to be here in the lowest position, he vowed silently, so be it. The archivist recalled the regulations of Pope Paul VI that ordered the electors to change their handwriting if necessary to preserve secrecy. How aware of human frailty Pope Paul had been, the archivist thought, with this knowing instruction. But it smacked of the rules of grand lodges of masonry or the clubs of boys. Solieri wrote Bouyer's name in his undisguised hand, looked up at the solemn faces of the cardinals on the opposite side of the chapel. Features that Leonardo would have sketched or that Fellini would have photographed. Still, they were not all Italians anymore. The church universal was here in a touching spectrum of color and age, each elector as earnest about his responsibilities as on his First Communion day, each, no matter his experience or expectations, awed to some extent by the mystery, ancient and new, of choosing a successor to St. Peter.

The cardinals were to vote according to seniority in the college. Maestrini rose, walked slowly toward the altar, holding up his folded vote, the small white ballot like a Communion wafer in his brown-spotted hand. The *camerlengo* paused for a moment, knelt before the altar, lowered his head in silent prayer. He rose in the tense quiet, spoke in clear, decisive, almost admonitory tones: "I call to witness Christ the Lord, who will be my judge, that my vote is given to the one who, before God, I consider should be elected." The *camerlengo* then placed his ballot on the saucer-like paten that covered a large gold chalice, lifted the paten, and deposited the voting card into the chalice itself.

Time slowed, throttling its humming power as a great locomotive does entering a famous city. As the voting proceeded the quiet was broken only by such homely sounds as chairs scraping and men coughing. Solieri was the last elector to vote. As he turned away from the altar he was aware of the attention focused beyond him on the gleaming chalice now filled with 96 votes. He scanned the cardinals as the official scrutineer shook the chalice vigorously to mix the ballots. The silver-haired Kiejson sat impassively submerged in his own depths. A few places away, Cardinal Casey leaned a few inches forward, raised his eyebrows slightly, touched his ringed hand to his temple as the scrutineer uncovered the chalice and began to remove the ballots. He handed them to a second scrutineer who counted them aloud before placing them in a second chalice. Ninety-six ballots. A stir of relief among the cardinals as this first hurdle of protocol was cleared successfully.

Solieri leaned forward as the three scrutineers sat down at a table below the altar, the historian absorbing the details of a great event. The first of the counters unfolded a card, made a note on a pad, passed it to the second who gravely did the same and handed it to the third who studied it momentarily, then called out the name, "The Lord Cardinal Kiejson." Solieri pulled back an inch, looked toward the unmoving Dutch cardinal. His features seemed to constrict, Solieri thought, as if he felt the first hint of the weight of what had until then been only a possibility. Solieri turned back to watch the last scrutineer pierce the ballot with a needle and draw a thread through it, as he would with every ballot, making a circlet of them before they would be burned in the old-fashioned stove at the far end of the chapel.

The second vote was read out, then the third, Kiejson on both of them. The archivist returned his gaze to the Dutchman as his name was called for the fourth time. In the archivist's vision, shadows descended on the other prelates and he saw Kiejson in a circle of light just as he had viewed birds as a child through a rolled paper spyglass. The crying of the tallies became vague and muffled as Solieri found himself drawn into ever finer concentration on the unblinking patrician face of the Hollander.

Cardinal Kiejson, the old man asked internally, what is it that I am trying to understand about you, what is it that I am missing? I should have talked to you, Solieri whispered to himself, growing uneasy, wondering if this preoccupation with the Dutchman was a symptom, some message from the worn vessels in his brain that he was really old, dizzied by the shifting weight of useless information inside his head, betrayed by circuits overloaded by fifty years of saving things. My mind, Solieri judged wistfully, is like an attic that has never been cleaned out. An attic . . .

The atmosphere changed subtly and Solieri broke free of his absorption as the third scrutineer began to read off the results of the first round of voting.

"The Lord Cardinal Kiejson, thirty-two votes. The Lord Cardinal Casey, twenty-four votes . . ." It would not last long, Solieri sensed, for the prefect of the Congregation for the Doctrine of the Faith had a commanding lead even on the first ballot, when by tradition many votes were cast symbolically to recognize and compliment certain cardinals who were not serious candidates. Bouyer of Marseilles received 15 votes. That accounted for 71 of the 96 ballots. The rest were scattered honorifically among various national groups. Three for Cardinal Caldwell of Boston, while the rest went to places as distant as Tokyo, Cape Town, Sydney, and Rio de Janeiro. Solieri blushed, shifted uneasily as one vote was recorded for him. He was conscious of eyes, some curious, some amused, turning briefly toward him. Some former student of mine, Solieri decided, or God's playing a joke on me again.

The mood seemed easier as the second round of voting began. Solieri forced his attention on Casey but could read little in the expressionless face of the Chicagoan. The second ballot should identify the next pope if it did not actually elect him. Sixty-five votes were needed and switching would begin to take place. Kiejson was bound to gain votes, but could he gain enough? It was more likely, the archivist concluded on the basis of conclave history, that the decisive votes would not come until the afternoon. He looked from the altar crucifix up to the panorama of Judgment Day on the wall behind it. Judgment Day, yes, he thought, in a way it really is. Almost out of his control his glance fell, as the second round of balloting began, on Cardinal Kiejson.

I thought, the old man complained, as he felt free to do with God interiorly, that I had settled this, that I . . . He broke off, feeling suddenly as if the occasion were invading and taking possession of him, that whatever was going on, he must pay attention, that he must strive, as he had throughout his life with even fragments and bits of documents, to listen to them, to give them a proper chance to speak to him. That is why my head is so stuffed with facts and information. I have cherished all these messages from the past, kept them as people keep newspapers, it is indeed like an attic . . .

Cardinal Kiejson rose from his chair, stood for a moment as if contemplating the fatefulness of his next step. Even the incidental sounds of men in congress diminished as the Dutch cardinal moved deliberately around the long table, clutching the folded card aloft in his powerful right hand. The temper in the ancient chapel shifted again and the other cardinals were drawn out of their private thoughts to follow his movements. Initially becalmed with solemnity, the atmosphere had turned tense and anxious as the ritual of voting began. Now, halfway through the second vote, the air tingled with the anticipation of a conclusion.

Solieri inspected Kiejson's face as the favorite stood motionless on the cusp of the raised platform. The pale scar, the badge of his suffering and symbol of his asceticism, was almost invisible against his taut sailcloth features. Kiejson looked toward the gold chalice on the altar. The other electors seemed to suspend their breathing as he hesitated before stepping down into the aisle. One second, two seconds. Kiejson appeared frozen, a man fully informed of the terror that went with the glory, hesitating to accept his destiny. Four seconds, five seconds. He remained fixed in place, the lightning flashes of history playing around his heroic figure.

Solieri thought of how the Dutch cardinal would be remembered by his brother princes in this moment, humbly shrinking from the burden of the papacy. Six seconds, seven seconds. The archivist felt a prickle of dread riffle the hairs on the back of his neck. What, he asked himself urgently, is it, feeling an unexpected destiny parallel to Kiejson's building up inside himself, what *is* it? Twelve, thirteen seconds. Why, Solieri wondered, am I, born out of due time, the least of the apostles, here at this moment? Kiejson stepped down, proceeded as if in a majestic trance, toward the altar. Solieri felt his heart beating faster, closed his eyes on a flood of half-forgotten images, opened them on Kiejson, erect, unmoving before the altar, his ballot still held just above shoulder level. *Yes,* the old man said almost aloud, *yes,* Lord, now I understand why you called me here.

Jimbo was just turning away from the main desk of the Excelsior when he almost collided with Max Hampton. The lawyer was as wrinkled as his pale summer suit and the light in his eyes seemed hard and dark as a gas ring, capable of exploding into full flame. The cardinal's lawyer, Jimbo thought, his own spirits lifting, I must be doing something right after all. "Max," he said cheerily, "how are you?"

The startled Hampton searched Jimbo's face momentarily, "Oh, you're Tracy, aren't you?"

"Do you want to take your money," the journalist asked, "or spin the wheel again?" Jimbo grasped the confused lawyer's arm, suggested breakfast, steered him toward the dining room, talking steadily in a low, confidential voice until they were seated, wearing down the lawyer's reluctance with a stream of information he had learned from reading Casey's dossier. Hampton summoned up courtroom gravity, sipped some water, watched the merry-eyed Jimbo over the rim of the glass, wondering where and how Tracy could have discovered such material. Casey had scoffed at the notion of a federal investigation before he headed into the conclave, confident that he would emerge beyond the reach of any law. Now *Time* had at least parts of the story of the Chicago archbishop's alleged misdeeds. Casey wasn't worried because he had a plan for gaining personal immunity. No, Hampton calculated bitterly, Casey doesn't have to worry. But *I* do, my name is on a lot of the documents that could be uncovered, *my* name . . .

"Come, come, Max, this is no time for woolgathering." Jimbo lit a cigarette, brushed powdery residue from his sleeve.

"You have nothing but rumor and innuendo, Mr. Tracy." Hampton's tone was brittle and harsh. "I suggest that you know that yourself."

"What's the old saying, Max," Jimbo asked as he signaled for a waiter, "when you don't have the facts, argue the law, and when you don't have the law, argue the facts, and when you don't have either . . ."

"*You* are the one lacking either facts or law, Mr. Tracy, and there really isn't anything to discuss."

"What do you know about Casey's involvement in the death of Pope Jean?"

Hampton's mouth fell open, his eyes flared, he spoke in a tight, strained voice. "That's an outrageous question, a goddam outrageous insinuation."

"We're both from the city of outrage, Max, Chicago. The city that doesn't even pretend to moral aspiration." Jimbo drew on his cigarette, balanced it on the lip of the ashtray. "Anything *can* happen there, Max, and everything *has* happened here. I think these stories are connected. Casey was there when Pope Jean died, you know that. You also know he was on the hook about the Vatican Bank. Who stood to profit from the pope's death if not our esteemed—strike that—our archbishop?"

Hampton lowered his head, spoke in as controlled a manner as he could to the tablecloth. "You have *no* proof of any of this. It's all wild conjecture."

"Look at me," Jimbo said, adrenaline reaching flood stage inside him, "look at me, Max. All you need to do is arrange for an IBM-compatible computer to be brought to your room here and I'll give you a look at my proof. Then I think you'll be interested in cooperating."

Hampton's facial skin stretched tight and smooth as scrimshaw. He seemed unable to speak, his eyes flitting from Jimbo's face to his hands, back to his face again.

"You know, Max," Jimbo said genially, "I'm beginning to believe in the power of prayer again. You ought to try it sometime. You converts are supposed to be good at it."

Hampton's gaze settled on something beyond Jimbo at the far end of the restaurant. His features slackened, he sipped his water, seemed more at ease, more confident, as he asked, almost smiling, "A computer? Why do you need a computer?"

"Because nothing's on paper. Doesn't that mean anything to you?"

"No," Hampton responded, his eyes following movement beyond Jimbo's shoulder.

"Maybe we ought to order breakfast in your room," Jimbo countered, feeling a seed of anxiety sprout in his stomach. "Let's go upstairs and see . . ."

A hand touched Jimbo's shoulder. He caught a flash of Hampton's relieved grin as he turned his head upward. Owen Wingate gazed down unpleasantly at him. "Well, Jimbo," the ambassador said, lowering himself into the extra chair at the table, "imagine meeting you here."

Jimbo looked back and forth from Hampton to Wingate, twisted toward the entrance. Wingate's driver stood next to the maître d's podium. Jimbo looked back at the grinning ambassador, his insides turning molten.

"Imagine that," Wingate said in an arpeggio of contented tones, "schedule a breakfast with Max Hampton and you never know just who will show up."

SIXTEEN

Cardinal Solieri paced in a jagged ellipse outside Cardinal Kiejson's conclave quarters. Several princes of the church had made arrangements to see the Dutchman following their communal meal after the second ballot had been completed and the wreaths of votes had been burned in the stove to send black smoke floating over the piazza, the signal that no pope had been chosen. Kiejson had gained on the second ballot, reaching a total of forty votes. But, surprisingly, Casey had increased his tallies by the same number and stood at 32. Bouyer had dropped to nine votes and the remaining 21 were as scattered as before.

Kiejson's election still seemed certain but an unspoken thought seemed to permeate the air of the luncheon: If Kiejson did not reach 65 by the second vote of the afternoon, some invisible, unmeasurable factor might come into play among the electors and things could move in an unanticipated direction. Everything depended on what Cardinal Casey and his Third World supporters decided to do. Solieri stared hard at Kiejson's door. Behind it, Casey was now alone with Kiejson. Perhaps, the archivist thought as he searched for his rosary beads deep in his cassock pocket, perhaps it will all be settled while I wait here in the corridor. Waiting, he thought uncomfortably, what a mystery lies in waiting . . .

The old cardinal inspected the handsome dark wooden door for a long moment, let his rosary slip back into the well of his pocket, took a deep breath and knocked. The door opened a crack, revealing a section of Casey's face and a softly lit book-lined wall behind him. "I have been wanting to speak with both of you," Solieri said firmly, "and I have waited long enough." He pushed the door open and the astonished Casey stepped aside. The archivist closed the door, looked into the rigid, frowning features of Cardinal Kiejson.

"Eminenza," Kiejson said in a voice of restrained hospitality, "Cardinal Casey and I, as you must understand, are discussing matters of utmost importance for Holy Mother Church."

"Yes, yes," Solieri said, taking a step forward, "I do *understand,* as you say. That is precisely why I am here."

Casey scowled, remained standing. "Cardinal Solieri, we really cannot give you time right now. If it's a question of money for the archives . . ."

"No, Your Eminence," Solieri said in a pure, simple tone, "as I told you, you have been very generous. As a matter of fact, I invited you to visit the archives one day. You recall?"

Casey shook his head, let his hands fall to his sides in exasperation.

"But you could not find the time. And neither, surprisingly, could you, Cardinal Kiejson. I understood and felt that I was the lowliest of all of you and held silent, like the father in the story of Jacob and Esau. Now I understand that I am one of the weak through whom God wishes to confound the powerful."

Casey rolled his eyes upward. "But . . ."

Solieri raised his hand, shuffled forward a few steps as the Chicagoan sat down. "Bear with me. I wanted you, Cardinal Casey, to come to the archives to see the draft of the statement the late Holy Father had prepared about you."

"There was no draft," Kiejson said authoritatively, "only the original. It was Pope Jean's policy . . ."

"It was Pope Jean's policy," Solieri said, cutting across the Dutchman's statement, "to have me read the drafts of all of his papers in advance. You didn't know that, did you?"

Casey's face looked like cracking plaster as he focused on the old cardinal, "Why, *why* didn't you tell me?"

"You never listened to me, not for long, anyway." Solieri paused, wrinkled his forehead, smiled gently. "I am not here to accuse you, *Eminenza,* or to condemn you . . ."

Kiejson's eyes glinted in his reddening face. "You must be mistaken, you cannot have seen . . ."

Solieri raised his hands, spoke in the untroubled voice of a confessor who has heard all the world's sins and is no longer surprised by anything. "I know that it is my own failing that has kept me back. Do you know what St. Thomas Aquinas said about the proud and the hesitant man?"

"Never *mind,*" Kiejson cut in, "what do you want *now?*"

Casey frowned, removed his glasses, felt discomfort thread through his chest as the string had through the used ballots. What, he wondered, what in God's name is going on here? "Missy," he whispered hoarsely, *"Missy . . ."*

Kiejson glared briefly at Casey, turned his eyes back to the old man in the ill-fitting cassock. "What, I ask again, for we have little time, what do you want?"

"The truth," Solieri answered calmly, gazing sympathetically at the front-running cardinals, "the truth before it is too late." He shifted his weight from one foot to the other. "Cardinal Casey, you apparently did not know that the Holy Father, in as compassionate a way as possible, intended to remove you from your post in Chicago and bring you to Rome in an honorable but not very influential position."

"What?" Casey looked savagely at Kiejson. "That's not what you told me. You said the Holy Father had cleared me."

Kiejson ignored Casey, looked coldly at the archivist. "You've no proof of this. This is something you have imagined. As the other cardinals say, you have been in the archives a long time . . ."

Solieri looked around the room, ordinarily part of a library. "And we meet among books," he said softly, pulling a folded sheaf of pages from his cassock pocket, "and *this* is the draft. You can see for yourselves."

Casey took the document, put his glasses on, began to read. The pages rattled lightly in his hands.

"I wondered," Solieri said, turning toward Kiejson, "why you hadn't told Cardinal Casey of this."

"I, I," Kiejson stumbled, "the document disappeared."

Solieri furrowed his brow skeptically. "I wondered why you would wait when you knew the truth all along."

Kiejson swallowed hard, said nothing.

"Then I realized that the only reason to wait would be to use the document, if needed, at the last possible moment. To keep it and, if I am correct, to allow Cardinal Casey to be a candidate. With his popularity in the Third World he would block out many other candidates."

"I did everything I could to dissuade him," Kiejson responded evenly. "Ask him yourself."

Casey let the pages describing his proposed exile fall into his lap, turned a hard gaze on the Dutchman. "Never, Franz, *never* did you tell me this . . ."

"If I am right," Solieri interjected, "Cardinal Kiejson felt that he might never need to. Perhaps to spare your feelings. Still, I think the original is here in this room. I don't think it ever disappeared, although I heard people say that it had. Everything that was in the pope's room went to the archives. But this document was not there. That, Cardinal Casey, was what I wanted to tell you about, and to show you this draft." He paused, looked directly at Kiejson. "You do have the original, don't you? I guessed that because you never came or sent anyone to the archives to see if it was there. You knew where it was all along. And you were about to show it to Cardinal Casey as a clinching argument in getting him to withdraw." His tone was infinitely kind. "That *is* the truth, isn't it?"

The Dutch cardinal's face was subtly transformed as if the laces that had held its classic lines and planes were slowly loosening, restoring play to an area where no give had been allowed for years. A rigid, highly controlled mask was crumpling, revealing the long-hidden natural face behind it. Kiejson seemed confused and uncertain as the layers of an inflexible external self dissolved like latex makeup held to the fire. Solieri watched almost tenderly, as one would a birth, as the structures collapsed and a long-lost Dutch farmboy face appeared. Kiejson seemed to be journeying silently back through the decades, jettisoning the burdens of achievement and expectation, a man on pilgrimage to a simpler identity.

The gasping Casey, the pages of the draft still spread on his lap, watched with Solieri as the confessional change worked its way across the Dutch cardinal's face in a symbolic response to the archivist's question.

"It's all right," Solieri whispered softly, "you do have the decree, don't you?"

Kiejson looked back blankly, reached for a folder on a side table, handed it to the old man, watched Solieri inspect it. "I wanted," the Dutch cardinal said slowly, regaining his composure, "to avoid causing scandal to the church."

Solieri nodded, glanced at the hard-breathing Casey whose eyes seemed to reflect the enormity of the loss the Chicagoan was beginning to grasp. He had never truly been cleared and now he never would be, the safe port he had hoped to enter by nightfall had been closed to him.

"When I watched you carrying your ballot," the archivist said, addressing Kiejson, "I remembered something that made sense out of the broken images and scattered facts that filled my head. I recalled you, just as you were today, standing hesitantly holding something in your right hand. That was when I had gone to hear Pope Jean's confession. When I arrived you were standing at the entrance of the chapel, not moving, frozen it seemed, just like this morning. I pushed past you and saw the poor pope lying dead on the floor."

Kiejson watched the archivist with unblinking eyes as the old man touched his head with one hand and continued. "That image came back to me this morning. And suddenly I *knew* what it was that you were holding in your hand that day." He paused, closed the folder. "When nobody would even listen to me I thought my concerns about its absence from the archives was exaggerated. It worried me. I prayed at Pope Jean's tomb every night, trying to understand what I was supposed to do. It only came gradually to me that God was testing me through all this, yes *me,* of all people. Are you brave enough, God seemed to be saying to me in my prayers, are you brave enough to find the truth?" He looked down at the two cardinals. Casey had lowered his head but the farm boy was disappearing again from Kiejson's face, the Dutchman was searching for his discarded armor.

"Then," Solieri continued, "when I was examining what records I could find about both of you in the archives, I came upon a note I had copied from Aquinas. What would he do, he had asked himself, if he had to choose between a proud man and a fainthearted one? Aquinas would choose the proud one because then he would be sure that at least *something* would be done. So, at the risk of sinning against pride, I decided that I, Angelo Solieri, the farmer's son, was weak enough in God's eyes to confound the strong."

A determined knock sounded on the door. The archbishops of London and New York seemed surprised when Solieri opened it and told them that Cardinal Kiejson would not be seeing anyone else before the afternoon session of the conclave. He closed the door, turned again toward the ironically bound princes of Chicago and Amsterdam. These two, Solieri thought, catching some mood of returning confidence in the air, these two did not get this far without possessing resilience and the intuitive gift of all powerful men to nose their way swiftly out of the avalanche that claims the lives of the innocent. They seemed more self-possessed, as if the sight of powerful colleagues in the corridor had set the machinery of calculation ticking inside them again. The archivist paused a beat before speaking. "You think, my brothers, that even if what I say is true, it is too late to alter the reality of the day, that for the sake of Holy Mother Church I should not expose her to the scandal that the revelation of this information would bring to her. Am I right?"

Kiejson and Casey stared dispassionately at the archivist, the membrane of control had sheathed the Dutchman's features again. "I would say," Kiejson responded, as if testing the steadiness of his voice, "that your options are very limited. You may, for example, tell your story to the other cardinals this afternoon." Casey nodded as the Dutch cardinal, his tone firming, continued, "I will arrange it for you. How do you think they will react? What do you think they will do?"

The room became quiet and musty, as if a frightening storm had passed over the hills and the villagers could safely forget the fervent resolutions that its rage had stirred out of their souls. Solieri compressed his lips, shrugged. "I think," he said simply, "that they would do the right thing."

"Yes," Kiejson responded, the magisterial gloss returning to his manner, "yes, they would. And the right thing, for the good of the church in this time of international peril, would be to ignore what you had to say. You are correct, you know, in your understanding of how the other cardinals perceive *you*. And we are right in accepting their votes as a clear indication of how they perceive *us*. They do not want this kind of trouble for the church. How harsh do you think they would be in judging my decision not to tell Cardinal Casey of a dead pope's decree? I felt the Holy Father was wrong at the time, that he should be more concerned about the Communist threat than unfairly judging the Vatican Bank matter. Don't you understand that these other cardinals would side with *me*? They know that Pope Jean was a holy man. They also know that he was naive. How do you think *you* will sound, waving this document, an old man looking into the doubting eyes of a hundred cardinals, dwarfed by the surroundings, seen in proper perspective? Go ahead, *Eminenza,* this very afternoon. I will indeed arrange it so that you may address the conclave." The fiber in Kiejson's voice toughened as he concluded. "Tell them everything, yes, and tell them your quaint story of St. Thomas and his choice of the proud over the hesitant man, too." Kiejson permitted himself a mocking smile. "Let us see if they do not count all of this favorably in my regard, let us see if they do not agree that I made a good judgment."

Solieri frowned, opened his mouth to speak, was preempted by a rejuvenated Casey. "Cardinal Kiejson is correct. The other cardinals will see this just as they see your patched and misbuttoned cassock—the sign of a man who has been too long with books and, if I may put it this way, too little with the real world."

"So, *Eminenza,*" Kiejson added in a mellowing tone, "think of the consequences of what you propose. There are greater issues that strong men must deal with resolutely if the church is to move into the next century. Your notion is very dramatic, I must say, but each one of these cardinals has had to make decisions just as hard and ambivalent as mine. So what if I kept the document? Do you think they are strangers to doing difficult, sometimes inexplicable, things for the good of Holy Mother Church?"

The archivist's shoulders sagged. He lowered his head. Casey's eyes met Kiejson's. The Dutch cardinal spoke patiently, soothingly, as if to an old parent. "Why don't you give me that file now?" He rose, took a step toward Solieri. "For the good of the church . . ."

"Where did you get this information that you shared with Mr. Hampton?"

"Oh, Ownie, for Crissake, stop these ambassadorial manners. You're still the king of Mazda to me, 'A hell of a car,' remember?"

Wingate tapped a well-manicured hand on the desk in Hampton's suite, scanned the lawyer for reaction, removed a cigar from his inside coat pocket, worked his jaw muscles as he fiddled with it. "Jimbo," he said impatiently, wearily, "the time for bright repartee is over. We know that you have appropriated confidential government materials. You could spend the rest of your life in a federal prison for that." He flashed a sickly grin. "And that's a fact."

"Ownie, you don't have thing on me. You had your goon search me after breakfast and *he* didn't find anything. You've been questioning me for almost three hours and *you* haven't found anything. You've probably been through my apartment and my office by now. And from the look on your face when you took calls in here, you haven't had any luck in either place. So we are, as they say, at an impasse. And that's a fact."

Wingate narrowed his eyes, *"Au contraire.* We did get our uniform back." He lit and puffed his cigar. "Do you deny that you had possession of a confidential computer disk, that, in fact, you reviewed it with Mr. Fred Harshar of *Global Travel* earlier this morning?"

"What did you do, put bamboo under Freddie's fingernails? Or was it the Chinese water torture?"

"Just like your old man, aren't you? Harshar, in case you're interested, admitted seeing this disk and some of the material it contains. Once we located him, he seemed anxious to cooperate. Even told us he threw you out."

"Your kind of guy, Ownie."

"And somewhere between there and here you ditched the disk." Wingate exhaled a jagged halo of smoke, leaned across the desk. "Why don't you cooperate, Jimbo? We're going to find it sooner or later."

"You've been watching too many FBI training films. Or maybe Warner Brothers out of the thirties." Jimbo shifted in his chair. "Why are you so worried, Ownie? Your ass if this gets out, right?"

"Mr. Tracy," Hampton said in a self-lubricated voice, "I'm sure that we all want to be reasonable. We don't want any harm to come to you or to your career. Or to the church through the improper use of raw, unverified files. That doesn't seem too much to ask, does it?"

"What is this," Jimbo asked with a grin, "good cop, bad cop? You know, Max, when you say those things, you must sound just like your father talking to my father just before he screwed him. Like father, like son."

The military guard at the door started, touched his holstered gun as Jimbo reached inside his coat. "Easy there," the journalist said, "you've already frisked me, remember. Ownie, you're going to have to do something about the attention span of these guys." He kept his hand inside his jacket as he continued. "You know, until I met you two this morning I really couldn't figure out what this was all about." He withdrew his hand slowly, sniffed the cigar it held, put it into his mouth, leaned toward Wingate. "Light, Ownie?"

The ambassador's eyes focused on Jimbo's cigar as he handed him his lighter.

"A Willem II, eh, Ownie? Just like yours." Jimbo flicked the lighter, drew on the cigar. "A little strong, these Dutch cigars, don't you think?"

"Let's get back to what you did with the disk."

"Oh, no," Jimbo said jovially. "Oh, no." He switched to a harsh tone. "We both got our cigars at the same place. I pinched one of Cardinal Kiejson's cigars after a real blow-out. No doubt you got yours on a more formal occasion."

Wingate looked uncomfortably at the thin cigar in his hand. "I brought this from Chicago."

"Like hell you did," Jimbo snapped, "it's a Willem II, right out of the Dutchman's silver cigar box. If you hadn't pulled it out, I never would have connected you two. But the cigar, of course, does that nicely. You've been to see him." Jimbo puffed on his own cigar. "*You* gave him the disk, you, shall we say, recruited him." Jimbo's eyes turned to Hampton as the lawyer stirred anxiously. "And you, Max, what a break. You're a marriage broker, just like your grandfather was in the old country. You brought us all together here. Without you, Max, I would never have known that you and Mister Ambassador here were joined at the hip in this. And well acquainted with the same confidential material. Breakfast mates besides. Making some kind of deal connected with it, and with Cardinal Casey, that's how I see it."

"You don't know what you're talking about," Wingate responded angrily, quashing his cigar in the ashtray.

"If I don't, what the hell are you so interested in me for?"

"Mr. Tracy . . ."

"Ah, Mr. Hampton," Jimbo said, holding his cigar like a dart, "how would you two like to hear my theory about Ownie's fucked-up efforts to elect a cardinal so anti-Communist the gun lobby would turn Catholic for him?"

"I'm sorry," Cardinal Solieri said softly, looking down at the carpet, "I can't tell you how sorry this makes me."

"That's all right," Kiejson said, extending his hand for the folder, "we'll just forget that this ever happened. Then you'll be able to get back to the archives, a place more congenial for you than the world of action."

"Yes," Casey chimed in, "you needn't worry that we'll let anyone know about this."

Solieri slowly raised his head. Tears welled in his eyes. "I'm afraid you misunderstand me," he said gently. "I am not sorry that I have spoken to you. No, no, not at all." He tucked the folder firmly under his arm. "Sit down, Cardinal Kiejson, please."

Kiejson's face clouded with irritation. "Cardinal Solieri," he said as if speaking to a nursing-home patient, "we have given you precious time. Other cardinals wish to meet with me . . ."

"Sit down," the archivist said again in a grieving voice, standing firm in the center of the floor. Kiejson backed away, took his seat again, exchanged impatient glances with Casey.

The old man rubbed a tear from beneath his right eye. "What I am sorry about is not what I have said, although you want me to feel foolish about it." He shook his head. "That is a terrible thing about so many powerful people. They try to shame other people in order to control them." He sighed. "I am sorry for what I'm about to say. I did not want, you see, to cause shame to you . . ."

Kiejson frowned, started to get up again.

"Sit, please. I have been trying to understand what happened to Pope Jean. And I have spent many hours in the archives lately reviewing the records of his life, his seminary reports, everything." He paused, looked directly into Kiejson's eyes. "And yours, too. And I found certain things missing. That puzzled me. Then I sent for more records from my colleague in The Netherlands. And I reviewed the dates and the times." He paused again. "I reconstructed the era, you see, so that I knew everything that was going on, the things you must have experienced or known about in a small country in wartime. And I matched that with the only period for which all information about you has disappeared."

Kiejson took a deep breath as the old man surveyed him with his searching brown eyes. Solieri spoke benignly, directly, to the Dutch cardinal. "What I am sorry about is what I think I came to understand. But now we must speak about it. For I think I not only understand how you received your scar long ago, but also how the pope died. Would you like to hear what I have to say? Or would you like to tell me about it yourself?"

VII

WISDOM

ONE

Mother Hilda braced her hands against the table, pushing the room away, pressing against Mike and Ann, hoping to dodge behind a pile-up of time and place. A quiver moved across her face as swiftly as a gull's shadow. Her wide eyes seemed fixed on demons. The table skidded on the polished wood floor. She let go of it, sighed, "No, no," and fell in slow motion against the back slats of her chair.

Mike reached forward, grabbed her shoulders, felt a flaring twig of pain in his right hand, pulled her upright. "Mother Hilda," he said in a strong, soothing voice, sounding as he once did at accident scenes and hospital bedsides, any place with the repentant and the defiant where the stakes were life and death. "Mother Hilda, you *can* tell us, you *must.*"

Ann moved around the table, placed her hands on the sighing nun's shoulders, turned to her husband. "Easy, Mike, take it easy." She held her gently. The seeress opened her eyes, looked directly into Ann's. Her visions of doom seemed to recede, she caught her breath like a swimmer out of the deep, streaming water. The two women's eyes locked, Ann's probing, calming, reassuring; Mother Hilda's at first all harsh blue defiance, then softening, the fierceness running out of them as quickly as the tide as she grasped that Ann would not hurt her. "You were just a girl," Ann asked tenderly, "weren't you?"

Mother Hilda nodded, her eyes still fixed on Ann. "Yes," she said, "only a girl." She sniffed, hesitated, began to speak directly to Ann as, a few miles away, Cardinal Kiejson did the same to Cardinal Solieri.

"You cannot know," the seeress began, bobbing in Ann's arms as if in a life jacket, "you Americans could never know what war in your own country is like. But we knew. At home, we knew. I was twelve, almost thirteen, when the Germans came out of the skies." The seeress became calmer, eased out of Ann's embrace as she descended into a dream of the past.

"It was mild that night in May, 1940. I was raised by my uncle and aunt. My parents had died in an accident. I was awakened in the night to this droning sound and then by noises in the distance. It was like a summer storm rolling along the flat land far away from us. Then there was a great excitement, my uncle came in, lights went on, there was excitement everywhere. I crowded with my cousins around the crackling radio. But the news was as confused as the static. Germans were coming out of the skies, coming down with bicycles, and dressed like the Dutch, or dressed like fishermen, farmers, even nuns. The terror, the uncertainty ended when the queen spoke, our beloved Queen Wilhelmina, telling us that the Germans had invaded but the Dutch army was fighting back."

She paused, looked at Ann and Mike, pleading in a contorted facial dumb show for some sign of understanding. Ann touched her forearm lightly, half said, half asked, "That's when you first saw death riding into the streets of the city . . ."

"Yes, yes," Mother Hilda sobbed, "it was terrible. We taped the windows, put up black curtains to hide the lights. Then a few days later we heard that Rotterdam had been bombed, that the dikes had been ruptured, the land was flooding, that the Germans would bomb Amsterdam, and Utrecht, too, if we did not surrender. And it was over the next day. The queen left for England with Prince Bernhard. And soon the streets were filled with the green uniforms of the Germans . . .

"Their trucks and motorcycles, their arrogant looks, I remember watching from a bridge over one of the canals as they rode along the cobbled streets. I looked down into the waters and saw the reflections of the sky, the brick houses and the church steeples, but not of the Germans. In the waters I could see our beloved Amsterdam drowned.

"It was not long before everything was a nightmare. The only world I knew was gone and the Germans were everywhere in the city, their eyes filled with death. Soon, you see, they closed their grip on everything. And I, a fearful young girl, thought that God was punishing us for our sins. But I could not believe that he could punish sin with sin. The worst part for me was to see, just before the Germans came, some neighbors burning anti-Nazi newspapers, anything that suggested that they loved freedom more than the Nazi occupation." She paused again. "You have never seen this, have you, the loyalty of everyone suddenly suspect, good people beaten and punished for being true Hollanders? You cannot imagine how a failure, even a hesitation about loyalty, gives the devil just the room he needs to make his entrance."

Mother Hilda sighed, lowered her head and slipped away from them out into the moving but unmoving current of the past. "They began then on the Jews. The Jews, they said, contaminated everything. So they had to register, then they could not go to the cinemas, then the Jewish professors—friends of my uncle—were forced out of the university, and one night they began the raids. Four hundred young men were taken to a concentration camp. Then the Jews were forbidden membership in the professions, they could not be directors of businesses.

"Evil lay on the city as the fog sometimes did. And while some of our neighbors formed the Dutch Nazi Party—and we did not know whom we could trust—my uncle became active with all those who helped the Jews secretly. I remember the day the Jews were forced to wear yellow stars with *Jood,* Jew, printed on them. So many of us wore yellow, too, or yellow flowers to show our support. And for a few days we felt proud and sure of ourselves.

"Then the Germans started to squeeze the life out of us, wanting to divide us, and if we did not live by fear, we lived by suspicion. We huddled together as the Germans, still victorious everywhere, began taking more Jews, and then more Jews. And then my uncle was caught helping some Jews find a hiding place. And we never saw him again. Can you understand how I felt? I had lost my mother and my father, my motherland, then my beloved brave uncle . . .

"And I, I was a young girl just becoming a woman, being touched by the mystery myself. And I did not know what to do with myself or make of myself. But I did not believe that God could preside over all this hatred and death. And I would sit on the white bridges and listen to the sweet bells of the Westerkerk and look down to see the Amsterdam I had lost looking back at me from the murky waters, hidden, gone, it seemed, forever.

"So I resolved to do what I could, as a young girl who had lost God along with country and family, to help Jews who were by now going into hiding. I cannot tell you the stifling feeling of it, I cannot . . . But I didn't care about life, I was trying to lose my own restless self, I could not breathe except when I helped smuggle clothing or food to one of the contacts who would bring it to one of the Jewish families.

"I lost myself with the lost, I did not care what happened, I only wanted to strike back at someone, to be too tired at night to think or dream or hope for any future. Death would have made no difference, for I drew inside myself and closed myself off and ignored the blood and the longing, the life of my own life . . .

"And then, when I was sixteen, in those long months when the old men argued about when and where the Allies would invade Europe, when the droning sound over the city was that of bombers heading for German cities, when the Nazi soldiers began to look afraid, and the streets were sometimes filled with them retreating, the smell of death on them, when all I cared about, all I lived for, was the work of the Underground, one night at my aunt's door, a young man came, bringing messages from Rotterdam and from agents along the seacoast. I looked at him once—tall, blond-haired, handsome—and he looked back at me, yes, just like that, in the vestibule of my aunt's house with the world pressing its darkness and hatred down on us all around. In that instant I felt everything that I had denied about myself, every pore and deepest part of me, came to life. I loved and wanted, as fire wants wood, this young man, this Franz, Franz Josef Kiejson . . ."

Something eddied across Mother Hilda's face so that it seemed to glow and darken at the same instant. "I loved Franz," she said slowly, "recklessly, foolishly, wholeheartedly. I was just becoming a woman and he was just becoming a man, each of us on errands to outrun evil and death. And yet, for each of us, in that shadowed world where death and separation and denial were the common experience of everyone, when it was too painful to think of the past and too uncertain to think of the future, we recognized each other." She opened her eyes, fires behind a filmy coating, looked at Ann, then at Mike. "You think you are the only man and woman to fall in love in desperate circumstances? And you found each other in a world without war, with food on your table, and death and sin not even thought of anymore."

She closed her eyes again, floated into a reverie about Franz, the handsome blond knight who had been a seminary student and had in his bag only a charred crucifix as a memory of the fiery gutting of Rotterdam. That, and a crystal paperweight with a snowfall inside from his dead parents' house. Franz moved into her aunt's cellar. She knew by their glances that despite the war, despite the messages they carried on their bicycles, they were thinking only of each other, and of how they could meet and be together, however dangerous, and let the war-ridden world around them be forgotten. For Franz, she said, with his perfect face and strong body had risen from the waters of lost Holland to rescue her.

"We felt," she said wistfully, "just as all lovers do. And although we were Catholics it made no difference to our becoming lovers. Not then. That is how *all* lovers feel when they find the great love of their lives—that it is different for them, that they have been trapped by fate or chance or by the church. Yes, by the church, as stern and unchanging as the face of the cathedral, and dark and cold, too, for the sun does not warm it easily. But lovers are of the sun and lovers are always misunderstood. True lovers are always in exile . . ."

She curled her fingers, clenched her fists as if she had never worked some old anger out of them. "And to be with Franz, to feel Franz in me, and our bodies young and strong and smooth, against each other in the night when the rest of the house was sleeping and the war was just the faint hum of bombers going one way or the other . . ." She paused, this time for over a minute, holding close inside her or being held by memories that filled the room with the unbearable pressures of sexual longing, with the aches of its urgency and passion, its strange territory of intimacy, its blinding light and its little deaths.

Mother Hilda, her eyes closed, spoke in a voice of sweetness and melancholy, the tones of the living recalling the love of the dead. "The more we were together, the more we seemed like innocent children playing outside of time itself. That we took risks delivering food, that we play-acted as we rode our bicycles past the Nazi soldiers, that death was on the other side of

day as surely as night was, all that only heightened the certainty, the excitement, and the purity of our love. The world had never known love as we
had. We could only find hints of it in poetry and in Shakespeare and we did
not care if there was a border of tragedy on all of life as on a card of
mourning. Let it consume us with its fire, we thought eagerly, let us die in
each other's arms. Even if the world misunderstood, even if we were found
naked together in the wreckage of the house, or killed together by the Nazis,
let us die, we thought, let death affirm the intensity of our sacred love . . ."

Mother Hilda grew silent, passive, withdrawn, the afterglow of memory
slowly dissolved and her translucent skin stretched tautly on her bones. "But
it was not us," she said, her voice flooded with sadness, "it was not Franz and
I who died . . ."

Mike and Ann leaned closer. "The Allies had come. Radio Orange, the
Dutch Free Radio from London, told us the news every day, and the old
men put pins in their secret maps, and freedom seemed near at last. Franz and
I were still lost in our love, lost anyway in our ecstasy, the fervor of each
night, that gift of the evil war. The war slowed down and Holland became a
corridor for the Nazi troops. Paris was freed but we were not. The Germans
struck back more viciously as they sensed that the war, once gloriously won,
was now being disastrously lost. And Franz and I sensed that this interval of
sweet darkness, this long night on our straw bed that seemed of crystal, was
also ending. What would we do? We were both seventeen that summer.
Franz gave me a paperweight as a gift, our own world, he called it. And one
long night when the bombers throbbed across the sky and there were thuds
and flashes on the horizon, we spoke of the future for the first time. My own
parents had married at an age not much older than ours and as I said that to
Franz, I could sense the slight change in his body as he lay next to me. He
did not answer me. Franz, I whispered, we must speak of this, we love each
other. Still he was quiet, unsure, a boy, I thought, a boy afraid of being fully
a man. Franz, I asked, what is it?

"But he could not answer right away. Finally, he said, Betje—for that
was my name—Betje, I may return to the seminary. I feel I must, or that I
must at least find out if that is what God wants of me.

"I was terrified, for I felt that he was rejecting me, *our* love, that, even if
it did not seem so, he would become more different every day, that the
freshness of our love was already lost, that something in his uncertainty was
pulling him away from me, that he might find the God who had hidden

during the war but that I would be left with neither of them. I could smell and taste the ashes of my life. Franz, I almost pleaded, Franz, we love each other, we cannot live without each other. But he was silent for a long time. I don't know what to do, he said at last, I do love you but I must love God more. I pulled him to me, fighting with whatever spirit God had put in him, trying to wrest him back, ravishing and being ravished in the long wordless hours until dawn.

"We were up and about as though we had slept like the most innocent children through the night. My aunt Grieje seemed frightened. She told us that the Nazis might strike out at anyone these days, especially because there had been an attempt on Hitler's life a week before, and that we must be careful, especially since Mr. Pieter from the Resistance had some important deliveries for us that afternoon. We must be very cautious, the war might be ending but things had never been so dangerous, there was nothing, she said, more dangerous than the last slap of the dying dragon's tail.

"Franz did not seem to be paying much attention. He was in another world and I knew what it was. I could see desire in the sideward looks he gave me and I could sense conflict, the battle I had plunged him into between his distant God, who might or might not be calling him, and me who wanted him urgently, here and now, all of him, and let God find other Dutch boys to give up their manhood before they understood it.

"I did not see him until the afternoon when we came back to my aunt's house from school. Mr. Pieter was there, very agitated. There had been a *razia,* looking for Jews, the night before. The Nazis, Mr. Pieter emphasized, might be losing the war but they would show no mercy, they would keep up their deportation of Jews until the end came. I remember how Mr. Pieter ran his finger inside his collar, how he perspired as he pulled us close. There was an informer at work, he whispered, someone giving the names and addresses of the hiding places of the Jews, the places we knew well because we helped with the deliveries. This, he said, was the moment of supreme danger for everyone. He did not know who the informer was so we could trust nobody. You, Betje and Franz, you must speak to no one, trust no one, no matter how long you have known them. Because you are young, you can get about the city without being noticed as much as some of us.

"He pulled us closer still. Listen, he said, and promise, as God is our judge, that you will do this and tell nobody of it. We listened and watched closely, for this was the excitement in which our love had been born and grew, and I felt it would strengthen it again now. We were to visit the hiding places, warn the Jewish families to be vigilant, tell them to admit only those whose loyalty they could swear to. If they could get through these few days, the traitor would be identified, and things would be safe again.

"There will be others doing the same work but pay no attention. Better that people are warned twice than not at all. Now, Mr. Pieter said, do not attract attention by hurrying. Are you ready? I nodded eagerly but Franz looked blankly at him for a moment. Yes, Franz is ready I said for him. He nodded as I took his hand and we headed for the door. I felt the pulse of Franz's inner conflict, the tension between flesh and spirit as I swept him along with me. Looking back, I saw Mr. Pieter sitting there at the table, his eyes bright, anxious, hopeful, as he watched us leave.

We each took half the list and agreed to meet at nine o'clock by the statue of Erasmus on the way to the railroad station. When we were away from the house Franz looked into my eyes and kissed me. I love you, he said, I will always love you. He seemed full of longing, of need for me in the coming night and I felt better, I felt as if I had won this day's struggle. We pedaled down the brick-paved road looking to the fat Nazi guard on the corner just what we were, teenagers in love.

"But it was a difficult afternoon and evening. The green uniforms of the Germans were everywhere and it was not as easy as I had expected to make the necessary contacts. I recognized other young people on similar missions but we ignored each other. The mood was dangerous and the worst perfume of Nazi terror—it was more evil because it was dying—filled the air. I thought only of Franz, and of winning him, body and soul, as my complete possession. I fought off the doom of the muggy August night by thinking of him, of his body, of how it would be to lie with him after all this was done.

"I waited until I saw Franz pedaling from the direction of the railroad station. I wheeled out of the side street and joined him as casually as I could. It was not the watching Germans that made me tremble, nor the danger I had just been through dropping messages at four hiding places. It was desire inside me and I sensed, as we pedaled along in the last of the evening, that Franz felt the same way. He could not wait until we had scraped our cycles into the yard behind my aunt's house, pretended an interest in the clipped code messages that poured out of Radio Orange, and descended, almost numb with craving, to the cellar, dark as the blacked-out city, and fell into each other's arms, undressing each other, scattering our clothes, kissing each other with longing that was its own light, moving slowly, free of time and death and danger, toward the simple bed in the corner. I have won, I grasped, too delirious, too close to abandon to think about it. I have won Franz for my own . . ."

Mother Hilda stopped as if her air supply had been abruptly cut off, stared, blind to Mike and Ann, back in Amsterdam during that last August of the war, her eyes straining to follow her lover as he lifted away from her in the darkness. "Franz?" she asked plaintively, "Franz, what is it?" The nun paused again, took up her story in the soft voice, "Franz was anxiously fumbling for a candle. He lit it and I watched him unclothed in the shadowed bath of yellow light. What is it, Franz, I asked as he searched for his shirt which lay like a fallen battle flag just by the steps.

"He pulled a twisted piece of paper out of the pocket, inspected it by the flickering candlelight. I could only drink in the sight of his handsome face, his tousled blond hair, his deep chest, then I saw him frown, lower the candle, hurriedly gather his clothes. I did not finish my list, he told me, I forgot, I forgot . . .

"He trembled as I touched him and tried to reassure him that Mr. Pieter had sent out more messengers than just us. But Franz was excited, as if the outcome of the war depended on him. I dressed quickly and we opened a blacked-out cellar window and climbed into the gray night. It was after eleven and I was afraid we would be caught for breaking curfew. Franz signaled to me to leave the bikes and follow on foot. We hurried, silent as thieves, through back ways north toward the western part of the central city, with its collar of old canals. We stood, hardly having spoken, at the end of Rozengracht. Across the glittering canal I could make out the tower of the Westerkerk against the ash-colored sky. Franz looked down at the slip of paper in his hand, squinted as if to pierce the slate shading on Prinsengracht, the street which, just past the church, crooked slightly out of sight.

"It is in the back, he said, if I can get to the back. But his voice drifted off. I stood by his side holding him, feeling the tension. Was it because of me or because of what he was supposed to do? Franz, I whispered, surely everyone has been warned. Nothing will happen. It is quiet all along here. One of the boats moored in the nearby canal scraped against another. Franz strained to see into the night again. As we edged along across the canal from Prinsengracht, I could make out the narrow steepled silent houses, the hump-backed bridges. We moved quickly along to the bridge a block beyond the Westerkerk. Franz turned to me, took my hands in his, told me to stay where I was, that he would be back in ten minutes. But what are you going to do, I asked, where are you going? He moved away, I could see him as he ducked his head to hurry across the bridge.

"I felt a bolt of fear in my heart and set out after him. On the other side of the bridge I could make him out crouched behind a tree. I slipped beside him, touched his arm. He did not seem to notice me. The houses thrust up above us, quaint ramparts against the night. I began to tremble myself, to worry at the lateness, at the strange quiet emptiness of Prinsengracht. Franz would have been done with this earlier, I thought, if . . . Franz stirred at my side, looked at me. I could not see his eyes but I felt his thoughts. He stood up, pressed against the tree, inched away from it toward the brick paving beyond the grass. And then he stopped as one stricken by fear, and more than fear, by that knowledge of the source of fear and the poisoned root of dread. Franz stood as if he were being judged, as if God were raking his soul for its lusts and indecision, flaying his spirit in the windless dark.

"The command to raise his hands sounded like a pistol-shot in the darkness. Before Franz could move, two Nazi soldiers had emerged from the shrouded housefronts, moving swiftly to grab him from either side. Two more stepped out of the shadows, their rifles held across their chests. There was no sound but that of boots on brick, the slap, creak, and metal clink of military equipment, the light laughter of the soldiers as they asked Franz where he was going. He did not answer, struggled to pull away. I held back, paralyzed in body and soul, the enormity of what was occurring and the foolishness of its cause washed through me in a searing rush of comprehension.

"One of the soldiers pulled the slip of paper from Franz's shirt pocket. He struggled to free himself from the soldiers holding him, found his mouth quickly covered by a dark-gloved hand. The soldier spread the paper on his knee as another played a flashlight on it, then straightened up, looked over his shoulder as if checking an address, seemed pleased with himself, laughed, curtly commanded the others to let Franz go. He shook free, called out, that is nothing, nothing, I tell you, surged toward the soldier who turned and brought his rifle down on Franz's head, sending him to the street senseless. He rolled over once, then lay still. I could see the blood on his face even in the dark . . .

"After a few moments I heard a car ignition and a German army truck pulled out of Wester Street. I waited again, for how long I do not know, wondering if my desire had killed Franz, if I had not sinned terribly in tearing him away from God, and if God on this dread August night was not taking his revenge on me. I struggled to his side, felt his pulse, smoothed his hair, a lank of which was soaked in blood from the blow to the right side of his face. I got water in my hands from the canal, bathed his face, bound it as best I could with a piece of cloth I tore from my dress, knelt holding him as tenderly as I could until he began to stir, my heart and soul empty as the street itself. Finally, we managed to hobble back across the bridge. Franz was too weak to go farther so I settled him at the base of a tree behind some bushes, and with them as our shield, we stayed through the rest of the night.

"It was only as dawn came that I realized what we had done. The eerie mood of quiet still gripped the street even though people were out as usual. I got more water, cleaned and rebandaged Franz's face, got some fried cakes from a nearby baker, and in an hour or so, when the crowds got thicker, I thought we might begin to make our way back to my aunt's. Franz, with his face bound and his head aching, could say nothing. His dazed eyes told me that we both felt the same judgment on our sins, that the brief insane life we had as lovers was over for good . . .

"As I stood up I saw a large official car, quiet and ominous as a cat stalking a bird, stopping by one of the houses. A green army truck pulled up behind it and men in dark suits followed by soldiers hurried through one of the doors. The Germans were making a raid, searching for hidden Jews in the very house, number 262, that Franz was to warn . . ."

Mother Hilda raised her head. Tears streamed down the crags that denial had worked into her features. She sobbed, spoke haltingly as she regained possession of herself. "I saw death riding in the streets of the city, you see, death for which we, Franz and I through our lust, had prepared the way. The concentration camp for the Van Daans and the Franks and their daughters Margot and Anne, the poor Jews hiding in the annex up behind the house on Prinsengracht. And death later for most of them. Who could have foretold it? Who could ever cry enough for it?"

Cardinal Kiejson, the binding lines of his face strained to the breaking point, his dried-out blue eyes with the stunned, depleted look of the freshly dead, finished his story in the calm tone men use after the guns have stopped or the storm has passed, when they no longer need fight to be heard. "I have not been able to cry for years about this. Or anything else. My whole lifetime of tears was shed then. I never knew, you see, whether the Germans had already found out about the annex through another informer, or whether they would never have known, except for us and our sins that begot worse sins . . .

"Betje and her aunt nursed me but I have carried this reminder always of the sins of my youth." He raised his hand stiffly, automatically to his cheek. "So we renounced our love and, as our penance and reparation, gave ourselves to God, gave ourselves completely to the service of the church. We would be as absolute in our renunciation of pleasure as we once had been wholeheartedly abandoned to its pursuit.

"You may think it strange, but I have tried to keep my vow of rejecting pleasure for myself in every decision I have made since. I even force myself to smoke, which I have never liked, so I will *have* to remember Amsterdam every day. With the same willpower I battled communism. I learned in Amsterdam, you see, that you cannot compromise with evil. I had tasted the evil of nazism in the saltiness of my own blood that terrible night . . ." He gestured involuntarily toward his facial scar, stared as if seeing deep into the mine of his past from which words could only be hauled out slowly. "There was nothing but evil in nazism. But many during the war thought they could find good parts in it, parts that would justify their closing their eyes and going about their business as if the Jews weren't being hounded to death all around us. And later I felt the same about communism. You couldn't make peace with it . . .

"That is why I was critical of Pope Jean and his romantic notions about the Communists. And why I felt that, whether the world understands it or not, we must battle that system more determinedly now than ever. The devil is in that system, the same timeless devil who vanquished me and left on my head the price of the most innocent of people in the worst crime of war.

"Otto Frank survived, you know. He said that he never wanted to learn who had betrayed them . . ." Kiejson closed his eyes, drifted back in time, lowered his head. After a long moment, he looked up, gestured toward Cardinal Casey, pale, absorbed, filled with his own thoughts. "I have always felt that Thomas, whatever his faults, was an unshakable opponent of communism. His own problems were minor compared to the good he did by supporting the church in the Third World, and by being orthodox. Believe me, I asked him to stand aside reluctantly because . . ." He stopped, frowned, his mouth agape.

"Because," Cardinal Solieri said gently, "you entered into an understanding with a group that seemed to stand for freedom."

"Yes, yes," Kiejson agreed, tired, bewildered, dogged in finding his way to the end of his story. "I thought they wanted only to defeat communism. But the devil was disguised there, too. I saw his face in the dossiers they drew up on my brother cardinals. I came to understand, like the Nazis, they could go too far . . ."

Casey remained immobile, trying to digest everything he had heard in the last half hour. Solieri stepped closer to the Dutch cardinal, touched his hand to his shoulder. Kiejson looked up expectantly, white with need, into the old cardinal's Umbrian earth eyes.

"You thought," the archivist responded easily, "that this anti-Communist organization had financed the New Century Movement only to hold demonstrations and only to threaten terrorist violence. Isn't that so?"

Kiejson nodded agreement in fractional, tremorlike movements.

"You did not expect the bombings, the death of children. You thought they were only going to underscore the Communist threat, make the cardinals, especially the weak ones like your friend from Boston, aware of the Marxist enemy. But you had made your pact and you felt, if I am not mistaken, that you had to become pope yourself, not so much for your own glory . . ." The archivist glanced briefly, meaningfully at Casey ". . . but to gain control over this new face of the mystery of evil you had known all through your life. You thought that as pope you could control them, didn't you?"

Kiejson nodded again, an exhausted pilgrim near the end of his journey.

"I reconstructed this in the quiet of the archives," Solieri continued. "Why, I asked, would nobody want to speak to or listen to me? Was it only because I was insignificant? Or were the answers in my care, hidden perhaps, but in my care nevertheless? And because of that, nobody wanted the old archivist to raise any questions. When I could not find, even through my contacts with other European archives, any history of the New Century Movement, I became puzzled. I needed this finding to speak to me, to reveal itself and its meaning. And gradually—in prayer at Pope Jean's tomb and through my own instincts that these terrorist bombings were too well timed, that access was too easy to the Vatican itself, and that the innocent died while we cardinals were only frightened—its nature became clear."

Kiejson sat numbly, a man past sorrow letting the rain fall on him, hoping for cleansing. The breathless Casey began to speak but Solieri fended him off with a teacher's reproving hand. "You found yourself caught in the tentacles of the same evil. That, I think, is why you hesitated, found yourself paralyzed almost, as you did on Prinsengracht that night, as you did in the Sistine Chapel this morning . . ."

Kiejson focused on the wise old man, spoke in a voice freeing itself of its constriction, a man letting go of his last defense. "And the other time, too?"

Solieri nodded, "Yes, the other time, too."

Mother Hilda had wailed and cried, her slender body heaving and shaking, spilling tears on her habit, clutching Ann's hands in her own, bony, clawlike, unpeaceful for all their years of touching the brows and wounds of the afflicted. Finally, she raised her head, tried to control her sobs, gulped for air. Mother of sorrows, Mike thought, feeling a great pity for her. Ann freed her hands, put an arm around Mother Hilda's steepled back. "There is something else," Ann half stated, half asked, still the doctor in the emergency room. Mother Hilda caught her breath, waited a moment before she spoke, punctuated her clauses with diminishing gasps.

"It was the evil in me, the fiery longing that I have never completely subdued, that ensnared Franz, poor good Franz, in evil too. All across these years, as we kept our pledge of doing penance, we never communicated by letter or in person. When he was ordained I sent him the snowflake crystal, our lost world. But I *felt* him, yes, I sensed him inside me every time I read or heard of him. How strange, I thought, that I should come to be thought a saint and that Franz should become a prince of the church. How little, I thought, people knew of what I was behind this mask I have worn like a habit every day."

"But you have done great good," Mike said, "the world has been better for your sacrifice."

"The world does not know me."

"The world," Ann said softly, "responds to what you have made of yourself for its sake."

Mother Hilda shook her head slowly. "You could never have helped anybody," Ann continued, "if you hadn't been loved greatly."

The nun sighed, things seemed too broken for her to put them together again. "The Lord have mercy on us . . ." Then she focused her clearing eyes on Mike. "And *you,* you who I could sense was leaving the priesthood, you reminded me of Franz. I felt it, yes, and I did not want you to repeat the sin that Franz and I had committed. I wanted to save your soul . . ."

"And keep him," Ann added evenly, "from me."

Mother Hilda seemed too weary to hold up her armor any longer. "Yes," she said in a scoured-out voice, "yes, to keep him from you. And to keep him from invading my life, discovering my weaknesses, my pretense, my unworthiness . . ." Her voice trailed away. "I am no saint," she continued finally, "I am a penitent. I have only tried to do penance for our sins."

"But," Michael interjected, "you didn't want Franz to become pope either."

"No, no," she replied, releasing her grasp on her last defense. "I felt—I *knew*—that Franz was in some way cursed. Perhaps by me, by my lust.

"I could *see* these things. I came to feel that Franz's fatal imperfection was not of the flesh but of the will. Just as he delayed, then froze in hesitation on Prinsengracht, so he would at the other times. He had given me his body and as a result carried forever, like the thorn in the flesh St. Paul spoke of, this terrible uncertainty. It was all the devil wanted, just that little space—that moment of delay, that inch of territory—that is all the devil needed from Franz to use him for his own purposes. I tried to warn Pope Jean when the feeling became stronger to me, but he did not understand. Then, when I heard that he had died, I saw death, as I had warned him, death in the city streets again."

Cardinal Casey's imagination streamed with images, his head pounded, at one moment he saw his mother's face, at another Missy's. The film of his life was being played on some giant beehive screen, its scenes multiplied even as they were divided. He would only stare, his face bleached out, the cracked china cup of his heart rattling inside him.

"Dear Cardinal Kiejson," Solieri said, addressing the Dutchman almost sweetly. "I *do* understand how the pope died. For what I saw that sad afternoon was the mystery revealed before my eyes. I only came to understand what I saw later. And I am sorry that we have had to come to speak of it today. I did not want to but . . ."

"Yes, yes," the worn-down Kiejson responded, "perhaps it must be so . . ."

"The pope was alive when you came to the chapel door," the old cardinal went on. "He did not feel well. He asked you to get the medicine in his apartment where he had left it. And you did. When you returned, the pope was much sicker. He had fallen to the floor, his hand shoved into the pocket where his medicine should have been. You came, heard his cries, saw him look up at you. That is so, isn't it? And you could not move, you *did not move.*"

"Yes," Kiejson said, choosing, "yes, that is so . . ."

TWO

Jimbo looked straight ahead as he hurried through the Excelsior lobby. No telling who might be looking and he didn't want to give any hints by a nervous glance toward the registration area that he had hidden the disk in a safe deposit box. He affected bravado, the perfect Chicago cover when a man wasn't sure what to do next. This, Jimbo thought, is when I need my little brother and his contacts inside the Vatican, damn him and that crazy marriage. "The Hilton," he said as he climbed into a taxi.

Mike and Ann had returned to their hotel sharing the same troubling thoughts, saying little. "Mother Hilda," Mike said as they walked toward their room, "does not wear off easily."

"Mike," Ann asked tentatively as he unlocked the door, "why did you go to Mother Hilda's, what was the real reason?"

Mike held the door open, sighed. "Because she expected us, because of the kids who died, because . . ."

"Because we're not free of the church yet."

Mike closed the door, embraced Ann, shuddering slightly. "The chill of

Holy Mother Church's spurned cheek," he said, his voice too strained to transmit redemptive irony. They walked out onto their balcony, stared through the milky haze at the squat magnificence of St. Peter's, a Buddha unmoved by the glaze of summer sun or the strange drama that was being enacted inside it. I embrace everything, its sullen, complacent silence seemed to say, all lives and times.

"Mother Hilda," Mike whispered, keeping his eyes on the basilica, "probably is a real saint. Despite everything. Maybe that's the way the really holy people are."

"What do you mean?"

Mike chuckled. "I don't know what the hell I mean." They fell into each other's arms, held each other for a long time. "That even the best of us humans," he said, raising his head away from Ann's, "even the best of us may be all screwed up. It's in the striving that you find the goodness."

"I don't think you've quite got this idea worked out," Ann replied playfully as they re-entered the room.

"No," Mike responded, feeling some relief, "no, my theory needs work, I'll admit that." He scooped up the messages, began to read them off. Roger Tansey was better, Josef Beck wanted Mike to attend another press conference, a Mr. Hickey had called. The *Times* had left a long message. Mike crumpled them, dropped them into the wastebasket. "Here I am," he said in a bittersweet tone, "with the story of the century. By God, Jimbo was right." He paused, gazed deeply into Ann's eyes. "But it *is* the knowledge of good and evil. It's too sacred—I mean, the memory of the dead is too sacred ever to tell this story. It would be like violating a tomb to go back to World War Two. Besides, this story has a life of its own, it's still working itself out. I wish I hadn't learned about it . . . There isn't anything I can *do* about it . . ." He sighed. "Besides, there are too many missing pieces. We really don't know how the pope died, or who's responsible for the bombings. We only know why Mother Hilda and Cardinal Kiejson are the way they are."

They embraced again, comforting each other as if they could hear the long ago sounds of the droning bombers and the distant explosions, wondering why this unfinished story had crossed their own like a river snaking out of the past, gurgling with intimations that their lives were somehow parallel to those of the seeress and the cardinal, and that an unsettling mystery still hung over all of them. "Now I understand," Mike said slowly, "why the best remembrance of the dead is a moment of silence. There's nothing you can say, there's too much you don't know. Their destinies are complete. The only respectful thing is silence." Ann touched the side of his face lightly with her hand. "And maybe that's why the Irish, always embattled with the fates, talk so much," he continued gently. "They're always trying to talk their way out of their destiny, escape on a magic carpet of words."

"Mike," Ann interjected brightly, "talk like that tells me it's time for us to get out of here."

Mike laughed, hugged Ann. "Okay, Mrs. Tracy, let's get the hell out of here. Let's go this evening, let's not wait to find out if the next pope is a Dutchman . . ."

There was a knock on the door. A disheveled Jimbo grinned impishly as Mike opened it. He nodded neutrally to Ann as he stepped inside, the wild light in his eyes telling her that he was going to have another go at his little brother. Mike eyed him warily, reassured him that Wingate's man Hickey had not shown up yet, hurry up, Jimbo, Ann and I are leaving Rome.

The journalist took a deep breath, rattled his story out as Mike and Ann moved about the room, packing their suitcases. He touched Mike's arm, his tone becoming enthusiastic, hortatory. "So this New Century Movement is like arms to Iran, they came out of the same playbook. Wingate helped set it up, mock terrorists to scare everybody about Communism. And Wingate, your superpatriot—Christ, never trust a car dealer starts getting a manicure —Wingate, whose old man along with Hampton's old man screwed *our* old man, he's going down for the count on this. Come on, Mike, this is Providence, God's giving us a chance to get even after all these years. But I need your help, there's lots I don't know yet—how the pope died, for example— and we don't have much time. We're at the two-minute warning. Come on, Mike, for the old man, we've got these sons of bitches on the run . . ."

Mike held a pair of socks in midair. "I just told somebody else who knew more about this story than either of us that the dead should bury the dead." Ann watched Jimbo's tense, frustrated expression as Mike continued. "So, Jimbo, I'm sticking with what I told you. This *is* the knowledge of good and evil. And we both ought to stay out of it."

"But the old man, think of the old man . . ."

"Denny was never much for revenge. He used to say people took revenge for you, if you waited long enough, they'd do it worse to themselves than you ever could."

"I used to believe that but now I think God needs a helping hand. They had it right in the Old Testament, they didn't mess around with this long-range philosophy . . ." Jimbo moved closer to Mike, closed his hand on his arm, his words tumbling out urgently. "Look, Mike, do this *for me.* Help me, for Crissake, help me get into the Vatican, help me take another step with this . . ." He was breathless, almost crying, a rumpled exorcist making one final effort to cast out the spirit that was taking Mike away just when he needed him.

Mike felt in his brother's grip a last-minute intensity not only for this story but for their relationship, felt a need deeper than he had realized before. "Have you noticed, Jimbo," he asked slowly, "that you've never said even hello to Ann since you came in here? Do you realize that you hardly ever look at her? What do you think you're doing to Ann and me? It isn't just me anymore. I'm married. I know you don't like it but it's true. We'll never be kids again."

Jimbo released his hand, stepped back, glanced at Ann who continued calmly with her packing. The journalist looked back to Mike, his eyes glassy. He opened his mouth but his throat was suddenly too dry for speech.

"I love you, Jimbo," Mike said, feeling sorry if he had hurt his brother, sorry their good-bye had come to this. "I love you, Jimbo, but I'm not going back into that world, not even for you."

Jimbo turned aside, lowered his head, gagged on the brine of remembrance, saw his wife Maureen's face, heard her speak words very much like those his brother had just uttered, I love you, Jimbo, but you haven't grown up, you'll never grow up, you don't want to . . .

Mike moved closer to him, put his arm around his shoulder. They stood together for a moment, then Jimbo embraced him, pulled back, snuffing away the blinding emotion of the instant. "Okay," Jimbo said, his voice firmer. He looked toward Ann, dipped his head an inch, the best he could do in saluting Mrs. Tracy, she's taken me on points, he thought, as he forced a loser's smile into position. He paused, regrouping his internal forces, turned toward the door, stopped. "One thing, Mike."

"Yes?"

"What *did* you find out, what spooked you so?"

"Sorry, Jimbo."

"Come on, now, I gave you everything I had." Jimbo was fighting to keep some kind of handhold, some way to make Mike feel he still owed him something, if not as brothers then as rogue Irishmen together. "I'm just curious. From a human standpoint."

"Yes, I'm sure you are." Mike looked at Ann. She kept her head down as she zipped her bag. He looked again at Jimbo, a string loosening in his heart, what harm would there be, he wondered, in telling him, it might even convince him to drop the story . . .

A heavy, insistent rap on the door haled Mike in from the sentimental seas. Ann stopped, her hands stilled in the act of zippering the seam of her bag. Jimbo spun swiftly, the sudden pain in his stomach counterpointing the twitch of discomfort in his forehead. Mike walked to the door, the pageant of his life unrolling like a tapestry over a balcony with his big brother at its center, Jimbo whose whole life depends on being a boy forever, on escapes justified by the trick of pulling them off.

A thin, white-faced, middle-aged American, smiling falsely below the narrow incisions of his eyes, held an old-fashioned boater in hair-matted hands. Next to him stood a short, rocklike Italian with a badge and a credential tag pinned to the collar of his tan summer suit. His smooth bald head glistened as brightly as an ornamental ball in an old-fashioned garden. "You remember, Jimbo, Bert. Bert Hickey," the American said somberly. "We have some serious questions for all of you to answer." He stepped across the sill, nodded toward his companion. "Inspector Malnotti has signed complaints from Count Rafallo regarding James Tracy about materials removed from his Vatican office. You two—you are Michael and Mrs. Tracy, I presume—are named as accessories in that and in the unauthorized removal of materials from the apartment of Cardinal Kiejson. We would like you to cooperate with us." He seemed bored but intense, burnt-out but dangerous despite his small town undertaker's looks.

"And you," Jimbo sneered, "the illustrious Hickey, the station chief under cover as an art dealer. Do you investigate by the numbers, the same way you paint?"

Hickey ignored him, studied the room, let his eyes come to rest on Ann. "You might as well leave your bag here, ma'am, we've got to detain you for a while."

Mike put his arms around Ann. "Where," he asked, "are we going?"

Hickey looked glumly at Inspector Malnotti, who spoke up in acceptable English. "These charges concern activities in Vatican City. We will take you to their security office."

The silence in the Sistine Chapel was almost absolute. The afternoon sun flooded through the high windows below the barrel-vaulted ceiling. The princes of the church seemed lost in their separate concerns and thoughts, each sensing that a climactic event was building and that instead of directing it, they were being shaped by it, driven inside their own souls, straining, as prophets of old, to hear God's voice in the subtlest sign, the movement of the air, the slightest flicker of transcendence. But there were no evident signals from the God, only a great stalled silence from which ordinary anxiety had been winched dry. The cardinals were in their places, their eyes focused on the voting cards before them.

Cardinal Solieri swallowed hard, looked from his vantage point at Cardinals Kiejson and Casey sitting a few places away from each other. They looked, as the third ballot was about to begin, just as they had earlier in the day. Solieri inscribed the name of the archbishop of Marseilles on his ballot, sat back, wondering what God had gotten him into. If I ask to speak, he thought, I will be looked at just as Cardinal Kiejson said, an old man with a wild tale out of the library stacks, and who would really believe me? And Cardinal Kiejson? He had wept like Peter over his sins but he had lived with them a long time, he had lived a life of penance, what would he do now? Near the front of the chapel, Cardinal Maestrini rose, began to walk stiffly toward the altar, his vote held above his head like a miniature dove.

Monsignor Lanza looked up sternly, thanked Inspector Malnotti and the lugubrious Hickey for their assistance, said that he would handle matters now. "We'd appreciate hearing something," the American said.

"This is a matter for the sovereign Vatican State," Lanza countered, indicating by the finest shading of his manner—that Hickey and Malnotti were to depart. After the door closed, he shook his head as he smiled. "I did not expect to become so involved with the Tracy family. I only witnessed the marriage, I did not enter one." His face became grave as he explained his surprise when he was told that an American agent and the Rome police were bringing in suspects. "It is only to keep you out of the way until the conclave is safely over. They can't hold you. But what is it that you know that has them so concerned?"

Jimbo and Mike began to talk at the same time, stopped like men who had different reasons for wanting to defer to each other. "I'll tell you," Ann said, moving into the moment of hesitation, "I'll tell you because I've heard both sides. And I'll tell you what I think, too."

Lanza sat, his lips compressed, his brow contracted, as Ann summarized Jimbo's tale of a U.S. government-aided plan to ensure the election of an anti-Communist pope; the out-of-control New Century Movement; the involvement, willing or not, of Cardinal Kiejson; and the story, still filled with lingering sadness, of the Dutch teenagers and their tragic love and even more tragic involvement in the Resistance movement, as well as their lives of reparation since then. "But," Ann concluded, "there are still aspects of this that we don't understand. And there doesn't seem to be anything we can do about it."

Lanza brooded for a moment, bent, unlocked a drawer, pulled a plume of handkerchief above the level of the desk. "I still have one of the missing pieces," he said calmly, "and I suspect that Count Rafallo, who made one of these complaints, will tell us what he knows. He was only doing what Wingate told him to do. I learned that he has been taking payments from Wingate, who made out the other complaint. Rafallo was of use in order to obscure the reasons for the pope's death. They wanted a mystery to hang over the conclave, a hint that evil powers had a hand in this death. Rafallo is no fool, he was playing his own game. But it was no accident that the pope's organs were, shall we say, put beyond even the possibility of further examination."

"Great," Jimbo exploded. "I knew the son of a bitch was crooked."

"Yes," Lanza replied wryly, "and he detoured you quite successfully for a while. He was keeping Wingate informed. He even knew you were seeing Miss Tomai."

Jimbo looked at Mike, blushed. "The actress," he muttered. "I interviewed her . . ."

"When," Mike asked, ignoring Jimbo's embarrassment, "when can we get out of here?"

"I think we have to think about this a minute," Lanza responded coolly, "for we four have information that, in some form or other, must be communicated to the conclave."

"Are you serious?"

"I have been thinking seriously all day. Do you think that we can allow this election to go forward? Do you think it will remain a secret that the American government, at somebody's orders, financed an imitation terrorist gang, and attempted to influence this election the way European powers did routinely until this century? Kiejson may have hidden his past so far, but he won't as pope. No matter how much penance he has done, it is unthinkable . . ."

"But," Mike said uneasily, "we can't get into a conclave . . ." There was a long pause. "Let the dead bury the dead, I really mean that."

"You forget," Lanza said, notes of anxiety feathering the determination in his voice, "that I have a conscience too. As to the conclave, I am in charge of security. All I have to do is give some orders in the right tone."

They laughed grimly. Ann and Mike understood from each other's eyes that they shared the same queasy feeling, generated by a subterranean tremor that ran out jaggedly from the institution that would not let them go, that kept breaking up the pavement in front of them, sending trees down to close the roads behind them.

"I've been trying to break out of the church," Mike said, forcing a smile, "and you tell me we're going to break into it."

"Hot damn," Jimbo said, "I knew it, Mike, I knew we were destined to do this together."

"You," Lanza said, addressing Jimbo, "will have to produce the disk with the information. We will need proof of this story if we are to get anywhere."

"That's easy," Jimbo replied airily, "it's in a safe spot. I can get it any time."

Everyone became quiet as if a many-armed goddess of fate had enfolded them and they needed a moment to pull themselves free of its grasp. "I can get it now," Jimbo said, "right now. It's at the Excelsior."

"Yes," Lanza said, lowering his eyes, "yes, we do not have much time."

"How about Wingate's men?"

"I'll send you in one of our cars."

"Come on, Mike," Jimbo said excitedly, "this one last ride. I don't have to leave you off at school yet. Come on with me . . ."

THREE

Rome seemed languorous in the summer twilight, more the old actress taking advantage of the shadows than the dazzling seductress showing her limbs in the light. They pulled away from the giant tongs of the Bernini colonnade, barriers parting, guards saluting their officially bannered car. "No smoke yet," the driver said, gesturing back across the piazza toward the Sistine Chapel, "no white smoke, no black smoke." He shook his head as if to ward off some unlucky emanation coming from the locked-in princes of the Church.

"I *like* this," Jimbo said in drawn-out tones of mock contentment. "It's like Palm Sunday, everybody getting out of the way for us." He kept twisting in his seat next to the driver, burning off his excitement as a refinery does its lisps of excess fuel. Mike and Ann huddled together. Mike thought that going to the hotel with his brother was a compromise that Ann had accepted more out of love for him than any enchantment with Jimbo's schemes. He caressed her wordlessly, trying to communicate his gratitude by touch, I appreciate what you're doing, letting me go while Jimbo collects his evidence. But what Ann picked up was Mike's own need for a lark, Mike's need to go camping one last time with Jimbo.

"Do you know," she asked in a voice of both comprehension and tolerance, "what Teddy Roosevelt said when he went hunting in Africa after he left the White House? This is my last chance to be a boy again, that's what . . ."

"I'll be grown up and off to college before you know it," Mike responded, "then you'll wish the little boy was still around."

The car eased itself into the turgid river of evening traffic, made its way into the blue valleys made by the buildings along the Via Veneto. People were coming out of buildings, calling to each other even though it was the time of siesta. Is it our car, Mike wondered, or is there a fire somewhere? People were shouting to each other, gesturing, excitement was sputtering fuse-like alongside them, overtaking the car. The driver turned on the radio. An agitated voice was speaking in Italian. "But whatever is going on, there is white smoke. Yes, it is confirmed, there is white smoke, a new Holy Father has been chosen. We do not have any information yet on who it is. There is great excitement in the area . . ." The driver turned, his face lightened as if a curse had been removed, smiled.

"Shit," Jimbo growled, "shit, shit, shit . . ."

"It's over," Ann said, relieved, "it's over . . ."

Mike leaned forward, touched Jimbo's shoulder. "I'm sorry, big brother."

Jimbo ignored him, bolted out of the car as they stopped in front of the hotel, pushed through the crowd buzzing about the election on the sidewalk. Mike took a breath, it really is over, he thought, no matter what we've learned, no matter what we've been through on the edges of this. "We're free, Annie," he said, felt fraternity peeling away with each step Jimbo took away from him, and the church, too, with its unknown new pope and its thousands of years of glory and fixes, the church's tight wrappings were unwinding like those of Lazarus, it really was over. The car radio crackled, the commentator's voice grew shrill, his words tumbling over each other as Mike and Ann alighted with the driver's assistance. Jimbo's progress into the hotel had been arrested by the wild-eyed, bristling Max Hampton, who was talking, gesturing, like a man waiting for something he dreaded. Or, Mike thought, like a man who knows that an escape helicopter will land in the prison yard any minute. Strangers and tourists, caught up in the suddenly

carbonated atmosphere, called out, asked questions, no, nobody knew anything, not yet.

Mike and Ann edged up the steps, watched Jimbo and the static-filled
lawyer pass into the lobby together. People streamed up and down on either
side of them as Mike and Ann, still letting the sudden end of the long day
settle, climbed the steps like secret witnesses who arrive too late to testify at
the murder trial. They passed through the hotel doors as an emergency
vehicle trumpeted somewhere in the streets behind them.

The lobby was filled with guests and visitors, some in evening clothes,
mingling, chatting, hurrying as if on the promenade deck of a great ship just
before sailing time. Near the center of the floor Jimbo and Hampton, their
tensed backs to the entrance, were engaged earnestly with someone they
were obscuring. Mike and Ann made their way toward them through the
casting call crowd. "That's Florence Roberts," Ann said, catching a glimpse
of her, grave and anxious as the lawyer and the journalist edged momentarily apart, "what's going on I wonder . . ." They joined the group as the
gesturing Hampton was attempting to reassure her.

"No, I'm confident that everything will be okay."

"Dr. Coleman," Florence Roberts blurted out as she caught sight of Ann,
"is that you? Oh, I'm so glad to see you . . ." She broke away from the
men, threw her arms around Ann, sobbed as she spoke. "It's Tom . . ."

"Tom?"

"The cardinal," Hampton cut in, "Cardinal Casey. He's ill . . ."

"Yes," Florence Roberts said, "isn't it awful? Mr. Hampton got a call.
Tom was taken ill just as the conclave ended, his heart, they think."

Jimbo and Mike stood next to each other, almost unaware of each other's
presence, absorbed in the sharp sudden drama. Mrs. Roberts dabbed at her
eyes with a handkerchief. "He apparently insisted on coming here, he
wouldn't be treated there. So, Dr. Coleman, would you take a look at him
for me?"

"That's about the situation," Hampton said before Ann could make any
response. "The cardinal insisted that he be brought here, that he wanted to
see Mrs. Roberts here . . ."

"And he's on the way?" Mike asked incredulously, looking at Ann, feeling that the mystery they had thought finished had billowed up again, dark,
surreal, enveloping. "Ann," he blurted out, "shouldn't he go right to a
hospital?"

"Let's see how he is," she said, putting her arm around Florence Roberts, the trim, well-dressed woman whose age lines were suddenly being kneaded out of her face by the worry of the moment, overcoming the makeup, the discipline, the achieved presence of a lifetime. She was publicly expressing the depth and the strain of all her years of relationship with the cardinal, the price, higher than Mike had supposed, of something more than friendship. Images of Mother Hilda and Cardinal Kiejson, Mrs. Roberts and Cardinal Casey, himself and Ann, linked in an unlikely mystery, love was the unlikeliest mystery of them all . . .

"I couldn't get him to go to a hospital," Hampton fussed. "When the old man gets determined on something, there's nothing anybody can do."

Mike surveyed the lobby as Jimbo tried to get more details out of Hampton. Who was the new pope, had Casey told him that? Hampton shook his head, No, no. Ann spoke softly with Mrs. Roberts, Yes, we'll see that the cardinal is well cared for. The great space of the lobby was a triumph of artifice, a temporary setting for intervals of lives, a stage or an ocean liner rather than a cathedral, a place charged with the intensity and drama of time more than the serenity of eternity. A commotion at the main entrance broke his uneasy reverie.

The thinning crowd hushed as a gray-faced Cardinal Casey, supported on one side by Monsignor Hawkins and on the other by the doorman, haltingly shuffled into the hotel. Mrs. Roberts gasped, moved toward him, Ann at her side. The cardinal stopped, trying to catch his breath. His Roman collar was missing and the top buttons of his cassock were open below his wattled neck. He was bareheaded; a lock of slate-colored hair fell across his brow. "Missy," he whispered, his eyes brightening, "Missy . . ."

"It's all right," Mrs. Roberts said soothingly, "it's all right, you'll be all right now . . ."

Ann took the cardinal's wrist, felt his pulse, nodded toward Hawkins. "Let's have him sit down for a moment." She turned toward Mike. "Make sure," she said calmly, "somebody has ordered an ambulance. He's too sick right now to stay here."

"Ann," Mike said, trying to compress concern, anxiety, and love into one word, but Ann had turned back to Cardinal Casey who had been lowered into a leather chair. Mrs. Roberts leaned over him, placed her hands on the sides of his face, spoke so quietly that only a few words of what she said could be heard. But there was no mistaking the timeless depth of her attention, the concentration of her energy, the fierce, fearful, protective stance of a woman who had loved a man for a long time.

"I already sent for an ambulance," Hampton said in the worn-out voice of a man who had used up all the responses he knew and felt helpless in front of love and death.

Mike could see the cardinal's eyes just above Ann's lowered head. They made contact with him, transmitted some message to him, what is it, Mike wondered as he advanced automatically toward his former archbishop. Monsignor Hawkins looked nervously toward Mike, back to the cardinal. Casey opened his mouth, spoke slowly but clearly to his priest secretary. "I want to go to confession . . ." Hawkins reached into his side pocket for a small purple stole, started to put it around his neck as Ann and Mrs. Roberts straightened up, backed away. "Not to you," Casey whispered, "to Mike there . . ." Mike and Hawkins glanced briefly at each other and, wordlessly, the secretary handed the stole to the former priest. Mike held the narrow silken band in both hands, looked at his brother, Hampton, Mrs. Roberts, and Ann. Their eyes were fixed and staring as they moved back, making a semicircle several feet away from the old man. They watched, just out of earshot, as Mike donned the stole and lowered his head close to Casey's, made the sign of the cross.

"I was to confession," the old man said, struggling for breath, "at retreat last . . ."

"That's okay, that's okay," Mike said gently, "just take your time."

"Not much time, Mike. But I'm sorry for whatever I've done to hurt people." He paused, took a deep breath. "I always did what I thought was right. But I've done things I knew were wrong, too, mostly being selfish, I don't know . . ." He grabbed Mike's arm with surprising strength, pulled him closer. "I hope what I did today makes up for my sins . . ." Mike turned his head slightly, looked directly into the old man's eyes. They seemed to be pleading for some intuitive comprehension as they moved past Mike's head toward Florence Roberts and back again. Do you understand me, they asked urgently, can you catch what I'm trying to say? Casey's glance ranged out toward Florence Roberts again.

"You loved her, is that it?"

The cardinal nodded eagerly, his washed-out eyes begging for yet more from Mike.

"You still love her . . ." Yes, yes, the frail Casey's head bobbed. "Always," he whispered, "always . . ."

"But you're sorry about something, is that it?"

Casey bowed his head, spoke feebly. "I didn't want you to marry because it, it . . ." He paused, gulped breath. "It made me feel guilty . . ." The cardinal released his grip on Mike's arm, rested his head on the back of the chair. "I'm sorry for these . . ." His voice trailed off.

"And for all the sins of your past life," Mike finished for him, speaking softly into his ear. "God understands," Mike said softly, "God wants you to be at peace . . ." He raised his bandaged right hand, made the sign of the cross as he spoke the sacramental words, "I absolve you from your sins in the name of the Father and of the Son and of the Holy Spirit. Amen."

He looked into Casey's face as he lifted himself away from the chair. The cardinal half smiled, seemed lighter, at ease. Florence Roberts hurried forward, followed by Ann as excitement flared freshly at the entrance. A squadron of policemen, followed by several priests and crimson-robed ecclesiastics poured through the door into the lobby which, except for the group around the cardinal's chair, was now almost empty. "The new pope is coming," one of the priests called out. Cheers flooded in from the street, the priests spread out from the entrance in ragged formation, the policemen strung themselves out in front of them. There was the slightest moment of quiet as the cheers outside died down. Then the door began to open.

FOUR

Mike and Ann exchanged glances quickly as Florence Roberts, oblivious to every other stimulus, hurried to Cardinal Casey's side. Jimbo looked quickly toward the desk, an image of the disk secure in its copper box rising and falling in his imagination. He turned toward the opening door. Max Hampton stood, the light of events beyond his control reflected faintly in his eyes, like a man held back behind the fire lines. Ann stepped next to Florence Roberts, put a comforting arm around her shoulder.

The door opened. The papal master of ceremonies, his swarthy face accented by the snowmass surplice he wore over a violet cassock, came through, looked back uncertainly. A young priest entered, scurried to join the flank of clergymen. There was the slightest break in the dramatic rhythm as the lobby noise, except for Casey's labored breathing, boiled away. Mike felt a tingling sensation of expectation as he focused intensely on the empty space.

Angelo Solieri, his plump figure testing the seams of the white papal cassock, walked into the lobby as confidently as if he were entering a library.

Mantled in a red cloak, a gold-trimmed flat black ceremonial hat in his left hand, he raised his right hand, now wearing the ring of the fisherman, blessing and greeting everyone. His glowing eyes and easy smile dominated the room gently, as if his deepest instincts and sympathies were free at last to gaze benignly on the faulted world.

He ignored the ecclesiastics, dropping to their knees like felled crows around him, headed directly to Cardinal Casey. "My friend and benefactor," he said mildly, looking down at Casey, then at Florence Roberts holding his hand in hers, and back into the Chicagoan's eyes. Mrs. Roberts did not seem to see the new pope, nor to hear his words of greeting. "Thomas," the pope whispered, "you must take care of yourself. My first official act is to come to see you." Casey's eyes brightened, he swallowed, attempted to speak. "No, no, save your strength, the pope makes that his first official order."

The new pope's twinkling eyes surveyed the group, caught Michael's, then Ann's eyes. He nodded to her, then reached out, touched Mike's shoulder as a father might, confirming hard-bought understandings of the heart. He's the old priest, a dizzied but happy Mike said to himself, I went to confession to him in the crypt, the one who showed me holiness without trying. Mike looked into Ann's upturned eyes. The church through this new pope, they grasped simultaneously, has blessed our marriage.

"I have taken the name Jean," the pope said contentedly to Mike. "I am Pope Jean II . . ." Then he turned back to Casey, leaned down to embrace him as best he could without disturbing Florence Roberts. "Thomas," the pope said, "you were a brave and generous man today, and I have come to ask you, as soon as you are better, to come with me on my first journey. I am going to Beirut, I just announced it on the balcony at St. Peter's. We must give a sign of peace and friendship in that city where the Christians have been killing each other for so long they can no longer remember why. We must begin with ourselves . . ."

"Yes," Casey said, mustering his strength, "peace, yes. You will be a good Holy Father . . ." The pope looked gently at Florence Roberts, then at Ann, turned his head toward Michael, his patient brown eyes radiating an old man's appreciation, if not approval, of the complexities of life. He smiled, touched Mike's arm again as another flurry of excitement broke out at the entrance. Two police officials, heavily braided and booted, entered the lobby, giving off signals of danger, spoiling the mood of the area with their quick movements, their darting eyes. The papal master of ceremonies intercepted them, was pushed forward ahead of them toward the waiting pope.

"Holy Father," the master of ceremonies said urgently, "these officials tell me that we must leave here immediately. There is a bomb threat and the entire hotel must be evacuated." Behind him, police were filing in, commandeering the desk, heading for the elevators and stairs. "There can be no delay . . ."

The pope frowned, feeling suddenly the weight of the office that had come to him that evening and the turbulent wake of the paranoia that had been loosed on Rome when his predecessor died. "Hurry, Holy Father," one of the officials said as the other ordered the priests and police to follow the pope out of the building. A muffled loudspeaker outside the hotel could be heard issuing echoing orders for the hotel and street to be cleared.

The pope paused to speak a few words to Casey, looked up again toward Michael. "Holy Father," the master of ceremonies said, pulling at his red cape, "please . . ." The pope's eyes surveyed the group quickly, he blessed them, and was bustled in a vanguard of officials and policemen toward the door.

"Please," a police officer said to Florence Roberts in Italian, "you must go now." She stared back at him not comprehending anything he said. He took her arm.

"Leave her alone," Ann said in English, gesturing the officer away, "I'll see to her." She turned to Mike. "Can you check on that ambulance?"

The police officer gazed at Cardinal Casey whose breathing was a little smoother, shrugged, and moved away. Mike surveyed the lobby, now growing noisy as guests, some of them half clothed, clattered down the stairways or flooded excitedly out of the elevators. A stout policeman blew a whistle, wigwagged his arms to impose order on the traffic, was swept along to the doors like a chip on a river. Ann bent closer to Cardinal Casey, talked to him in a low voice. "The ambulance, Mike," she called, turning around, "see if it's here yet, will you."

"I'll check," Jimbo said, looking toward the exit, estimating his chances of getting out of the lobby and back in. Hampton remained standing mutely, unmoved by the fire-drill commotion. "Come on, Max," Jimbo said, "there's nothing you can do here." Hampton started like a man shaken from sleep, followed Jimbo as he made his way through the nervous, pushy crowd.

Mike knelt on one knee next to Ann, asked with his eyes how the cardinal was doing. Ann answered clearly with hers, not well and we need that ambulance.

Another police official stopped, urged all of them to get out of the hotel.

"We need a stretcher," Ann replied calmly, "can you help us?"

"Yes, yes," the officer countered, "but you, and the lady here, you must leave. We will take care of the cardinal, believe me . . ."

"I'm a doctor," Ann responded. "I'm going to stay with him until you can move him."

"And I'm her husband," Mike said, "I'm staying, too."

The officer nodded gravely, touched Florence Roberts on the arm. Ann touched her, too. "Go ahead, Florence," she said, "I'll see that he's taken care of."

"Go on, Missy," Casey said hoarsely, "please . . ."

Florence Roberts hesitated, embraced Casey, kissed him. "I'm staying with you, Tom. I'll be right here."

Jimbo returned from the front door. The crowd of departing guests thinned out, leaving the air disturbed, the chairs and tables askew, edges of the carpet turned up, Flying Dutchman quiet descended on the hotel. "Things are all tied up outside," the returning Jimbo said breathlessly, "but there's an ambulance about a block away. I told them to get a stretcher and bring it along . . ." He broke off as he focused on the tableau. "I mean, they'll be right here. I think you ought to go . . ."

"Everyone out, everyone out," a police officer cried in the cadences of a bellboy.

Jimbo leaned down next to Mike and Ann. "For Crissake, they'll be here with the stretcher in a minute. Come on." He edged around, crouched next to Mrs. Roberts. "Look, lady, if you go, maybe they'll go, too. Come on." Florence Roberts turned toward him. "You go ahead, young man." She tightened her grasp on the cardinal's hand. "I wouldn't know where to go."

"Come on, Mike," Jimbo said, "let's see if we can carry him." The brothers worked around Casey, began to lift him. He groaned, began to tremble and perspire. Florence Roberts gasped.

"You'd better put him down," Ann ordered. "We'll have to be careful." They settled Casey in his chair again. Ann wiped his brow. He gradually opened his eyes, focused on Mrs. Roberts.

"Look, Missy," Casey said between breaths, "you have to think of Ed and his family. I'll be right along. Please, for me . . ."

Florence Roberts rose slightly, kissed Casey on the cheek. "I don't want to leave you."

"They'll take care of me," Casey said, gesturing toward Mike and Ann. "Okay, Missy?"

She took a deep breath, kissed him lightly again. Casey looked toward Jimbo, his watery eyes asking him to see Mrs. Roberts out. The journalist took her arm as she moved reluctantly away, steered her across the deserted lobby.

Mike put his arm around Ann's shoulders, brushed her face with his. "I love you," he said softly. Ann seemed to relax, responding to Mike's tone as much as his words. She looked into his eyes. "I love you," she said. Their eyes held each other tenderly as if, as silence settled again on the lobby, they sensed the profound rightness of their caring for the dying cardinal. As if their journey, begun so long before with the mysterious meeting of their eyes in a hospital room, had always been destined to bring them to this disordered and dangerous place, that love had been given to them not just for themselves, but to be given away, freely and without fear.

Ann took Mike's bandaged hand, kissed it lightly, rubbed her cheek against it, kissed him again. Mike looked at the ragged bandage. Love is God's gift to the wounded, he thought, nobody else would recognize it. But you couldn't keep it, there was no way you could keep real love for yourself, love kept breaking itself open, there was no fix for it. Mike kissed Ann again, sensed that she was feeling the same things. Love, they said with their eyes, love, in one form or another, linked and pulled together as securely as a cobbler's thread the patchwork of their days. A harsh amplified voice barked orders on the street. They put their arms around each other, felt a deep and unassailable peace spread through their souls.

The door burst open, swung shut on the gasp of outside noise. Jimbo hurried across the eerily quiet lobby. "The goddam stretcher, it'll be here . . ." He frowned, hunched down at Mike's side. "Come on, Mike," he urged, "you don't owe anything to the church anymore."

"You go, Jimbo," Mike said, his arm still around Ann. "Maureen and your kids'll be worried. We'll be out in a few minutes."

Jimbo studied his brother and Ann in profile as they huddled in front of Casey. He had never before noticed how their faces seemed to match. They seemed serene together, they fit together. "Goddammit, let's get out of here." He pulled at Mike's sleeve, looked at the cardinal, gray, his mouth open. "Goddammit, Mike . . ."

"Go on, Jimbo," Mike said softly, "I'm a big boy now."

Jimbo leaned down anxiously, hugged Mike impulsively, kissed him. "You were always a good kid. I love you." He paused, leaned across and bussed Ann on the cheek, pulled back, tears welling in his eyes. "Goddammit, why don't you two leave? Come on now, for Crissake, come on . . ."

"Go on, Jimbo," Ann said evenly, "we'll take care of each other."

Jimbo straightened up, looked down desperately at Mike and Ann, then at the desk and toward the door, where the hell is that stretcher? He took a deep breath, hurried across the floor, stopped at the entrance, gazed again at the peaceful group at the center of the lobby, plunged out into the noisy, roped-off street.

Jimbo reached the police lines as light flashed across the crowds and thunder erupted inside the hotel. He was thrown forward by the rush of blistering air as with a throaty, drawn-out roar the hotel collapsed on itself inside its thick walls.

After

Numbly flying across the Atlantic afterward, I dreaded telling my mother about Mike and Ann and how they died in each other's arms. I planned to skip the marriage part, and to tell her that Mike died as a priest hero. Why not let her think that she still had Michael and the glory of his priesthood in some way, I asked myself, and what difference would it make, really? And Ann's family, well, I didn't know what they felt or what they knew, didn't know what to tell them, either. Mike and Ann were called heroes by the media but, of course, Michael was described as Monsignor and they called Ann Dr. Coleman, "a physician visiting Rome." Florence Roberts said she had asked Ann to step into an emergency with her "cousin" Cardinal Casey. It was sad enough as it was and, as I looked down from the plane window at Chicago, lashed by summer heat, I thought of the whole story, as rich in buried secrets as the city itself. One more secret couldn't make any difference.

As I climbed the creaking steps to my mother's flat I changed my mind. There had been enough secrets, enough truths buried and half buried already, enough fixes. Mike and Ann *were* married, they were as married as man and woman can get. That was the truth I had wanted to ignore, that I had wanted to obliterate as if it had never happened. As I paused on the landing I thought of the old man. Denny said always tell the truth, it's easier to remember and it's better for you. Mom didn't let me say anything at first, just led me, thinner and more gray-haired than I remembered her, into the kitchen, made some tea, the Irish chicken soup. She added sugar to hers, avoiding my eyes. Then she looked across the table at me and asked, very softly, "Michael and Ann were married, weren't they?"

I lowered my eyes, whispered yes in a tight, hoarse voice. She looked relieved. "I knew Mike loved her," she said after a long while, "I knew it by the way he changed after he met her, there was no hiding it. It came out all the time. I could tell by the sound of his voice when he talked to her on the phone, no matter how formal he tried to be or what church business he discussed. And by the little hurry in his step when she would come to visit here . . ." I just watched her as she sipped her tea. She had made some kind of peace with their love long before.

We buried Mike and Ann together in the Tracy family plot, right next to Denny. It's a nice place, if you can say any of these places is nice, and when I'm in the States I try to visit, bring fresh flowers, even. I just sit there, trying to pray, but I don't really know what to say. Not that I haven't tried, but the old schooldays stuff just rattles through my head and doesn't touch what's going on deep inside me. But I'm not sure what that is, either. The only thing that seems to work is time, the thing I hate to have pass and need to have pass. I sit by a tree not far from their grave and I just keep quiet and try to let things settle down. There's a lot of peace for me in doing that.

They gave Cardinal Casey a great send-off at Holy Name Cathedral, of course, and Florence Roberts, dressed in black, walked right behind the coffin and sat weeping like a widow in the front row along with little Eddie and the family. Some people say that young Ed, the great financier, looks an awful lot like Casey. I don't know about that but in death Cardinal Casey's reputation has improved considerably. You'd think he had spent his life healing lepers, comforting the sorrowing, in short, being a real priest. The investigation of him was dropped, naturally, a noble death putting the fix in better than anything else yet devised, even in Chicago. As I entered the cathedral I heard a young priest being interviewed about the characteristics he would like to see in the archbishop who would succeed Casey. "I'd like a man," the boyish priest said in rather self-pleased tones, "who is really human." Holy Christ, I thought, what do you think you just had? But I kept my mouth shut as I shuffled, all sixes and sevens anyway, inside.

Casey's new ecclesiastical esteem arose from the totally unexpected and out-of-character action he had taken at the conclave when he asked his own supporters to switch their votes to Cardinal Solieri. All that stuff is supposed to be kept secret but Pope Jean II talked about it himself, saying the truth was more important than secrecy, things like that being one of the ways he has become the pope even the Protestants love. Just as the afternoon balloting was about to start, Casey asked for the floor. He said that he wasn't worthy of the votes of his brothers but that he knew a man who was. Everybody, of course, expected that he would urge his peers to switch to Cardinal Kiejson. But Casey surprised them by proposing the old archivist. Then Kiejson himself spoke, saying that he, too, wanted the cardinals to vote for Solieri. The Dutchman said that the papacy would be too much for him and that he wanted to enter a monastery to lead a life of prayer and sacrifice "for the good of the church." Pope Jean didn't let any of the rest of the story out, however, and Kiejson is back in Holland, praying for us in silence, his biggest secrets and his inner sorrows unknown to the world.

Mother Hilda went back to Hilfen Haus and she's still taking care of the prostitutes, still pissing off the pimps. She doesn't give interviews anymore and she refuses to travel. They say that there is something subdued about her. The pope stopped to see her when he was in Munich, had a private conversation with her. My guess is that she's been more at peace since then, that the pope somehow made her feel understood, he has a way of doing that with people. In any case, she's living with her secrets, too. Everybody, the old man used to say, ends up where they belong.

My computer disk was destroyed when the hotel went down. One of the areas rigged with explosives was the safe deposit boxes, those symbols of capitalist degradation. So my secrets and my story—the story of a lifetime, not to mention my great chance to revenge Denny on Wingate and Hampton—disappeared irretrievably, too. But the old man was right about revenge. Stay out of the way and give people time, they'll supply their own rope, build the scaffold, too. That's what Wingate and Hampton did for each other, trading charges of all kinds when word leaked out about the New Century Movement and its crackpot origins inside the United States Government itself. They let some former commando recruit real terrorists for what they called Operation White Russian. Psychopaths Incorporated, they should have called it, since the loonies in it got out of hand, trying out new explosives, blackmailing and screwing each other, it was like letting the Chicago City Council run World War Two, a real fuck-up.

And Rafallo sang like Caruso to the investigators, claimed that Wingate had tried to involve him in an anti-Communist plot, had offered him money, but that he was only too glad to cooperate with the authorities, especially if they didn't extradite him. Which they didn't. But Pope Jean II fired him and even took away his title as a papal count, another move that has endeared him to the world. But Rafallo, along with Angelica Tomai, is in a new business, running a combination fat farm and drying-out place for celebrities somewhere in Tuscany.

The government, of course, disowned poor Ownie, said that Operation White Russian was a plot arranged without the knowledge of the president. The former king of odometer resetting on the South Side was fed to the congressional committees that were just looking for some sucker to hang in public. The sad part was that Ownie thought that he would be greeted as a hero, the honest man who tried to do right by his country, and that he would get a presidential pardon. Having that big used-car business didn't help him any, believe me. And Max, well, his bickering with Ownie brought a lot of attention to Hampton's other dealings in Chicago. He went down as the man responsible for transferring diocesan funds out of the Lincolnland Bank, using inside information from DioGuardia. The Feds are very hard on inside trading these days. They went to jail, Ownie and Max, for other people's sins, it seemed fitting.

They went to a gentlemen's prison up in Wisconsin. The word is that Max hasn't adapted very well, the work in the laundry never having been in his line, although it had been his grandmother's. Ownie Wingate, however, even though he hadn't had a manicure in a long time, seemed to have gotten along well working on the farm, jogging and doing push-ups, and looked forward to returning to the car business, Toyotas this time. "A hell of a car," he had already started to say that. They were his last words when, with a shovel in his hands, looking fit and trim, the angels made a cardiac arrest of him and he fell, kind of surprised-looking, head first into the pig shit. Things have a way of rounding themselves off.

And me, well, I thought a lot about love, and that sticking together was what you did in life, that maybe it *was* life. So I tried a reconciliation with

Maureen. The kids, the old house in Chicago, it was a great idea. Which is why I wish it had worked out better. It was something I longed for, something, after what happened in Rome, I vowed I would work at. But they don't make fairy tales the way they used to, it didn't work and we're separated again. I think Maureen is better off without me. Maybe there's something about me that wasn't made for, well, for the kind of love I think Mike and Ann had. But my marriage was too broken to make it work again, maybe that's my revenge on myself. *Time* was very nice to me, said I could stay in Rome, or go somewhere else, London maybe, or a war zone if I wanted. War zone, I said, you've got to be kidding. I decided to retire. I live and write in Rome now and once in a while one of my kids comes through and even calls me and we have dinner together and life isn't so bad.

But I stay away from the Via Veneto, and I can't even look in the direction of the rebuilt Excelsior Hotel yet. I guess I just haven't worked it all out. I met Monsignor Lanza the other day, he's kept his secrets, too, and, although I've been tempted to ask him what he did with the papal medicine, I never have. He says he's not really sure how you tell whether people are saints or not anymore, that in this life it's awfully hard to see anybody whole. He's an archbishop now and he's been very nice to me. He tells me that I should be glad that Mike and Ann had found such love in this life. And that now they can never lose it.

That's not what bothers me, though.

Seeing them whole, that's what I wish I had done with Mike and Ann. I wish I had gotten myself out of the way so that I could have seen them just as they were, and not as I wanted them to be. They loved each other, that wasn't hard to see, I understand that now. And that they belonged together. Ann wasn't stealing Mike from me, I understand that now, too.

I only wish that in that last minute I had been able to tell them that I understood how much they really did love each other and that it was okay by me. The trouble is, you never know that it is the last minute. So I keep replaying that last interval, thinking about what I could have said, what I should have said. Archbishop Lanza says they do understand now and I guess he's right.

What I miss, you see, is *them*. Son of a bitch if I don't.

EUGENE KENNEDY is the author of many books, including the prizewinning novel *Father's Day* and the biography of Chicago's Mayor Richard Daley, *Himself*. He is a professor of psychology at Loyola University in Chicago.